**Suddenly, Runa found herself
against the wall of the building.**

Both of Shade's hands were on her shoulders...

"I can smell your desire, Runa," he murmured in a coaxing, seductive tone. The man was sex on legs, an overwhelming mass of muscle, testosterone, and sensuality for which she had no defense. Nothing had prepared her for something like this. She doubted any woman could be prepared for Shade. At least not mentally.

Her heart pounded frantically against her rib cage. The situation was rapidly tumbling out of control, and as his tongue swept along her neck and his hands stroked her hips, she found she couldn't care.

A low, sensual rumble came from deep in his throat as he kissed her. Not a proper kiss, but a lick across her lips and then a deep, hot meeting of tongues that had her panting and clinging to his jacket like she would never let him go...

# ACCLAIM FOR
## LARISSA IONE'S NOVELS

### DESIRE UNCHAINED

"4 stars! Rising star Ione is back in this latest Demonica novel...Ione has a true gift for imbuing her characters with dark-edged passion...thrilling action and treacherous vengeance...a top-notch read."

—*RT Book Reviews*

"Warning! Read at your own risk. Highly addictive."

—FreshFiction.com

"Wicked...decadently sinful...prepare to be burned!"

—Gena Showalter, *New York Times*
bestselling author of the Lords of
the Underworld series

### PASSION UNLEASHED

"4½ stars! The third book in Ione's supercharged Demonica series ignites on the first page and never looks back... Adventure, action, and danger leap off every page. The best of the series to date!"    —*RT Book Reviews*

"Fast-paced from the onset and never slows down until the exhilarating climax...Readers will be enthralled by the action and the charmed lead couple."

—*Midwest Book Reviews*

## PLEASURE UNBOUND

"Very dark, very sexy."
>—Emma Holly, *USA Today* bestselling author

"Dangerously erotic, wonderfully satisfying...Ione knows how to make your heart race."
>—Cheyenne McCray, *New York Times* bestselling author of *Dark Magic*

"4 Stars! [Ione's] hard-edged style infuses the story with darkness while taking it to sizzling heights."
>—*RT Book Reviews*

"Larissa's storytelling is compelling and raw. She is truly gifted and you will fall madly in love with the characters in this series."
>—Jaci Burton, national bestselling author of *Hunting the Demon*

"5 Stars! Fascinatingly innovative...full of fervent encounters and shocking disclosures...compelling scenes and dynamic characters. Never has the paranormal world been more intriguing. *Pleasure Unbound* will leave a lasting impact on the reader, as this unforgettable story will evoke emotions long after the last page is read."
>—SingleTitles.com

"This is a dark, sexy, and adventurous story...has everything a paranormal romance book needs, and it will have a lot of readers coming back for more."
>—ParanormalRomance.org

# DESIRE UNCHAINED

# DESIRE
# UNCHAINED

## LARISSA IONE

**GRAND CENTRAL**
**PUBLISHING**

NEW YORK    BOSTON

Grand Central Publishing
Hachette Book Group
1290 Avenue of the Americas
New York, NY 10104
www.HachetteBookGroup.com

Grand Central Publishing is an imprint of Hachette Book Group, Inc.
The Grand Central Publishing name and logo are trademarks of Hachette Book Group, Inc.

The Hachette Speakers Bureau provides a wide range of authors for speaking events. To find out more, go to www.hachettespeakersbureau.com or call (866) 376-6591.

The publisher is not responsible for websites (or their content) that are not owned by the publisher.

Printed in the United States of America

Originally published in hardcover by Hachette Book Group
First mass market edition: July 2008
Reissued: December 2014

10  9  8  7  6  5  4  3  2  1
OPM

**ATTENTION CORPORATIONS AND ORGANIZATIONS:**
Most HACHETTE BOOK GROUP books are available
at quantity discounts with bulk purchase for educational,
business, or sales promotional use. For information,
please call or write:

**Special Markets Department, Hachette Book Group**
**1290 Avenue of the Americas, New York, NY 10104**
**Telephone: 1-800-222-6747  Fax: 1-800-477-5925**

For Karen Boss, who is always willing to drop everything to give me a read, to brainstorm, and to lift my spirits. Girl, you have been there for me for years, and I don't know what I'd do without you.

For my mother-in-law, Lynn Estell, who has been a cheerleader since she read my first manuscript (which will never see the light of day).

For Karen, Warren, and Lauren Allen, who have been a big part of my life for years. Karen, you're one of the strongest people I've ever met. Warren, hey, at least I didn't kill you off in this book. Lauren, sorry about the chocolate-covered garlic.

To Robyn Thompson…we don't see each other nearly enough, but you're always in my thoughts.

For Ann Martin and Michelle Willingham, whose lunch and dinner dates have been an oasis of sanity in an otherwise insane world.

To the wonderful Writeminded Readers Yahoo group, who are always enthusiastic, fun, and supportive. Y'all rock!

And as always, to my family, who put up with my constant tapping on the keyboard, my Crock Pot cooking during deadlines, and my tight schedules. I love you.

# Acknowledgments

Writing can be such a solitary process, but to make a book come together, so many people are involved.

Thank you to the wonderful art department at Grand Central Publishing—you are truly amazing.

And a huge thanks to my wonderful agent, Roberta Brown, for making this book possible, and ditto to my brilliant editor, Amy Pierpont—your guidance has been invaluable. I'm so lucky to have both of you.

I am also blessed with friends who will drop everything to give me a quick read or critique, so I need to offer my deepest thanks to Lara Adrian and Stephanie Tyler. I owe you!

# Glossary

*The Aegis*—Society of human warriors dedicated to protecting the world from evil. See: Guardians, Regent, Sigil.

*Carceris*—The jailers of the underworld. All demon species send representatives to serve terms in the Carceris. Carceris members are responsible for apprehending demons accused of violating demon law, and for acting as guards in the Carceris prisons.

*Council*—All demon species and breeds are governed by a Council that makes laws and metes out punishment for individual members of their species or breed.

*Dresdiin*—The demon equivalent of angels.

*Guardians*—Warriors for The Aegis, trained in combat techniques, weapons, magic. Upon induction into The Aegis, all Guardians are presented with an enchanted piece of jewelry bearing the Aegis shield, which, among other things, allows for night vision and the ability to see through demon invisibility enchantment.

**Harrowgate**—Vertical portals, invisible to humans, which demons use to travel between locations on Earth and Sheoul.

**Infadre**—A female of any demon species who has been impregnated by a Seminus demon.

**Maleconcieo**—Highest level of ruling demon boards, served by a representative from each species Council. The U.N. of the demon world.

**Orgesu**—A demon sex slave, often taken from breeds bred specifically for the purpose of providing sex.

**Regent**—Head(s) of local Aegis cells.

**S'genesis**—Final maturation cycle for Seminus demons. Occurs at one hundred years of age. A post*s'genesis* male is capable of procreation and possesses the ability to shapeshift into the male of any demon species.

**Sheoul**—Demon realm. Located deep in the bowels of the Earth, accessible only by Harrowgates.

**Sheoulic**—Universal demon language spoken by all, though many species speak their own language.

**Sigil**—Board of twelve humans known as Elders, who serve as the supreme leaders of The Aegis. Based in Berlin, they oversee all Aegis cells worldwide.

**Ter'taceo**—Demons who can pass as human, either

because their species is naturally human in appearance or because they can shapeshift into human form.

*Therionidryo*—Term a were-beast uses for a person he or she bit and turned into another were-beast.

*Therionidrysi*—Any survivor of a were-beast attack. Term used to clarify the relationship between the sire and his therionidryo.

*Ufelskala*—A scoring system for demons, based on their degree of evil. All supernatural creatures and evil humans can be categorized into the five Tiers, with the Fifth Tier composed of the worst of the wicked.

*Classification of Demons, as listed by Baradoc, Umber demon, using the demon breed Seminus as an example:*

*Kingdom: Animalia*
*Class: Demon*
*Family: Sexual Demon*
*Genus: Terrestrial*
*Species: Incubus*
*Breed: Seminus*

# DESIRE
# UNCHAINED

# Prologue

―⌒―

*Three Years Ago...*

"He's gone. Let's call it."

Shade ignored his partner and crunched another series of compressions into the shapeshifter's chest. Beneath his palms, cracked ribs grated with each downward stroke.

One–one thousand, *crunch*. Two–one thousand, *crunch*. Shade's own heart was pounding, pumping enough blood per minute to fuel Underworld General's lava-thermal generator, but the patient's heart didn't so much as spark. Three–one thousand, *crunch*. Shade's thigh muscles screamed with pain, cramping after Gods knew how long kneeling in blood next to the patient. Four–one thousand, *crunch*. A tingle spread down the *dermoire* that encased his arm from his right shoulder to his hand as he used his specialized gift to force the patient's heart to beat.

"Shade. Stop." Skulk, Shade's half-sister and paramedic partner, put a dainty gray hand on his arm. "We did all we could."

Knowing Skulk was right didn't make giving up any easier, and Shade didn't have enough breath left in his lungs to curse about it. Panting, he ceased CPR and sat back on his heels on the filth-strewn floor of the abandoned brewery. His arms trembled from exertion, and his stethoscope hung heavily around his neck.

He ground his teeth as he looked into the glassy eyes of his deceased patient. The vic was just a kid. Fourteen, maybe. He'd probably only recently learned how to shift out of his human form to whatever species his family belonged to. The telltale birthmark of a true shifter, a red, star-shaped mole behind the left ear, had barely formed.

"This is bullshit," Shade muttered, standing. Nearby, the two False Angels who had called in the report to the hospital stood, their sweet, virginal appearances belied by the sinister glint in their eyes.

"You didn't see who dropped him here?" he asked.

One of the angel impostors shook her head, her golden hair swishing against her white gown. "He was just lying there. Peaceful."

"He looked peaceful with half his organs missing?"

The other False Angel smiled. "Touchy, touchy." She trailed her fingers suggestively along the low-cut neckline of the gown no true angel would wear. "How about we help you relax, incubus?"

"Yes," the other one purred. "I've always loved a man in uniform."

The first False Angel nodded. "Veragoth does so enjoy haunting police stations."

"Mmm…" The female called Veragoth twirled a strand of hair around a finger and swept her hungry gaze from

Shade's face to his feet. "But I'm starting to think I should be hanging out with paramedics."

Yeah, his black, BDU-style medic uniform made all the females hot even when he wasn't casting off the fuck-me pheromones that came standard issue for Seminus demons. But for once, Shade didn't feel like getting naked with two beautiful females. He was exhausted, angry, and damned sick of the newest rash of demon mutilations. Worse, no one gave a rat's ass that someone was chopping up demons for their parts and selling them on the underworld black market. It had been going on since time began, but few cared.

Shade did.

He was the asshole who got called to scenes where he rarely made a difference in whether or not the vic died. Most were too far gone. Or dead.

Skulk holstered her radio and dug through the jump bag for a fresh pair of gloves. "Since shifters don't disintegrate aboveground, Doc E wants the body. Let's scoop it up. We're done here."

*We're done here.* Too many calls ended like that lately.

Cursing, Shade helped Skulk load the kid's body onto a stretcher and wheel it to the rig. The black ambulance, one of two servicing Underworld General Hospital, was protected by a spell that rendered it unnoticeable to humans, but here, the cloak wasn't needed. They were in a quiet part of New York City, a formerly industrialized area that had been abandoned during Prohibition and was only now starting to build up again as a residential neighborhood.

"Let's roll," Shade said, and slammed shut the rig's rear doors.

It was Skulk's turn to drive, so Shade climbed into the

passenger seat, popped a stick of gum into his mouth, and concentrated on filling out the run sheet.

Patient's chief complaint? *Deadness due to organ removal.*

Patient's response to treatment? *Still fucking dead.*

"Sonofabitch." Shade pinged the pen at the dash. "This sucks—" He cut off, suddenly shaken by a rumble deep inside him, an earthquake in his very soul. Pain rolled up from the epicenter, spreading through his body until the tsunami of agony slammed him backward in his seat.

"Shade? What is it? *Shade?*" Skulk shook his shoulder, but he barely noticed. He threw open the door, thankful they hadn't taken off yet, and fell from the vehicle.

His knees hit the pavement with a crack he heard through the roar of blood in his ears. Doubled over, he wrapped his arms around his gut. Blackness engulfed his vision, his brain. One of his brothers was dead. Who? Gods, *who?*

He reached out with his mind to connect with Wraith, the brother who couldn't be more his opposite, but with whom Shade had a unique connection. Nothing. He couldn't feel Wraith at all. Struggling for each breath, he felt for the weaker connection with Eidolon, but again, nothing. He couldn't sense Roag, either.

In the background, he heard Skulk talking on her cell phone with Solice, the on-duty triage nurse at the hospital. "Where are Shade's brothers? I need to know. Now!"

"Skulk…" he gasped.

She knelt next to him. "Hold on." She listened into the phone for a moment. "Okay, Solice says Roag went to Brimstone. She's all mad because he wouldn't take her with him, but she's getting ready to head there now. She doesn't know where E and Wraith are. They refused to go with Roag."

Not a shock. No Seminus in his right mind would step inside a demon pub where female lust could hold you prisoner for days, or worse, send you to your death at the claw-end of a jealous male. But then, Roag had never been in his right mind.

Shade groaned, swallowed sickly. Gradually, a pinpoint of light pierced the darkness. Wraith. He could feel Wraith's life force. Thank the gods. Relief made his shoulders sag, but only for a second. He couldn't sense Eidolon. Blindly, he reached out with his hand as though he could touch his brother. Skulk caught his arm, twined her fingers through his.

"Breathe, Paleshadow," she whispered, using the childhood nickname she'd given him over eighty years ago. "We'll get through this."

Not if E was dead. Shit, he was the brother who kept them all level, who kept Roag in line and Wraith alive.

Awareness sifted through him. *Eidolon.* He was safe.

The pain faded, but a gnawing, aching emptiness drilled one more hole into Shade's soul. Seminus demons were connected to all their brothers, and when one died, he took a chunk of his surviving siblings with him. Thirty-seven deaths later, Shade felt like a colander.

"Who was it?" Skulk asked softly.

"Roag." He drew in a deep, shuddering breath. "It was Roag."

"I'm sorry."

"So am I," he said, but it was an automatic response. As much as he hated to admit it, the world was now a better place.

# *One*

~

**When walking through the "valley of shadows,"
remember, a shadow is cast by a Light.**

**—Austin O'Malley**

It had been at least two decades since Shade had awakened on a strange floor, hung over and without a clue to his whereabouts. The heavy weight of a manacle around his wrist and the sound of a rattling chain made him smile. It had been even longer since he'd been in this situation *and* chained up.

Cool.

Sure, he preferred the females to be the ones in chains instead of him, but he'd roll with it.

"Shade."

The female voice sounded familiar, but he couldn't place it through the ringing in his ears. He couldn't open his eyes, either.

"Shade. Wake up." A hand shook his shoulder, not gently, as he'd expect a female to do after a spending a night with him. Hell, she should be waking him with her mouth on his—

"Shade, damn you, *wake up!*"

Groaning, he rolled onto his back, wincing at the dull ache pounding against the back of his skull. "I'm awake, baby. I'm awake. Climb on. I'll catch up."

"Thanks, I'll pass. But call me baby again and I'll rip your lips off."

Shade peeled his eyes open. Blinked at the blurry face peering down at him. Blinked again.

"Runa?"

"You remember my name? Pardon me while I pass out from shock."

The sarcasm wasn't necessary, but yeah, he remembered her name. She'd been the hottest human he'd ever brought to his bed. Long, caramel brown hair that felt like the softest silk on his chest, abs, thighs, as she kissed her way down his body. Full, sensual lips that had curved into wicked smiles worthy of his wildest dreams, pale champagne eyes that complemented smooth, golden skin that had melted like brown sugar under his tongue.

But he hadn't seen her in nearly a year. Not since the night she ran away and fell off the face of the earth.

"Why are you here? Why am I here?" He squinted in the hazy darkness. "Where *is* here?" His first thought was that maybe The Aegis had captured him, but this place was too creepy even for those demon-slaying bastards.

"Can you sit?" Runa helped him up, too quickly, and his head swam. She pushed him back against a wall with more strength than he'd expected. He didn't resist, grateful for the cool, damp stone that eased his nausea.

"Answer my question," he said, because he now suspected that this wasn't a sexual hangover, which meant that there could be no good reason to be chained up and feeling like shit with a woman who probably wanted to cause him some damage.

Runa snorted. "You're still an arrogant ass."

"Shock, huh?"

"Not really." Her hand came down on his forehead, as though checking for fever, but as a human, she'd have no idea that his normal body temperature ran high, and he pushed her away. Besides, her touch made his temp jack up even more, something he definitely didn't need.

"Well? Where are we?" They seemed to be in some sort of cell inside a larger enclosure, maybe a dungeon. Something dripped incessantly, straw littered the floor, and candles burned in iron sconces on the stone walls.

Hell's bells, he'd been cast in a cheesy horror movie.

"I don't know where we are. We seem to have four captors... at least, four different demons have been down here to feed us. They call themselves Keepers."

Yeah, this was definitely bad. "Us?"

"I've been here a week. There are a few others in cells. The Keepers take out some and bring others in."

For the first time, Shade looked down at himself, saw the heavy chains connected to his left wrist and ankle. Runa was secured to the opposite wall with a manacle around her right ankle. She wore jeans and a tight, sleeveless sweater he'd have appreciated if it weren't for the fact that he was being held prisoner. She looked different than he remembered, too. When they'd dated—if screwing like rabbits could be called dating—she'd been shy, needy, and easy to control, which had fed his need to dominate, but had ultimately grown boring.

Beneath the conservative dresses and slacks she'd worn, she'd been a little round, soft, even. But now... *holy hot*. She'd put on muscle, and he swore she'd grown taller. Her well-worn jeans fit like a glove, and the black sweater stretched across breasts that were definitely smaller than they had been, perfect for his hands. His mouth.

And this line of thinking was doing nothing but making him hard in an extremely inappropriate situation.

Then again, as a Seminus demon, he was pretty much always hard.

"When was I brought in?"

"Last night."

He shook his head, trying to loosen the congestion that had jammed up his thoughts and memories. Last night...last night...what had he been doing? Wait...he was wearing his paramedic uniform. He remembered going to work, checking in with Eidolon, and getting into a scuffle with Wraith. Their newest doc, a human named Kynan, had broken it up by dousing them both with a bag of saline.

Same old, same old at the one and only medical treatment facility for demons.

Shade and Skulk had gone out on a call, an injured vamp at a New York meat packing facility. They'd entered the building, but from there, his memory took a leave of absence.

"Was anyone else brought in with me? A female?"

"The Umber demon?"

His heart thundered like a trip-hammer. "An Umber came in with me?" Runa nodded, and he didn't stop to think about how she even knew what an Umber demon was. "Where is she?"

"You sleeping with her?" Her sharp tone cracked in the dank air.

"She's my sister, and I don't have time for your jealousy."

"Seems to me you have nothing but time," Runa said, but her voice had softened. "I'm sorry. I don't know what they did with your sister. They took her away a little while ago." She shifted away from him, and he realized she was at the very end of her chain. "You don't look like her."

He didn't offer an explanation for the fact that he and his sister were different species, and she didn't ask. Instead, she watched him as he eyed the bars in the door to their cell and wondered how sturdy they were. Then again, they could be paper for all it mattered if he couldn't break the chains that tethered him to the wall.

"Our best chance to escape won't happen until they come for us," she said.

"You said they feed you."

"Yes, but they push the food and water in with a stick. They won't come close."

"Who are they?"

"I think…I think they're what you demons refer to as Ghouls."

Shade's blood pressure bottomed out. "What? How do you know?"

"That's what someone in another cell called them."

Ghouls. Not the kind humans feared, the flesh-eaters of lore. No, Ghouls were what demons feared—well, second to Aegis slayers, anyway. *Ghoul* was the name given to anyone—demon or human—who kidnapped vampires, shifters, and demons to harvest body parts for sale on the underworld black market. The Ghouls had always been vicious, but their operation had taken an even more sinister turn in the last couple of years. Now, instead of merely taking body parts, they did it while the victim was alive.

Last year, Shade and his brothers had crippled the operation. Eidolon's mate, a half-breed named Tayla, had helped root out humans who had been secretly working with the demons heading the organ-harvesting ring.

The demon population had enjoyed a few months of breathing room, and then suddenly, a couple of months ago, the disappearances and mutilations had started up again, as bloody as ever.

A door at the end of the dark corridor burst open, and the sound of footsteps echoed through the dungeon. Shade braced for a fight, but the intruders stopped before they reached the cell where he and Runa sat quietly. Waiting.

It wasn't until the screams started that Shade truly realized just how much trouble he was in.

Runa Wagner sat on her little pile of straw, listening to the screams of some female as the Keepers dragged her away to what would probably be a horrifying death.

Shade's rugged, masculine features gave nothing away, such as how he felt about what was going on around them, and she carefully schooled her own expression to match. Except there was no way she could make her eyes go as flat and cold as his nearly black ones could, no way she could make her jaw do that grating, rigid thing that made him appear as if he was sharpening his teeth on bones.

Menace radiated from him, as palpable as the danger surrounding them. He tugged on his chains, but discovered, as she had, that they were designed to take more serious punishment than either of them could dish out.

He turned to her, and though his perusal of her body from toe to head was anything but sexual, she felt a stirring in places she'd long thought dead. Dead, because he'd been the one to kill them.

"Have they hurt you?"

"Not since they brought me in." She figured she sported a shiner from the whack across the face she'd taken, but other than some scrapes and bruises, she was fine.

"You're sure?" He shifted to his knees and grasped her calf with his free hand.

Runa recoiled, but he held her easily. "Don't touch me."

"Easy, sweetheart. I'm just doing a system check." His voice was rough and resonant, sensual without even trying. "You used to like it when I touched you."

"Yeah, well, that was before I caught you in bed with two vampires. Oh, and before I found out you were a demon."

"Only one was a vamp."

She sucked in an angry breath. "That's all you have to say for yourself?"

"I'm not the talkative type."

"Unbelievable," she muttered. "You deceived me, cheated on me, and you can't even bother with an I'm sorry?"

He removed his hand and sat back on his hip, one leg tucked beneath him, the other cocked at the knee. He stared at the wall, his shoulder-length black hair falling forward to conceal his expression. "I'm sorry you thought I was human. I never said I was."

"Call me crazy, but is that really something I should have thought to ask?" she spat. "I guess I should have, because I might not have been so shocked to see a real-life vampire and a... whatever it was in your bed."

"You weren't supposed to come to my place that night. You said you were busy."

"I wanted to surprise you."

And she'd done that, all right. She'd walked into his apartment, arms full of makings for a romantic meal.

As soon as she'd stepped through the door, she'd heard the noises coming from his bedroom. Stomach roiling with foreboding, she'd crept down the hall to the open door.

Shade had been on his back, sideways on the bed, his legs dangling over the edge. A naked woman straddled him, rode him slowly, her face buried in his throat. Runa must have made a sound, because he'd turned his head and looked at her with glowing golden eyes. Crazily, the first thing that came to mind was that she'd never seen his eyes when they'd made love. He always closed them, buried his face in her neck, or took her from behind.

"Join us?" he'd asked, and that's when Runa had noticed the other woman kneeling on the floor, her face between his legs.

The woman on top of him raised her head. Blood ran down her chin, and when she smiled, her fangs flashed. A spiked leather collar ringed her neck, the chain connected to it ending in Shade's fist.

As Runa stood there in shock and horror, the woman bent, tongued his nipple, and picked up her pace. Shade moaned, gripped the woman's hips, and arched into her.

Runa had fled. Sobbing, she'd run—from one nightmare into another.

"You said you were busy," Shade repeated, fixing her with a penetrating stare. "I wasn't expecting you."

"So that made what you did okay? When did you start screwing around on me?"

He propped an elbow on his knee, somehow managing to look casual, as if he got captured by Ghouls all the time and maybe enjoyed it a little. "Don't ask questions you don't want to know the answers to."

"Oh, I want to know."

"I don't think you do."

"You're an ass."

"Tell me something I don't know."

"I was in love with you." Silence fell like an executioner's ax. Oh, God. Had she just said that? Out loud? If the way the blood rushed from his face was any indication, then yep, she'd opened her big yap and made a fool of herself. "Don't worry," she said quickly, "I'm over it. Over you."

He leaned forward. "Good. Do you know what I am? What I *really* am?"

"You're a Seminus demon." She glanced at the black markings that ran from the fingers of his right hand all the way up to his neck, tattoos she'd thought were just that; tattoos. But she'd since learned that they were something he'd been born with, a history of his paternity going back dozens of generations. The very top symbol, an unseeing eye just beneath his jaw, was his personal mark, which would have appeared following his first maturation phase at the age of twenty.

"And?"

She smiled tightly. "I spent months researching your species after that night." Not that much information had been available. Oh, incubi had been thoroughly documented, but his particular breed, Seminus, was so rare that she'd unearthed only sketchy details.

"Then you know my nature—"

"Your nature?" Anger flooded her, anger she thought she'd buried. "I get that you pretty much live in a state of perpetual arousal. I get that your need for sex is all but uncontrollable. But you know what? I don't give a crap. You tricked me into having sex with you. Used your incubus tricks and pheromones. You lied to me, made me think you were human." She could go on, about how betrayed and sickened she'd been when she'd learned the truth, but ultimately, what had happened after she'd fled his apartment was what mattered. "You ruined my life," she snapped.

Well, she'd done that herself long before Shade had walked into her coffee shop, but he'd definitely made things worse.

"Shit," he muttered. "See, this is why I make it a rule to not sleep with a human more than once. Your females are clingy."

She stared. Sputtered. "Are you kidding me? You think my life was ruined because you seduced me and then broke my heart?"

"Well, yeah," he said, shrugging one broad shoulder.

What. An. Ass.

Snarling, she leaped into an aggressive crouch so fast he reared backward. Her chains rattled as she trembled with the force of her rage. Her skin prickled, tightening, her gums ached, and she knew she was dangerously close to letting out the inner beast.

"You arrogant son of a bitch." She slammed her palm into his chest, was thrilled to hear him grunt. "I was upset that night, but I'd have gotten over it. Too bad I never got the chance. See, after I left your apartment, I was attacked, torn up, and left to die. You might have known that if you hadn't had some skanky vampire shouting your name. You might have heard me scream."

Shade's gaze sharpened on her, points of midnight flint. "Someone hurt you?"

"Am I supposed to believe you care?"

His hand came up to curl around hers. "Believe it or not, I'm not a monster."

She laughed, a hard, bitter sound. "No, but I am." She got right up in his face. "Because of you, I'm a monster, Shade. I'm a goddamned werewolf."

# *Two*

A werewolf? *Not good.*

Shade closed his eyes, hoping that when he opened them, he'd wake up in his own bed and Runa would be gone.

"Well?"

So much for that. This nightmare wasn't going away. He opened his eyes. Wished he hadn't. Runa was glaring at him, her pale eyes sparking. Gods, he'd bet she was beautiful in beast form... shiny, toffee fur, glowing champagne eyes. She'd be big; would probably stand taller than him. And now the fact that she seemed taller and leaner made sense. Those bitten by werewolves, or wargs, as they usually called themselves, put on muscle and grew an extra inch or two in human form.

Now that his head had cleared, he could smell her as well. Her scent was no longer flowery and sweet. No, she smelled earthy, like a late summer rain in the forest. Oh, and she also smelled really, really pissed.

"Isn't the full moon in two days?"

Her eyes narrowed. "Why? You think I have a raging case of PMS?"

"It occurred to me." Weres might joke about Pre-Moon Syndrome, but those who weren't were-creatures didn't find anything funny about their hair-trigger tempers, mood swings, and out-of-control sex drives.

"Oh, right. My anger wouldn't have anything to do with the fact that of the two people I hate the most in the world, I'm chained in a cell with one, and in two days when I morph, I'm probably going to be skinned alive for my pelt, which is apparently worth a mint on the under-world black market." She jerked her hand out of his with a snarl. "So excuse me for being a little pissy."

"A little?"

She yanked on her chain as though hoping it would break so she could launch at him. "I should bite you."

"Demons are immune to lycanthropic infection."

"It'll still hurt." She bared her teeth, and he had no doubt she'd rip into him if she could. "I'd planned to hunt you down and cause you some serious pain, you know. Unfortunately, the Ghouls caught me before I could do it."

"How did they catch you?"

She drew her knees up to her chest and wrapped her arms around them. "I went back to the place where the werewolf attacked me. It was a long shot, but I was hop-ing to find some clues. Since it was close to your place, I went by your apartment afterward. You weren't there, but a man approached me from the street as I was leaving. He asked if I knew you. Asked too many questions. I got sus-picious and tried to leave, but he jabbed me with a needle. I woke up here."

Shade frowned. "How'd they know you're a warg?"

"They didn't until another warg came to interrogate me," she said, which made sense. Usually it took a were-creature or shapeshifter to recognize another.

"What did they question you about?"

"You, Shade. They kept asking what I was doing at your place and how I knew you."

Oh, fuck. She wasn't taken off the streets for her pelt. She was taken because she knew him. But *why*?

Runa still glared at him, her delicate brows angled in a severe line. He inhaled her again, took in the sharp aroma of her anger and the softer, feminine scent that tapped into his protective male instincts. She didn't belong here, trapped with demons in a dungeon that smelled of mold, urine, and layers upon layers of despair.

Neither did his sister, and the knowledge that both Skulk and Runa were here because of him drop-kicked a sick feeling into the pit of his stomach.

His track record for protecting females was the stuff of nightmares.

A harsh grating noise accompanied a draft of cold air as the iron door to their cell swung open. Runa crowded close to Shade. A male Nightlash demon entered, his humanoid appearance broken by clawed feet and sharp teeth. Two imps—one male, one female—followed, eyes and mouths disproportionately large for their small, round heads. They carried chains, a cudgel, and a bamboo cane.

"Take him," the Nightlash said.

Shade lunged at the imps. The Nightlash tripped one of two levers on the wall. Instantly, the grind of turning wheels rattled the cell, and Shade's chains shortened, tugging him until he was hanging sideways, plastered to the wall.

He gritted his teeth against the pain wrenching through his shoulder and hip. One of the imps clamped a metal collar around his neck while the other installed leg irons. His curses echoed off the damp walls, but through them, he heard Runa pleading with the Nightlash to leave him alone. Surprised, Shade slid her a glance as the imps lowered him to the floor.

Rage glittered in her eyes, and maybe she didn't hate him as much as she'd said. Then again, maybe she wanted the Keepers to leave him alone so she could kill him herself.

"Where are you taking me?" Shade thrashed against his bonds, which earned him a strike to the back of the head by the imp with the cudgel.

The Nightlash didn't answer, merely curled his lips in a nasty smile and wrapped the chain connected to the collar around his fist, yanking Shade to his feet. The imps wrenched his arms behind his back and slapped restraints on his wrists.

They dragged him toward the door. When he struggled at the threshold, a caning to his hamstrings dropped him to his knees. A cool breeze caressed the back of his legs—the cane had torn through his pants. His flesh would be next.

Behind him, Runa spat curses and threats that were as creative as they were ineffective. He couldn't imagine the Runa he'd bedded saying those things, not the shy creature she'd been. Seemed the little human truly had grown claws and teeth.

Freakin' sexy.

Or it would have been if he weren't being dragged

toward one of three whipping posts. Sure, Shade could appreciate a good whipping as much as the next guy, but he had a sneaky suspicion that he wasn't in for a good time. Still, better the post than the water wheel, the rack in the corner, or the meat hooks hanging from the ceiling. And those were the tamer pieces of the torture equipment that littered the cavernous space.

At the rear of the dungeon, an arched opening into a smaller chamber revealed a sight that sent blades of ice right into his spine. Medical equipment filled the room—cutting tools, an autopsy table, a bone saw, and a chest spreader. Fresh and dried blood stained the floor.

Gods, this was beyond sick.

The demons strung him up, facing outward, his hands stretched tight apart and above him, his legs forced wide by a spreader bar and fastened at the ankles. The female imp stroked his thigh, working her way up, and he quickly started working on a plan to seduce her into letting him go...until the Nightlash cuffed her in the head. Still, the fact that some of the Keepers were female was something to keep in mind.

"Where is the Umber female?" he asked.

"Cooperate, and you'll see her."

Shade hadn't expected an answer, so the deep, gravelly voice shocked him. He thought he detected a touch of an accent...Irish maybe, but he couldn't be sure. A hulking figure veiled in black robes stepped out of the shadows, its chuckle as cold as the air.

"And what do I have to do to cooperate?"

"Suffer."

An icy tremor crawled across the surface of Shade's skin. "Maybe you could be a little more specific."

Motion flashed in his peripheral vision. Something struck him in the chest, and blood splattered on the wood post next to him. The Nightlash stood there holding a thorny flail, looking all proud of himself.

"Was that specific enough?"

"Worked for me," Shade said glibly, though he did so through gritted teeth. "It'd be more effective if you removed my shirt, though."

"And everyone says Wraith is the smartass of the family."

Shade's mind screamed. How did this sonofabitch know about Wraith?

"That's a common misconception. Dickhead."

The insult earned him more specific suffering. Blood ran freely down his chest through the shredded remains of his medic shirt. His only consolation was the knowledge that because they were busy torturing him, they were leaving Runa alone.

"Remove his clothes," the dickhead said, "and fetch the fluffer."

Fluffer? One of the imps skittered away while the Nightlash cut away Shade's uniform and stripped him of his boots.

"You know, it's not fair that I have to be naked and you're hiding in that drama-queen robe."

Robe Man moved forward, just a little, but enough for Shade to feel the male's vibe on his skin. It was familiar, like a scent that brought back a memory but couldn't quite be placed. The vibe felt diluted, or maybe masked. A spell, perhaps, had been used to cover it up. But why? So he wouldn't be recognized?

"You're close to *s'genesis*," Robe Man said. "The

Change. I can sense it. Are you ready? Or do you plan to fight it, like Eidolon did?"

Hell, no, he wasn't going to drag out the final maturation process, the one that would allow him to shapeshift and impregnate females, among other, less pleasant things. But how did this asshole know what E had done to try to stave off The Change?

"If you're trying to get me to ask how you know about my brothers and about my species, it won't work, asshole. You got something to say, fucking say it already."

"Not yet." Robe Man circled him, his face hidden in his cowl, but the way he moved...again, very familiar. He stopped behind Shade, and then the tickle of a finger trailed down his spine. Shade fought the urge to shudder. "So? Are you going to fight it? Or take a mate? Oh, that's right, you can't take a bond-mate because you might fall in love and consummate your curse." Hot fetid breath heated Shade's ear as the creature leaned close. "Youthful indiscretions always come back to bite you in the ass, don't they?"

The son of a bitch knew about the *Maluncoeur*, a curse that promised if he fell in love, he'd slowly fade away until he became invisible to everyone. He'd live forever, wracked with stabbing hunger pangs, debilitating thirst, and unbearable sexual desire for all eternity.

Shade closed his eyes and tried to figure out who could know such intimate details about his life. The list was short, and those on it wouldn't talk.

Unless they'd been tortured.

*Skulk.*

"Again," Robe Man said. "Inner thigh."

Shade barely had time to brace himself before the Nightlash's flail ripped into his flesh.

Robe Man laughed. "Doesn't this seem a bit like karma, given how many females you've strung up like this?"

Shade didn't bother to argue that this was different, because sometimes the line between pleasure and pain blurred far too much for Shade's comfort.

"More."

The flail bit into Shade's other thigh. Sweat popped out on his forehead, his vision dimmed, and *damn*, that hurt. How could E stand going through this once a month when he paid for Wraith's sins?

"You're wondering how Eidolon deals with this every time Wraith goes over his limit of human kills."

Shade's head snapped up and around, but Robe Man had retreated to the shadows. "I've had enough of your bullshit," he roared. "Who the hell are you?"

A sinister cackle echoed through the dungeon. "I'm the demon who is going to make you beg for death. Starting now."

"Hello, Shade." The female voice Shade knew well brought his gaze back front and center.

"Solice?" He stared at the brunette vampire nurse who had been working at UG for years, and suddenly everything made sense. Skulk hadn't talked—Solice had. "You bitch."

Her sultry smile revealed long fangs as she leaned in and licked up his chest in a warm, wet lash. Her raspy tongue caught on shredded flesh. Pain streaked through him, but he'd suffered worse while playing with some of his rougher bedmates.

"I've wanted to taste you for so long," she murmured

against his nipple. "But you never so much as looked at me."

"That's because after years of fucking my brother," he growled, "you were damaged goods."

She continued to tongue his chest, even sucking lightly on his caduceus pendant, and he wondered just when the torture would begin, because all this was doing was turning him on. Yeah, it was messed up, but shit, he was an incubus, capable of getting it up under the worst of circumstances, and the female in front of him was throwing off arousal like she was in heat.

"We'll see who is the damaged one." She dropped to her knees, eyeing the blood on his thigh. And he knew. Oh, shit, he knew exactly how his suffering would go down.

Every noise that filtered through the wood and iron door made Runa flinch. She should rejoice at the knowledge that Shade was being tortured. She should volunteer to help. But damn her heart, she wanted to save him.

So she could kill him herself.

Except, she hadn't come back to New York to kill Shade. She'd returned to her hometown with military orders to gather intel on a demon hospital, and to locate an ex-soldier and Aegis Guardian who hadn't been heard from since reporting the existence of the hospital. The Army feared he might have become a traitor not only to the United States, but to the entire human race. And when the U.S. Army's Raider-X Regiment issued an order, you followed it—and not just because they'd planted a micro-detonator in your brain. No, the supersecret military unit inspired loyalty by giving "special humans" a purpose and a sense of belonging in a world that had rejected them.

She hadn't been rejected, but her situation had guaranteed that, without help, The Aegis would have killed her, but probably not before she slaughtered countless innocent humans. Fortunately, her brother, a high-ranking officer at R-XR, had known exactly what to do the night he found her bleeding to death in the alley where she'd been attacked. The Army had saved her life, had even attempted to prevent the lycanthropic virus from taking hold. They'd failed, but the side effects of their experimental treatment turned out to be handy.

She still turned into a giant, slavering beast three nights out of every month—a beast with no control over her actions and very little memory of what took place while she was in beast form. But thanks to the Army, she could also turn into the beast any time she wanted to. Even better, when she changed form intentionally, she retained her humanity and could control her actions and remember everything once she returned to her human form.

Laughter bubbled up from somewhere, female laughter, followed by a long, drawn-out noise. An erotic growl. *Shade*'s erotic growl. She'd know that sound anywhere. So what, they were torturing him with sex?

That bastard. She hated him. But she was pretty sure that just before the werewolf attack, he'd saved her brother's life. And, truth be told, probably hers, as well.

Runa had met him when she'd been at the lowest point in her life. Twenty-five years old but feeling double that, she still hadn't gotten over the death of her mother four years earlier—how could she when her mother had died alone and miserable, thanks to Runa? But more recently, her best friend had moved to Australia with her new husband, Runa's coffee shop had been only days from closing, and her brother had been dying. Arik had, in fact, been dying in her house, and the only reason she wasn't with him was that he'd insisted that she tend to her shop and employees, who would soon be jobless.

One of her employees, a pierced, green-haired girl who called herself Aspic, had been razzing Runa about never taking risks, which was probably why her business had failed in the first place. No risks in love, business, or life. And where had that gotten her?

Arik might have been dying, but he'd *lived*. Should she be struck by a mysterious disease that killed her by slow measures, would she know the satisfaction of having truly lived life to the fullest?

The answer to that had been painfully obvious, especially because guilt had been killing her as surely as whatever had struck down Arik. She had denied herself anything that even resembled pleasure with the ruthlessness of a religious zealot. How could she allow herself to experience what she had denied her mother?

Not a day had gone by that she didn't think about how she'd ruined her parents' marriage and sent her mother into a downward spiral of depression. No matter how many times Arik tried to tell her that she needed to forgive herself for telling their mother about finding their father with another woman, she couldn't. Because Arik didn't know her secret—that deep down, Runa feared that she hadn't done it out of concern for their mother.

She'd done it to hurt their father.

The day Shade walked into her life had been the day

she'd wondered, for the first time, if she would have anything to live for once Arik was gone.

He'd sauntered into her coffee shop, huge, impossibly gorgeous, black motorcycle boots thudding on the floor, his leather pants and jacket making that soft rasp, the pirate earring in his left lobe glinting in the light. His right hand had been tattooed, as well as the right side of his throat, and she'd wondered if tats on his arm had connected the two.

*All female eyes latched on to him. All male eyes had averted.*

*"Oh, fuck me," Aspic whispered. "All. Night. Long."*

*There was no looking away from him as he moved to the counter, his gaze locked onto Runa's.*

*Aspic started to pant, honest-to-God pant. "Here's your risk, Runa. Take it. Make a move or I swear I will."*

*He stopped in front of Runa. "Coffee." The word rolled off his tongue as if he'd said, "I'd like to give you an orgasm."*

*"Yes," she whispered, because he could give her...oh, right. Coffee. She cleared her throat. Twice. "Regular, tall, or grande?"*

*"Whatever your largest size is."*

*"Do you have a brew preference?"*

*"Strong and hot."*

*"Milk? Soy or dairy? Cream?"*

*"Hell's freakin' bells." He planted his palms on the counter and leaned in. "Just. Coffee." His intense gaze roamed over her figure in a blatant appraisal that should have infuriated her but only made her heart beat faster. "Though I might be tempted to try something sweeter."*

*Aspic nudged her with an elbow and then stepped for-*

ward. *"Runa's a little shy. Do you have a motorcycle? Because she loves motorcycles. Bet she'd love to see it."*

*"Aspic!"* Runa's cheeks burned with mortification.

*"Runa,"* the leather man said softly, as though testing the feel of her name on his tongue. *"Would you like to take a ride?"*

*"She'd love to,"* Aspic said, and plopped his coffee in front of him.

Runa shook her head. *"I don't think—"*

*"Good,"* he said, as he threw down a ten-dollar bill. *"Keep the change. Let's go."*

Before she could utter a protest, he grabbed his coffee, came around the counter, took her hand, and led her toward the back door. She planted her feet at the threshold. *"Look, Mr...."*

*"Shade."*

Odd name. Then again, she worked with a girl who called herself Aspic. *"Mr. Shade."*

*"Just Shade."*

*"Shade, then. I'm afraid I can't go anywhere with you."*

He cocked one black eyebrow and pushed open the door. *"Who said anything about going anywhere?"*

*"But, you said ride."*

Her flowing skirt whirled around her calves as he whisked her into the side street and toward the alley. *"Yep."*

Panic flared. This man could be a serial killer or a rapist, and here she was, half his size, be-bopping into an alley with him. *"I can't—"*

Suddenly, she found herself against the wall of the building, his body pinning hers, his mouth against her *ear. Both of his hands were on her shoulders... what had he done with the coffee?*

*"I can smell your desire, Runa," he murmured in a coaxing, seductive tone. "You're blooming for me like a flower."*

*He rocked his hips into her. The erection behind the fly of his pants massaged her belly, promising an experience she'd never forget. The man was sex on legs, an overwhelming mass of muscle, testosterone, and sensuality for which she had no defense. Nothing had prepared her for something like this. She doubted any woman could be prepared for Shade. At least not mentally. Her body was preparing itself without her go-ahead.*

*Her breasts tingled and tightened, her heart pounded frantically against her rib cage, and a rush of liquid dampened her panties. She squeezed her thighs together to relieve the ache between them, but that only made things worse.*

*The situation was rapidly tumbling out of control, and as his tongue swept along her neck and his hands stroked her hips, she found she couldn't care.*

*He fisted her skirt and drew it up to her hips. "Do you want this?" He nuzzled her throat and pressed a thick thigh between her legs, creating the most delicious pressure. "Tell me to stop, and I will."*

*This was her out. Her chance to get away from him. To go back inside her failing shop and then home to her dying brother. On the way home she could get robbed and shot. Run over by a taxi. Stabbed in a subway station.*

*And she'd die knowing she should have taken a risk for once in her life.*

*Shade's fingers slipped between them, stroking her core over the wet fabric of her panties. "Well?"*

"*Don't stop. Please don't stop.*"

A low, sensual rumble came from deep in his throat as he kissed her. Not a proper kiss, but a lick across her lips and then a deep, hot meeting of tongues that had her panting and clinging to his jacket as if she would never let him go.

The rip of fabric registered in her ears, alongside the hum of passing vehicles, the laughter of someone on the sidewalk. None of it mattered, not even the flutter of her panties against her legs as they fell to the pavement.

God, this was crazy. Sex with a stranger in an alley. In the middle of the day.

A moment of clarity punched through her sexual haze as he unzipped his pants. She stopped him with a firm grasp on his wrist. "Why me?" she rasped. "There were other women in there, prettier, sexier—"

"I sensed your need."

It was a strange answer, but then he was pushing against her entrance despite her restraining grip, and she didn't care why this whirlwind had happened. Instinct took over, and she wrapped her legs around his waist and groaned as he eased the tip of his erection inside.

"Oh, man," he breathed. "You're so tight." He pulled back a little, and then pushed inside again, just the head. The mild stretching sensation eased into a shimmer of pleasure as the crown of his penis worked the ring of nerves at her entrance.

"Wow." She arched her back, and he slid his forearm behind her, cushioning her spine. "More. I want more."

As though he'd been waiting for permission, he thrust deep, destroying her pleasure with a wave of pain. He froze, his expression tight. "You okay?"

"Fine," she managed, as the pain faded. "It's just been a long time." Years, in fact. She'd lost her virginity her senior year of high school to a boy who swore he loved her, but two days later he'd loved someone else in the same way.

"You should have told me," he growled. "I could have been gentler."

"Just finish it," she said, and with a harsh curse, he started moving inside her.

There was no slow buildup like she'd expected. No mildly pleasant stirring of sensation. No gradual warming.

There was an instant shattering, an explosion that would have had her screaming if he hadn't slapped a hand over her mouth. His powerful thrusts rammed her into the building but she didn't care, couldn't care, because she was coming again and he was shuddering, moaning, jerking in a powerful release.

When they could both breathe again, she lowered herself to her feet and he pulled out, tucking himself swiftly back into his pants. Warm, tingly fluid dripped down her leg, blasting her back to reality.

"Oh, my God. You didn't use a condom."

"I'm sterile, and I'm not a carrier for diseases."

"Still—"

He silenced her with a kiss. When he drew back, she felt dazed. He took her hand and led her toward the shop's rear entrance. Just before she reached the door, a flash of lightning sizzled through her veins.

"Oh!" She gasped as another orgasm rocked her body. Shade held her through it, his massive body taking the impact of her spasms.

"That's going to happen a couple more times. You

*might want to hide out in an office or break room for a few." He waited until she was steady on her feet, and then sauntered off. At the corner, he glanced back over his shoulder. "By the way, I drive a Harley."*

*Frowning, she stepped inside the building. Aspic grinned. "So? What kind of bike did he have?"*

*Runa laughed. "A Harley. He had a Harley."*

Shade had contacted her later, and they'd dated for a few weeks. Then her brother's medical condition worsened. Shade had come to her house, spent a few minutes with Arik, and within days her brother had made a full recovery.

It was only days after that that she'd been attacked by the werewolf, and Arik had taken her to the R-XR for life-saving care.

The secret military installation had been a shock—she'd thought her brother was regular Army, just another soldier. But he'd been working for the R-XR for years, along with a select group of about a hundred others, some active duty, some civilians. And a handful were even wargs—military members who had survived attacks and been snatched out of their regular units to work for R-XR.

Because of their lycanthropy, they'd felt isolated from their fellow soldiers, and they'd formed a pack, as their new instincts demanded. They'd allowed her into their inner circle, but without a military background, she'd still felt like an outsider no matter how often they'd invited her to their backyard barbecues and nights out at the base bar.

Arik had *not* been happy about any of that. He'd been convinced the alpha, a too-hot-for-his-own-good male chauvinist named Brendan, had his sights on making her his alpha female, but then, Arik had always worried about her. From the time they were children, he'd been her watchdog, dragging her away from their father's fists. Then later, when Arik had been awarded guardianship of her, he'd made sure every high school boyfriend understood the consequences of hurting her.

A grinding noise yanked Runa out of her thoughts. The door to the cell swung open, and the Nightlash and the two imps dragged Shade inside. He was naked, his arms and legs bound, his chest and thighs caked with dried blood.

His eyes, glowing gold, fixed on her. An instant, uncontrollable urge to go to him had her straining against her chains. He bellowed, battled his captors as he struggled to get to her, and although she didn't know why he wanted her so badly, she could feel his desperation right down to the way her body heated in response.

The Nightlash slammed a thick club down on Shade's skull. The sharp crack echoed through the cell like a gunshot. Shade grunted and settled down, but his eyes still glowed, and he still watched her...

Watched her with the single-minded intensity of an aroused male who wanted one thing.

And wanted it now.

# Three

"Talk to me, Shade."

Runa stretched to the end of her chain. Their captors had left him secured to the wall with a collar around her neck and just out of her reach. He'd gone crazy at first, leaping at her like something possessed, giving her a glimpse of the demon beneath the human appearance. Eventually, when his throat began to bleed from the struggles, he'd curled into a fetal position and lain there, panting and moaning, for what had to have been half an hour. His vulnerability broke through the barrier of anger she felt for him, until her fingers had itched to smooth his hair away from his face, where sweat had beaded on his brow.

*Idiot*. The man...creature...whatever...had tossed her away like garbage. She didn't give a crap about his you-know-my-nature bullshit. For the first time in her life, she'd taken a risk, had believed that maybe it was time to put aside the past and let herself be happy.

Her anger roared back, and she welcomed it like an old friend.

"What did they do to you?" she asked, her voice steely.

"Need..." He broke with a shudder. "Pain."

"I know it hurts. What can I do?"

"Pain. Hurt...me."

"Yes, they hurt you—"

"No." His face twisted into an agonized grimace as he stretched until his toes made contact with her fingers, at which point he hissed. "I need you...to cause me pain. Make it...hurt."

"What? No." She jerked away from him. "I've been dying to do that for a long time, but if you want it, it sort of takes the pleasure out of it."

"Please." He opened his eyes. Dark shadows framed them, and the gold was gone, replaced by the near-black that always sucked her in.

She stared at his foot, wondering what she could do. There was nothing within reach she could strike him with. But maybe...no, if she shifted into a werewolf, the manacle around her ankle would hurt like hell as her size doubled.

"Runa." He shuddered so hard his chains rattled. "I'll die...if you don't."

Oh, damn. No matter how angry she was at him, she couldn't let him die. He fell still as she stripped off her shirt, as though he knew she'd decided to help. She peeled off her jeans, as well, but had to leave them hanging off the cuff around her ankle.

Bracing herself, she shifted. Skin stretched. Bone popped. Excruciating pain ripped through her face as her jaws extended and teeth erupted. Sure enough, the ankle manacle squeezed like a vise, sending such intense waves of agony up her leg that her vision blurred. Shade watched with wide eyes as she leaped to the end of her chain. Her larger size and canine muzzle gave her the extra length she needed to clamp down on Shade's foot with her mouth.

He yelped, a brief shout of pain before he smothered the sound with a moan. Between her teeth, she felt bones give but not break. His skin didn't fare as well, and she tasted blood.

"Enough," Shade growled, and she released him.

Her leg throbbed as she shifted back to human form. She lay on the ground, exhausted from the transformation, feeling spent and hoping no one had seen. If their captors learned she could voluntarily shift form into a warg, they might not wait until the full moon to take her pelt.

She gagged at the coppery taste of blood in her mouth and spat into the straw.

"Thank you," he said hoarsely, and if she didn't know better, she'd think his shredded voice was the result of hours of screaming. But he'd endured his torture and suffering in silence. He sat up, pulling gingerly at his foot, but he seemed much better despite the amount of pain the wound must have caused. "Why can you shift at will?"

Weakly, she faced him, her gaze dropping to his naked body before she could catch herself. Even sitting there, chained up and injured, he radiated masculine power. She raised her eyes to his caduceus pendant. She'd recognized it as a medical symbol back when they were dating, but now that she knew where he worked and what he was, the odd design made more sense. The common staff had been replaced by a dagger circled by two sinister-looking vipers, and the wings above their heads were batlike and tribal.

"You first," she said, as she pulled her jeans up. "Why

do you feel better even though I just gnawed on you like a Rottweiler's chew toy? What did they do to you?"

He threw his head back against the wall and stared at the ceiling. "They forced a female on me. It's a curse of my species that once we're aroused beyond a certain point, we need release, or the pain becomes disabling. If it goes on long enough, we die."

"Oh. So the female…" she trailed off, not wanting to know what the female had done to him.

"She pleasured me with her mouth until I was crazy with lust, and then she stopped."

"So… didn't the fact that you're in a chamber of horrors put a damper on your libido?"

"My mind wasn't willing, but my body responded." He drilled her with a hard look. "I'm an incubus, and she was as aroused as I was. I couldn't help it."

Right. His *nature* again.

"So if you sense arousal, you have to respond?" When he nodded, she bit her lip, thinking. "The day we met, you said you sensed my need. Is that what you meant?"

He nodded again. "It's why I generally avoid public places. A nightclub, especially a demon nightclub, can be hell. No pun intended."

That would explain why they'd never gone anywhere during the month they'd dated. Their entire relationship had revolved around his place or a hotel, sex and food. Once, they'd taken a walk in a park—at night when the area was deserted. At the time, she'd thought it romantic. Now she knew better.

"Then, no matter where you are, you have to stay if you sense need? You can't leave?"

"Not if a single female wants sex. I'm compelled to

find her. If she's with another male, the results can be violent."

"Why not just, um—"

"Release can't come by my own hand."

Which was why he'd tried to get to her when they first brought him in. He'd been frantic with pain and lust, needing release, and she'd been the only female in sight. They'd chained him just out of reach to torment him. Sick bastards.

"And you needed me to hurt you . . . why?"

"It was a gamble. I hoped the pain would overwhelm the lust-agony." He studied his foot and applied pressure to a gaping wound that was bleeding badly. "Your turn. Why can you shift at will? Wargs only shift during the full moon. And shapeshifters turn into true animals, not were-beasts."

"I'm not sure why," she lied. "I was hoping maybe your hospital could help me find out."

He cocked an eyebrow. "How do you know about the hospital?"

"I've been hunting for my sire, which means I've met some nonhumans. And your uniform pretty much gave you away." More lies, but the truth wasn't an option. He couldn't know that the R-XR knew about his hospital and that one of the reasons she'd been looking for Shade was to learn more about it.

Shade had told her he was a paramedic, but it wasn't until the R-XR was given a caduceus pendant taken from a shapeshifter doctor The Aegis had killed that she realized Shade must work at the demon hospital. The shapeshifter's pendant had been identical to his.

Normally, her job with the R-XR was to literally sniff out other were-creatures. The military would then secretly tag them, and their information would be added to a giant database, allowing for monitoring.

But Runa's familiarity with New York City, as well as her past association with Shade, had earned her this assignment.

"You shouldn't hang out with nonhumans," he growled. "You aren't ready."

"I didn't ask for your permission."

"You're a baby in my world, Runa. Stay out of it."

She waved her arm in an encompassing gesture. "Look around you, Shade. I can't get in much deeper. I certainly don't have a choice." She narrowed her eyes at him. "It's your fault I'm in this world in the first place."

"You do realize that as a warg, your lifespan has quadrupled, right? So you should be thanking me."

"Assuming I don't die in the next couple of days. Or get killed by The Aegis. Or by other wargs." She huffed. "If you're expecting gratitude, you'll be waiting a long time. Not that we have a long time."

"We're going to be okay."

"And you know this how?"

"My brother can sense me. He'll find us."

Too bad her brother couldn't sense her. Heck, neither he nor the R-XR would know she was missing until after the full moon when she was supposed to check in. She watched as Shade checked his bleeding foot and returned pressure to the wound. He didn't so much as flinch, his movements precise and coldly efficient.

"How many brothers and sisters do you have?" She'd asked him the question a long time ago, but his answer had been vague—*a few*—and then he'd changed the subject as deftly as a politician.

"One sister—the Umber. Two brothers. Wraith and Eidolon."

"Are they Umber demons, too?"

He shook his head. "No. They're Sems like me."

"How is it that you have an Umber sister?"

"We share a mother. With my brothers, I share a father, but our mothers are all different species."

"So . . . you're half-breeds?"

"No. All Seminus demons are purebred and male. There are no female Sems, so after *s'genesis*, we impregnate females of other species. The offspring are born purebred Seminus demons, though everyone inherits minor traits from his dam."

Interesting. "Why would these other species volunteer to have Seminus children?"

"They don't. Sexually mature Seminus demons gain the ability to shapeshift into the males of other species. So basically, we trick them into having sex with us. If that doesn't work, rape does."

"Nice."

Shade rolled his eyes. "We're *demons*. But if it makes you feel any better, most of us are disgusted by our destiny until we go through *s'genesis*. Then we don't give a shit anymore."

"So you do care?"

"Right now, yes. The idea of deceiving or raping any female in order to knock her up disgusts me. So does the reality of what happens to the infants."

"Which is?"

"Most are slaughtered at birth. Few demons are willing to raise a demon of another species, let alone one that was conceived through trickery or rape."

"So I'm guessing the fathers don't have anything to do with the children."

"Most of us never meet the male that sired us. All we know is the family that raised us, though we can sense our brothers."

"So you never knew your father?" She shifted to get more comfortable, wincing at the dull ache in her ankle.

"All I knew of him were secondhand stories."

"Do all sexual demons reproduce like that?"

"Nope. Most incubi and succubi use humans for reproduction, but Sems can't. Impregnating humans results in cambions."

"Cambions?"

"Sterile half-breeds." The way he said it, with a slight sneer, told her what he thought of breeding with humans.

Apparently, screwing them was just fine, however. She tried to keep the bitterness out of her voice as she asked, "So your mother's an Umber, right?"

Shade nodded. Runa didn't know much about the cave-dwelling species, had only skimmed the information she'd found while researching demons to identify Shade's breed. Apparently, they were gray-skinned and humanoid, though they avoided contact with humans. They were extremely social in their family orders, but were isolated within the demon world—probably because they were the natural prey of some of the more vicious species of demons.

"What about your brothers?" She leaned forward, intensely curious. She'd had a rude introduction into the demon world, but once she got over the shock, she'd dedicated every spare minute to learning as much as she could. "What species are their mothers?"

"My older brother, Eidolon, was born to a Justice demon, and Wraith's mother was a vampire."

She blinked. "I didn't think vampires could breed."

"They can't. Wraith's an anomaly."

Somewhere in the dungeon, something screamed, and Runa shivered.

"What about your parents?" she asked quickly, and a little shakily. "Was what you told me when we were dating true? Your mother lives in South America and your dad is dead?"

A long, awkward silence filled the cell. Finally, just as Runa was about to give up on getting an answer, Shade said, "My mother was killed a couple of months ago."

"Oh. I'm sorry."

"Did you kill her?"

Her voice cracked with astonishment. "No."

"Then don't be sorry."

"Am I annoying you with my questions?" she snapped.

"Yep." He shrugged. "But it's not like we have a lot else to do."

As if on cue, footsteps pounded outside. Runa crouched, ready to attack, but Shade remained where he was, looking for all the world as if he was lounging on a couch with a beer. If the fact that he was nude bothered him, it didn't show.

The door swung open. The Nightlash who had dragged Shade out of the cell earlier entered and dropped a gym bag on the floor. A robed figure slid inside behind the other demon, its face hidden inside a deep hood, though she thought she caught a glimpse of some sort of mask. Only the creature's hands were visible—clawlike, skeletal things wrapped in leathery skin. Some of its fingers were missing, but that didn't stop him from holding a wicked-looking spiked club.

It turned to Shade. "I see you've recovered from your ordeal."

"That's what happens when you hire second-rate whores like Solice. You should have instructed her in the proper art of blowjobs."

The thing hissed. "I'm going to make you suffer."

"Promises, promises," Shade drawled, turning away to study his fingernails.

Runa could practically feel the rage billowing like steam from the robed creature. "I will make what I did to your sister look like fun."

Very slowly, Shade lifted his head, his dark eyes narrowed and gleaming with hatred. "Where is she? What did you do to her?"

"Do you really want to know?"

Shade leaped to his feet. "Tell me!"

The creature nodded to the Nightlash, who opened the bag on the floor and pulled out what looked like a leather blanket.

*Oh, God.* Runa's stomach lurched. She felt the blood drain from her face as the robed one cackled.

"Umber skins are worth a fortune on the underworld market. She's going to make someone a fine cloak."

A blast of darkness hit Runa a second before the icy wind, and then Shade let loose an agonized wail that would stay with her for the rest of her life.

Kynan Morgan was probably the biggest pain in the ass on staff at UGH. Scratch that. Not probably. He was, and he knew it.

He also didn't give a shit. He didn't give a shit about much

anymore. His give-a-shit meter had broken nearly a year ago
when his wife betrayed him and then died at the hands of
her lover. One of her lovers, anyway. The human one.

Then there was Gem, with her black and blue hair, Goth
clothing, piercings, and tats. He'd forgiven Tayla for being
a demon. Mainly, because she hadn't known the truth of
her paternity until Eidolon figured it out. But Tayla's sister, Gem...not so much. He'd met her a few years ago at
the New York City hospital where she'd worked, pretending to be human. She'd talked to him, laughed with him,
seen him nearly naked during exams.

Truthfully, it wasn't a betrayal; she'd owed him nothing. But he'd liked her, trusted her, and all along she'd
been the enemy.

But even that wasn't entirely true. Since the violent
night nearly a year ago, he'd come to the disturbing real-
ization that not all demons were evil, that some strove to
be good. The knowledge, on top of his wife's betrayal,
had shaken his moral, spiritual, and emotional founda-
tions. He'd pulled away from The Aegis, from one of the
two things he was good at: killing.

Which had left him with only one skill remaining,
something he hadn't even been sure he had the stomach
for anymore.

Healing.

At that point, Eidolon had stepped in and offered him a
job at UGH, as one of the half-dozen humans already on
staff. The irony was flat-out, fucking funny. He'd spent years
killing demons, and now they wanted him to heal them.

He'd accepted, but on the condition that he chose who
he helped. He would not be responsible for putting evil
back on the streets. Eidolon had understood, and he'd even

made Kynan a doctor, since the hospital was short on physicians with degrees, and Kynan had a shitload of medical experience thanks to his Army medic training and years of patching up Guardians after battles with demons.

Still, this was a temporary gig. Hanging out with demons was a perfect mirror for where he was mentally, but he had to believe it would come to an end, that he could find himself again. He wasn't sure he could go back to being the Regent of the New York Aegis cell—hell, he didn't think they'd even want him. If the Sigil—the twelve supreme leaders of The Aegis—knew he'd been working with the enemy...well, he'd *become* the enemy. They could never know what he was doing at the hospital. And if they knew that the New York City cell's temporary Regent, Tayla, was half demon and mated to a demon, he and Tay would both end up with death warrants hanging over their heads.

Apparently, the Sigil didn't yet know about Tayla's new approach to demon-slaying—she'd educated the Guardians in her cell to recognize the difference between evil demons and harmless ones, a move that had rewarded them with a handful of demon informants. She'd also instituted a capture-instead-of-kill policy when it came to were-beasts. Another good move—some weres didn't cause harm intentionally—they had escaped their cages, or were new enough to not understand what had been happening to them three nights a month. Only those with no regard for human life were put down.

Kynan had to admit that after a shaky start in The Aegis, Tay had turned out to be an excellent Regent.

"Hey, grunt."

Kynan ground his molars at the sound of Wraith's voice as he snipped the thread of the last stitch he'd put into his patient. The Neethul had been remarkably quiet during the procedure, even though her species' standard mode of operation seemed to be stuck on snarl. Neethulum weren't his favorite species of demon to patch up, but they focused their cruelty on other demons, not humans, so he had no problem sending the Neethul back into the general demon population.

Besides, this one had been injured when she was attacked and raped by a post *s'genesis* Seminus demon, and he wanted her to find the bastard and rip him apart. She was probably pregnant, but there was nothing he could do about that.

Kynan looked over at Wraith, who was looming in the cubicle doorway, his cocky grin begging to be knocked right off his face. "What do you want?"

"Mainly? To irritate you."

"I swear to God—"

"Uh-uh." Wraith waggled a finger at him. "You can't do that in a demon hospital."

Ky breathed deeply and counted to five, something Eidolon said helped him deal with Wraith. It might help E, but then, Wraith hadn't slept with *his* wife. Sure, Wraith denied screwing Lori, but Wraith wasn't exactly Mr. Straight and Narrow. And if he was this bad now, before *s'genesis* hit him, he was going to be seriously off the rails afterward.

"If it weren't for the Haven spell, I'd kick your ass," Ky snapped.

Wraith laughed, because it was an idle threat. Kynan was a trained fighter, both for The Aegis and before that, the Army, but the Seminus demon was not only a master of every fighting method known to man and demon, but, at ninety-nine years old, he had about seventy years of experience on Kynan. Wraith could wipe the floor with him without breaking a sweat.

"You crack me up, human. I'll let you keep breathing," Wraith said, as he said every day, in that deceptively easy-going way of his. "Has anyone heard from Shade?"

"No." And that couldn't be good. Last night, Eidolon had sent a team to find Shade and Skulk when they hadn't returned from an ambulance run and hadn't answered their radio or cell phones. The team had arrived at Shade's last known location, but hadn't found a trace of the para-medics. "Can't you sense him?"

"If I try hard enough. But unless he's trying at the same time or in severe enough pain—" Wraith broke off on a gasp. Dropping to his knees, he clutched at his gut, dou-bling over. His blond hair concealed his face, but his mis-ery was obvious in the way his voice cracked. "Fuck," he moaned. "Oh, *holy fuck*."

Kynan spun, hit the intercom button. "Eidolon! ER two, STAT!" He kneeled next to Wraith. "Hey, man, what's wrong? Tell me what hurts."

"Shade." Wraith lifted his head, his blue eyes, so differ-ent from his brothers' dark ones, watering. "Shade hurts."

"You bastards!" Shade lunged at the robed sonofabitch, the chains jerking him up hard. Raw, grinding grief flayed him open like a slayer with a *stang*. It had been eighty years since he'd felt this, since his actions had cost the lives of all but one of his Umber sisters. Now that one sur-vivor, the sister he'd sworn to protect, was dead.

"Who are you? Show yourself, you coward."

"Who am I?" The robed thing moved forward. "Do you really want to know?"

Again, snarling, Shade leaped against his chains. "No. I asked to hear myself talk, you fuck."

"So dramatic." Robe Man reached up and removed his mask, a nasty thing made of hide and hair, but his face was still concealed by the cowl.

"*Who are you?*"

Slowly, the figure pushed down his hood. "I'm your brother."

Heart pounding wildly, Shade looked into Wraith's face. His blue eyes. His sun-streaked blond hair. His cocky grin that exposed vampire fangs. But the vibe was wrong. As before, when Robe Man was torturing Shade, the vibe was muted. "You aren't Wraith."

"I never said I was." He flicked his tongue over one fang in a move that was pure Wraith. "But if it's any consolation, it was Wraith I was after. Not Skulk. Why was she on duty instead of him?"

A chill crawled up Shade's spine. Wraith rode the ambulance only one day a month. How had this bastard known that yesterday was Wraith's day? Had Wraith shown up as scheduled, Skulk wouldn't have been called in and Wraith would have been taken by the Ghouls along with Shade. So how had Robe Man known, unless...of course. Solice. How long had that vampire bitch been spying on him and his brothers?

"I'm not telling you shit." Shade spoke slowly, deliberately, making sure every word dripped with the hatred he felt.

The Nightlash stuffed his gruesome trophy back into the bag, and Shade nearly collapsed with grief.

"She screamed your name, you know," the fake-Wraith

said. "Cursed it, really." Smiling, he closed his eyes and breathed deeply, as though taking in the sound of her screams, the smell of her agony.

This was a creature who fed off misery, and Shade didn't play that game. He'd had a lot of experience with demons like him, and as much as Shade wanted to tear the bastard apart, he knew he had to play smart right now.

And after he got what he wanted, he would make sure that this sonofabitch paid a million times over for what he'd done to Skulk.

Runa felt the icy-burn of hatred seeping from Shade's pores as he held himself motionless, his weight balanced on his injured foot as though her bite amounted to nothing more than a scratch.

"Get on with whatever you came to do." His voice, strong and deep, cracked like a whip.

The other male hissed and lunged, halting just out of Shade's reach. "I've always hated you. Nearly as much as your pathetic little brother."

Shade bared his teeth. "That might mean something to me if I knew who you are."

For a moment, their captor stood there, a vein in his temple pulsing. He'd said he was Shade's brother, but Shade didn't seem to be buying it. Still, it was weird how much he resembled Shade, except for the blue eyes and blond hair. When he tore off his robe, revealing a sculpted, athletic body, she noticed other differences, mainly that Shade was broader in the shoulders, but slightly shorter—which, at around six-three, wasn't short. The markings on his right arm were the same, but where Shade sported an unseeing eye on his neck, this other demon had an hourglass.

Suddenly, the muscle-bound demon shimmered and morphed into some sort of humanoid creature, withered and hunched over, its cracked skin wrinkled in some places and stretched tight and shiny in others. Whatever it was, it looked as if it had been dunked in a deep fryer and cooked extra-crispy.

"I can't hold on to an adopted form for long," he said. "A couple of hours, at most. I have all the limitations of a Seminus after *s'genesis.*" His gaze caught Shade's and held it, the newly brown eyes glinting with more than a touch of insanity.

The blood drained from Shade's face so fast she thought he might drop.

"Yes," the thing rasped. "You know who I am now, don't you?"

"No." Shade stumbled sideways, catching the wall with his shoulder. He'd gone deathly pale, his skin glyphs pulsing starkly against the ashen tone of his skin. "You can't be…"

Scarred lips twisted into a grotesque smile. "Look at me. We heal quickly and well, but look what fire does to us."

"Fire," Shade whispered. "Fire destroyed the Brimstone." He shook his head, his dark hair whipping into his eyes. "But you were killed. The place was burned to the ground. I felt you die."

"I died for a time," the burned thing said, "so the bond we brothers shared was broken that day, but you know it's me."

"Shade?" Runa's voice broke into the tense air hanging in the cell. "What's going on? Who is he?"

"He's my dead brother," Shade bit out. "It's Roag."

# *Four*

*Roag was alive.*

Shade tried to process the information, but he didn't get very far. Nothing was making sense. "Why? Why are you doing this?"

Roag waved his shriveled arm. "This? The demon parts harvesting? You'll find out soon enough."

"How long?" Gods, Shade had visions of Roag running an operation for decades, right under their noses.

"Couple of years. I'm the new kid on the block, but my operation has all but put the others out of business."

"But why did you let us think you were dead?"

"*Why?*" With a roar, Roag swung the club. Shade ducked, but his chain restricted his movement, and he caught a glancing blow on the cheek. "You have the gall to ask me that? You tried to kill me."

Blood dripped down Shade's face in a stinging rivulet. "What the fuck are you talking about?"

"Brimstone, you dumb shit. You, Wraith, and Eidolon arranged for me to die. The only thing I don't know is who made the final decision that I was too insane to live."

Actually, Shade had decided that decades ago. It had been 1952, and all four of them had just spent thirty-six hours sharing a Bedim demon harem. Sated, exhausted, and still feeling a sexual high, they'd discussed what life would be like after *s'genesis*. Unlike E and Shade, Wraith and Roag had been looking forward to it. But Roag not only looked forward to it, he truly hadn't cared how he'd come out of it. Sane or not, it made no difference to him.

Eidolon had been surprised by Roag's attitude, but not Shade. He'd always thought Roag was one rat short of a plague.

"It wasn't us. For some reason, no matter how batshit crazy you went, E looked the other way."

"I'm not insane," Roag snarled.

"Right. Because sane people cut up other people to sell their parts."

That earned Shade another whack with the club, this time in the shoulder. "You dare judge me? I had nothing until after I healed from the fire and started up this operation, but now I stand to take all you and our brothers took from me."

"It wasn't us," Shade repeated.

"Liar! I know it was. And for that, you will all suffer. Just like your sister."

Roag signaled to the Nightlash, who came forward with his own club. Runa screamed, but Shade just closed his eyes. Fighting would be pointless, and Roag would get off on it. Instead, he bore the beating until his knees gave out.

At some point the blows stopped and Roag and the Nightlash left, but he had no idea how long ago that had been. Felt like days. Stones and straw bit into his knees as he knelt on the floor of the cell. His head throbbed and his mouth was dry, and he was only now coming around again.

Runa's touch, light and feathery, might have had something to do with that.

"How long?" he croaked.

"I don't know. A while." She pulled her hand away. They were still chained to the walls, barely able to touch and only if they stretched.

"Son of a bitch," he breathed, settling painfully onto one hip. "That son of a bitch."

"That demon...Roag...you thought he was dead?"

"For three years now."

Shade stared past her, at the stone wall that oozed moisture, but in his head, he was seeing a replay of the day he'd learned Roag had died. Only later had it come to light that The Aegis had somehow located the magic-cloaked demon pub and slaughtered everyone inside. When the Guardians were done, they burned Brimstone to the ground. How Roag had survived was a mystery, but the fire damage explained why Shade hadn't recognized his voice, which was now so gravelly and deep that his Irish accent had been distorted.

"I'm guessing that when he looked normal, with the blond hair, he was impersonating one of your other brothers? Wraith, right?"

"Yeah." He glanced over at Runa, wondering how she was handling all this, but man, she was a trooper, sitting there all calm and cool when Shade just wanted to go as batshit loco as Roag.

"Is...is there anything I can do?" she said softly.

"Only if you can bring back my sister."

"I'm so sorry."

He risked another glance at her. "I thought you hated me."

Her head snapped back as though he'd slapped her. "I would never wish this on you." She looked down at her hands, which were folded in her lap. "I know what it's like to love a sibling."

Shame shrank his skin. He remembered her brother, her devotion to him, her misery as she watched him waste away. They'd been close—she'd told Shade how her brother had been awarded custody of her when she was sixteen, after their father disappeared and their mother had been hospitalized. Arik had protected her as a brother should.

As Shade should have protected Skulk.

"How is Arik?" he asked, needing something—anything—to keep from screaming.

"He's great." She slid him a sidelong glance. "Thanks to you."

Shade cranked his head around. "I don't know what you're talking about."

"You healed him." She searched his face, but he didn't know what she was looking for. "I know you did."

"I didn't—"

"Don't. I know it was you. Arik was dying, and then you came over... and after you left, his condition began to improve."

Shade sighed. Three days before Runa found him with the two females, he'd gone to her house, an older two-story in New Rochelle, to drop off the jacket she'd left at his place. He'd also planned to make a clean break from her. He'd sensed her growing attachment, her need for more than he could give. The moment he walked through the door, the rank stench of death had assaulted him. Runa had been on the phone, so he'd wandered through the house until he found the master bedroom, where her brother had been lying in bed, a living skeleton.

"He was suffering from a demon-inflicted disease," Shade said, when her stare made it clear that she wasn't going to let this drop.

"What did you do?"

"Shit." He scrubbed his hand over his face. He hadn't wanted her to know any of this. He hadn't wanted her to feel grateful or that she owed him. The last thing he needed was for her to harbor any kind of tender feelings toward him.

"Shade? How did you cure him?"

A scuffle broke out in a nearby cell, followed by obscenities, a few barks of pain, and then things settled down. The silence, with the exception of the nerve-wrackingly incessant dripping noise, was enough incentive to keep Shade talking. Anything was better than listening to the sound of his own thoughts.

"I have the ability to affect bodily functions. The primary purpose of my incubus gift is to force a female into ovulation, but I can also enter the body at a cellular level, reverse some diseases." He shrugged. "Your brother's disease was an easy fix, actually."

"The doctors were amazed," she murmured. "I took him to the hospital the next morning. He walked in on his own two feet for the first time in months."

"Happy to hear it."

"Thank you."

And there was the gratitude he'd been hoping to avoid. "Don't thank me. I did it for purely selfish reasons," he growled.

"How can saving a life be selfish?"

He forced himself to meet her gaze with as much malice as he could muster. "I didn't figure you'd give it up if you were grieving over his death."

She gasped, and he felt a twinge of guilt for lying to her. He'd saved Arik because that's what he did. He was a paramedic, and even though the guy was human, he'd been suffering.

"You're a bastard."

"Yep."

He winced as he made himself more comfortable—hard to do after Runa's bite and the torture he'd been subjected to. Abruptly, he felt like a piece of shit for wincing at his discomfort, given what Skulk had probably gone through.

"So how did you survive the warg attack?" he asked. "How did it happen?"

She remained quiet for a moment, as though the silent treatment was a punishment, and he supposed in a way it was. "It happened the night I went to your place and found you with those...whores. I ran out, wasn't paying attention to anything going on around me, and the werewolf attacked me." She flinched so violently Shade swore to kill the warg if he ever caught him. "He tossed me behind a Dumpster when he was done. I don't know how long I lay there, but I did manage to find my cell and call my brother. He came for me. Took me to the hospital. The doctors wanted to keep me for a couple of days, but Arik checked me out against medical advice the next evening. I didn't know why, but I trusted him."

"He knew you'd been bitten by a warg."

"Yes. He didn't tell me that, though. He took me home

and locked me in the wine cellar. I thought he'd lost his mind. The next morning, when I woke up in the destroyed cellar, he explained."

Shade shifted forward, his aches momentarily forgotten. "How did he know? And how did he contract a demon virus?"

She jerked her gaze away, and he wished they were closer so he could force her to look at him. Then again, it was probably best if they didn't touch. He had too many memories of how good she felt under his palm. Under his body.

"Runa?" When she didn't answer, he tested the limits of his chains. "Dammit, he's Aegis, isn't he?"

She shook her head.

"Military?"

Her gaze snapped to his, eyes flashing with surprise.

"What? You think demons aren't aware that governments all over the world are working on the *great underworld scourge*?" He scrubbed his hand over his face. He was so freaking tired. "I don't suppose we can count on the military swooping down to save us?"

She just stared.

"Didn't think so." He blew out a long breath. "Wraith might be a no-show, too. Looks like we'll have to save ourselves."

"How?"

"That," he said grimly, "is the question of the day."

⌒

"The problem with having evil minions is that minions are stupid." Roag looked down at a slimy little drekevac that looked like a deformed, hairless ape, cowering at his feet.

"But I brought you the Seminus demon, one of the

brothers you asked for." The drekevac whimpered, his spindly fingers stroking Roag's boots.

"And torturing him with an unfinished blowjob and the death of his beloved sister was amusing, but ultimately, Shade is useless to me. He's cursed. Which means his body parts could be cursed. I need Wraith."

Eidolon would do in a pinch, but Roag had already set him up for a lifetime of torment. Logical, loyal Doc E was being tortured once a month by vampires who would eventually maim or kill him. Besides, he'd need E's surgical and healing skills to carry out his plan. Since Shade was useless, that left Wraith. Which was bloody fine, because he was the one Roag wanted to suffer the most anyway.

Poor little Wraith, so broken and tormented, so sheltered by his idiot, clueless brothers. Fools. Roag had seen through Wraith from the beginning. His youngest brother was a waste of good organs, but Roag planned to remedy that.

"Once again, you fail me." He kicked the drekevac so hard it flew across the ancient keep's great hall and slammed into a trestle table. As it scrambled toward him again, Roag morphed into Wraith's form, reveling in the transformation that made his stiff, scarred skin turn soft and supple. "Since you obviously need a reminder, this is what he looks like." And what Roag would look like once he'd harvested Wraith's skin and reproductive parts.

"Lover?"

He wheeled around, thanking the Great Satan that he'd changed form before Sheryen entered the room. The Bathag demon had never seen him in his true form, and if he had his way, she never would. He needed Wraith, and he needed him soon. Eventually, Sheryen would grow resistant to the mind-sex and would realize that despite all her memories and orgasms, they had never once had intercourse.

"What is it, Sher?"

"I see you have a Seminus in the dungeon. I want to take him out to play."

Jealousy nearly unhinged him. "You are to stay out of the dungeon, *lirsha*. How many times have I told you that?"

Her pretty pout made him grind his teeth in frustration. He still experienced the same urges he'd always had, but thanks to the loss of his sexual organs in the Brimstone fire, he could do nothing about them. It was a torture of the worst kind, being aroused but unable to fuck. He'd given Shade a taste of that earlier, when he'd set Solice to work on him, but clearly, she'd not worked him up enough, because he'd come down from his arousal rather than suffering to the point of death. The plan had been to let Shade agonize for hours, until he was nearly dead, and then send Solice back in, give Shade the release he needed . . . and start the cycle all over again.

A few moments of pleasure, punctuated by several hours of agony. Over and over. Beautiful.

And all ruined because Solice sucked dick as poorly as she performed surgery to remove the body parts from the demons his Ghouls captured. Which was why he needed Eidolon. Finding good medical help was even more difficult than finding good minions.

"Hmph." Sheryen tossed her long, silver hair over her shoulder. "Then I'm going to Eternal. Care to join me?"

Damn her. She knew he wouldn't go to any kind of club, let alone a vampire bar. The very idea made him break out in a cold sweat. "I'll see you tonight in our lair."

She blew him a kiss and sauntered away. "Follow her,"

he snapped to another minion, who had been gnawing on a bone near the blazing hearth. "I don't want her taking a side trip to the dungeon on her way out." Shade would gladly seize the opportunity to screw her brains out and then use her to escape.

Roag should kill him. Or slice him up. Seminus parts were damned near priceless on the underworld market.

Problem was, there was no way of knowing if Shade's curse, one of the most sinister and ingenious Roag had ever heard of, would affect the parts.

He was doing all of this for Sheryen, so he could bond with his true love and keep her in his bed—but he couldn't risk transplanting organs cursed by an antilove spell onto himself.

But killing Shade outright would be too quick. No, he had to be made to suffer like Eidolon. But how? Roag had killed Shade's mother, which had been fun even though Roag hadn't told Shade about his role in it yet, and Skulk's death would haunt him, but it wasn't enough.

"What has my brother been doing down there? Is he miserable?" Probably not. Shade had always been into whips and chains.

The drekevac shrugged one misshapen shoulder. "I... think not. The she-warg is keeping him company."

Roag narrowed his eyes. "They'd better not be able to touch." If that bastard was finding pleasure in his dungeon—

Wait... that was it. The ultimate torture for Shade. And if all went well, Shade wouldn't just be tormented for the rest of his life...

He'd be tormented for all eternity.

# *Five*

Satin sheets. Down pillows. Chocolate-covered strawberries and champagne. All of it was too decadent for Shade, who preferred a lot less comfort and a lot more leather and chains, but the luxury suited Runa. Her soft skin deserved silky sheets. Her long, thick hair fell in shiny waves across the puffy pillow. And the way she licked strawberry juice from her lips set him on fire.

Somewhere in the back of Shade's mind, he suspected this was a dream, but he didn't want to fight it. Being with Runa felt too damned good.

He moved against her, buried deep inside her wet heat. It had been so long since they'd been together, so long since he'd let himself enjoy being with a female instead of just getting off in one.

It was dangerous, allowing sensation like this. If she hadn't caught him with the two females last year, he'd have sent her packing, not because she'd grown clingy as he kept telling himself, but because *he* had been growing clingy. If not for the curse, *Maluncoeur*, he might have been tempted to hang on, see where their relationship might go, even if bonding with a human was out of the question. Even if, with her inexperience and shyness, she wasn't his type.

Something about her had drawn him, had him thinking about her long after he'd left her at her coffee shop, had him hunting down her phone number and calling for a date two nights later.

"*I've missed you, Shade.*" Runa's voice was sweet nectar, bubbling in his veins like the sparkling wine he'd sipped from the small of her back a few minutes earlier, when she'd lain on her belly, spread out before him like a feast. "*Take me inside you.*"

His head snapped up. Her eyes, glittering with lust and love and everything in between, gazed into his and he knew she meant what she'd said. She wanted to bond with him. To become his mate and help him through the *s'genesis* so he wouldn't go through it alone, so he wouldn't have his life turned upside down.

The right side of his face throbbed, the dermal markings trying to punch their way to the surface and declare that he'd gone through The Change. He was weeks away, days or hours, even, from becoming a shapeshifting demon who forgot his old life and spent his days in the mindless pursuit of females to impregnate.

Bonding with a mate would stop the insanity—literally. Post*s'genesis* males often went insane, Roag being an example of that. Bonded post*s'genesis* males kept their sanity, became fertile, and could shapeshift, but the only females they could sleep with were their own mates.

The fact that they would be limited for life to one female was the reason many Sems didn't bond, especially after *s'genesis*—who wanted to spend six hundred years with the same mate? Worse, there was only one way out—the death of one of the partners. And since demons, in general, held a serious disregard for life, finding a mate you could trust not to kill you in your sleep two hundred years into a bond was next to impossible.

Still, Shade would be willing to take the chance...if not for the curse. He couldn't risk falling in love with the female he bonded himself to—and he knew he *would* fall, and fall hard. The desire for a loving family had been bred into him on his mother's side, and every day he ached for what he couldn't have.

For now, though, he had Runa.

Her legs locked tight around him. She arched up, taking him to the root, moaning robustly. He'd forgotten how tuned she was to him in bed, always responding to his every desire with enthusiasm. Her curiosity had been limitless, and he'd enjoyed introducing her to various positions, toys, and acts.

Reaching low, she dug her nails into one butt cheek, forcing him into a rhythm of her choosing. "*Harder*," she growled. "*Until I scream, demon.*"

Surprise rang through him; she'd never shown any kind of aggression during sex, had catered to his desires and needs, had been pliable and perfect.

This was even better.

He pounded into her, giving her what she wanted, making her whimper as they climbed higher. The scent of her arousal rose up, intoxicating him with lust. Making him so drunk that the room began to spin, and when she commanded him to "*Drink me*" and dragged a long nail across her clavicle and drew blood, he did, without thinking.

She threaded her left fingers through his right ones, stretched their arms high above her head. Pain shot through him, lovely, delicious pain that radiated from his shoulder where she'd sunk her teeth. The *dermoire* that extended from his fingers to his neck began to glow with liquid heat, seeming to melt their limbs together.

Hell's rings, they were bonding. Oh, shit, it was happening and he couldn't stop it, not when her blood flowed like wine down his throat and she drew his blood with strong, erotic pulls. Not when his orgasm was barreling down on him like a freight train and she was screaming and...

He roared in his release as her climax milked him, her slick inner walls contracting around him and holding him prisoner.

*Prisoner*...

Blinded by the orgasm that went on and on, he couldn't see straight, but something wasn't right. The smells in the room were off, no longer chocolate and arousal, but mold and sewage. His knees weren't sliding on satin. They were scraping on hard stone.

"Runa," he whispered, and she moaned, rousing herself with the same dreamy fogginess that affected him.

"What happened?" She blinked up at him. Out of the corner of his eye he saw the *dermoire* on his arm stop glowing. He felt her inside him, in his soul, his heart. They were bonded.

And with growing horror he realized where they were.

"You bastard." Rage nearly boiled Runa's blood as she glared up at Shade. "What did you do to me?" She shoved hard at his bare shoulders. "Get off me!"

To his credit, he seemed as bewildered as she was. He scrambled off her, his movements jerky and awkward. But then, she wasn't exactly moving with grace and finesse, either. Her limbs felt heavy, as though her veins ran thick with lead instead of blood.

"Shit," he breathed, kneeling beside her. "What happened?"

"You don't know?"

"I know we just bonded. But I have no idea how we got to that point."

Bonded? She winced at a twinge of pain in her head. She must have been drugged. Her mind worked furiously. Nebulous images swirled through her head. The Keepers had brought them food and water. They'd eaten, and after that...her mind was a black hole. She vaguely remembered hearing Roag's voice, but then she was in a hotel room with Shade, and they were making love...

*Bonding.* The biting, the blood...some sort of mating ritual?

A tingling shock of arousal washed over her, purged her of coherent thought. Oh, she remembered this, remembered how sex with Shade left her enjoying orgasms for long afterward. She bit back a moan, ashamed that under the circumstances, she could possibly find another release.

As it swept over her, Shade drew her into his strong arms. "I love this part," he murmured into her ear. "After I've taken you, and you come apart while I watch."

She arched against him, clinging to his broad shoulders, clinging to the exquisite ripples of pleasure she didn't want to end. His hard slabs of muscle buffered her body's spasms. Dimly, she realized his thigh had spread hers and she was rocking against him. He held her tight, driving the hard length of his erection into her belly.

His lips brushed the rim of her ear as he talked her through the orgasms that came one after another. His words were graphic, hot, a verbal aphrodisiac that kept her shuddering in his embrace.

When it was over and her head had cleared, she shoved him away again, though with less force than before. "This is insane," she said, her voice as hoarse as she'd ever heard it.

"So is Roag." Shade shoved his hand through his hair, watching her as though gauging her ability to handle everything that had happened.

"I remember hearing Roag's voice. They must have drugged us. But why?" She glanced around the tiny cell, only now realizing that they were no longer chained to the walls. Hope sang through her. She welcomed the feeling until a dark hunger made her realize that it wasn't hope she was experiencing.

It was the pull of the full moon. The time was near.

"Why, I don't know. But Roag has the power to make us think things that aren't real. It's the same gift Wraith has. He got into both our heads and made us want to bond."

"And what, exactly, is bonding?"

"It's what Seminus demons do if they want to either avoid or reverse the worst effects of *s'genesis*. We still go through The Change, but if we have taken a lifemate, we don't sink into a life of violence, and we don't have the urge to impregnate every female on the planet." He leaned forward, his eyes dropping to her exposed breasts, which tightened under his hot gaze. "We only have the urge to impregnate our mate."

She swallowed and wrapped her arms around herself. "Did you..."

"I'm not fertile yet." He frowned. "Do I have a ring around my throat?"

"Yes." It was an extension of the *dermoire* running up his arm...a knotted collar around his neck. She reached out to touch it, but he shied away.

"Don't." His voice was low and rough. "I'm having a hard time controlling myself. The things I want to do to you..."

Her heart thundered in her chest. Jumped to her throat so she could barely find her voice. "Is...is that normal?"

"I've heard that taking a mate before The Change brings it on faster." His gaze darkened until the whites of his eyes had nearly been consumed by the black. "Because of the permanent supply of sex."

The mere word, the possessive intensity in his expression, nearly had her moaning. "Think again, buddy. I'm not going to be your little sex slave." She hoped that sounded more convincing to him than it did to her.

Shade put more distance between them, but the way his body was coiled, the way he watched her, reminded her of a panther ready to pounce. "That's not how it works." He fingered his throat. "Are there one or two rings?"

"One."

"There will be two once the *s'genesis* is complete. The first one means I'm bonded. The second means I'm fertile. You'll develop arm markings that match mine in a few minutes. Since the lycanthropy altered your DNA, you're no longer fully human, so the bonding shouldn't kill you."

*Shouldn't?*

This was really, really not good. She shoved to her feet and started to pace, the wolf blood itching just beneath the surface of her skin. "Okay, how do we unbond?"

He scrubbed a hand over his jaw. "We don't."

"What do you mean, *we don't*? There has to be a way. A spell, a ritual—"

"*There isn't.*" He rubbed his jaw again. "Fuck."

It occurred to her that she should be more upset, but since they were probably both going to die sometime in the next day or so, mating for life didn't seem like a big deal.

"For fun, let's say we survive the Ghouls. What does being bonded mean for me? For us?"

He stood, paced for a moment, his toned body a thing of beauty as he walked. "Forced fidelity, for one thing. Neither one of us can willingly have sex with another. You'll feel pain if you try. I won't be able to get it up. It means we will sense each other's arousal no matter how far apart we are. We'll feel each other's emotions. I can feel your anger right now."

"I'll just bet you can." She glared at him. "So this all sounds pretty shitty. Why would anyone do this? I mean, I get that it might make things easier on you, but why would women do this?"

"Not women. Our blood is toxic to humans, so we can't bond with them."

"Fine. Females, then. Why would demon females bond with you?"

"Demons do fall in love, you know," he snapped.

"Females do want to keep the male they love from going insane and fucking everything that moves." He took a deep breath, and when he spoke again, he was calmer. "Some species get longer lifespans out of the deal. Prey species get a protector in a mate. There are lots of reasons a female might bond with a Seminus demon."

"What about werewolves?"

"Out-of-this-world orgasms."

She stared. "*That's it?* Great sex? I'm forced to deal with you for the rest of my life and all I get out of it is great sex?"

"*Better* than great sex," he said, sounding a little put out.

She reached for her clothing, scattered around her. "This is just great." And she wasn't talking about her panties, which had been shredded.

"I'm not real happy either, princess."

She resisted the urge to snap at him. This wasn't his fault. "What's up with your brother? Why is he so ..."

"Psycho?"

"That works."

"He's always been off kilter. He was born to Neethul slavemasters, an extremely cruel race. When he went through his *s'genesis,* he lost what few marbles he had."

She tugged on her jeans, and at some point she must have growled, because he shot her a curious glance.

"You're close, aren't you?"

In answer, her muscles tightened painfully, as though they were being separated from the bones. "The full moon is almost here."

"Shit."

"Yeah. As soon as I change, they're going to skin me."

Shaking his head slowly, Shade fingered his earring. "I don't think so. Roag bonded us for a reason."

"So he won't kill me?"

He met her gaze. "Oh, he'll kill you," he said quietly. "But not yet. I think he has something far worse planned."

Doctor Gemella Endri stood in the physicians' lounge at Underworld General, watching Wraith pace while Eidolon and Kynan tried to calm him.

The futility of their efforts was heartbreaking. Wraith had been coming apart at the seams for hours now. Even his clothes hadn't been able to stand up to the stress. His T-shirt had been stretched irreparably at the neck from his hands' constantly tugging at it as though it had been strangling him. She figured that as much as he'd been pacing, his combat boots' soles should be completely worn down.

Shoving both hands through his hair, he stopped walking and threw his back against the dark gray wall covered with incantations written in blood—protective spells that prevented violence. Mostly. He and his brothers were exempt from the violence restriction.

"I still can't locate him. Dammit, I can't find him!"

Eidolon looked up from where he sat across from Gem, his dark eyes haunted. The ambulance Shade and Skulk had been driving had been found, but there had been no sign of the demons, and everyone in the hospital was operating in worry mode. "Can you feel him at all?"

Wraith stared at the ceiling, which was as dark as the walls. "I get blips of him when he's in pain, but they don't last. Someone must have put a masking spell on him or something."

"It's the Ghouls, isn't it?" Kynan voiced what they had all been thinking, and Gem drew an anxious breath.

"*No.*" Wraith shot across the room and slammed Kynan against the wall, which began to pulse as the threat of violence rose. He shoved his forearm into Ky's throat, putting pressure on the jagged scars running from Ky's jaw to his clavicle. "Don't say that. Don't even *think* it."

Kynan didn't react, other than to watch Wraith with calm eyes. What he'd said was right on target, and they all knew it. Just this morning an Oni demon had been brought in, her tongue and three eyes harvested by Ghouls, which only intensified their worry.

"Let him go, Wraith," Eidolon said in a soft, soothing voice. "Concentrate on Shade."

Several agonizing heartbeats ticked by before Wraith finally shoved away from Kynan. "I gotta get out of here."

Eidolon stood, adjusting his stethoscope to keep it from sliding off his neck. "Wraith..." The warning in his voice was as sharp as a scalpel blade.

"Spare me the just-say-no lecture, bro." Wraith stalked out of the lounge, and with a curse, Eidolon followed, leaving Gem alone with Kynan.

"That is one messed-up demon," Ky muttered, rubbing his throat as he snagged a Red Bull from the staff fridge. Gem had to pry her gaze away from the way his scrubs hugged his fine ass as he bent over.

"I think we're all a little messed up," she said tiredly.

"You mean everyone? Or just demons?" Ky popped the top while watching her with those denim-colored eyes that always made her breath come a little faster. "Like you."

The blunt reminder put her in her place. He was a human who used to kill demons for a living, who now had every reason to hate them. Yet he worked with them, socialized with them, and at UG, he healed them. Still, he couldn't see beyond what she was. Couldn't see how badly she wanted him.

Granted, the wounds he'd suffered when his wife betrayed him were still raw, but Gem wanted desperately to heal him, if only for her own selfish reasons.

She loved Kynan Morgan, and had for years.

Didn't matter that he was no longer the man she'd fallen in love with. The demon half of her rejoiced at the loss of his purity, his *goodness*. The human half wept, longed to see him whole again.

"Gem?" Kynan's hand came down on her shoulder, startling her out of her pathetic musings but soothing her with his heat.

God, he was hot. Dark, spiky hair, blue eyes, deeply tanned skin. His athletic build was made for marathons both in and out of bed.

"Ah, Gem?"

She blinked. "Sorry. I'm distracted."

"We're all worried about Shade and Skulk."

"Are you? Truly?" Her question came out more sharply than she'd intended, and she carefully leveled her voice with the next one. "Do you honestly worry about them?"

"You think I don't care because they're demons?"

"It occurred to me."

"I've known humans who were more evil than either of them."

The answer gave her hope, a light, fluttery feeling in her belly. "Could you...could you ever, um, be with a demon?" The question was out of her mouth before she could take it back.

Vocal cord damage sustained during his Army days had left him with a rough, gravelly voice, but now it went even lower and rougher. "What are we talking about? Sex?"

Her mouth went dry, and a shiver of both desire and anxiety raced through her. "I—I don't know. I just...could you see yourself with one?"

One long finger trailed along her jaw, the most intimate contact they'd ever had. "Never."

With that, he stalked out of the room.

Kynan ground to a halt just outside the lounge door, his heart pounding, his breath searing his throat. The shadowy hospital halls closed in on him, and he had to brace himself against the wall as a dizzying sense of vertigo bore down on him.

What the hell had just happened back there? In all the years he'd known Gem, he'd never caught more than a friend-vibe from her, but suddenly, she'd seemed... wanting.

Wanting *him*? Why? He was damaged goods and a Class-A asshole. Not to mention the fact that for over eleven months, his libido had been as dead as his wife.

But suddenly, as he stood there with Gem, his body had resuscitated as if it had been jacked up by a defibrillator.

*She's a demon.*

"Half demon," he muttered to himself.

*But the demon half is as bad as it gets.*

Jesus Christ. He stood there warring with himself

in the hallway, his scrub bottoms revealing his current aroused state, and why? He'd just made clear that he could never become involved with a demon, not even for something as shallow as sex, because sex had never been shallow for him.

Man, the incubus brothers would laugh their asses off if they knew *that* about him. How he'd always considered sex to be something special, to be shared between two people who cared for each other. But it wasn't as if he was judgmental of those who didn't feel the same way. He'd grown up the son of a call girl who had gotten out of the business when his wealthy, married father paid her a large sum to keep quiet. He'd seen the best and worst of people growing up and then again in the Army during battle. People did weird shit when they were stressed or hurt or just because of their upbringing.

So no, he didn't judge, and he didn't jump to conclusions.

Maybe he'd simply misinterpreted Gem's question. Maybe she hadn't been talking about sex—or, at least, sex with *her*.

Maybe he was a fucking idiot, because he knew damned good and well what the conversation had been about, and his dick knew, too.

Not that it mattered, because nothing could happen between them, no matter how sexy she looked in her leather miniskirts and thigh-high stockings—which he just realized at this very moment were unbelievably hot.

Fuck. He was in a shitload of trouble, and he had no idea how to dig himself out.

# Six

Shade paced, thinking of a plan to get them out of the dungeon. He watched the Keepers who came and went, trying to get a bead on their patterns, species, and sex. Seducing a female would give them their best shot at escape, and so far, he'd seen two—the female imp who had taken him from the cell earlier, and another who fed them.

Runa had fallen asleep a few minutes ago, so he sat next to her, back against the wall, and thought about Roag, hoping to remember something that might shed light on why Roag blamed Shade and his brothers for what had happened to him in the fire at Brimstone.

Runa's soft snores lulled him as he thought about the last day he'd seen Roag alive.

*The first ambulance run of the day had been a bust. By the time Shade and Skulk had arrived at the alley where a Soulshredder had been injured, he'd died, leaving behind only a thin, greasy oil slick on the ground.*

*Returning from the run, Shade had turned into the con-
demned parking garage, spiraling down several levels
beneath the New York City streets. Deep underground,
a garage door shimmered, invisible to humans, but a
beacon for demons. Shade had punched a button on the
ambulance's dash, and the gate opened, allowing the rig
to enter. They'd emerged inside a giant parking lot adja-
cent to the hospital.*

*After parking in an ambulance stall, he'd headed for
the break room, where Eidolon was arguing with Wraith,
over something stupid, no doubt. Roag was propped
against one wall, eyeing Solice, a vampire nurse, as she
bent to raid the fridge.*

*"Shade," Roag said in his Irish brogue, "I'm trying to
talk our brothers into going to Brimstone. They're refus-
ing. Again."*

*"Why do you even try? No one wants to go."* Not even
Wraith was crazy enough to hang out in lust-filled demon
bars.

But Roag no longer cared about consequences. He
was a slave to his instincts and libido. Even now, as he
watched Solice, the scent of lust rolled off him in waves.
Licking his lips, he crossed to her, hauled her against
him, and shoved her face-first into the wall.

*Eidolon cleared his throat. "No sex in the break room.
You know the rules."*

*As though he hadn't heard, Roag continued to caress
the nurse, and Shade braced for a battle. But when Eidolon took his first step toward the pair, Roag backed down.
"You're so uptight, E."*

*"I'll meet you at the bar when I get off shift," Solice
purred, and Roag grinned.*

*"We'll play spank the naughty nurse."* He nipped her earlobe and released her. She swayed, affected by his incubus pheromones as he stalked toward the door. Most females would avoid a posts'genesis Seminus demon if they recognized what he was, but since vampires couldn't conceive—except in Wraith's mother's lone case—vamps had no reservations about screwing them.

*"Idiot,"* Shade said as the door closed behind Roag. *"He's going to get himself killed."*

*Once he was gone, Wraith came to his feet, a wicked gleam in his eyes. "One can only hope."*

"Shade?"

Shade blinked out of the replay of the day Roag had been killed. He'd dozed off, and gods, he'd much rather be back in the dream than in the reality he'd awakened to.

He looked at Runa as she stared down at him and his heart pounded. It was only a matter of time before he fell for her, and the consequences of his emotional weakness would make a lingering death seem fun in comparison.

Shade had never feared anything, but the *Maluncoeur*, cast on him by a pissed-off warlock eighty years ago, scared the ever-living crap out of him, and if he wasn't careful, Runa would be his doom. Because even now, his body was surging to life, demanding that he possess her over and over, until she became addicted to him. And it *would* happen. With every orgasm, his semen would bond her more strongly to him, a chemical process that would result in more powerful, longer orgasms and a release of endorphins that would linger for hours. In short, she would learn to crave him as much as he craved her.

If only he hadn't given in to the needs of the human female so long ago, the beautiful silent film starlet who had fucked her way to fame and who demanded rough, violent sex from Shade as a form of penance. If only he'd not killed her husband when he found Shade naked with his tied-up wife. If only that husband hadn't been a warlock who'd thrown the curse at Shade in his last, dying moments.

> I call thee, servant of Evil, Demon of Vengeance, I call thee, Arioch, who giveth revenge, who taketh away life. I command thee, bind this demon to the *Maluncoeur*, to a life eternal of unslakable thirst, relentless hunger, unending pain, unrelieved desires. He shall not know love, lest he pass into shadow and *Maluncoeur*. Come hither, Come hither. Accomplish my will.

Eighty years later, the warlock's words were as clear as the day they'd been uttered through bloodied lips.

Runa patted his cheek with a cold hand. "Hey. You awake?"

He brushed her hand away before he did something stupid, like pull her down on top of him. It didn't escape his attention that she still didn't bear the mate markings on her arm. "What is it?"

"Someone's coming."

"Finally." Snapping out of his haze, he came to his feet and slid, naked, against the cold stone wall. Footsteps rang out—soft, light. Definitely female.

Fucking perfect.

He eased toward the cell door, where the shadowed corner would hide him. He gestured to Runa, who fell into place on the floor as they'd discussed, a length of chain wrapped around her neck.

She did a damned good job of looking dead.

Shade was going to do an equally good job of looking invisible.

As he slipped into the splash of darkness near the door, he shivered, his skin cells shifting and darkening until he couldn't see his own hand. Very few beings could detect him now, thanks to the inherited Umber demon ability to turn to shadow in the presence of shadow.

The footsteps fell harder, louder. A second pair.

Breathing slowly, evenly, to keep his heartbeat steady, he waited, hoping whoever was approaching wasn't sensitive to the sound of beating hearts and rushing blood. Vampires, especially, were a pain in the ass that way.

"Master said you no come here!" Desperation bled into the harsh whisper of a male outside the door.

"I want to see the Seminus," the female voice purred. "Roag and I aren't bonded yet, so I can do what I want. He doesn't know I've returned from Eternal. I have time to play."

Through the bars on the door, Shade could scent her lust, and for the first time in eighty years, he didn't experience even the smallest stirring of arousal.

He slid a glance at Runa, and his dick jerked. Damned bond.

The female peeked through the bars. Her pale, translucent skin, violet eyes, and pointed ears identified her as a Bathag, a cave-dwelling species. So...Roag had found himself a female to bond with.

"He's gone. Who let him out?" She rattled the door. "He killed the warg."

"No do this," the male cried. "No!"

The iron lock clicked. The door swung open, and the

female stepped inside, looked directly at him. He held his breath, tried—and failed—to keep his heart rate down. After a long moment, the Bathag turned away.

As she moved toward Runa, Shade struck, both hands clamped on either side of her head—but at the last second he didn't snap her neck. He should, but if what she said about bonding with Roag was true, his brother was in love with her.

She could be useful.

Runa leaped to her feet. "Behind you!"

He whirled, blocked a strike from the male who'd followed the female inside. In three moves, he had the skeletal demon broken and dead, and Runa had the female face-down on the floor. Runa straddled the Bathag, one hand holding the back of her neck, the other wrenching the Bathag's arm behind her back.

Though he scarcely had time to dick around, he stood back for a moment and admired the sight of his mate overpowering and—

Shit. He shook himself out of it. "We've got to go."

Runa's eyes shot wide. "Shade!"

Two Darquethoths burst into the cell, their fluorescent eyes, lips, and slashes in their obsidian skin glowing bright orange in the dim dungeon light. They moved fast, but he tore through them, making an opening for Runa as they spun away.

"Come on!" he shouted, and grunted as a rope wrapped around his neck. One of the Darquethoths slammed him into the cell door. Pain sliced up his spine.

A roar of rage echoed through the dungeon, and then Runa was there in a flurry of fists and feet, ripping some impressive moves on the Darquethoths. The rope slipped free, and he planted his fist in a Darquethoth's face. The male crumpled to the ground at the same time as the other, who had taken a blow to the head from Runa's foot.

The Bathag struggled to her feet. When she locked eyes with Shade, she hissed, and the ground began to shake. A stone in the ceiling crashed to the floor in a cloud of dust, and shit, she was going to bring the entire place down.

Runa's pupils dilated and narrowed wildly. Her fingers elongated. Night was falling as fast as the ceiling. Shouts came from somewhere. More Keepers.

"We have to go!" He grabbed Runa's arm. He wished they could take Roag's female with them, but the Bathag would slow them down.

The ground beneath them rolled and bucked as they dashed out of the cell.

Ahead, two Keepers fought to stay on their feet. Shade went through them like a bowling ball through pins. Without slowing, he dragged Runa up the narrow, winding staircase. They burst out of the stairwell and out onto a grassy expanse. Gray mist surrounded them, featureless save for the thick tendrils that swirled at their feet. Here and there, the veil thinned, allowing a view of rocky cliffs and scraggy trees in the distance. Behind them, a stone wall rose sharply, disappearing into the fog.

They'd been held in a castle.

"Where are we?"

"Ireland, I think." A guess, based on the landscape, but also on Roag's background. Upon his first maturation, he'd emerged from Sheoul, the demon realm deep inside the earth, to live among humans in various Irish cities, eventually becoming involved with the IRA. Nothing excited him more than causing trouble.

Runa doubled over, panting, though he suspected her respiratory issues had less to do with exertion than with her impending change into a warg. "What was all that about? The shaking."

"The Bathag . . . they have control over earth and water. They can cause tsunamis, earthquakes, all kinds of shit if they're riled. She was pissed." Angry shouts interrupted, sending him into his own bout of spastic breathing. "We gotta go, babe. I'd love to stay and play, but it seems like this stupid bond has brought out some seriously protective instincts."

"I can take care of myself." Her voice was soft but infused with steel. Just like her gaze.

He took her in, aware that time was running out, but not wanting to deprive himself of this moment. She had a warrior's soul, a fighter's resolve. It called to him, over-riding his common sense.

He grabbed her around the waist and tugged her up against him. At the same time, his skin tightened and his blood flushed hot. He wanted to take her right then and there. Hell's fires.

"I know you can. But I can make sure you don't have to."

Knowing the smart thing would be to leave her here to get herself killed, he cursed the bond, took her hand once again, and dragged her toward the forest.

⌒

Runa kept up with Shade, welcoming the stitch in her side and the way her lungs burned with every breath. She was free, and the fresh, crisp evening air ignited an urge to run, howl. Hunt.

"It's coming."

He stopped so suddenly she nearly ran into him. "Roag?"

She inclined her head toward the horizon, where a sliver of the day's last light peeked through the curtain of mist. "Night. I'm turning."

"Where do you usually go?"

"Does it matter? We're thousands of miles away from the United States."

"I can get us anywhere in minutes. Now, where do you go?"

She had a comfortable cage on the Army base, a secret installation beneath Washington, D.C., that ingeniously used the pentagram and hexagram layout of the city to its advantage. The symbols of Masonic significance, mistakenly believed by some to be satanic in nature, provided protection against evil while enhancing defensive magic.

Obviously, she couldn't tell Shade about it or take him there. Civilians weren't allowed anywhere near the operation. Demons were, but only if they were restrained, part of the R-XR program... or dead.

"My house in New York. I have a setup in the basement."

Not that she'd been there in months; she'd been too busy working with the Army to go home. Who'd have thought there were so many were-creatures in the world? She spent most of her days traveling the globe to were-beast hot spots, mostly coming back to D.C. only for the full moons. She loved the travel, the challenge of tracking down others like her, most of whom were tagged and left unharmed. The military seemed to think that in the event of a battle between humans and demons, weres and shapeshifters could play a vital role, and the military wanted them fighting on the side of humans.

Shade shook his head, but his alert gaze never ceased scanning the area around them. His muscular body sang with restrained power, and his sharply defined tribal *dermoire* lent an uncivilized, predatory quality to him. Amongst the haunting, untamed landscape, he fit right in. All he needed was a broadsword, and he could have been an ancient warrior, built for two things—fighting and sex. She shivered in a primal, feminine response to the image of Shade claiming a victory in battle, and then claiming her.

"Roag might know who you are," Shade said. "I don't want the Ghouls finding you."

Panic flared, making her heart thunder violently in her chest. Or maybe the tight, strung-out feeling inside was just the werewolf wanting out. "We have to do something. If I change..."

She trailed off, not wanting to voice the problems that could come from changing into a slavering, murderous beast that would probably kill Shade and then run off in search of human victims.

"I know." Shade lifted his face to the sky, as if he wanted to let loose a howl. She knew the feeling.

"What are you doing?"

"Probing for a Harrowgate. Roag wouldn't base his operation far from one."

*Harrowgate.* An underworld transportation system. The Army had been trying to figure out how they worked for years.

"Got it. This way." He started moving in the direction from which they'd just come.

"Uh..."

"We'll be fine. Once we're inside the gate, we'll transport to an exit near my place."

They slipped quickly through the trees. Shade moved like a cat, all sleek grace and light steps, and if his injured foot troubled him, he gave no sign of it. Her own steps grew heavy as her body tensed, preparing for the change. Part of her wanted to give the wolf side free rein, a danger for every warg.

Once a month she battled the desire to become a beast and run free, killing at will and for pleasure. This was the monster she'd become thanks to the bastard who had bitten her.

And thanks to Shade—something she'd do well to remember.

"We're here."

Runa peered into a glimmering space between a boulder and a crumbling stone wall. She'd seen similar curtains of light before, but she'd written them off as a trick of the eye.

Less than a dozen yards stood between them and the gate. But something wasn't right. The air had gone unnaturally still, as though evil had leashed the wind against its will.

Shade must have sensed it, too, because they weren't moving, and he'd gone motionless, except for his eyes, which seemed to be taking in everything at once.

"The gate is being guarded," he murmured.

"By what?"

"I don't know."

The rapid thump of multiple footsteps carried to her ultrasensitive ears, and she knew they were out of time. "We're going to have to risk it. Bad guys, eight o'clock."

They dashed toward the gate. Something rose out of the ground, a nebulous, smokelike creature, and they skidded to a halt, mere feet from the entrance. White wisps of mist wove together, slowly taking form as a beast about twelve feet tall, with gaping jaws and sharklike teeth. Red slits formed its eyes. It had no legs that she could see, but what it lacked in legs it made up for in claws the length of her arms. Runa had no idea what it was, but it smelled like feces and rotten fish. And it was scary as hell.

"Not good," Shade grumbled.

"Aren't you the king of understatement."

Behind them, three Keepers and the Bathag crashed from out of the brush. Shade leaped into action, taking one of the Darquethoths down. The Bathag leaped on Runa, her face morphing into something horrible and vicious, with a mouthful of sharp teeth and a forked tongue. Runa had trained hard with the Army, and while she was no Special Forces commando, she could hold her own. More or less.

Less, in this case.

The world spun as they rolled down an incline and crashed into a stone fence. Runa grunted and plowed her own fist into the demon's face. Teeth scraped her knuckles, and Runa sucked air.

"That hurt." Runa hooked her leg over the demon's back and flipped her. The female's snarl broke off when Runa struck her in the jaw.

The demon froze, momentarily stunned. Runa dragged herself to a thick, dead branch. The sickening crunch of something hard striking flesh, followed by Shade's pained curse, breathed new life into her fight. She leaped to her feet and swung the branch like a golf club.

"Runa! Don't kill her!"

Too late, the crack of wood on the Bathag's skull rang out, and the thing went limp.

Runa couldn't spare a single tear for the bitch, but she did spare a second to feel for a pulse. Nothing. Why would Shade want the Bathag alive? Wiping her bloodied hands on her jeans, she looked toward him, but he was fully engaged in battle again. She raced to the crest of the hill, found two dead demons, and Shade, taking down the last Keeper. Behind him, the smoke-creature snarled, but it floated back and forth, unwilling—or unable—to attack.

It was shocking, seeing Shade fight like that, a mass of hard muscle and tats spinning like a tornado. Her impression a minute ago was right; he was built for battle. Battle and danger and trouble all in one powerful package. He crunched a kick into the Darquethoth's back. It went down, a boneless puddle.

Shade didn't miss a beat as he turned to her. "The Bathag's dead?" She nodded, a weird sense of foreboding falling over her when his expression turned grim. "Damn. You ready?"

"For what?"

He took her hand. "We're going to make a run for it. The vapor wraith is bound to the Harrowgate, and it's male, so I can't seduce it."

She eyed the thing, straining to get to them but pulling up short, as though it was tethered to an invisible leash. "I thought you said that since we're bonded, you can't do that anymore."

"I can't go all the way with another female, but I still have an excess of incubus charm."

"Charm?" He had to be kidding.

"Fuck-me pheromones."

Now, *that* she believed. "Why would the vapor wraith be bound to the Harrowgate? Are all gates protected?"

"No. This is Roag's handiwork. To prevent his captives from escaping, and to prevent enemies from finding him." He squeezed her hand. "How are you doing?"

She knew what he meant, and almost as if his words reminded her inner werewolf that it should be starting to shift, her joints began to pop in excruciating bursts of pain.

"We have to go," she gasped. "But how?"

"We run right through it."

Voices rang out in the fog. They were out of time. *She* was out of time. She might think that running headlong into one of the scariest-looking demons she'd ever seen was a bad idea, but she'd have to trust Shade if she wanted to live.

"Whatever you say," she breathed.

He cocked an eyebrow at her, and then they were running. Shade threw out his arm as though to push the thing out of the way, and his *dermoire* began to glow. They hit the beast, and the sensation of a million jellyfish stings exploded all over Runa's body. She fought the urge to scream in both terror and agony. Tears burned her eyes, and she stumbled. Shade caught her, held her upright against the solid wall of his body.

The vapor wraith screeched, and suddenly they were past it. Shade dragged her inside the Harrowgate. Darkness closed on them, the pitch black broken by glowing symbols and maps etched into the smooth obsidian walls surrounding them.

Pain still rolled through her body, and beneath her skin, her muscles stretched tight, tugging on her joints as her body began to morph into her beast form. *Hurry, Shade.*

"What happened to the demon?" Her voice sounded

rough, guttural, and she knew she was speaking through a half-formed muzzle.

"I used my gift to scramble its insides. Didn't kill it, but it stunned the creature enough to get us through." He cast her a sideways glance. "Oh, hey...let's not do that yet. Sit. Stay."

Oh, he was hilarious. She was going to bite him as soon as the transformation was complete.

Shade tapped some etchings. A heartbeat later, the gate opened, and they stepped into a wall of heat and humidity. A jungle. Instantly, the sense that she was going to explode out of her skin faded. Her blood tingled with the upcoming full moon event, but the immediacy of the change had vanished. Best of all, her body parts had popped back into place.

"Um, where are we?" A cacophony of sounds surrounded them, bird calls and insect buzzing, as well as unidentifiable creatures screaming in the treetops.

"Costa Rica."

"Central America?"

"You know of another Costa Rica?"

Smartass. She jumped at the sound of something hissing. This place was going to give her a heart attack. Bad enough that demons were after her. Now she had to worry about poisonous snakes and hungry jaguars.

"Will those demons follow us?"

Shade shook his head and started moving through the brush.

She hurried after him. "What about Roag?"

He halted, his dark eyes scanning the surrounding jungle. "It's difficult to track someone through Harrowgates unless you can sense them. You need a hellhound."

"Okay, so why here?"

"You'll have a few extra hours of daylight. And," he added, "my second home is here. Roag doesn't know about this one."

Well, color her stunned. "You never told me you had a second home."

"It's not someplace I take humans."

Lovely. She pictured him bringing his demon sex partners here, to this steamy jungle where they probably rolled around like wild animals. All the reasons she hated him came roaring back, along with hackle-raising anger. That, combined with the premoon jitters, made for one caustic mood.

"It's not someplace you're taking me, either," she snapped.

"You have a better idea?"

"You can do what you want. I'll move in with my brother until this thing with Roag blows over."

Displeasure wafted off him in waves. "Out of the question. You stay with me."

"Think again." She crossed her arms over her chest, trying to ignore the trickle of sweat running down her back as the tension between them grew thicker than the sticky air. "I'm not the naïve, spineless little twit I was when we were dating."

"I liked you a lot more when you were spineless," he muttered.

"Yeah, well, I liked you more then, too."

"Dammit, Runa. The thing with Roag won't blow over. You killed his female. He will stop at nothing to get at you. And once he has you…" Shade's hands fisted at his sides, and he swallowed hard.

Her imagination took what he hadn't said and went to all kinds of horrific places as she cast a worried glance back at the Harrowgate. The shimmering arch hung between two rocks, identical to the one they'd entered in Ireland. Except this gate didn't have a creepy demon guarding it.

"Why can't I sense it?" she asked, more to get her mind off the reality of what Roag would do to her than to satisfy her curiosity.

"Newly turned werewolves are still too human. As your humanity fades with time, your nonhuman instincts will sharpen."

"How long? I mean, it's been almost a year."

He shrugged, a tense roll of one shoulder. "We have a warg paramedic on staff at the hospital who can sense them, and he's a hundred years old, was turned in his twenties. So he started sensing Harrowgates somewhere in that eighty-year time frame."

She shot him an irritated glare. "How helpful."

"Come on." He grabbed her hand, the one that had been shredded by the Bathag's teeth, and she winced. "You're hurt." He drew her knuckles closer to his face, bringing her body in as well.

"It's nothing."

Shade ignored her, running his fingers lightly over the raw, torn skin. A breeze rattled the trees, bringing with it Shade's scent, a potent mix of earth and sweat, battle and sex. Dirt and blood streaked his chest, and a bruise darkened one cheek, but he was all the more gorgeous for it. She hated her primitive response to the way he'd fought for her, hated *him*, in fact. But she couldn't stop staring any more than she could stop her heart from beating.

"Let go of me." She bit the words out viciously, desperate to get away from him, but he held her with his hypnotic gaze and slow, soothing passes of his thumb across her knuckles. When a low-level buzz shot through her hand, she gasped. "What are you doing?"

"Speeding up the healing process. I can't do what Eidolon does and heal you on the spot, but I can nudge your body's natural curative abilities into high gear." His voice was husky, reminding her of the way he sounded when he was inside her, murmuring sexy, naughty things in her ear.

He must have been reminded of the same thing, because he cursed and dropped her hand. "Follow me." He moved off without another word.

Frustrated by both her mercurial feelings for him and his unpredictable behavior, she watched him go, tempted to try the Harrowgate on her own.

"You won't be able to work it," he called out, and dammit, how had he known what she was thinking?

He led her along an overgrown trail, his movements swift and sure. Leaves sliced at his skin and branches clawed at him, but he didn't seem to notice.

She didn't know how far they'd walked with her jumping at every noise, but she sensed at least an hour had passed when he began to slow. The sound of rushing water reached her ears about the same time as a swarm of mosquitoes attacked her.

"God, I need a shower." She slapped her neck, squishing one of the bloodsuckers. "How can you stand living here?"

"The native wildlife doesn't bother me, and only the most extreme temperatures affect me."

She remembered how, in the cold dungeon, he hadn't so much as shivered after he'd been stripped of his clothes. She, on the other hand, had thought she'd freeze to death at times.

The thick weave of mossy trees and lush plants thinned, opening into a clearing bordered on one side by a sheer rocky cliff and a massively tall waterfall, a sparkling paradise in the middle of hell.

"Let me guess, the entrance to your cave is behind the fall?" Too cliché.

He said nothing, merely kept walking. She followed, slapping mosquitoes and brushing aside branches that snagged her sweater and tugged at her hair. They passed between the cliff and a giant rectangular stone, the path angling sharply upward for about thirty feet, until they ran into a dead-end tangle of brush and vines. Shade reached into a section of vegetation, fumbled with something until she heard a click, and a large chunk of rock slid sideways, revealing a narrow opening.

"Who built this?"

"Demon contractors."

There was something you didn't hear every day.

They stepped through the opening into a cool cavern. Soft light flooded the cave from fixtures mounted in the polished white stone ceiling.

"The waterfall powers the place," he said before she could ask.

Behind them, the stone slid back into place, but she barely noticed, was way too fascinated by this lair of his.

Open and surprisingly airy, the natural features of the cave had been used to create living space. Stone benches lined with plush fabric were scattered around the cavern.

A hearth had been set into a deep recess in the smooth, dark walls. There was even a large flat-screen TV hanging over the fireplace.

"It's mainly to watch movies," he explained, as he moved toward the rear of the room. "I don't get cable here, so I've got a helluva DVD collection."

Yeah, she had noticed that. One entire wall had been carved into shelves that held more DVDs than a video store. And for God's sake, could he get dressed? The way the muscles in his back rippled, the globes of his ass flexed as he walked...she couldn't help but stare, and he definitely didn't need that kind of ego boost.

He disappeared through a doorway, and she followed him. Tiny pinpoint lights had been set into the walls of the short hallway, which opened up into a kitchen of sorts. Again, natural cave features had been used, brilliantly, to define the room. The table, which could seat eight on two long benches, had been carved from stone. So had the counters and double sink. Stainless steel appliances, while compact, were state-of-the-art, and had been set into the walls for minimal profile.

"This is so cool." She'd been impressed by his New York apartment, with its modern, masculine decor, but this...wow. "Why would you live in the city when you could come home to this every day?"

"How do you know I don't live here?" He gestured for her to enter a narrow opening that jagged to the right, concealing whatever lay beyond the kitchen.

"There's not enough here to keep you busy," she said, and stepped into...oh, God. She clapped a hand over her mouth to contain a startled yelp.

He snorted. "If I come here, I plan to be busy." She came

to a halt, her feet turning to lead. His hands came down on her shoulders, and his mouth dipped to her ear. Her heart skittered in an erratic rhythm. "As you can see."

Oh, she saw.

They were in some kind of bedroom. Though she could use that term loosely. "This—this is a torture chamber."

Shade brushed by her, the heat of him practically burning through her clothing. "I prefer to call it a pleasure chamber." He swung around to her and she expected a smile, but strangely, he looked...sad. "This is where you'll stay tonight."

"What?" She backed away from him, bumped into the cave wall behind her. Something rattled. Chains. Holy crap. "You took me from that dungeon only to bring me to another one?"

She scooted away from him, sliding her back along the cold wall, but he tracked her with the predatory intent of the jaguars she'd been afraid of on the walk through the jungle. *Fool.* Shade was far more dangerous than any jungle cat.

He caught up to her, halting so close she had to crane her neck to look up at him. His voice was a deep, erotic growl as he murmured, "It's a play room, Runa."

"One man's play room is another man's torture chamber," she said hoarsely.

"Look around."

Swallowing her terror, she dragged her gaze away from his dark one.

A massive bed took up the entire back of the room and, like everything else, it had been built into a recess so that it sat in its own little cave. Pulleys, chains, and leather cuffs hung from the ceiling above the bed.

Elsewhere, sturdy wooden structures had been placed randomly, though she had no doubt there was nothing random about the way they were meant to be used.

"Stocks," he explained. "Spanking benches." His hand drifted over the lid of a chest in one corner. "Whips, flogs, gags. There's more, but I doubt you want to see."

Runa's mouth went dry. She had no idea how to respond, but she did know that for the first time since meeting Shade and learning he was a demon, she was afraid.

Shade left Runa alone in the bedroom, unable to stomach the scent of her confusion and fear. He hated that room, hated everything in it. Hated that he'd had to bring a woman as gentle and caring as she was into a place where he'd spilled both his semen and the blood of countless females during sex. They'd wanted it, and he'd given it to them because his nature forced him to do it, but he'd hated every minute with those demon females. They always left his cave satisfied, but he would be scrambled on the inside, so rattled that only immersing himself in work would level him out again.

Knowing his brothers would be freaking out, he used the satellite phone to call Wraith's cell. Wraith answered on the first ring.

"*Shade?*" Static warped Wraith's voice so Shade could barely hear, but he didn't want to step outside for better reception. He'd rather keep tabs on Runa.

"Yeah, man, it's me."

"Where are you? Are you okay? E and I have been climbing the fucking walls."

"I'm good. I'll head into UG in a few."

"I'll come to you. Tell me where you are."

The concern in Wraith's voice cut Shade like a scalpel. He and Wraith had always shared a deep connection, almost too deep. Wraith could sometimes read Shade's thoughts, which would be bad enough even if Shade didn't have any secrets he was keeping from his younger brother. But he did have secrets, and one of them was this cave. Tortured and caged for years, almost from birth, Wraith had a serious issue with anything resembling bondage or torture. He definitely wouldn't understand Shade's extreme sexual needs.

"Bro, I'm okay." He heard the shower turn on, imagined Runa stripping, pictured water running down her naked body, and his own hardened. "I need some down time, if you catch my meaning."

"If you aren't here by midnight," Wraith growled, "I'm coming after you. *If you catch my meaning.*"

Shade grinned. When Wraith made a threat about coming after you, he meant that when he caught you, he was going to kick your ass.

"Chill, 'kay? I'll fill you and Eidolon in on everything when I get there." He hung up before Wraith could argue and slipped out the hidden side entrance between the living room and kitchen. Immediately, a warm breeze wrapped around him like a lover's embrace—the only kind he'd ever truly allowed.

The exit took him to a flat, well-concealed stone platform behind the waterfall. He'd never brought any of his sex partners out here, but he wanted Runa to see his favorite spot in the world. Runa, who was naked in his shower. Shade's skin grew hot, so hot that the fine, cooling mist from the pounding water did nothing to ease the burn.

Sucking in a breath and a curse, he stepped fully into the waterfall. Water crashed over him, washing away the grime from the dungeon, but it couldn't scour away the darkness in his soul or the pain of losing Skulk.

His little sister had been the one beacon of light in his life, the soft to his hard. She'd been gifted with the Umber ability to see darkness inside anyone, had possessed the power to lessen or even remove it with a touch. That she couldn't heal Shade, couldn't come close to removing the darkness inside him had been a constant source of worry for her, but she'd been convinced that both his curse and the regret surrounding it could eventually be banished.

She'd been wrong about Shade, but right about Roag.

"There's so much evil in him, Paleshadow," she'd told Shade once, using the nickname he'd never hear again. With his tan skin, he'd stood out among his twenty sisters, all of whom were purebred Umbers, with cement-gray coloring, charcoal hair, and gunmetal eyes. He'd been the firstborn—a product of his father's rape of his mother when she was barely out of puberty—and ten years older than the oldest sister. Umbers were extremely gentle and maternal, so he'd been treated as well as his sisters. As the eldest, it had been Shade's responsibility to care for them. To keep them safe.

He'd failed miserably.

His mother had left him in charge while she went hunting, something that often took days. While she was gone, he'd been struck by his first maturation cycle, had left his sisters alone to satisfy his sexual urges, and when he'd returned to the cave, he'd come upon a slaughter. Khilesh devils in search of a meal had targeted the unprotected den, and it had been clear that even after they'd filled their bellies, they'd continued to kill. Skulk had been the only survivor, had escaped death by hiding inside a narrow cave shaft that was her favorite spot during their games of hide-and-seek.

Shade closed his eyes and turned his face up, hoped the water would pound him until he was numb, but he knew it wouldn't help. Nothing helped. He'd hunted down the Khileshis, but even their deaths hadn't helped. His remorse over what had happened was something that ate at him like acid, and it didn't matter that he'd left his siblings during a period of madness. Hell, he barely remembered leaving the cave. Barely remembered the days of nonstop sex that followed.

And yet, neither Skulk nor his mother had blamed him. It had been their love and comfort that made him want a family of his own, sons he could raise with a mate he loved.

Thanks to his curse, that wouldn't happen. It *couldn't* happen.

Shaking off the thoughts that were taking him down a well-worn path he didn't want to walk today, he stepped out of the water and strode into the cave. Runa was in the kitchen, wearing one of his T-shirts and a pair of draw-string boxer shorts she must have cinched to the limit at the waist. The shirt dwarfed her, fell to midthigh but didn't cover nearly enough.

"I found some soda in the fridge," she said. "I hope you don't mind."

"Help yourself to whatever you want." He slipped past her to get to the bedroom, where he changed into leather pants, a tank top, and boots. When he finished, he was surprised to find Runa standing in the doorway.

"I want to know what all this is," she demanded, her eyes full of that new stubbornness he wanted to hate, but admired no matter how hard he tried not to.

"I'd think it would be obvious."

"You never...you never used anything like this with me."

An image of Runa spread-eagled on his St. Andrews Cross and at his mercy licked at him, and his pulse pumped in an erratic rhythm. He might hate the room and everything in it, but only because he *had* to use it. Wanting to use it was a different thing entirely.

"No, but I wasn't the gentlest lover, was I?"

"I don't know." Her gaze dropped to her bare feet. "I don't have much basis for comparison. There was just that one guy before you..."

Something caught tight in his chest. He forced himself to inhale and exhale because he really needed to stay upright and a sudden lack of oxygen, combined with what she'd just said, would put him on his lid right now.

"You haven't been with anyone since me?"

Her brows framed a fierce glare. "I've been a little busy, what with being a werewolf and all."

A fierce, possessive instinct surged through him, swelling him with pride, swelling other parts with arousal. *Mine. Only mine.*

He ground his molars. Good gods, they'd been mated for all of a day and already he was growing close to her. Wanting her.

It could *not* happen.

Anger replaced the anxiety, summoned from that dark place inside that was a bottomless well. He grabbed her wrist, dragged her into the room. "Time for a little lockdown," he growled.

"Shade! What are you doing?" She struggled in his grasp, but the additional strength her lycanthropy had given her didn't come close to matching his. At least, not while she was in human form.

As gently as he could, he took her down to her hands and knees, held her immobile with one hand on the back of her neck as he reached for the *morphestus* chain that had been secured deeply in the rock. The links, reinforced with demon magic, had been designed to hold even the strongest beings, and the cuff he snapped around her ankle would adjust to the correct size automatically, so when she shifted, it would expand to accommodate her larger frame.

"Nightfall is coming."

"Yeah," she snapped, "in what, a couple of hours?" Her foot struck out, nearly catching him in the thigh.

"Something like that."

His gaze drifted over her, the way her head was down so her hair formed a curtain around her face, hiding what was no doubt an expression of fury. Her perky ass was raised up, rubbing against his hip with every angry motion. He could take her like that, right here, right now. A flick of his wrist would tear the flimsy boxers away. A twist of his fingers would free his throbbing shaft.

His instincts fired even as his mind screamed at him to resist his urges. Cursing, he released her and leaped away. She let out a furious, base curse of her own and lunged, grabbing for his leg. She missed, but barely. "Don't do this!"

"You've given me no choice!" he thundered, knowing it wasn't fair to punish her for his lack of self-control, but fair wasn't something he was concerned about at the moment. "You make me want you, and that can't fucking happen."

She recoiled, her mouth falling open. "Well, excuse me for being in your brother's dungeon and having absolutely nothing to do with any of this."

Now he felt like an ass. He stared down at her, the way she sat back on her haunches, the huge T-shirt hiked up enough to reveal the cotton boxers stretched tight over the hills and valley of her sex between her spread thighs. She looked vulnerable and sexy at the same time, but mostly vulnerable. This had to be terrifying for her, mated to a demon without her consent, chained up in a strange place, and on the verge of changing into a werewolf.

Oh, hell. He squeezed his eyes shut, willed himself to come down a little. "Look, I don't like this any more than you do. But I've got to head to the hospital. I'll bring you back some steaks or something. Before morning."

He knew, thanks to Luc, their werewolf paramedic, that if wargs didn't feed in beast form, didn't feel the tear of flesh and crunch of bone between powerful jaws, they woke up in their human bodies feeling ravenous, grumpy, and still craving the taste of raw meat. An unsatisfied were-beast would rampage in human form even after changing back at sunrise.

Runa looked away from him. "I don't want you to see me like that."

"Like what? A warg? You think I've never seen one? Honey, I'm a hundred years old. I've seen them, treated them, screwed...ah, yeah, I've been around a warg or two." She said nothing, and since he still felt like he'd just kicked a dog, he sighed. "I'll toss the food through the door and I won't look. Okay?"

"Whatever," she muttered. She tugged on the chain. "This is going to hurt when I shift."

"The cuff will expand."

"Of course. One size fits all is probably a necessity for you, isn't it?"

Feeling her angry gaze on his back, he stalked to the kitchen, grabbed a pack of gum from the cupboard, and wondered what he was going to do now. Wondered how he was going to tell his brothers that he was bonded, that Skulk was dead, and that their deceased brother was not only alive, but behind the organ-harvesting ring that had recently been plaguing their people. E would probably go all stiff and silent. Wraith would hit the ceiling. They'd react differently, but he had no doubt they'd agree on one thing.

In order for Shade to live, Runa would have to die.

Kynan stood in the staff break room, listening to Wraith and Reaver, a fallen angel and damned good healer, poke fun at the slasher movie playing on the large-screen TV. It wasn't Kynan's first choice of brain-drain programming, but he wasn't going to complain, since this was the first time in days that Wraith had done more than pace and snarl. He was just happy Shade had called and was okay.

He glanced up from grabbing a sandwich from the fridge in time to see one onscreen couple go at it, which pretty much guaranteed they were going to get slaughtered at any moment.

Wraith shot Reaver a grin. "Bet that's one of the bennies of falling, huh? Pleasures of the flesh?"

The ex-angel shrugged. "It doesn't suck."

Wraith cocked an eyebrow at the action on the screen. "She does."

Reaver's mouth turned up in the smile that made every female in the hospital think thoughts the poor ex-angel couldn't even begin to comprehend. "That's the best."

"I wouldn't know," Wraith said.

Kynan nearly choked on his peanut butter and jelly. "You're almost a hundred years old and you get laid a dozen times a day. The math doesn't add up."

Wraith rolled his eyes. "A, a twelve-pack is a slow day. And B, most of the females I hang with have teeth like razors. If you think their mouths are getting anywhere near my di—"

"*Code silver, ER.*" The female voice crackled over the intercom.

"Cool." Wraith grinned, and Kynan shook his head. Only Wraith would get excited about some sort of creature going apeshit and wreaking havoc in the hospital.

The Haven spell discouraged violence by causing extreme pain if anyone tried to hurt another intentionally, but an angry, hurt demon on the rampage could tear the hospital apart and cause a shitload of collateral damage.

Kynan shot out of the break room with Wraith and Reaver on his heels. They rounded the corner to the ER and, as a group, skidded to a halt. A massive, black-furred werewolf stood in the center of the room, holding his head and howling. A male nurse stood nearby, hand pressed against a bleeding wound near his occipital horn.

"The warg tried to attack me," he said.

The were, still cradling his head and making so much noise that Kynan's own head was starting to hurt, was definitely paying for his mistake. "What's taking so long with the trank?" he shouted at Ciska, the triage nurse, who was fumbling with the emergency med box at her desk, kept stocked with tranquilizers for exactly this type of situation.

Reaver ran a hand through his mane of golden hair. "That's a big-ass wolf."

"Bigger than Luc," Wraith muttered, which was saying something, because Luc was a tank on legs.

The warg finally brought his claw-tipped paws away from his head. Saliva dripped from his jaws and rage burned in his eyes. Kynan had battled dozens of unusually large werewolves in his Aegis career, but this one would have been considered a trophy kill.

Not anymore, thanks to Tayla. At least, not in the New York City Aegis cell.

Ciska slammed the drug box closed, the noise drawing the beast's attention. It leaped, knocking over equipment and chairs.

"Shit!" Wraith dived for the werewolf's leg, catching it near the shin. "Shoot him!"

The beast swung. The blow caught Wraith in the shoulder and sent him flying across the room. For a heartbeat, everyone except the werewolf froze. Holy...crap. The beast shouldn't have been able to strike Wraith without experiencing pain. It seemed to realize it had found a target, and in an instant, it was on top of Wraith and the two were tearing into each other.

Cursing, Kynan snatched the trank from Ciska and nearly got himself laid out as he jammed the needle into the creature's flank. It howled and spun around, but went down with a thud before it could attack.

"What. The. Fuck?" Wraith leaped nimbly to his feet,

his mouth and nose bleeding. He didn't miss a beat as he landed one well-aimed kick in the unconscious beast's belly. "You'd better not have rabies, you bastard."

"I thought only you and your brothers could beat on each other without feeling pain." Gem stood at the entrance to the emergency department, playing with one black and blue braid.

"Yeah," Wraith muttered. "Me, too..." He trailed off, frowning. "Something's not right."

Kynan kept his eyes on the warg, mainly to keep them off Gem. "Ciska, where did the warg come from?"

She used her red, whiplike tail to gesture at the Harrowgate, which was invisible to Ky's human eyes but which he knew existed between two polished marble pillars on the far side of the emergency room. "I heard a noise, looked up, and saw him in the middle of his change."

Wraith crouched next to the beast and laid his hand on its head. "Oh, man," he whispered. "Oh, shit. I know this vibe. His thoughts..." His palm smoothed the fur between its ears in a way Ky swore was almost loving.

"Wraith? What is it?"

"It's Shade," he said. "This werewolf is Shade."

# Seven

Blackness swirled around Shade, pinning him down as he drifted in and out of consciousness. He tried to roll over, but something more solid than the oppressive darkness was restraining him. He groaned. If he opened his eyes and found himself in Roag's dungeon again...

"Shade, man, wake up."

"E?" Shade dragged his lids open as far as they'd go, which wasn't much. He peeked through slits at Eidolon, who was unbuckling the straps holding him down. Shade looked up at the chains and pulleys hanging from the dark ceiling, and felt a rush of relief. UG. He'd made it to the hospital.

Wait—why didn't he remember anything, and why had he been restrained? How long had he been here? Where was...*Runa!*

Panic flared, but dimmed when he sensed her life force through the bond, sensed that she was safe, if angry, in beast form.

"What happened?" he asked, and shit, his throat was sore. He felt like he'd swallowed a spiny hellrat. Whole. And backward.

"Ah, well, looks like you got yourself mated."

One hand came free, and he reached up to rub the tell-tale ring around his throat. "Wasn't intentional." When E's brows rose, Shade shook his head. "I'll explain later. Why am I strapped down?"

"You aren't. All done." Eidolon helped Shade sit up and offered him a cup of water, which he refused.

"You gonna tell me what happened?" And why was he naked? Even his necklace was missing. Man, he was sick of waking up in strange places with no idea how he got there. Someone had laid a set of scrubs on the chair beside the bed, so he dressed while his brother ignored the question. "E? You're freaking me out."

"What do you remember?"

"Not much," he said shakily. "I remember chaining Runa up." Right after that, he'd hiked a few miles to his mother's cave, something he did out of respect, making sure no other demons had set up shop, but that was a secret he kept to himself. "I entered a Harrowgate, and…and that's all I remember." He swore. "How long have I been here? She's probably starving. I need to get food to her."

"Runa's your mate?" At Shade's hesitant nod, E asked, "Werewolf?"

"How'd you know?" Sure, the fact that Shade had locked her away on the night of a full moon was a dead giveaway, but the way E was hedging, not meeting his gaze…it wasn't like his brother. Something was seriously wrong.

"Last night, you stumbled into the ER. Do you remember that?"

"Vaguely, now that you mention it." He struggled to put together the fragments of memories floating around in his head, like the one of him stepping out of the gate and into the reddish light that allowed for day-dwellers to see inside the hospital as well as those who lived in the dark... but after that, the image broke apart like smoke in the wind. "It's pretty much all a blank."

"That's because the moment you exited the Harrowgate, you turned into a warg."

Shade froze as he tied the drawstrings on his pants. "That's a joke, right?" When E didn't crack a smile, Shade inhaled sharply. "E, come on. We're immune to the lycanthropic infection."

"I'll be sure to remind you of that tonight when you're doing tricks for Milk Bones."

Shade couldn't swallow. Could barely breathe. Seminus demons were not prone to "turning." The only way his species could become part of another species was to be born to it. Like Wraith, who was a full-blooded Seminus but also a vampire. Under the right circumstances, had Shade been born to a werewolf, he'd be a pure-blooded Seminus who would crave Kibbles and Bits three nights out of the month. But you couldn't *turn* into a vamp or a warg.

"Tell me what happened, Shade. Where have you been for the last couple of days?"

Shade sank down onto his bed before his knees gave out. "Hell, E. I was in hell."

A long silence dragged out. The familiar, muted blips of hospital equipment had nearly calmed him when E finally spoke. "You said your mate is chained. Where?"

"My place."

E nodded, knowing exactly which place. "That's why

you changed so suddenly. The time difference between
Central America and New York. All it took was stepping
out of the Harrowgate. You completely missed the transition period."

Yeah, Shade had seen a were or two shift from human
to beast and vice versa, so he knew they didn't just poof
into shape. Apparently, he had. He must have been one
pissed-off puppy once his shift was complete.

"Did I hurt anyone?"

"There were a few scrapes and bruises, but nothing
serious."

"Bro!" Wraith strode into the room and yanked Shade
into a bear hug.

"Someone was a little worried about you," Eidolon
drawled as Wraith released Shade.

"Like you weren't." Wraith punched E in the shoulder
and turned back to Shade. "Now, big bro, you have some
explaining to do. Starting with what the fuck you were
thinking getting yourself bonded."

Shade shook his head. Which felt like it had been
whacked with a baseball bat. "Trust me, that's not where
I need to start."

"Where have you been?" Wraith crossed his thick
arms over his chest, obscuring the raunchy phrase on his
T-shirt. "We know you were in pain, and we know you
were shielded."

"Shielded? Yeah, I guess that makes sense. I couldn't
feel you. Wondered why you guys didn't come rescue me."
Roag would have been smart enough to install a damping
spell around his castle to keep demons inside from sending
out telepathic pleas for help, as well as to weaken the waves
of misery that would be felt by those sensitive to it.

"Wraith nearly came out of his skin, he was so stressed." E made it sound like he hadn't worried, but the puffy shadows beneath his brother's bloodshot eyes said otherwise. "Everyone here was worried about you and Skulk." His voice lowered. "She *is* okay, right?"

"No." Shade's chest tightened around the empty hole Skulk's death had left. "The ambulance run we went on was a trap. Skulk and I were taken by Ghouls."

The temperature in the room plummeted as his brothers went dead still.

"Skulk?" E's voice was barely a whisper.

Shade couldn't say it. Not with the way his throat had closed up.

"Ah, fuck," Wraith rasped.

Eidolon said nothing, merely closed his eyes and hung his head. He'd be offering up a prayer in the tradition of his Justice demon upbringing, a prayer asking for fair judgment of her soul and a satisfactory return to a new physical body.

Shade, whose religious upbringing had been less fundamentalist than Eidolon's, wasn't sure what to believe about the state of Skulk's soul, but like many demons, humans, and vamps, Wraith didn't pray to anyone or anything, and curses began to fall from his mouth, nasty invective in several different human and demon languages.

"I'll kill the bastard who did it, Shade. I swear to you, I will mount his head in the specimen room."

More curses spilled from him as his rage gathered. Wraith had two switches—I-don't-give-a-fuck and I'm-going-to-kill-something—and any intense emotion threw one of them.

A voice screamed inside Shade's head—Roag's crackling,

hoarse words saying that Wraith had been his target, not Skulk. "We've got to find him first." He patted his shirt out of habit, seeking a pack of gum.

"Tell us everything," Eidolon said, and Shade braced himself for their reactions.

"I woke up in a dungeon. Runa was with me."

Wraith scowled. "Runa? That human you were boning last year?"

"Yeah. She's not so human anymore. And now I'm bonded to her."

"Why? How?"

This was so humiliating. "We were forced into it. By someone who knew about my curse. Someone who wants us all to suffer." He patted his shirt again. First chance he got, he was putting in an order for a damned vending machine in this place.

"It was a vampire, wasn't it?" Wraith asked.

It was a logical conclusion, given what had gone down between vamps and Seminus demons thanks to their father's insane indiscretion. The vampires considered what he'd done to be the worst kind of offense, and Shade had to agree. What kind of sick bastard raped a woman during the transition between human and vampire, impregnated her, and then used his gift—the same gift Shade had—to keep her body alive so the fetus would grow, until she gave birth? He'd violated her repeatedly during her pregnancy and kept her in what had to have been a hellish stasis, not quite human, not yet vampire.

Not surprisingly, the female had gone mad, and Wraith had paid the price. Eventually, so had their father, once the vamps caught up to him.

"I wish the fiend responsible was a vampire." He realized his hand was still at his chest, but he was rubbing it instead of patting for gum. The hole Skulk had left hurt, and talking about it only made it ache more. "It was Roag."

Wraith's eyes narrowed, and he waved a hand in front of Shade's face. "E? Did you order a CT scan? Did he hit his head?"

Shade swatted his brother's hand away. "Roag lives. And he's more twisted than ever. He's been behind the black market operation for the last couple of years."

Eidolon went taut, his expression haunted. Wraith took a second longer to absorb the announcement, but when he did . . . shit. Shade had never seen his brother go so deathly white.

"Not funny, Shade." Wraith's voice was a harsh growl. "Not. Fucking. Funny."

"Do you see me laughing?" Shade exhaled slowly, needing a moment to make sure he could keep his shit together, mainly because as unstable as Wraith was on a good day, this could get real ugly, real fast. "Roag survived the fire. I don't know how. He's damaged—skin like beef jerky, no nose, missing half his fingers."

Eidolon, ever the logical one, shook his head. "We felt him die. We'd feel him if he was alive."

"His death severed the connection," Shade said, "but when he was resuscitated, the connection wasn't."

"How was he resuscitated? By whom?" Wraith dug one hand into his jeans' pocket, and Shade knew he was comforting himself by feeling up one of his weapons. His brother was never unarmed, not when he was sleeping, fucking, not even in the safety of the hospital. No doubt there were a half-dozen more blades concealed on his body.

"Solice. She was there, with Roag. No doubt she's been spying for him." Shade clenched his fists at the memory of how she'd gone down on her knees and tortured the hell out of him in the dungeon.

"*Solice?*" Wraith's lip curled into a nasty snarl. "She's so fired. Like, with real fire."

Eidolon was totally revved, grinding his teeth, tugging on his stethoscope. "This doesn't add up. He was massively touched in the head, but why would he want to hurt you? And Skulk?"

"He killed Skulk to torture me. The rest . . . he thinks we're responsible for the fire at Brimstone. He wants revenge."

Wraith's eyes shot wide open, and E shook his head. "The Aegis did it."

"I know, but he's convinced we wanted him dead."

"I sure as hell want him dead," Wraith ground out.

"You won't get an argument from me." Shade pegged E with a look, daring him to disagree, but his brother only nodded.

Wraith paced in a circle, his boots striking the obsidian floor so hard Shade expected to see sparks. "You say Roag forced you and Runa to bond?"

"He made us think we were dreaming."

E cursed. "He really is sick. He knows that if you have a female tethered to you, you'll fall for her."

"And activate the curse." Wraith wheeled around. "It's an easy fix. We just kill Runa—"

A low growl erupted in the room. The writing on the walls began to pulse, and Shade realized the noise and aggression was coming from him.

"Easy, Shade," E said. "You know Wraith is right."

Yeah, he knew that. But the fierce, possessive instinct to protect his mate was burning inside him.

"I'll do it." Wraith's voice was hard, decisive. "Where is she?"

Shade was in his brother's face so fast he didn't remember getting there. "Touch her, and I'll lay you out like roadkill."

Wraith held up his hands, smiled with a flash of fangs. "See? This is why I'm never, ever bonding with a female. Makes you stupid." He shot a meaningful glance at Eidolon. "Or pussywhipped."

Pissed as Shade was, he had to give Wraith that one. Not that Eidolon being whipped was a bad thing. His mate, Tayla, had kept him from going insane, but she also had him wrapped around her slender little slayer finger. When she crooked it, he came.

Pun intended.

"Shade," Eidolon said softly, "would it be easier if Tayla did it? Tonight, after Runa changes?"

"No!" Shade backed away from Wraith, ran his hands through his hair, and left them clutching his skull as if doing so would help him keep his head on straight. "Nothing will make it easier. You think I want to know that Wraith is getting off on killing my mate or that your slayer is beating the hell out of her?"

E nodded as if he got that. "I can do it. I'll sedate her first. She won't feel a thing."

Anguish twisted Shade's gut, and he dropped his hands. His body and emotions were so tweaked out. "That's not like you, offering to kill someone." Then again, it was the logical thing to do, and E was all about logic.

"Better her than you." Eidolon's dark gaze sharpened.

"I won't risk losing you, Shade. Not to that curse. We've already got the werewolf thing to deal with, on top of your impending *s'genesis*."

The *s'genesis* that was clawing at him even now. He could feel the throbbing in his throat, right above where his mated mark had set into his skin. His groin throbbed in time with his neck, and he knew he'd need to be with Runa, and soon.

"No one touches her until I've gone through it," he growled. "Having a mate will make it easier, and with the lycanthropy complications..." What a nightmare. If *s'genesis* struck during a full moon, he could only imagine the horrors he'd inflict on the females he'd attack for sex.

Eidolon blew out a breath. "I agree that it makes sense to wait, but you're taking a chance."

"I'm not going to fall in love with her anytime soon, bro. She's annoying as hell. I have time."

"I don't like it," Wraith said.

Shade snorted. "You just want an excuse to kill her."

Wraith didn't deny it. "How did she infect you, anyway?"

His body cramped, as though it remembered the agony he'd been in when he'd begged Runa to hurt him.

"She shifted to bite me." He frowned. "She can shift at will. She doesn't need the full moon."

Eidolon started. "How is that possible?"

"She doesn't know."

"This isn't good, Shade. Were-beast infections are human diseases. We're not meant to catch them. Who knows what the lycanthropy is doing to your body. And what happens during a full moon when you need sex? You could rip your partner apart."

"I'll have Runa."

"For now."

Shade clenched his fists and changed the subject. "Maybe you should run some tests on her." The tests might reveal why she didn't sport the mating markings, too. Though that was something he'd keep to himself for now.

"Good idea."

Wraith picked up a scalpel from a nearby tray and tested the edge with his thumb. "You two are acting like she'll be alive long enough to find out what's wrong with her. Are you forgetting that she needs to die, and the sooner the better?"

Shade's hackles raised. "You're a little too eager to put her in the ground, brother."

Eidolon stepped between them. "I need to see Runa. If she can shift at will, she might have some unique antibodies to the lycanthropic infection. If I could isolate what makes her different—"

"You might be able to develop a cure for me," Shade murmured.

"Exactly."

Shade tried to ignore the sense of relief that took pressure off his chest, tried to pretend the relief was due to the fact that he might be cured of his lycanthropy and not that Runa had been given a temporary reprieve.

The relief didn't last long though. A wrenching, agonizing sensation slammed into his midsection, and his skin screamed as though he were being pricked by a million needles.

"Shade?" Wraith's voice vibrated with alarm. "What is it?"

He heard the scalpel clatter to the floor and felt two sets

of hands on his arms, felt his body being braced between his brothers' large, sturdy frames.

"I'm okay," he breathed. "It's Runa. I felt her shift back. Burn of re-entry, I guess." He shuddered as the sensations eased away, was suddenly very glad he'd been drugged for his transformation. "She's hungry." A stirring in his groin told him food wasn't all she craved.

Hell's teeth.

"Go to her," E said, in a tone that said he knew exactly what was going on. "Bring her in later."

Shade pulled in a ragged breath. "We need to deal with Roag. He's after us, and he might have more spies in the hospital. And Runa killed his female. He'll be after her, too."

"I still can't believe he's alive." Eidolon picked up Shade's chart and tucked it under his arm. "Do you know where you were being held?"

"It was a castle. Ireland, I think."

Wraith bared his fangs. "I'll find it. I swear to you, I'll nail his ass to the wall."

Shade nodded. If anyone could find Roag, Wraith could. His job at UG was to research, locate, and retrieve rare artifacts, spells...anything that might come in handy during the course of treating demons. He had experience, instinct, and single-minded focus that couldn't be easily broken. When he wanted something, he got it.

"Be careful, bro. Roag has always had a real hard-on when it comes to you." And speaking of hard-ons, Shade's punched painfully against his scrub bottoms. He needed to get to Runa.

"That's flattering," Wraith said wryly, "but he's still going to die."

The door whispered open, and Ciska entered. "Doc E? We have a new trauma patient in the ER. Gem is asking for your assistance."

"Got it." Eidolon slapped a hand on Shade's back as he passed. "Go to Runa. When you bring her in, we'll get this figured out." He disappeared down the hall, but before Ciska could follow, Shade stopped her.

"Got a second?"

"For you?" she purred, sliding seductive glances between him and Wraith. "Always. Are we going to party?"

Wraith shrugged, the motion casual, but he still looked a little wigged about everything. "I'm game."

Wraith was always game if the female wasn't human or vampire, and since the nurse was a pretty little Sora demon both Shade and Wraith had tapped, Wraith's enthusiasm was a no-brainer.

"Come here." Shade pointed at his brother. "You. Stay."

Ciska sauntered up to him, pressed her ample chest to his, and began to rub in a way that should have triggered an electric tingle. But it didn't. "Is he just going to watch?"

"Touch me," Shade commanded.

Smiling, she reached down, grasped his cock. For a moment, he stayed hard. Hope soared. Maybe he wasn't truly bonded to Runa. Maybe...she began to stroke, and he deflated like a punctured lung.

Fuck.

He wheeled away. The need for sex was still there, raw and persistent, but his groin felt as if it was connected to Runa by a rope. It tugged, bringing his erection back, making him burn.

Runa might not be marked, but he was definitely bonded

to her. She wanted sex, and by the way his adrenaline was surging, she wanted it in a way she hadn't before.

Damn her, she was going for his jugular, and it was only a matter of time before he bled out.

⌢

"Ky, buddy, would you mind checking on Wraith?"

Eidolon strode into the ER, where Kynan and Gem had been treating a Trillah demon—a sleek, catlike species—with a mangled foot. Gem had just come on shift, so they still hadn't dealt with how Kynan had practically run out of the break room yesterday, and the air between them crackled with unacknowledged tension.

"What's wrong with Wraith?" Ky tossed some bloody gauze into the trash.

"Remember the dead brother I told you about?"

Kynan nodded. "Roag, right?"

"He's alive."

"What?" Gem looked up from spiking a bag of saline. "That can't be right."

Fury flared in Eidolon's expression, quickly snuffed by the doctor's usual cool façade. "I'm having a hard time believing it myself." He snapped on some surgical gloves, all business, which was, Ky had discovered, how the guy handled stress. "Shade says he's behind the newest black market operation that's been filling our ER and morgue. He captured Shade, forced him to bond with a warg, and...and he killed Skulk."

"Jesus," Kynan muttered. He watched Eidolon assess the patient as though nothing out of the ordinary had just happened, but his eyes, flecked with red that came out when he was extremely pissed off, were flashing.

"I don't know how Wraith is going to react to all of this once it sinks in. I'd appreciate it if you could help me keep an eye on him."

Great. Just his luck to get tasked with babysitting detail. "No problem." He stripped off his bloody gloves and checked his watch. Six hours. He'd be off duty in six hours and drunk as a skunk in seven. Couldn't happen soon enough.

He'd wanted to get lit last night after the encounter with Gem, but there'd been a minor crisis at Aegis headquarters, a rookie Guardian who'd fallen apart after her first battle. Tayla could handle pretty much anything that came up during normal operations, but she was a little too hard-edged to deal with meltdowns. The traumatized Guardian had also required medical attention, so he'd pulled double duty as medic and shrink. Afterward, he'd gone straight to the tiny bachelor pad he'd moved into after his wife left him and crashed out of exhaustion rather than an alcohol binge. Tayla had offered to let him stay on the couch at headquarters, a six-bedroom house where two dozen Guardians lived, but he couldn't bear to stay where he and Lori had been happy.

*Happy.* What a joke. He had no idea how long Lori had been cheating on him before he caught her, but now their entire relationship was in doubt, all the way back to his first military deployment. She could have been screwing anyone while he was getting his ass shot at in deserts and jungles.

"I left him in Shade's room," E said. "Thanks, man. I owe you."

"Damn straight." Kynan stalked out of the emergency department, made it to Shade's room a minute later.

The door opened as he reached for it, and Ciska

brushed past him, a secret smile on her lips. The secret became less of one when he entered the room and saw Wraith zipping up.

Wraith rolled his eyes. "E sent you, right?"

"Yep." Kynan closed the door.

"I don't need a babysitter, so take a hike."

Ignoring Wraith, Kynan sank down in a chair. "Where's Shade?"

"Probably fucking his *mate* by now."

Yeah, that news had spread like hellfire through the hospital. Ky wasn't sure why Shade taking a mate was such a big deal, since E had done the same, but apparently it was a Very Bad Thing.

"It'll work out, Wraith. It'll be fine."

"Whatever. I don't care."

"Don't give me that shit. You care a lot."

Wraith snorted. "I don't care about anyone or anything, human." He jabbed Ky in the chest with one finger, leaned in close to growl in his ear, "I'd sell out my own brothers for the right price. Get that through your thick skull."

With that, Wraith stalked out of the room. As the door shut, Kynan heard him shout, "Hey, female! Come here!"

Kynan stared at the door. Wraith might not be looking for a fight or making a beeline for a junkie right now, but he had a tendency to use sex in place of drugs or violence when he was upset.

When the sex ran out, Wraith was going to go for one of his other two vices, and then things would get ugly fast.

Wraith waited until the lab technician he'd just screwed closed the door to the supply closet in which they'd just bumped uglies. Strike that—*he'd* bumped ugly. With her underbite, overgrown lower canines, and patchy fur, she wasn't the most attractive Slogthu he'd ever banged.

As soon as she was gone, he slid to the floor, spine against the wall, and buried his face in his hands.

Fucking Kynan. What made him think Wraith cared about anything?

*I'd sell out my own brothers for the right price.*

His words rang through his head, a harsh truth because he *had* sold out a brother. He'd betrayed his own kind, his own flesh and blood.

And he'd fucking gotten off on it.

Three years ago, while hunting New York City street gang members for sport more than out of a need to feed, he'd run into an Aegis slayer. Naturally, the moron had tried to kill him. Wraith supposed the guy had been an adequate enough fighter, but there wasn't a being on earth or in the demon realm of Sheoul who could take Wraith in hand-to-hand, and within seconds, he had the guy on the ground, dagger at his jugular.

It had been tempting to kill him, to drain him dry with his teeth. Instead, he'd given the guy a tip. Well, more than a tip. Wraith had practically drawn the Aegi a map to Roag.

Roag, who'd had a tenuous hold on sanity before *s'genesis*, and who had gone about as evil as could be after. Wraith and his brothers had agreed that none of them should have to live like that, but no matter what Roag did, Eidolon demanded full investigations before any severe punitive action was taken.

But the investigations took too long, and finally, after finding the remains of a human female Roag had raped to death, Wraith took action.

He could have killed Roag himself, but E would have figured it out. Wraith hadn't counted on The Aegis taking out the entire demon bar where Roag had been hanging out. Not that it had been a big deal—so what if a bunch of vamps and demons got whacked? But didn't it just figure that the one who was supposed to have died was the one who survived.

And now, because of Wraith, Roag had tortured Shade, nearly killed him, and had killed Skulk, one of the few females at UG Wraith hadn't screwed—and not because Shade would have blown a valve. Wraith had kinda liked her in a big-brother way.

And now she was dead, and Shade was suffering. Because of him.

"I'm so sorry, Shade," he whispered.

He threw his head back against the wall, eyes closed, mind jonesing for the mellow blotto of a drug binge or the cranked-up rush of a battle high. Sex wasn't working; he could screw every female in the hospital and it wouldn't be enough. He needed more.

Balling his fist, he punched it into the wall. The pain gave him a momentary buzz, but dammit, nothing was going to fix his life. He figured he still had a year left before *s'genesis*, and then he wouldn't give a shit about any of this.

But right now it hurt. And with the exception of self-inflicted pain, he didn't do hurt well.

"This is like the plot from a bad comic book," Roag growled. "I'm surrounded by complete incompetence."

A Drec minion knelt before him, his head bowed. It

had been nearly a day since Shade escaped, and the mess still hadn't been cleaned up. Several of his Ghouls were missing, and Sheryen hadn't returned from Eternal yet, which wasn't unusual, but which pissed him off nevertheless.

"Only two of our other captives escaped when their cell doors were damaged by falling stone," the Drec said.

Roag's withered hand curled into a fist. He wasn't concerned about the *other* escapees. What really chapped his cracked hide was that Shade and the warg bitch had broken free.

Fury seared him, shivered painfully across his ruined skin. Wraith was going to pay for ruining his life. For turning him into a burned-out shell.

Because he had no doubt Wraith was ultimately responsible. The night at Brimstone played over and over in his head, a movie that was stuck in a permanent play-rewind-play cycle. He'd been minding his own business, fucking a couple of faeries in the back of the pub, when the place had been overrun by Aegi. Roag noticed that one slayer, a Mohawk-haired punk, had been searching for someone in particular, and when he laid eyes on Roag, he'd zeroed in.

Roag had known, in that moment, that he'd been targeted. Instantly, he used his gift to enter the slayer's mind, and he'd seen a memory in the slayer's head. One where he'd been tipped off by Wraith, given directions to Brimstone and a description of Roag. His little brother had even sweetened the pot by telling the Aegi that he'd pay for proof of Roag's death.

Thanks to *s'genesis*, Roag had been able to shapeshift into something bigger and meaner, and he'd ripped that Aegi apart. When the pub erupted in flames, the only thing that had saved his life was that the demon he'd shifted into was immune to fire. Shifting into another species didn't bring with it the special gifts unique to the species, so Roag hadn't been completely immune, but he'd received enough resistance to prevent him from burning to a pile of ash. Still, if not for Solice showing up after the slayers left, he'd have died.

He'd always despised Wraith, despised the attention showered on him by E and Shade, but since that day at Brimstone he'd wanted Wraith to suffer as no one in history ever had. And when Roag was satisfied that Wraith had suffered enough, he would die. But not before playing skin and organ donor. Wraith would give back what he'd taken from Roag.

A commotion at the end of the hall grabbed his attention, and when he looked up, his heart, what was left of it, stopped.

"My lord," a Nightlash minion said, "we found her near the Harrowgate..." The Nightlash carried Sheryen's crumpled, broken body in his arms.

Roag stared at Sheryen as she was placed at his feet.

A bloody, injured Darquethoth limped forward. "We chased your brother and his female. They attacked—"

"Who killed Sheryen?" he rasped. "*Who?*"

"Your brother's mate, my lord."

Rage rolled through him, rattling his bones, stretching his joints, making his leathery skin crack until blood streamed from the fissures.

"Summon a necromancer."

The Darquethoth hissed. "But master—"

"Do it!" Roag roared. "Now!" He would have his lover back. Consequences be damned. "And get a new spy into the hospital."

"Yes, master."

"I will have Wraith," he swore, "and I will ruin my brothers' lives, but first I will have that bitch's head on a spike."

Roag kneeled next to his beloved, his entire body shaking as he pulled her into his arms. Thank the Great Satan she'd died near a Harrowgate, where the demonic energy prevented her body from disintegrating.

With a silent prayer, he willed the necromancer to hurry. Sheryen must be reanimated before her body began to decay, and the clock was ticking.

"Fear not, my love." He brushed his mouth over hers, glad she couldn't feel his scarred, stiff lips. "Soon, I will be wearing Wraith's skin, and you will feel the pump of Runa's blood in your veins."

He smiled at the thought, the delicious irony that only the blood of the one who had killed her would bring Sheryen back to life.

# *Eight*

Runa lay on the floor of Shade's cave, her body aching with residual postshift tenderness, her stomach knotted with hunger. She also ached with arousal, an inconvenient side effect of the shift from beast to human after a full moon. The effects usually lasted an hour or so as the primal animal hormones raged inside her human body. It didn't help that she'd awakened naked on a blanket that was steeped in Shade's scent.

Bad enough that he affected her when he was with her. Now he was doing it from a distance.

Need twisted her insides, made her clench her thighs and her teeth. She hated this phase of the werewolf change, when no amount of self-gratification was enough. Raw, violent urges roared through her, and it was probably a good thing Shade wasn't here, because she knew damn good and well she'd attack him.

For sex.

Where was he, anyway? she wondered. Her stomach rumbled, and her mouth watered. Why had Shade not delivered food last night as he said he would? Had something happened to him? She sat up, only to feel the heavy tug of the chain attached to her ankle.

She was tired of being chained. From one dungeon into another in a matter of hours. In her heightened sexual state, she studied the whips, canes, and flogs that decorated the walls of Shade's bedroom. The masks and gags and cuffs. Disgusting. Disturbing. And yet...what would it be like to be at Shade's mercy, to have his strong, talented hands wielding the tools he could use for pleasure...or pain.

He'd always been relatively gentle with her...relative to all of this, anyway.

*I wasn't the gentlest lover, was I?*

No, she supposed he hadn't been. He hadn't allowed her to touch him except during sex. He'd commanded her actions in bed, and some part of her had liked the way he handled everything. When he was in charge, she could relax. Between her brother's illness and her coffee shop's imminent closing, her plate had been full, her spirit all but broken.

So when Shade took her to his place for dinner and a few hours of sex, and then promptly brought her home, or when he'd meet her at a hotel, screw her hard and fast, and take off afterward, she'd been okay with it, for the most part.

And actually, hard and fast sounded really good right now. Just thinking about it brought a low growl into her chest and wetness between her legs. The wolf-beast in her wanted to get down and dirty. Wanted to submit to a powerful male, but only after a stimulating, hardcore battle.

She had never believed she would want to have sex with someone she hated, but maybe hating him would make it easier. It was just sex, right? No emotional attachments, no falling for him again. Just. Sex.

Except, could their relationship remain that way, now that they were bonded? He'd made it sound so... permanent. But maybe the R-XR could find a way to get her out of it. And if not, well, they had a few things to work out, because they couldn't spend decades—or even centuries—hating each other.

She shook her head, because she refused to believe this was permanent. There had to be a way out, and she'd do whatever she had to in order to find it.

*Where was he?*

The sound of footsteps vibrated in her ears, still sensitive from her shift. *Yes.* Heart pounding, she stood and swept up the blanket to cover herself. She'd stripped last night before she'd morphed into beast form, and now she wished she'd dressed this morning.

When Shade rounded the corner, she wasn't sure if she was relieved to see him or not. He filled the doorway, both massive shoulders brushing the sides of the stone frame, his broad chest expanding with each forceful breath. The scent of his arousal and anger came to her on a hot draft of air.

Excitement shot through her. Uncontrollable, shivery excitement.

"*Damn you,*" he said, in a voice that had been scraped over sandpaper. "Damn you for making me burn like this. For you."

Even dressed in scrubs, he stole her breath. He was carrying a bag of fast food, and his eyes were gold lasers that burned everywhere his gaze lit on her skin. He said nothing as he tossed the food to the floor and closed the distance between them.

She sighed his name, hating that she'd done it but unable to take it back. Not when she was already on fire for him. She closed her eyes, waited for him to kiss her, but he spun her, pushed her against the wall so his chest pressed against her back. His erection prodded her backside through the fabric of his scrub bottoms, and she couldn't help but rub herself against him like some sort of feline in heat.

"I hate how you do that to me," she whispered.

He popped her hips back with one hand splayed on her belly. "Do what?" He roughly kicked her feet apart.

"Make me forget how much I dislike you."

"Welcome to my world." He slapped his palms on the stone on either side of her head and covered her body with his. "I don't want this, but here I am."

For a moment she thought he'd take her like that, against the wall. But he remained motionless, dominating her in a primitive, animal message. The male animal was larger, stronger, and he would have his way with his female.

She began to tremble with forbidden, naughty anticipation. One of his hands tore away the blanket she still held uselessly to her breasts as the other clamped down on her hipbone and turned her to bring her hard against him. His erection ground into her belly, an immense, unyielding presence.

"Touch me." His fingers dug into her hip while the other hand came up to tangle in her hair. "Do it now." His pelvis arched into her, a not-so-subtle command.

Oh, yes. She wanted—needed—to touch him. But the beast still raged inside, desperate for more than a merely pleasant release. It wanted wild and erotic, with an edge of danger.

Her core went molten at that thought.

Feeling frisky and aggressive and more than a little stubborn, she nipped his collarbone hard enough to make him suck air. "Make me."

His body went steel-rod stiff. "What did you just say?"

She boldly met his gaze. "I said, make me."

He looked so floored, so utterly shocked that she almost laughed. Almost, because instantly, his shock veered sharply to anger. The hand that had been in her hair grabbed her wrist. She snarled, struggled against him, but he didn't give an inch. He brought her hand inside his pants and forced her to palm his cock.

"Now," he said, in a deep, guttural rasp, "stroke me."

Their gazes were still locked. The predator in her got all hackles-raised at the challenge in his eyes. The female in her got all shivery. The woman who had done a lot of growing up in the last eleven months decided that it didn't like being ordered around. It was time to show this male that she wasn't going to roll over and play the submissive.

Smiling, she closed her fingers around his thick length. It pulsed in her grip, the hot blood pounding in a raging tide against her palm. The head pushed up through the ring of her fist, which she couldn't close fully. He felt good, so good...she waited until the glint of triumph sparked in his eyes—and then she shoved him as hard as she could. He stumbled back. She sank into a crouch, ready to spring.

"You—"

She struck him in the gut with her shoulder, putting her entire body into the hit. He grunted and fell backward, coming down on the bed more gracefully than she'd have liked.

Her victory was short-lived. He came at her like a tank, spun her and slammed her face-first to the floor hard enough to knock the breath from her lungs. He pinned her with his weight, his long body stretched out on top of hers.

Hot breath fanned across her cheek as he growled into her ear, "What happened to my timid little Runa?"

Timid. The reminder of the power he'd had over her, the power to break her heart, really ticked her off.

"She died in the jaws of a werewolf, you son of a bitch."

Beneath him, she writhed, trying to break free of his grip but feeling her arousal grow with every motion. His cock ground against her ass, a hot brand between her cheeks. She could feel every ridge, every bump through the thin cotton of his pants, and now as she struggled, it was to push her hips up. To get him where she needed him to be.

"Would a son of a bitch make you moan?" His tongue swept along her jaw, a warm, wet stroke that forced a moan from her throat, just as he'd said.

"Yes," she panted. God, she was going to come like this.

"Yeah, you're probably right."

In an instant, his weight was gone, but his palm came down on the back of her neck to hold her cheek to the floor. His other hand slid beneath her hips to lift her so she was on her knees. She heard the rustle of fabric as he pushed down his scrub bottoms.

"I've wanted to do this to you since yesterday, when I

dragged you down to chain you here." He inhaled a great breath and let out an appreciative purr, and she knew he'd scented her desire. "I had you positioned like this, open to me. Vulnerable."

*Vulnerable.* In this position, she couldn't move, was completely dominated. It chafed, made her want to strike back, and yet, she quivered with excitement and her arousal ran down the inside of her thigh. She knew Shade saw, because he groaned.

"I want to lick you," he said roughly. "I want to start low on your thigh and drag my tongue up through that sweet juice until I hit the spot that makes you scream."

Oh, God. She whimpered, pumped her hips as his words triggered the beginnings of an orgasm.

"But I can't trust you not to fight me, can I?"

"Yes," she gasped. "Trust me." She wanted his tongue buried between her legs, wanted him to lap at her, to take her with his mouth until she collapsed.

His finger slid up the inside of her thigh instead, catching her slick juice. "Too bad I'm such a son of a bitch."

Straining, she jerked her head around enough to watch him suck his finger as he locked his gaze with hers.

The erotic sight tackled her, and she detonated.

"Oh, yeah." Shade released his grip on her neck and entered her with a swift thrust of his hips. Her core grabbed him, the spasms that rocked her body clenching and milking with such strength that he hissed, pushed deep, and just held on. "Fuck," he groaned. "Oh ... *fuck.*"

She felt him swell inside her, and then he was pumping so hard she was scooting forward on the floor. The front of his thighs slapped the backs of hers and his fingers gripped her hips with bruising force.

This was what she'd wanted since she woke up. She rejoiced in the furious pace, the brutal pounding, the wet sounds of erotic play...his shout as he released inside her.

Another climax took her by surprise, ripped through her body like a strike of lightning. Shade kept pounding into her, his hips jerking as his second release wracked his body. Another came for her, and another, until she was sobbing with pleasure and exhaustion.

She welcomed both, because all too soon, she'd be wide awake in a strange world with a demon who didn't want her, and another demon who wanted her...but wanted her dead.

Shade collapsed, slid bonelessly to the floor, taking Runa with him so they were on their sides, spooning.

Hell's freakin' rings. Was that the kind of mind-blowing sex that happened between mates? If so, he now understood why E got that stars-in-his-eyes look whenever he talked about Tayla.

The conversation with his brothers regarding Runa's fate came roaring back, along with scenarios that put a damper on the postorgasmic bliss. He could picture Tayla attacking Runa with silver-tipped weapons, beating her into a pulp before delivering the death blow.

Then there was Wraith, who could be brutally efficient or play with his prey like a cat with a mouse. He might take Runa down quickly, but would he feed on her? The image of his brother at Runa's throat, getting turned on and draining her of the last of her life as she lay limp in his arms, made Shade tense up and pull Runa closer. No fucking way was Wraith going to touch her.

Eidolon could do it with compassion, could inject a killing sedative while pretending to be taking blood or something... but no, if Runa had to die, Shade would drum up the courage to do it himself. She deserved that, at least.

She stirred, and he ran his hand up and down her arm. Her smooth skin, still curiously devoid of his *dermoire*, prickled with gooseflesh beneath his palm. Why hadn't the mate-markings appeared? Was it possible that he was bonded to her... but that she wasn't bonded to him? If so, he was looking at an eyeful of disaster. He required sex like humans required water. To live. Sex for a bonded male could come only from his mate. If the bond wasn't reciprocated, she could take off, have sex with whomever she wanted. If he couldn't get to her, he'd die.

He'd have to attempt her part of the bonding ritual again. He couldn't afford for her to be a free agent while he was tied to her.

"Runa?"

"Mmm."

He nuzzled her hair, inhaled her natural, earthy fragrance. "Come on. Let's clean up."

She didn't answer or move, so he unlocked the *morphestus* manacles with a command and carried her into the shower. Gently, he set her down. She smiled at him in a slightly dazed way, swaying on legs so shaky he worried she'd drop. Without thinking, he folded her into his arms and held her upright. When the spray from the double heads jutting from opposite rock walls hit her, she moaned, threw back her head, and damn she was beautiful.

Keeping one arm around her, he poured a stream of liquid soap over her shoulders, covered her in the pearly syrup until it dripped down her arched back and between her breasts. Carefully, tenderly, he washed her, all the while thinking what a moron he was for letting himself enjoy this.

She made an erotic sound, something between a gasp and a moan, and he pulled her closer, used his body as a buffer against her orgasmic spasms. Her noises, the feel of her slick, wet skin against his...it was enough to get him hard again. Not that it ever took much, but after the sex they'd just had, he should be sated for hours.

Hell's gates, he was in trouble.

He should never have brought her into the shower, should have cleaned himself up after the sex and left her to fend for herself. And she could. Of that he had no doubt.

Appreciation for her strength swelled in him, made him smile as he combed his hand through her hair. This new Runa threatened his world as no female ever had. Even if he couldn't sense her physical and emotional needs and moods, he'd find himself attracted to her. Sure, she was gorgeous, more so now that she had an edge about her, but it was more than that. Beneath the stronger, more aggressive personality she'd developed over the last year was the soft femininity and nurturing disposition he'd been raised to appreciate. He'd always told himself that he'd taken care of his sisters and mother, but truly, it had been the other way around.

Gods, why couldn't Roag have bonded him to anyone else? No other female tugged at his heart like Runa. No other female drew out his protective instincts the way she did.

No other female stood a chance of making him fall in love.

She was still only half-responsive as he rinsed and dried her, but as he tucked her into bed, she managed a yawn and a mumbled, "Food?"

"Yeah, I brought food. It's cold now, but I've never met a cold burger I didn't like." He fetched the bag he'd tossed to the floor earlier. She sat up, her gaze both groggy and dreamy as she dug into the fries and quarter-pounders.

"Thank you," she said between bites. "I'm starving."

"I can see that." He smiled when she stopped shoveling food into her mouth to glare at him, but it was a mock glare, because she chomped down on a fry and gave him a playful grin. Overtaken by a sudden urge to caress her pouty bottom lip with his thumb, he reached for her. With a curse, he checked himself at the last second and thrust a napkin at her to cover his actions. "You have ketchup on your mouth," he lied. "And ah, sorry about last night. I kinda got tied up at the hospital." He stretched out on top of the covers next to her. "That was a pun."

She froze midchew. Swallowed. "Tied up? Seriously?"

She looked so cute that this time when the urge to touch her made him itch, he gave in to it, trailing a finger along her exposed hip. "Funny thing. Seems that when you bit me in Roag's dungeon, you transmitted your lycanthropy to me. So last night when I stepped out of the Harrowgate into the hospital, I grew fur and fangs, and then tried to eat half the staff."

"But…" The color drained from Runa's face. "You said you're immune to it."

"Under normal circumstances, yeah. Eidolon thinks whatever allows you to shift at will affected your disease, and therefore—"

"Your resistance to it." She closed her eyes and fell back against the studded-leather headboard. "I'm sorry, Shade. I'm so sorry."

Emotion clogged his throat, a knotted mix of pleasure that she cared enough to be sorry, guilt that he'd gotten her turned into a werewolf, and anger that he'd let himself feel anything for her at all.

"Don't be," he said roughly. "If you hadn't bitten me, I could have died from the pain I was in."

"Still—"

"Don't," he barked. "Eat your food and get some rest. We're heading to the hospital in a couple of hours."

"Okay, Mr. Grumpy. Will we be coming back here?"

"We'll have to." He measured her response as he leaned in, some sick perversion wanting to get a rise out of her as he said, "We need to chain ourselves up."

And wouldn't *that* be interesting. They'd either tear each other apart or screw each other to death.

"Together?" The French fry in her hand began to tremble. "So we can touch?"

Touch, taste...Shade's body hardened as his mind filled with images of what it would be like to spend a night with both of them in beast form and nothing but pure animal instinct to guide them. Even now, his instinct was to put her flat on her back and drill her into the mattress.

"I felt your desire from New York," he gritted out. "I promise we won't spend another night apart as long as we both live. Last night I was heavily sedated, but tonight I won't be, and nothing will keep me from you." He rolled over so he wouldn't have to look at her and be tempted to take her again. "Finish eating and get some sleep. You'll need your strength."

Gem had just showered, stepped into a fresh pair of scrub pants, and fastened her bra when the unisex locker room door opened.

"Ah, sorry..."

"Kynan." She'd been trying to get him alone all day, but the man was a master of evasion, so she wasn't going to waste this opportunity. "Hey. Look, we need to talk about the other day..."

He held up his hands and made a point of not looking at her boobs. He looked everywhere *but* there. "It's fine. We're cool."

He turned away, but she grabbed his wrist. "No. Wait. Please."

"There's nothing to talk about." His already low voice dropped even lower, scraping gravel. "Let go. I don't like to be touched."

"I don't believe you," she said softly. "Tay told me how you and Lori couldn't keep your hands off each other."

Kynan went taut, but the pulse in his wrist bounded against her fingers. "Don't go there."

"I can see your scars, Ky. It's what I am. I can exploit them, reopen them, make them worse." She bit her lip, wondering if she'd just done more damage. "Or I can help you heal them."

"There's nothing here to heal, doctor."

"What happened to the Kynan I used to know? The one who laughed, the one who was gentle and caring and laid-back?"

He laughed then, but it was a bitter, cold sound. "He's dead, Gem. He died right alongside Lori."

His wife, whom he'd discovered in the arms of two different males in one night—one a trusted Guardian, and the other a demon with no moral compass.

Wraith. Who denied sleeping with Lori, but who had fed from her right in front of Kynan and who might have done far more had Eidolon not interrupted.

"He's not dead. He's just hiding—"

Suddenly, she found herself pinned against the lockers, one of the handles biting into her spine and Kynan's big hands on her shoulders. "He's gone," he growled. "Does this feel like someone who is gentle and caring?" He shoved a little harder for emphasis and then released her. "You're wasting your time with me, Gem. Find someone else to nurse back to health."

He stalked away, leaving her, heart pounding and chest heaving, in the middle of the locker room.

# Nine

⌒

The bed was comfortable, more so than Runa would have expected in a cave full of BDSM equipment. But Shade surprised her at every turn, and she wondered if she would ever truly know him. Then again, it appeared that they had a lifetime to get to know each other—not only as lovers, but as werewolves.

God, she hadn't seen that coming.

She remembered how pissed she'd been when she learned about her own infection, how she'd been terrified, lost, and alone, even though Arik had been there to help her through it. She hadn't understood the physical and behavioral changes that had taken place almost imme-diately. She'd been afraid for her future, for the innocent people she might hurt, and she'd been angry at how her life had been yanked out from under her so she no longer had any control over anything.

Shade had an advantage over her in that he'd been born

in this strange world, was already familiar with were-wolves. But, she thought, as she absently trailed a finger around a leather cuff dangling from the bedpost, this was a male used to being in control, both in and out of the bedroom. Having to give that up three nights a month couldn't be sitting well with him.

Yawning, she glanced at the bedside clock. She and Shade and had been sleeping for six hours. Careful to not wake him, she rolled over. He was facing her, his expression one of peace. The strange ring around his neck flexed as he breathed, the design's dark color the same as that of the *dermoire* running the length of his right arm.

She brushed his glossy hair away from his neck, where his personal symbol, the unseeing eye, seemed to, well, see her. With each breath, each swallow, it undulated, followed her no matter which way she moved.

Unsettled, she trailed her finger down his arm, followed the hills and valleys of his ropey muscles until she reached his hand. The *dermoire* went all the way to his long fingers, the ones that had stroked her, penetrated her, brought her to decadent orgasms more times than she could count.

Heat began to simmer in her veins at the thought. Geez, she was a hormonal mess. The werewolf thing had ramped up her libido, and the full moon made it worse . . . but being near Shade was like throwing gas on a fire.

A few minutes under cool water sounded good right about now.

She rolled to the side of the bed, kicked her feet over the edge—and in an instant found herself tugged back onto the mattress and tucked beneath Shade.

"Not so fast." His voice was sleepy and wonderfully

rough, and his half-opened, slumberous eyes burned gold. His erection lay heavily in the juncture of her sex.

"I was just going to take a shower. Would you like to join me?"

"After." He nuzzled her throat, nipped the sensitive skin there. "After I'm finished with you."

"Did you feel my, ah, arousal?"

His fingers delved between her legs to test her slick need. "Yep, I can feel it."

"You know what I mean."

He laved the area he'd bitten with his tongue. "It woke me up. Why?"

"Because," she moaned, tilting her head to the side to give him better access, "earlier you said you felt my desire from New York. I was just wondering if you will always feel it."

He lifted his head to look at her. No longer sleepy, his eyes burned with intensity. "We're bonded. I'm aware of everything you feel." He arched and slid inside her. "When you want sex, I'm compelled to give it to you."

"Even if we're in different states? Different countries?"

"Yes, but that won't happen again." He pinned her wrists above her head and began a slow, steady rhythm. "No mate of mine—" He broke off with a curse.

"You don't like that word, do you?" Just once, she wanted to be able to run her hands over his shoulders as they bunched with each of his powerful strokes, to dig her fingers into his back as she came, but his grip on her wrists tightened.

"What word?"

"Mate."

He shook his head, his thick hair falling around his face. "I don't like any of this."

She arched her back to take him deeper. "Not even *this*?"

An emotion she couldn't name darkened his expression. "You're aroused. The bond compels me to service you."

"Excuse me?"

"You heard me." He thrust faster, his movements almost mechanical. "Let's get it over with."

"If you think you're doing me a favor by screwing me," she snapped, "you can stop right now and go screw yourself."

He stopped, but he didn't withdraw from her body. "You would never have said that to me a year ago." His voice was a low, rough rumble. "No female I've *ever* brought to my bed would dare speak like that to me."

Glaring at him, she struggled to free her hands. "Probably because they're hanging in chains from your ceiling."

"Good point." He glanced at the implements of torture and pleasure hanging from his walls as though selecting one for her. The thought made her shiver, but whether with fear or excitement, she wasn't sure.

"I suppose you want to do that to me?"

He laughed, as if what she'd said was completely out of the realm of possibility. Which offended the hell out of her, because why would he enjoy other females like that but not her? And why in the world would she be upset about that?

"I like your spirit, little wolf. But it could use...discipline."

"My dad said the same thing." She winced, regretting

both the words and the memories that rushed in through the opening she'd made for them.

*The little brat needs discipline.* Her father'd say it right before he came at her with a belt or a wooden spoon or whatever he had handy. She'd been so spirited as a child, defying her parents at every opportunity, enraging her alcoholic father to the point of violence.

So how could she possibly view Shade's assortment of whips and other, unidentifiable objects as anything other than instruments intended to cause pain? What kind of messed-up sicko was she?

Shade stroked a thumb over her cheek. "Runa? Hey, you okay?" He finally released her wrists and shifted his weight as he prepared to climb off her. "We'll do this later."

"No." She tightened her legs around his waist. "I think...I think you *would* be doing me a favor if you just keep...you know." Now that her anger had faded, she couldn't be as crude as she wanted to be.

"Fucking you?"

Heat bloomed in her cheeks, and desire bloomed in her core. "Yes."

"You sure?" When she nodded, he sank against her once more, his hips rolling into her even as a sigh of relief escaped his lips. "Good, because stopping would put me in a world of pain."

"Like in the dungeon?" Lightly, so he wouldn't realize that he'd forgotten to restrain her, she settled her palms on the warm skin of his shoulders. "When you could have died?"

"Not that bad. We barely got started just now. I'm not that worked up yet. I'd have gotten over it eventually, but you'd have wanted to stay the hell out of my way for a couple of hours."

Her heart did a little flip that he'd have suffered for her, and dammit, it shouldn't be flipping for him for any reason. It seemed to be looking for any excuse to fall for him again. Clearly, it had a very short memory.

Shade tongued her nipple, shattering her thoughts. "Can you feel me?"

She smiled, because oh, yeah, she could feel him stretching her sensitive inner walls, sliding across the spot inside that made her wild. "Uh-huh."

He seized her left arm, the one he'd said should gain mate markings to match his, and her heart sank, because she wanted to be able to touch him, just this once.

"Not that. I mean, can you *feel* me? Did you sense my shift into a warg? Did you feel my mood this morning?"

Locking her ankles behind his back, she writhed against him, annoyed that the talk was interfering with the lovemaking. "No. Nothing. Am I supposed to?"

"I think so." He broke her leglock and pushed himself off up her. "Stay there."

Her body shook with need as he stalked out of the room, but he was back within moments.

And he was carrying a kitchen knife. "Um...Shade?"

"Shh." He mounted her, sank into her with a hard thrust. "I'm not going to hurt you."

"I know." How she knew, she wasn't sure, but in that moment, she just did.

For a heartbeat he froze, but then he was pounding her into the mattress with ruthless, delicious force.

Her climax came out of nowhere. Shade slashed his wrist and brought it to her lips as she peaked. Coppery wetness flowed over her teeth, her tongue.

"Drink." His voice was a husky command she couldn't

resist even though every instinct screamed against this. She remembered doing it in the strange dream-sex they'd had in the dungeon, the sex that had been imaginary but at the same time, very real.

Unable to stop herself, she took long, greedy pulls. With every swallow, her climax climbed higher, went on and on. His blood was like liquid sex, and as he pumped into her and found his own release, hers wouldn't stop. Orgasm after orgasm thundered through her, and each time she thought she was finished, another would overtake her.

Gradually, she became vaguely aware of Shade's weight on top of her, of his labored breaths, and of his rumbling voice.

"Runa?" He tried to pull his arm away, but she'd latched on with her teeth and was gripping him with her hands and no way was she letting go. As long as she drank, she came, and . . . "Runa!"

Ecstasy rolled over her and kept coming. A twinge of pain streaked across her cheek, but she didn't care. The pleasure had consumed her, taken her higher than she'd ever been.

The pain intensified, and through her orgasmic haze she realized Shade was squeezing her jaw, forcing her to open her mouth. Reluctantly, she released him, and he jerked away, clutching his forearm.

She moaned, unable to move as her amazing climax melted away. "What happened?" Her voice was a drugged, barely audible slur.

One corner of his mouth turned up in amusement, which surprised her, given the pain he must be in. "If I didn't know better, I'd say you were half vampire."

Sensation spun up again. Lust built, exploded, and she convulsed with another release, her body bucking wildly. Shade watched her with hooded eyes, his gaze shattering in its intensity.

"Beautiful," he whispered, his voice touched with awe. "You're so beautiful when you come."

She felt beautiful when he looked at her like that. Beautiful and vulnerable.

Panting, she fisted the sheets. "Why? Why make me drink you again?"

On some level, she knew she should be disgusted by the fact that she'd swallowed his blood, but after nearly a year of eating raw flesh three nights a month, she'd become a little desensitized.

"You don't have the mate marks yet. I'm hoping another try will make them appear."

"Maybe not all species get them."

Shade's gaze skipped away. "Maybe."

Sitting up, she grasped his forearm. "What are you not telling me?"

"Nothing you need to worry about." He stood, pulling out of her grip. "We need to go. We'll hit your place first to pick up some clothes. After that, we'll run some tests on you at UG, and be back here by nightfall."

Part of her mission for R-XR was to learn as much as she could about the demon hospital, so this was a great opportunity, but following that order felt wrong now. Like a betrayal.

God, she had enough to be concerned about without dealing with whether or not she should disobey her commander. Who also happened to be her brother. She'd have to check out the hospital and decide what to do from there.

"Don't tell me not to worry, Shade. Not when you are obviously concerned about something."

Dark shadows flickered in his eyes, turning them flat and black, making her shiver. "You're right, Runa. As long as Roag is still out there, we have every reason to worry."

No one liked a slow day in the ER, but they made Kynan climb the walls. He wasn't a kiss-your-boo-boo-and-make-it-better kind of guy. He wanted blood and guts, life or death. The kind of cases that dumped a gallon of adrenaline into the system. As an Army medic, that's what he'd been best at handling, under fire or in the eye of the storm. He hadn't even cared whether his patients were human. Car-struck dogs and bullet-riddled camels had received his care right alongside the humans.

And the demon.

Kynan exhaled slowly, the memory crushing in on his chest. He and Lori, who had also been enlisted, had been married four years. They'd been stationed at Fort Lewis, but he'd been deployed to Afghanistan. On the day his life had changed forever, he'd gone to the aid of a team of Rangers who had been ambushed and pinned down. When his team arrived on site, the Rangers were nowhere to be found, and with the amount of blood that had been splashed like paint on the mountain rocks, they couldn't have humped it out of there on their own.

Ky's team had conducted a search, an expanding square that turned up jack shit and landed his team in a firefight. In a hail of bullets and never-ending, ground-rocking explosions, Kynan had been separated from the team and pursued by Taliban fighters. He'd taken refuge in a cave.

Nursing a leg wound, he'd radioed for help. The transmission had been spotty, and he'd had no idea if the cavalry would be saving his ass any time soon. As he settled into a defensive position, he stumbled upon what was left of the Rangers. Alongside them were the bodies of enemy fighters, and scattered among the fresh carnage had been hundreds of human and animal bones.

Ky's mind had barely registered the horror when a two-headed monster—a demon, Kynan knew now—emerged from deep inside the cave. He shot it and then tried to save its life, mainly because someone somewhere would want the thing alive.

The enemy fighters had attacked while he'd been distracted, and he'd taken a shot to the throat. His memory from that point on was hazy at best, but later he'd learned that when fellow soldiers discovered him, they'd also found the men who'd attacked him torn limb from limb. There was no sign of the monster, but shortly after Kynan woke in the military hospital after life-saving surgery, the Men in Black—well, green, actually—had come for him.

With his enlistment nearly up, they couldn't force him into the Army's supersecret paranormal defense division, the R-XR, but the civilian equivalent, The Aegis, had approached him with an offer he couldn't refuse. They'd guaranteed double what the military paid, medical and retirement benefits, as well as his own cell, to be co-supervised with Lori. They'd also wanted him to travel, to train other Regents in both tactical fighting techniques and emergency medicine.

So the moment he was honorably discharged from the Army, he and Lori had signed on to fight demons.

Funny, since here he was, working in a demon hospital and saving their lives. At the moment, however, he was standing at the triage desk, filling out a chart for an infant Daeva who'd been brought in for a cough.

*A cough.*

Christ, demon parents could be as paranoid as human ones.

He heard footsteps, felt the warm swirl of air that accompanied Dr. Shakvhan, an ancient succubus who practiced Druidic medicine by day and stole human souls by night. Kynan had no problem working with her, but outside the hospital, Dr. Shakvhan would definitely meet the sharp end of his *stang*.

"Did you discharge the Neethul this morning?" she asked in a voice dripping with sensual promise she wasn't faking.

"Why?"

She shrugged one shapely shoulder, making the pale blonde hair draped over it shimmer. Little wonder that human men went willingly to their deaths with her. She was *Playboy*-centerfold gorgeous.

"Eidolon wanted me to take a blood sample for the DNA bank."

Kynan dotted his I's and crossed his T's on the chart. "Did it this morning."

Eidolon went ballistic if every patient wasn't checked against his list of catalogued species. Any species of demon not previously admitted to the hospital must be DNA tested and asked to donate blood to the bank for future use in others of the same species.

Dr. Shakvhan smiled and patted him on his head. "Such a responsible human. I think I'd leave your soul intact after

I drained you of your seed." She sauntered away, hips rolling in a rhythm that left most males panting.

Kynan hadn't panted for anyone since his wife died, and he wasn't going to start now, especially not for an evil succubus.

*You almost panted for Gem.*

Fuck that, he was not going there. Except his body *was* going there. It hardened at the thought of Gem, at the memory of how she'd stood in the locker room, her full breasts overflowing in the cups of her black bra, the tattoo of some sort of dragon covering her flat, trim belly, its teeth inked to appear as though they were clamping down on the piercing in her navel.

*Gentle and caring, my ass.* He'd done that gentle, caring thing with Lori, and look where it had gotten him. Maybe now that he'd made Gem intimate with the lockers, she'd get the message. She'd realize that some scars never heal.

He shoved his patient's chart into the filing box with more force than was necessary and reached for another as the Harrowgate hummed.

His adrenaline kicked in, and he welcomed the rush that washed away all thoughts of Gem. Technically, his shift had ended ten minutes ago, but he'd be willing to stay longer if something cool came in. Severed limbs and avulsions were always favorites.

The smell of blood preceded the patient, and yeah, this would be a trauma home run. Kynan jogged toward the gate, coming to a shocked halt as Wraith stumbled out. *Holy crap.* The demon must have gone a couple of rounds with a giant blender.

He was holding one shoulder, the arm hanging uselessly

to the side, blood running in a stream to the floor. Deep lacerations scored his entire body, exposing ribbons of tendon and white bone, but he was grinning as if he'd just gotten his first blowjob.

"Page Gem and call Eidolon at home," Kynan told the triage nurse. "Now." E had gone home an hour ago, but he needed to be here for this.

Kynan hooked an arm around Wraith's waist to keep him upright. "Shit, you weigh a ton." He guided Wraith toward one of the available rooms. "What happened?"

Wraith groaned as he sank down on a table. "Shot." He peeled his hand away from his shoulder, where blood oozed from a sharply defined hole.

"The other wounds aren't from guns, man," Kynan said, as he gloved up.

"Machetes."

Only Wraith would get himself chopped up by machetes. "Out hunting African rebels again?"

"Maybe."

"Keep pressure on that bullet wound." Obviously, Wraith's airway and breathing were fine, so he quickly checked the demon's pulses in all of his extremities. Everything looked good, but emergency medicine in a demon hospital was a hell of a lot different from in a human hospital, mainly because every demon species had different normal vital signs, constitutions, death thresholds . . . for the most part, Kynan winged it.

Kynan cut through Wraith's shirt with a pair of trauma shears and then carefully peeled the cloth away. Dried blood stuck the fabric to his skin in places, but this was the easy part. Those wounds were nasty.

The curtain separating the cubicles swept open, and

Gem entered. "Wow. You get into a fight with a really big cat?"

"Funny, Gem. Now why don't you get your funny ass over here and suck my—ow! Fuck!" Wraith glared at Kynan.

"Sorry." Kynan tossed the bloody shirt to the floor. "The fabric is embedded in the lacerations."

"My ass. You did that on purpose."

"Can't prove it." Kynan probed one of the deeper cuts. Seminus demons healed rapidly, and Wraith's bleeding had slowed, but not enough. "If it makes you feel any better, E's on his way. He'll have you all healed up and back out hunting genocidal maniacs in no time."

Gem thumbed up one of Wraith's eyelids. "You been draining junkies again?"

Wraith gave an indignant grunt. "No."

Kynan hooked his stethoscope's earbuds into his ears. "But you fed on the Africans, didn't you?"

"Well, duh."

When Gem shot Ky a questioning look, he said, "The fighters are feral. Completely wild, half out of their minds on kanif and harder drugs."

"That explains the glassy eyes."

"What happened?" Eidolon stalked into the room, dressed in tan cargos and a blue linen button-down.

"The usual," Gem said. She gestured to Ciska, who was preparing instruments. "Get a unit of blood. Any species."

"Dammit, Wraith," Eidolon murmured. "Why do you do this to yourself?"

Kynan slid the stethoscope's cold bell against Wraith's back. Wraith winced. "There were only, like, a dozen guys. And then all of a sudden I was fighting the entire fucking army."

"You were supposed to be looking for Roag."

"I was. I took a lunch break."

Eidolon bent to inspect Wraith's shoulder. "You've been shot."

Wraith snorted. "Cowards. Seriously. Who brings a gun to a knife fight? That's cheating."

"You don't have a gun?" Kynan asked.

Wraith made a face of disgust. "It's not very sporting to shoot people."

"So you're saying that you didn't shoot the people who shot you?"

"Hell, yeah, I shot them. Disarmed a punk and took out as many as I could before I hoofed it to the closest Harrowgate."

The *dermoire* on Eidolon's arm began to shimmer as he channeled healing energy into Wraith. Before Kynan's eyes, Wraith's lacerations began to knit together. Wraith groaned, baring his teeth. His fangs elongated, and Kynan could practically feel them throbbing. The healing process could be painful—Kynan had endured the pain a couple of months ago after being bitten by a Cruentus demon during an ambulance run.

Ciska returned with the blood and handed it to Wraith, who bit into the bag.

"That's disgusting," Kynan muttered.

Wraith cocked an eyebrow. "You volunteering to play Big Gulp?"

"You wish."

Wraith snorted, but before he could spew some smartass remark, E nodded in satisfaction. "Done. Now for the bullet wound." He glanced at Ky. "We'll need a local for this."

"I'm fine," Wraith said.

"This is going to hurt like hell, bro. Ky, get the shot."

"I said, I'm fine." Wraith's voice was a low growl that vibrated the air in the room.

Eidolon got right up in his brother's face, his eyes gold—which meant he was either aroused or pissed, and since Tayla wasn't around...

"We're not doing this tonight, Wraith. You got the fighting out of your system. Sex probably, too. And, I see, a little chemical assistance. It's time to chill out."

"No. Local. Anesthetic."

Narrow pinpoints of red began to poke through the gold in E's eyes as his anger hit the next stage of pissed. This was going to deteriorate into a critical situation, and fast.

"Get the shot, man," Shade said from the opening in the curtains, a new *dermoire* around his throat and a new female at his side. His mate?

Kynan couldn't be sure. She wore jeans and a short-sleeved silk blouse that revealed toned arms that were unmarked by the mate-*dermoire* Tayla had.

Wraith's eyes flashed ice—he'd obviously noticed the same thing. At least it took his focus off the issue of the injection.

"Get the shot," Shade repeated, his voice low and soothing. "If E says you need it, you do."

Wraith scowled, but if he was going to listen to anyone, it would be Shade. "Fine. Yeah. Whatever. Gimme the shot, human." As Ky brought the needle near the wound, Wraith grabbed his wrist. "Make it hurt."

"It'll make my day."

In the silence that fell, Kynan could hear Wraith's low, steady growl as he stared at the new female as if she was an enemy. Shade had picked up on Wraith's animosity, and the two brothers locked gazes. This was bad, though Kynan had no idea why or what the hell was going on. But a break in the tension would be a good idea right about now.

He knew he shouldn't do it, but as he injected the local, he said, "Hey, Wraith. I have a new X-Box game. Really violent. I plan to get seriously fucked up and play tonight. Want to try to kick my ass?"

Wraith's head swung around. "Why are you asking me?"

"Because you're always beating the hell out of me in the gym, and I want a chance to take you down."

Wraith's eyes narrowed, as if he knew this was a trick, but he couldn't resist the bait. "I do knock you around, don't I?"

That was a no-shitter. Kynan had been training with Wraith for months, learning new fighting techniques and honing the old ones, but he'd never acquire even a tenth of the skills Wraith had mastered.

"I'll kick your ass in the game, too," Wraith said, not so much as flinching as Ky pulled the needle out of his flesh.

"You don't stand a chance."

Wraith snorted. "I'm so going to grind you into dust."

Eidolon offered Ky a subtle nod, a silent thank-you for defusing an explosive situation. Ky returned the nod and made the mistake of glancing over at Gem. He might have snuffed the fuse from one stick of dynamite, but it was clear by the glint in her eyes that the thing between him and Gem still burned.

# *Ten*

Shade didn't wait around in the ER to answer questions or listen to lectures about Runa. He took her to the lab, plunked her into a chair, and gave the technician, Frank, one of the few humans on staff, orders to take enough blood to run every test available.

Then he waited just outside the door where he could see what was going on, because no way was that man going to touch Runa without Shade's being present. He'd have preferred to draw the blood himself, but he knew his brothers would be showing up at any moment to ask questions he didn't know how to answer.

He watched Runa through the window, inexplicably pleased to see that she was looking around the lab with curiosity, not terror, as he might have expected from someone who had never been inside a demon hospital. Then again, she knew he was right outside the door, and he'd assured her that nothing bad would happen to her as long as he was near.

What a big, fucking lie.

His gut wrenched as he dragged his gaze away from her. He was growing too close, too fast, and this morning's sex had made the situation worse. Not only had he lied through his teeth about servicing her—hell, he'd probably needed her more than she'd needed him—but the haunted look in her eyes when she'd brought up her father had been like an icepick through his heart.

There was a painful story there, and he had a feeling it was related to the darkness, the guilt, he sensed in her, but he didn't want to know. Didn't want to string her up as he had the females in his past in order to draw that darkness out through sex and pain. As long as she tried to keep it buried, he'd be okay. The moment she decided she wanted to open up about her past, the moment she decided she wanted to be rid of her guilt or whatever was staining her soul, he'd be forced to do whatever it took to extract it from her.

The thought made him queasy.

And what the hell was up with the lack of the mate-markings? Even after the second try this morning...nothing.

This was so not good.

E walked up to him, his concern obvious in his drawn brows and the tight set of his mouth.

"Where's Wraith?" Shade asked. "I figured for sure he'd want to be here to drill me."

"I sent him with Kynan. Told him you didn't need both of us drilling you."

"Bullshit. Wraith wouldn't buy that."

Eidolon grinned. "He didn't. But I explained that I know what it's like to have a mate, and I'd know how to deal with you. I told him anything he said would send you running for the hills and we'd never see you again."

"That's not going to happen."

A grim scowl replaced E's smile, bringing them both back to the place where Shade was royally fucked. "I know that. But he doesn't."

"Is he okay?"

"He's rattled. He's doing his best to deal with the Roag thing, and Skulk, and you being in the situation you're in, but he's taking things a little too well."

"Which means it's only a matter of time before he blows."

Eidolon dragged a hand through his short, dark hair. "You didn't say anything about Runa not being marked." When Shade shrugged, E continued. "Can she sense you? Or is this bonding one-sided?"

Shade glanced through the door window at Runa, who was smiling at the lab tech as he held her arm steady for the blood draw. *Mine*. Shade swallowed hard. Rage and jealousy had made a fine blockage in his throat.

"Frank's *touching* her. I should have done the draw. I still can—"

"Shade? Look at me."

He wrenched his eyes away from Runa and Frank.

"Why didn't you get the blood samples yourself?"

"Because I'm trying to keep my distance. But his hands are on her. I'm going to kill him."

"It'll get easier, bro. As the bond settles, the raging jealousy will ease up. Won't go completely away, but it'll get better. If it didn't, I couldn't have let Tayla keep working with men at Aegis headquarters."

"Let her? Something tells me you wouldn't have been able to stop her."

E looked a little sheepish. "Yeah, you're probably right."

Shade sucked in a shaky breath and avoided looking through the window again. "The bond is one-sided. I don't get it. I know we did it right the first time. And today I repeated her part of the ritual."

"This could be a problem."

"No shit." Shade braced a shoulder against the wall, welcoming the support. "Hey, can I ask you something?"

"Shoot."

Shade hesitated. Talking sex with his brothers had never been any different from talking sports. But this felt awkward and wrong, as if he were betraying Runa.

"Is sex…different for you since you took Tay as your mate?"

Eidolon's brows shot up, and a knowing grin split his face. "Oh, yeah. Much better. Definitely a perk of the bond."

"I was afraid of that."

There was a brittle silence. Finally Eidolon said, "We'll find a way to get you out of this. Both the warg thing, and the curse."

Shade laughed bitterly. "Even if we find a cure for the lycanthropy, the curse isn't going to end well."

"There's got to be a way. Something we missed."

"We've been looking for almost eighty years, E. There's only one way out, and it's not an option."

Yeah, the fun little love curse came with an out clause that was as demented as the prick who dreamed up the spell in the first place.

Shade could transfer the curse to a loved one, some- one he cared about in a nonromantic way. Which left only Eidolon and Wraith, and that was not going to happen. Even if he did decide to transfer the curse, he had no idea how to go about doing so.

An orderly pushing a cart with his tentacles passed by, and once he was out of earshot, Eidolon said, "Are you in danger of falling for Runa anytime soon?"

Shade closed his eyes, as if doing so would block out the truth. "No," he lied. He didn't want to freak out his brothers, and saying yes would put Runa in immediate danger.

"I know you don't want to kill her, but there might be another way."

Shade's eyes snapped open. "What?"

"We can keep her here. Or somewhere. A special room where she'll be comfortable. You can go to her when you need to—"

"You want to keep her caged like an animal? Like an *Orgesu*?"

"Shade, if she isn't bonded to you, she can take off. Go anywhere she wants, screw anyone she wants, and where does that leave you? A strung-out beast trying to track her down before you die. Even if she were bonded, you can't be together. You'll fall for her. It's inevitable. Then we lose you and you're stuck in a fate worse than death."

Way worse. He could picture himself as nothing more than a phantom, floating around with no way to commu- nicate with anyone, no way to touch anyone. Stuck in a permanent state of starvation, thirst, and pain from unre- lieved lust, he'd go insane. Hell, insanity was a family trait, and he was halfway there already.

"I can't keep her as a sex slave, E. I can't make her live out her life alone except when I come to her a few times a day for a quick fuck."

"I'm giving you an alternative to killing her."

Shade glanced through the lab door window, trying to imagine Runa locked away, alone in a room with nothing but maybe a television and some books to keep her company. Would she waste away, fade into a listless shell with nothing to live for as her bright spark fizzled? Would she just he there as he took her, her empty eyes staring at the wall until he finished? Or would she grow angry and bitter, becoming a rabid beast he'd have to rape in order to get what he needed?

Gods, he wanted to throw up.

As though she felt his gaze, she turned, flashed him a little wave with one hand as she held a cotton ball over the needle puncture with the other. Frank said something that made her laugh, and she turned to him, her smile innocent and flirty all at once, and Shade wanted to barge in there and crack open the bastard's skull.

"Fucking Roag," he snarled. "Man, I want to make him bleed."

"We all do."

"Really?" Shade whipped his head around. "Do you really? Because you and Roag were always tight. You never saw the bad in him."

Eidolon blinked a couple of times, as if he couldn't believe Shade had said that, and yeah, that was a low blow.

"Hey," Shade muttered, "I'm sorry. I'm frustrated. And pissed. I shouldn't be a werewolf, I shouldn't be bonded, and Skulk shouldn't be dead. Oh, and my neck burns."

Frowning, E brought his fingers to Shade's throat. "S'genesis. It's coming. Any minute now."

Naturally. He rubbed his eyes, wondering how he'd backed right up to a cliff edge so quickly.

Rotating lights on the walls began to flash, and the faint warble of ambulance sirens sent a jolt of adrenaline surging through Shade's veins. It never failed to amaze him how, when E first proposed building a hospital, Shade had resisted, having no desire to help anyone. But he'd quickly grown addicted to the excitement, the rush that came with every emergency.

He knew Eidolon was feeling the same thing, would be jonesing to sprint to the ER and take command of whatever was going to be exploding through the doors.

Shade scrubbed his palm over his face. "I need to get back to work."

"You sure?"

"It'll take my mind off things. Besides, who knows how my poor ambulances were being treated while I was gone?" He couldn't leave Runa alone, though, not when it would be so easy for her to run away. "Runa can ride along on the ambulance runs."

"As long as you think you can handle it."

"I'll work on the new duty schedule tomorrow and start runs as soon as the full moon phase is over."

The lab door opened, and Runa stood there, looking adorable and lost, and he wanted to drag her into his arms and hold her. He was in so. Much. Trouble.

"Frank said I'm done."

*Frank.* Not *the lab technician*. Or Mr. Williams. Frank. This raging jealousy was not good.

Eidolon knew, clapped a hand on Shade's shoulder. "It'll get easier."

"Whatever," he mumbled. "You heading home?" When E nodded, Shade added, "You're sure Wraith's okay."

"For now. Kynan is keeping an eye on him."

"Kynan Morgan, right?" Runa asked.

Eidolon cocked a brow. "You know him?"

Runa bit her lip in that way she did that made Shade want to kiss her. "My brother knows him. I thought I recognized him earlier. From pictures," she added hastily.

"He was the doc working on Wraith." Shade grabbed her hand, hating that she was asking about the man. "Back to the cave." Because the way he was behaving, he belonged in a fucking cave. He might as well take her by the hair and drag her there. To top it off, his skin had begun to tingle and stretch, and he had a feeling he was about to go canine.

"I'd like to run some more tests," Eidolon said, falling back into doctor mode. "An MRI, a bone marrow aspiration—"

"Bro, we stay much longer and you'll need to send her to a vet clinic for all that." Shade glanced at Runa. "We're going to hit the cafeteria on the way out."

"I'm not hungry."

"Did you notice the demon species on staff? They all have unique diets. Which includes raw meat."

She wrinkled her nose. "So you keep . . ."

"Not live animals. But we've got a walk-in fridge full of carcasses." Her expression of disgust made him smile. "You eat raw meat three nights a month and you're offended by our cafeteria?"

"It's not like I *want* to eat raw meat. Trust me, if I could cure the lycanthropy, I would." She glanced at Eidolon. "Do you think there's a chance, at least, that Shade could be cured?"

She wasn't supposed to care, and that she did made Shade's heart bleed. "He'll do his best," he ground out, and tugged her toward the cafeteria. To Eidolon he said, "If you learn anything from the tests, ring me. And let me know if you get any leads on Roag."

"I will."

"Be careful, Shade. Be really careful," Eidolon said, but he wasn't talking about Roag.

He was talking about Runa.

The cafeteria was like nothing Runa had ever seen. Strange, foul odors mingled with familiar, spicy scents that made Runa's stomach both turn and growl with hunger.

The tables and benches appeared to be made of massive slabs of granite, and a pit, maybe five feet deep and forty by forty feet in size, took up one corner of the cavernous room. Three demons of unidentifiable species were in the pit, tearing something apart with their teeth and claws. Around them, a half-dozen smaller creatures, grotesque, spiderlike things the size of Chihuahuas, were snapping up scraps.

Runa shuddered and clutched Shade's hand a little harder. "I hope those things aren't employees."

"The big ones are patients. The others are cleaners."

One of the demons, a green, winged, man-sized thing, turned to look at her, and she nearly froze at the intensity of the evil in its gaze. Except, it really didn't have a gaze, since it had no eyes.

Shade barked something to the creature in a language she didn't know, and it snarled, but it went back to crunching bones between its sharklike teeth.

"Don't antagonize the patients," he said to her, but she didn't have time to protest, because they stopped at a table where a pretty black-and-blue-haired woman in scrubs sat alone, reading a mystery novel and sipping coffee from a mug stained with her black lipstick.

"Gem," Shade said, and the woman looked up. "This is Runa. Keep an eye on her for a minute. No one is to lay a finger on her."

He didn't wait for a reply, simply strode off with the arrogance of someone who knew damned good and well he wouldn't be disobeyed. Annoyance and appreciation warred as she watched him walk away, all silent menace in his black leather and boots.

The female he'd called Gem stuck her pierced tongue out at him and then gestured to the bench across from her. "Have a seat. You must be Shade's—" she glanced at Runa's bare arm and broke off. "Or not."

"I am," Runa sighed. "I just don't have the marks yet. Shade's brother is trying to figure out why that is." She watched Gem take a sip from her cup. "Smells like a Kona-Colombian blend."

Gem's pierced brow shot up. "Wow. You're good."

"I used to own a coffee shop."

Pushing aside the mug, Gem gazed longingly at the lunch line. "I'd love you forever if you taught these morons how to brew a decent pot of coffee."

"Brewing bad coffee should be a crime," Runa said, smiling. She liked this woman. "So, are you a doctor here? Are you human?" She bit her lip. "Was that a rude question?"

"Not at all." Gem slipped a bookmark between the pages of her paperback and put it aside. "I'm a doctor. And I'm half human. Eidolon's mate, Tayla, is my sister. I'm sure you'll meet her soon. She can help you figure out what to expect from the bond—and from Shade."

Runa stared across the table at the Goth doctor, wishing she wasn't such a stranger to this world. A stranger to Shade. "How well do you know him?"

"I've known him for years, but honestly, I don't *know* him that well. He's a great paramedic, can run the hospital as well as Eidolon, but when it comes to his personal life, he's pretty tight-lipped." Gem lowered her voice. "You love him, don't you?"

"We hardly know each other," Runa said, which wasn't an answer. "I mean, we dated before...sort of. But I caught him with these—" She closed her eyes and blew out a breath. "I'm babbling."

"Yeah, you are." Gem grinned. "But you're allowed. You're in love." Gem's smile turned sad. "But he barely knows you exist, right?"

"Something like that," Runa said softly. She watched a red-skinned nurse walk by on her way to the food counter, where two human-looking servers dished up unidentifiable hot meals. "But I don't love him."

"Whatever." Gem rolled her eyes, making the silver and ruby-jeweled piercing in her eyebrow climb up her forehead. "But girl, you've got scars that run deep, and they have nothing to do with Shade."

"I'm not sure what you mean," Runa said, even though she did. Shade's betrayal a year ago had cut her deeply, but truthfully, she'd come to understand the situation, even if it still hurt.

But that wasn't what the other woman was talking about, and Runa knew it.

Gem's green eyes glowed with an eerie luminosity. "Shade can heal them, but only if you let him. Only if you trust him."

Utterly absorbed in Gem's words, Runa jumped when Shade's hand came down on her shoulder. In his other hand, he held a burlap sack.

"Let's go." He jabbed a finger at Gem. "Mind your own business and keep your Shredder-shit to yourself."

Gem stood. "I'm going to let that go because I know a lot has happened to you." She swept up her book. "But don't forget that I can see your scars, too, and the path you're on will give you a lot more."

"You're out of line." Shade's voice cut through the low-level buzz in the cafeteria, drawing a tense silence. Even the demons in the pit grew still.

The Goth doctor locked gazes with him, as if she wanted to press the issue, but the flat black of Shade's eyes promised zero tolerance. "I know what I see, Shade." She swept out of the room, a blur of black and blue and silver piercings.

With the way Shade had tensed up, Runa expected to hear a string of blistering curses from him, but he surprised her by saying mildly, "Come on."

She didn't move. "What's 'Shredder-shit'?"

"Gem is half Soulshredder. They can see weakness, scars, and exploit them. Let's go."

"Wait. What path was she talking about?"

"Nothing, dammit. Now, were you wanting to grow fur here in the hospital or back at the cave?"

"Nothing?"

"Runa, let it go. You don't want to know. Trust me."

God help her, she wanted to trust him, wanted to know that at least one person besides her brother cared about her.

She looked at him, at the demon she was bonded to. His eyes were narrowed into dark, dangerous slits, and his expression was as hard and unyielding as his body.

Yes, God help her.

Shade was not in a good mood when they arrived back at his cave. Runa tried talking to him, but his responses amounted to grunts and the occasional snappish yes or no.

He strode straight to the bedroom-slash-torture-chamber and hung the bag of what she assumed was meat from a hook on the ceiling.

She wasn't about to ask what else he had hung from there. Still, she crossed her arms over her chest and nodded at the equipment hanging neatly, arranged by type and size, from the walls. "Tell me about all of this."

Shade shook his head, the soft whisper of his hair brushing against his jacket collar joining the eerie squeak of the meat hook swinging back and forth. This was the strangest situation she'd ever been in, and when you worked for the U.S. Army's paranormal unit, strange situations were a daily deal.

The thought made her flush with guilt. Shade had been distant, not entirely open with her about everything, including what happened in this room, but she'd been keeping secrets, too, like how much the Army knew about his hospital, and why she'd truly come to New York.

And what the heck was she going to do once the full

moon was over and she had to go back to work? Shade wasn't going to let her walk away, but she wasn't about to give up the job she'd grown to love so he could keep her prisoner in his cave.

"You don't need to know."

"Yeah, I think I do."

"Runa, you don't *want* to know."

"You keep saying that, and I'm sick of it," she said, jamming her fists on her hips. "I'm not a docile little mouse anymore, buddy, and I want answers. Now."

Shade cursed, ran his hands through his hair over and over as he paced. She tore her gaze away from him, mainly to give him time to compose himself, because he seemed to be on the verge of exploding out of his skin.

So she stared at the walls, where the rows of whips, canes, and bondage equipment hung. Bottles and jars lined a shelf, alongside gloves and masks, and even some less-threatening toys such as feathers. God, how many females had he brought here? And what did he do with them?

"Shade? Do you force them?" Her gut tore up at the question, mainly because she was afraid of the answer.

"No." He swung around, his eyes so fierce she actually recoiled a little. "Never. I choose females who demand it. Who need it."

"What do you mean, need it?"

He began to pace again, his long legs eating up the length of the bedroom in fewer than a dozen strides. "Remember that first time at your coffee shop? I told you I could sense your need."

The memory of what they'd done in the alley made her flush hot. "That was sex. I can't imagine anyone *needing* to be beaten."

"They need to be liberated. I sense all sexual needs, including the need to be released."

Okay, now things were getting weird. Well, weird*er*. "Released? From...life?"

This time when he stopped pacing, he stared at her as if she'd grown fur already. "I'm not a monster. I don't kill them. *Ever*."

"Then what are you talking about? And would you stop pacing? You're wearing a hole in the floor."

Naturally, he ignored her. "Some females are into BDSM. They crave the submission. The rough treatment. The restraint. They might even get off on pain. They *want* it. That's one thing. Others *need* it." He reached up and rubbed the back of his neck, but his stride didn't falter, and neither did his concentration. "I told you my mother is an Umber demon."

"Yes, but I'm not overly familiar with that species."

"They can sense darkness in others—evil, regret, guilt, things like that. Makes them good judges of character."

Guilt. She wondered just how much of that she wore on her sleeve for everyone to see. And how much more of it was obvious to Shade. "Can you do that?" *Please say no...*

"Not in males. See, Seminus offspring inherit a few traits from their mothers' species, but not all of them, and what they do get is often mutated by the Seminus genes. Since I'm a sexual demon, I can only sense darkness in females, specifically, those who are tormented by it and want to be rid of it." He paused. "And I can draw it out."

"How?" When his gaze flickered to the equipment on the walls, she felt a sinking heaviness in her chest. "You torture it out of them."

"I told you, Runa. You didn't want to know."

"Do you—" She swallowed. Hard. "—do you sense darkness in me?"

A long, tense silence stretched between them. His eyes held her, never wavering or fluctuating in intensity. "Yes. Probably tied to the scars Gem was talking about."

The room shrank. Became a coffin, not a cave. "You wouldn't—"

"Release from it isn't something you need. Not now. Not yet."

Well, wasn't that a relief. But the way he'd said "not yet," didn't bode well. "I still don't understand this."

Shade made an impatient gesture. "I can't explain it. I just know when a female is tortured inside. She subconsciously wants and needs to be freed from whatever haunts her. Believe me, Runa, I don't force any female to come to my cave." He shot her a look of regret. "Except you. But that's different. When they're here, they get a safe word or safe gesture. If they use it, I stop. But some can take...a lot."

"Do you enjoy it?" she asked, despising the tremor in her voice, hating the way her gut cramped in dread. She raised her hand to her mouth, as if that would quell the nausea. The idea that he might get off on hurting others...God, her heartbeat pounded in her ears so hard she wasn't sure she heard him correctly when he finally answered.

"I hate it."

"E-excuse me?"

"I said—" He closed his eyes and took a deep breath. "I said I hate it."

*Thank God.* She pictured the females spread and bound, imagined Shade standing there with his fingers curled around the handle of a whip, but she couldn't reconcile the image with the man standing before her. "What do you get out of it, if you hate it so much?"

"I find my own release."

"But if you hate it—"

"I'm an incubus, Runa. My body doesn't care what my brain thinks. The females are here for sex, just as I am. I'm compelled to give it to them."

She closed her eyes, unable to fathom how he could be so casual about being with so many females and what he did with them. Then again, he was a demon, and she'd only been in his world for a year. She didn't understand it. But she wanted to.

"So if I want something, something other than sex, are you compelled to give it to me?"

He hadn't been looking at her, but now his head swiveled around to her, his dark gaze narrowed in suspicion. Even the unseeing eye on his neck, which peeked out from a part in his hair, seemed to take her in.

"That depends on what it is," he said, his voice husky and low. "What do you want?"

Nervous energy made her fingers tremble as she peeled off her shirt and pushed down her jeans until she stood before Shade wearing only lacy pink panties. Heat licked her between the legs at the sudden hunger that burned in his gaze.

"I want what you gave the others."

Shade had been raised among demons until he was twenty. He'd spent the next eighty years pinging between the demon world and the human one. He didn't shock easily. He never went speechless.

But as Runa shoved down her panties and sauntered to the St. Andrews Cross, he found himself unable to talk. Or breathe.

"Don't," he croaked.

She ignored him, turned to back up against the hard wood that had supported countless female bodies before her. The idea made him ill. Runa didn't belong there. Her delicate skin shouldn't even come into contact with something so tainted by the presence—and blood—of others.

She kicked her feet into the ankle manacles, and they snapped shut with an ominous metallic clang. Reaching up, she did the same with her wrists. Each closure made his heart jerk in his chest. His mind screamed at the sight and at the same time, his body purred.

How could it not? Her toned arms stretched taut above her, making her breasts ride high and firm. Her narrow waist flared at the hips as her legs spread wide, and between, that sweet, hot flesh taunted him, the female lips parted just enough to reveal a glistening hint of arousal.

Runa stared at him, a wicked challenge in her eyes. "Well, mate? I'm submitting to you. What will you do with me now?"

"Submit?" He shook his head. "You've barely begun to submit." In a bid to end this idiocy, he crossed to her, used his height and build to intimidate her as he loomed just out of arm's reach. "You're throwing down the gauntlet in a game you know nothing about, Runa."

"Then teach me," she said huskily, and he suddenly

saw himself covering her with his body, driving into her as she writhed against the bonds, helpless to do anything but succumb to the pleasure he'd give to her.

This was ludicrous. He should release her immediately, shackle her for the moon shift, and then go have a few beers until it was time to chain himself up. His fingers found the release mechanisms at one wrist.

"No." Her whispered word contained a mix of both command and pleading desperation. She inhaled, the action putting her breasts in contact with his ribs and sending a shock of lust straight to his balls. "I want what you give the others."

His body jerked under the force of her desire as the compulsion to give her what she craved began to take hold. Damn her. Damn her to hell, because now he wanted the same thing. The one blessing in all of this was that although he sensed a deep, dark guilt trapped inside her, she wasn't ready to confront or release it.

"Truly, Runa?" He skimmed his palm down her arm until he reached her breast. Dipping his head so his mouth brushed her ear, he closed his hand over the fleshy mound and squeezed until she gasped. "Do you truly want to know what it means to submit? To find that place inside you that wants to please another? Because I'll be straight with you—subs generally have more power than the doms. But not in my case. Never in my case."

Disgusted by his own words, but mind-fogged by the driving instinct to give his mate what she wanted, he broke away from her and snared a leather mask off the wall. It felt cold and wrong in his hand, but he forced himself to select a ball gag next. Her breath caught when he plucked a handful of clothespins from a basket on one shelf. She eyed the items in his hand, visibly swallowed, and then met his gaze with her defiant one.

"I trust you."

He broke out in a cold sweat. Other females had trusted him—to hurt them.

Runa trusted him *not* to.

She had no reason to trust him. She shouldn't. Trusting him had gotten her nothing but a broken heart, attacked by a werewolf, imprisoned by Roag, and into mortal danger—danger from Roag, from Eidolon and Wraith...and from Shade. She'd never survive in this world if she didn't throw up some damned walls and toughen up.

*She's a hell of a lot stronger than you give her credit for. Stronger than you.* The words were a vicious taunt in his head, as if some wicked part of him wanted to punish her for being stronger than he was.

"Shade? Did you hear me?"

Anger boiled up inside him, seared his blood and his thoughts. It didn't matter that he was furious at himself, at Roag, at everyone *but* her. He needed to strike out, and she was the only available target.

"Shut up!" he yelled. "Just *be quiet*."

He pushed the gag into her mouth, more gently than he'd intended, but hell's fires, he couldn't hurt her even when he wanted to. Which pretty much made all of this pointless unless he could scare her. Snarling in frustration, he threw down the mask and tugged on a leather glove studded on the palm with tiny, needlelike spikes, and on the back with larger, heavier ones. Next, he chose a nasty little whip with a barbed tip.

"What now, little wolf?" he asked, his voice going soft

and dangerous. "What happens when I really start to work you over? I didn't even give you a safe gesture."

She made a noise deep in her throat as she eyed the equipment he'd chosen. Her gaze locked on his gloved hand as he reached for her, halting a scant millimeter from one breast. She quivered, her nipples tightening in response.

"Do you still trust me not to hurt you?"

Her head snapped up, and the resolve in her expression made him stumble back. She wasn't going to back down. She didn't smell of fear. He was holding implements of torture that could make her scream in agony or pleasure or both, and she wasn't afraid at all.

He could love her for that.

Terror of his own cut through him in an icy blast. He hurled the whip to the floor, tore off the glove, and released her with clumsy, trembling fingers. He talked himself through it like a crazy man, unsure what he was saying, but hearing himself speak.

When she was free, he backed away as if she were a contagious disease. He knew how idiotic he must appear, but he didn't care. And if she knew what was good for her, she'd keep her trap shut and her hands off him.

For a moment it seemed as though she'd read his thoughts, because she just stood there, rubbing her arms vigorously to bring circulation back. Then, because she was, after all, Runa, she had to go and ruin everything by talking.

"What are you doing? We aren't finished."

He turned away, pretending he hadn't heard her. Maybe if he ignored her, she'd go away. He felt something strike his back, saw the ball gag hit the floor. She'd thrown it at him.

"I said, we aren't finished."

"Yes," he growled, "we are."

Something else bounced off his shoulder. A clothespin, fun little items for pinching flesh. "What's *Maluncoeur*?"

Shade jerked around. "What did you say?"

She stepped back, but she didn't drop her gaze. "You kept mumbling '*Maluncoeur*' while you were releasing me."

"Nothing." He took a deep, rattling breath. "It's nothing."

"Stop lying to me," she shouted. "Stop avoiding me!"

"Avoiding you? I can't get *away* from you!"

"You're such a jerk! Stop shutting me out." She made a sweeping gesture around the room. "You won't even let me be part of the things you've done with other females you say mean nothing to you. Does that mean I'm less than nothing?"

Hell's bleeding, freaking rings. How could he tell her that he didn't want to do to her what he'd done to all those females not because she meant less to him, but because she meant so much more?

"Remember what I said about not asking questions you don't want to know the answer to?"

She recoiled, crimson splotches mottling her cheeks. "You can be such a bastard sometimes, you know that?" She stamped past him and into the bathroom. Had there been a door, he knew it would have been slammed hard enough to take it off its hinges.

# *Eleven*

⌒

Wraith turned out to be pretty good company. He'd kicked Kynan's ass in a couple of video games and had entertained himself by going through Kynan's movie collection and making fun of it, but mainly, he just kept quiet while Kynan drank himself into a stupor.

Six beers and six shots of whiskey later, Kynan wasn't nearly drunk enough. He glanced over at the demon, who was sitting in the leather recliner next to the couch, throwing potato chips at David Letterman.

"You're getting grease all over my TV screen," he said.

Wraith snorted and fell back in the chair, legs spread, black button-down BDU shirt gaping open. His clothes had been ruined during the battle with the African rebels, so he'd borrowed one of Shade's paramedic uniforms to wear since he refused to wear scrubs—"damned pajamas," as he called them. He sighed, ran a hand over his muscular chest.

Christ, Kynan had never seen anyone as well-toned and built as Wraith. It was as though the demon spent twenty-three hours of the day working out. And it wasn't bulky muscle gained from countless reps with heavy weights— it was the functional stuff, the sinewy, ropey kind that saw regular use and not just from workouts.

Lori had rubbed against that chest, had used her face like a cat marking its territory. Her hands had smoothed up and down Wraith's body in intimate familiarity.

Seemed like yesterday, but it had been a year ago that Kynan had seen Wraith with his fangs buried in Lori's throat and his hands working her pants' zipper. Wraith had always denied sleeping with her, but the sight of them together had stuck with Kynan to this day.

"Human? I can smell your aggression. What's up?"

"Tell me again that you didn't sleep with Lori."

"Shit, are we back to that again? I don't bang humans. Want me to make a tape recording so you can play it over and over?"

"Why don't you sleep with humans? Most vampires love them."

"I have a pulse. I'm not like most vampires." Wraith leaned forward, braced his forearms on his knees. "I've got the thing with your wife figured out, though, if you can dig yourself out of the pity well for a second."

"You're an asshole."

"Ouch," Wraith drawled. "Hurt me."

"Fine. What do you have figured out?"

"It was Roag. He's the one who messed with your wife's head, probably for months."

"How?"

"He can shapeshift. After he recovered from the fire at

Brimstone, he probably used my form for his black market dealings to frame me so I'd take the heat. That's why that night at the zoo, when you saw me with her, she thought she knew me." Wraith shoved his hair away from his face. "Thing is, I don't think he actually had sex with her."

"You aren't making any sense." Kynan eyed the whiskey bottle. "Or maybe that's because I'm half lit. I saw her rubbing all over you. It was pretty obvious she'd screwed you—or Roag, if that's who she thought you were."

"Okay, listen. From what Shade said, Roag got toasted like a burnt marshmallow. He would have been nearly destroyed, right down to his junk. I'm betting he can't have sex no matter how badly he wants it." Wraith grinned. "Which is really fucking funny."

"You're sick. And how is he still alive if he can't have sex? You need it to survive, right?"

"If his testicles got barbecued off, he wouldn't need sex anymore."

"So why would Lori think she had sex with him?"

"Because he has the same gift I have. He could have made her believe it."

"Not buying it." Guardians had defenses against attacks on the mind, and besides, making memories like that would have left some sort of doubt, some sort of lingering feeling that something wasn't right.

Suddenly, Kynan was flat on his back in his bedroom, hands tangled in the sheets, and Gem was riding him. Her soft skin glistened with perspiration, and her strong thighs held him prisoner in their grip. Pleasure shot through him, sharp and searing. Gem's moans vibrated all the way to his balls, which tightened, ready to spill.

This was wrong, all wrong. He knew he wasn't here

with her, knew that somehow Wraith was doing this, but he couldn't escape. Wasn't sure he wanted to. Especially not when she did that thing with her lip, rolling it between her teeth as she threw back her head.

Light flashed in his eyes, and he was on the couch again, fully clothed, panting, a raging erection straining at his button-fly.

"Believe me now? And I wasn't that deep into your head. If I'd gone deeper, you wouldn't be aware that I was doing it. You'd buy it all as if it really happened."

Jesus. Kynan scrubbed his face with a trembling hand. "That's what Roag did to Lori?" And why the hell had Wraith used Gem in that fucked-up little fantasy, anyway?

"I'd bet my life on it."

Kynan shifted to make more room in his jeans. "Then why..."

"Why did I bite her? Try to get into her pants?"

Nausea rolled through him at the memory. "Yeah," he rasped.

"She was all over me, Ky. I'd been fighting and was half-crazed with bloodlust. I didn't want to, but I wasn't thinking straight, and I needed to feed. And unfortunately, since I'm an incubus, feeding and fucking go together when I'm with a female."

Great. Whatever. He needed a break from all of this, and he had to take a leak. He stumbled to the bathroom, and when he came out, Wraith was standing near the door.

"This was a riot, but I'm outta here, human. I need to get back to hunting Roag, and I need to feed."

*I needed to feed.* It was what Wraith had said about Lori. He'd bitten her, sunk his huge-ass fangs into her graceful, creamy throat. Her head had lolled back as though she were in utter ecstasy.

Dammit. Kynan sank to the couch and in a fit of childish, drunken rage, he swept his hand across the coffee table, sending the empty bottles and bags of chips flying. When the last beer bottle stopped rolling, clunked up against the TV stand, he flopped back onto the cushion and threw his feet onto the now empty table.

This was so screwed up. He knew better than to drink, because his thoughts always detoured to Lori. Sometimes he remembered the good times, the entire days they'd spend in bed, making love and talking about the future, vacations they wanted to take, the kids they wanted to have. Other times he'd think about seeing her in Wraith's arms, his fangs buried deep in her throat.

What had it been like for her? Had she been afraid for her life, or had she enjoyed it? Had she been waiting for Kynan to save her, or would she have let Wraith take her right there in front of him?

He wanted to scream at the top of his lungs and hope Lori heard him, wherever she was. She'd left him with so many questions and so much anger, and he wasn't so drunk that he didn't recognize that he needed help to get out of the quicksand of despair that was sucking him down slowly.

"Wraith," Kynan blurted, "bite me." Okay, maybe he really was drunk.

Wraith paused as he reached for the door handle. "Come on, Ky. I expect a better comeback from you."

"It's not a comeback. I want you to feed from me." *I'll take Things You Never Thought You'd Say for a hundred, Alex.*

One tawny eyebrow shot up. "How much have you had to drink?"

"Not enough to affect my judgment." That was a totally drunk thing to say.

Wraith snorted. "I don't care about your judgment. I'm wondering 'cause I get a righteous high from the alcohol in the blood."

"Do you ever have any thoughts that don't revolve around you?"

Wraith appeared to consider that for a moment. Then he shrugged. "Nope."

Which wasn't true, because the demon definitely cared about his brothers, no matter how vehemently he denied it.

"Just do it."

Wraith stepped away from the door, his eyes narrowed as if he expected Kynan to spring a trap. "Why do you want this?"

"I'm curious."

"Bullshit. You've hunted my kind for years, and now you want to let one suck you dry? And why me? Why not find some hot female vamp for a nice fuck and suck special?"

"I don't trust anyone else."

"You shouldn't trust me," Wraith growled.

"I don't. But I know you won't kill me. The hospital means too much to you, and I'm a damned good doctor you can't afford to lose."

"You're a fool if you think anyone or anything means anything to me."

"Whatever." Kynan crossed his feet at the ankles. "You going to bite me or what?"

"Not until you tell me why."

"I'm giving you a free shot at my blood and you're playing hard to get? What kind of vampire are you?" When Wraith just stood there, Kynan rolled his eyes. "Oh, come on. My blood's eighty proof. You want it. You know you do."

Wraith's eyes sort of glazed over, because, yeah, he wanted it. But the damned demon wouldn't be deterred. "Tell me."

"Fuck you."

"Not my type."

Ky sighed. "I hear you don't usually feed from females."

"Female *humans*. Demon females and male humans are on the menu."

"Why male humans, but not females?"

"Because men don't give me wood."

"That's a relief."

"Only if I plan to feed from you. Which I don't. Unless you tell me why."

"Because I want to know what my wife felt when you bit her, dammit!" Kynan roared, surprising himself at the ferocity and suddenness of his anger.

Wraith turned away. "I didn't want to," he muttered. "I swear."

Kynan slapped his hand over his face and rubbed his eyes. Shit, he was tired. "I know."

He heard a rustling, the creak of the chair cushion next to him. Wraith's hand closed on his forearm and brought it to lie, palm up, on the armrest. Ky's heart began to pound hard in his chest. He didn't look. Couldn't. Then came the pain as Wraith's daggerlike fangs sank into his wrist. A second later, warmth washed over him. Tingles spread through his muscles and nervous system.

God, this felt good.

He slid Wraith a glance. "This isn't like, vampire gay, is it?"

Wraith snorted and shot him the finger.

Vampires were freaking strange. But he was starting to see why some humans willingly allowed vamps to feed from them. The high was powerful, and probably addictive.

He could imagine how it would feel to have a female doing this. At his throat, pressed up against him, lying on top of him or under him. His body began to stir as Gem became the female crushed beneath him, her teeth latched on to his throat—except she wasn't a vampire, so the whole idea was ridiculous.

A stream of sensation shot up his arm when Wraith took a particularly strong pull, and damn him for putting the Gem scene in his head earlier, because now he couldn't get it *out* of his head. It had been so real it felt like a memory instead of a fantasy.

He could still hear her whispering sexy, naughty things in his ear. The sound of her voice took him deeper into relaxation, lulling him more than the alcohol ever could.

"What. The. Hell?" Gem's voice drifted to him, crisp and clear.

He peeled open his eyes just enough to see her standing in the living room, arms crossed over her breasts, which were pushed up into two plump mounds by the midnight-blue corset she wore. If she turned around, he'd bet her skirt would barely cover her ass. Her chunky, high-heeled boots came up over her knees, leaving only her thighs touchably bare.

She'd braided her hair into two ponytails, put on a spiked leather dog collar and black lipstick, and she looked

like she was ready to party. Why that thought sent a stab of
jealousy through him, he had no idea.

Then again, he was sitting on his couch, drunk, with a
vampire latched on to his wrist. Clearly, he was fucked in
the head.

———

*Holy shit,* Gem thought. This was…unexpected. Kynan
was sprawled on the couch, legs spread, left arm propped
on the armrest. Next to him, kneeling on the floor, was
Wraith, his mouth firmly attached to Ky's wrist. When he
looked up, his eyes glinted with mischief.

"And I repeat, what the hell? What is going on here?"

Kynan gazed at her with slumberous eyes that made
her body flood with heat. "What's it look like?"

She glared at Wraith. "Looks like someone was too
lazy to order a pizza delivery guy for dinner."

Wraith disengaged his hold and smacked his lips. "This
is better. Home cooking." He held her gaze as he licked
the punctures in Kynan's wrist to seal them. Slowly. Sen-
sually. She swallowed, her mouth suddenly dry.

Wraith *knew.* Knew she wanted Kynan, was toying
with her because he was aware of the fact that she wanted
to be the one licking the human. And when his nostrils
flared, she knew he could smell her arousal.

"Why are you here?" Ky's voice was husky, lazy, as if
he'd just woken up. He'd have a great morning voice.

"Wraith called me."

Ky shot Wraith a you're-going-to-get-it look, but
Wraith just shrugged and leaped nimbly to his feet.
"What? I called while you were in the bathroom. Didn't
think you should be alone. And I gotta go. I need more

than the measly pint you gave up." He headed for the door. "Later."

Throwing his head back to look at the ceiling fan as it spun in slow circles, Kynan heaved a sigh. "Shit."

"Shit, is right. What were you thinking? You didn't do something dumb, like ask him to turn you into a vampire or something, right?"

"I might be guilty of poor judgment, but I'm not stupid or suicidal."

"Well, don't *get* stupid or suicidal, because I don't think Wraith can turn anyone. He's not technically undead."

Kynan threw his arm over his eyes. "Ever think about that, Gem? You know, wonder what kind of person would trust a vampire enough to drain them to the point of death? I mean, what's to stop a vamp from just leaving them for dead instead of giving them the exchange of the vamp's own blood?"

"I'm sure that happens." She looked into his kitchen, which was basically a cove in the corner of his living room. "I'll get you something to drink. You need to hydrate. And a little tip? Next time you decide to donate blood, give to the Red Cross."

He said nothing as she searched his fridge, came up with Gatorade, and poured a glass. When she returned to him, he was in the same position, eyes closed, though he'd dropped his arm. She planted one knee on the cushion next to him, lifted his head, and put the glass to his lips.

He emptied half the glass before opening his eyes. "Thank you."

"Well, you couldn't very well hydrate on beer," she said, eyeing the bottles scattered on the end table and floor.

His smile was lopsided as he tugged on one of her

braids. Her pulse jumped wildly. "You ever get drunk, Gem? Ever lose yourself in a bottle and hope to drown?"

Abruptly, she became aware of the heat of his outer thigh against her knee, the stroke of his fingers over the braid, the hot fan of his breath across her cheek. "No," she whispered. "I can't."

"You get sick?"

"Yes," she lied, because she couldn't tell him the truth. Not now, when he seemed to have forgotten what she was.

Which was a demon of the Fifth Tier, the last, worst level on the Ufelskala, a scoring system for evil. If the demons of her species were tornadoes, they'd be F5s.

That she was only half demon made little difference to her, or to Kynan. She did what she could to contain her Soulshredder half, which included having ensorcelled restraining tattoos inked around her ankles, wrists, and neck. She also avoided alcohol. Drinking reduced her ability to control the demon within.

She'd learned that the hard way, when she'd gotten drunk at a frat party during med school. Something minor had sent her into a rage. Fortunately, she'd recognized the sensation that felt like claws scraping the inside of her skin, and she'd raced for the nearest Harrowgate. Somehow she'd ended up at UG, where Reaver had sedated her until the buzz wore off.

The fallen angel had prevented what would have been a bloody rampage.

Kynan's knuckles brushed her throat, and at her quick intake of breath, his hand stilled. She searched his face, saw a range of emotions playing out like a movie in fast-forward. Sadness. Fear. Arousal.

Confusion.

"You're so pretty," he whispered.

It was the alcohol talking, but she didn't care. For nearly a year he'd viewed her only as a colleague on a good day, as a demon on the rest. Right now he saw her as a woman, and it didn't matter that he was looking at her through beer bottle glasses.

Slowly, so as not to startle him or snuff the sexual spark arcing between them, she set down the drink. She lifted her hand to his face, marveling at how his cheek felt hot against her cold palm. He stared at her, and when she swiped her thumb across his full lower lip, his mouth opened, just a little. God, she wanted to kiss him. Instead, she kept stroking. Lightly. Gently.

His hand rested on her hip, nudging her closer. Nerves made her tremble as she leaned in, her gaze fixed on his mouth. He tipped his face up to hers. The hand that had been playing with her braid cupped the back of her head and pulled her down.

Their lips met. Hesitantly at first. His were firm, unyielding, and then, as though a dam had broken, he ravaged her. She gasped into his mouth, a sound of surprise and relief. *Thank you, God.*

He dropped both hands to her skirt and roughly hiked it up. A sweet, pinching ache began to pulse between her legs as he dragged her onto his lap so she was straddling him. She clutched his shoulders for balance, the rock-hard muscles not giving at all under her fingers.

As her core came in contact with the rigid length straining at the fly of his jeans, she went utterly wet. With a groan, he arched into her, using his grip on her hips to hold her against him.

Still he kissed her, his tongue alternately sweeping her

lips and thrusting deep to mate with her tongue. Need consumed her, and she found herself rocking in his lap, rubbing her sex against his, the thin layer of her silk panties creating a delicious, hot friction.

This was a dream. It had to be. She was kissing the man who starred in all her fantasies, was on the verge of orgasm, and they hadn't even removed any clothing. She wanted to reach between their bodies and release his shaft from its denim prison, but she was terrified to do anything that might make him change his mind.

His lips burned a path along her jaw and down her neck. "Gem," he murmured against the sensitive skin of her throat. "God, you're so warm."

She shuddered with delight at his words, at the way his tongue was a hot, languid caress down her jugular. Sensation raced in a circuit from where his tongue flicked over her throat to every point of contact.

A low moan dredged up from deep in his chest, the vibration buzzing through his entire body and into hers. Sharp, panting breaths marked the beginning of a new, frenzied rhythm of thrusts between her legs. A sheen of sweat broke out on her skin. Her thighs quivered and her breasts tightened and a powerful implosion took her apart from the outside in.

Crying out, she clung to Kynan with her hands as he ground against her. He hissed through clenched teeth, his big body jerking as his release took him. The orgasm had stolen coherent thought but not her vision, and as she watched him come, she thought she'd never seen anything so beautiful.

He bucked a final time, and as their breathing slowed and the hormones settled, her heart sang. God, he was perfect. A man made for sex.

"Ah, fuck," he groaned. "Gem...shit. I'm sorry."

"Sorry?" She smiled and drew a finger down his T-shirted chest. "The only thing you should be sorry about is that we're still clothed."

He averted his gaze, his expression tight, and she became aware of a new tension between them when all tension should have dissipated. Darkness fell over his face like nightfall, and he shoved her off his lap and stumbled to his feet. She opened herself up to what Tayla called her "demon vision" and gasped.

Kynan's emotional scars ran deep, but they'd been knitting together over the last couple of months. Now, centered over his heart like glowing, bleeding fissures, they looked as fresh as the day he'd received them, the day he'd found Lori in the arms of someone else.

"Kynan? What's wrong?"

He hooked his thumbs in his jeans' pockets and looked at the ceiling. "You'd better go."

"We should talk—"

"*Please*, Gem." His shoulders rose and fell. "I'm drunk, exhausted, and a pint low on blood. I need to be alone."

Awkwardly, she stood and tugged her skirt down, for the first time wishing it was a lot longer. "If you need anything..."

"I'll call."

She cast a glance over her shoulder as she left, knowing damned good and well that her phone was not going to ring.

He was taking a chance, hanging out in the hospital. Before he "died," Roag had hung out here because of the endless supply of nurses to screw, but he'd always hated this place, had never understood why his brothers had built it. Who gave a flying fuck about patching up demons? Taking them apart was a lot more fun.

But his Ghouls had been unsuccessful in finding someone who would spy for him, and he didn't have time to get one of his minions on staff. Revenge had taken far too long as it was, and now that Sheryen had been reanimated, he had only days to find Runa before Sher's zombielike body gave out. He needed Runa's blood, and he needed it now.

Wearing the form of a common Slogthu, he was practically invisible to the staff as he kept to the shadows, pretending to be visiting a patient. He wasn't worried about his brothers' discovering him—Eidolon didn't work nights, Wraith spent his nights carousing, and Shade would be dealing with his warg bitch.

Still, a few staff members possessed the ability to see through alteration magic. Not that they'd recognize him, since he resembled a charcoal briquette more than his former self, but any demon masquerading as another would arouse suspicion.

So he watched. Watched for the perfect victim for the next phase in his plan. He wanted to strike his brothers where it hurt—the hospital and its staff. Once his brothers were rattled, they'd make mistakes.

A female Sora—Ciska, according to her name tag—sauntered past, toward the Harrowgate, her red skin smelling faintly of Wraith. Roag's hackles rose. Too many of the females in this place smelled like his little brother, who was living the life Roag should be living, screwing females without a care in the world.

He'd start having a care. Right now. Because the Sora didn't know it, but she was about to become his next victim.

He took a deep breath, filling his nostrils with Wraith's scent and comforting himself with the fact that this would be the last time she smelled of his brother. Because in a few minutes, she was going to smell of nothing but her own terror.

# *Twelve*

~

Runa didn't remember much of what had happened the night before—at least, not much of what happened after she'd come out of the shower. She'd gone straight to the tether and chained herself up before Shade had a chance to. Everything after that was a blank, but she did remember shifting back to human form at the same time Shade did. Though she'd still been angry, she'd given in to her raging hormones. She definitely remembered the sheer ecstasy of finally having someone there to relieve the cravings that came every morning following the full moon.

Shade had taken her three times, wordlessly, ruthlessly. Afterward, they'd collapsed into bed, and they still hadn't spoken a word. Oddly though, he'd tucked her up against him and held her close as they fell asleep. It occurred to her that he'd wanted to make sure she didn't escape while he was sleeping, but that theory didn't track with the way his fingers had stroked her skin in long, lazy passes.

Six hours later, Runa awakened, but Shade still slept, so she wrapped up in a robe and padded around the cave, exploring the nooks and crannies, but mostly, she was looking for a phone. She found one in his TV room. Quietly, she checked on Shade to make sure he was still sleeping, and satisfied that he was crashed hard, she slipped outside the cave.

Steamy jungle heat engulfed her. How did he keep the cave so cool and dry, when it was obvious that he didn't have air conditioning? Odd.

That she was obsessing about how Shade kept his cave cool instead of making the call she needed to make didn't escape her notice. She had a life outside this weird one she'd stumbled into, and now she had to face it.

Stomach churning, she dialed her brother's cell phone. He answered on the third ring.

"Arik?"

"Runa. Where are you? I know you aren't due to check in until tomorrow, but I thought I'd hear from you before now."

That was because she rarely went more than three or four days without calling Arik. Working for R-XR was lonely; few coworkers wanted to hang out with her socially, and Arik was her only outlet. Apparently, being a werewolf was something of a roadblock to friendship with humans.

She eased away from the cave and propped herself against a tree. "I ran into some complications."

"Are you okay?" The strain in his voice was obvious even over the static crackle and echo.

"I'm fine. But I need you to research something for me. *Maluncoeur.*"

She heard the scratch of a pencil on paper, and then, "What is it?"

"No idea."

"You going to tell me what's going on?"

She peeked around the tree to the cave opening. All clear. "I was picked up by Ghouls."

"*What?* Where are you? Do you need help?"

"Calm down. I'm safe." Sort of.

His curses could have melted the circuitry in the satellites transmitting their conversation. "I told Davis not to send you on this mission. *Goddammit.* I should have been the one to search for Kynan."

Arik had been against her work with R-XR from the beginning, but with her coffee shop closed, her heart broken by Shade, and her new werewolfyness, there had been nothing to keep her from doing something interesting for the first time in her life.

And the work *was* interesting. Sometimes it was even a little dangerous, like the time she'd followed a lion-shifter through the streets of Madrid and walked right into his entire pride as they prepared to head to the country to hunt. Only her ability to shift at will had saved her.

"It's not the Colonel's fault," she sighed. "You were busy, and I jumped at the chance to come back to New York."

"You jumped at the chance to see that demon again, you mean."

She didn't waste her breath on a denial, partly because it would only lead to another argument about how crazy she was to have feelings for Shade, and partly because she no longer knew if she'd come to hurt him or to see him one more time.

"So what happened with the Ghouls?" Arik asked, when she didn't argue.

"It's a long story, but the gist of it is that apparently I'm bonded to Shade."

"What do you mean, *bonded*?" Runa knew her brother well enough to know he'd spoken through clenched teeth.

"I don't know. I need you to research that, too. Find out if there's a way out of it."

"Shit."

"Yeah. But it isn't all bad news. I found Kynan." She leaned her head back against the tree. "He's working at the demon hospital."

"You're fucking kidding me. He's the one who told us about it in the first place!" He was also the one who gave Arik the demon caduceus that had made her put two and two together to equal Shade's being involved with the hospital.

"I know. I saw him treating Shade's brother, Wraith."

"You were *inside* the hospital?"

She closed her eyes and listened to the screeches of some kind of creature in the canopy above. "Shade took me. He and his brothers work there. I haven't been able to talk to Kynan, so I don't know what his deal is."

"Where is the hospital located?"

A bird exploded out of the brush. She watched it, wishing she could fly away with it instead of walking the dangerous line she was straddling. On one side was the Army, and on the other, Shade. No matter what she said or didn't say, she was going to betray someone.

"Runa? Where is it?"

"I can't say."

"Can't, or won't?"

It was a fair question, and she didn't know the answer. True, she couldn't draw a map to UGH, but even if she could, would she? "I can't. We accessed it through Harrowgates, which I can't use by myself."

"I don't like this. You need to come home."

"That's not possible."

"Is Shade holding you prisoner? We'll send a team—"

"It's not that." Well, it *was* that, in a way. "It's the bond, Arik. He needs me."

Arik's voice went low and deadly. "Why?"

*Oh, because he needs sex a few times a day, and only I can give it to him.* But what would happen if she wasn't around? Sex was like air for his species, so if he didn't get it...could he die?

"He just does."

"Come. Home."

"I plan to. But I need to know more about this bond, like what will happen to me if I leave him. Just do the research for me. And hurry." Because each day brought her closer to Shade, and she had a feeling she soon wouldn't want out of the bond.

The forest around her went silent, and a chill ran up her spine. She scanned the area, saw nothing, but she didn't like the sudden vibe. "I have to go. I'll call again when I can."

"Wait—"

A branch snapped, stopping her heart and drawing her gaze to a shadowed recess in the trees behind her. *Oh, God.* She saw eyes. Burning, glowing, red eyes.

She stumbled backward, fumbled the phone. Her heel caught on a vine and she nearly went down. The darkness surrounding the red eyes began to shimmer and take form even as the eyes closed on her. A scream welled in her throat, clogged behind the lump of terror.

The shape solidified.

*Shade.*

Her brother's tinny, panicked voice blared from the phone, which trembled in her hand. "I'm okay," she said into the mouthpiece. "I'll call later." She disconnected, wondering, sickly, how much Shade had heard.

His eyes were little more than red, laser-intense slits now. "Mate," he rasped in a voice that sounded as if he'd forgotten how to talk.

"Shade? What's wrong?" She caught his forearm, and he closed his eyes and swayed.

"*S'genesis.*" A moan rumbled from deep in his chest, which was bare, like the rest of him.

Her eyes dropped to his groin, where his sex strained upward so rigidly he had to be in pain. She slid her gaze up, over skin that glowed, radiated scorching heat. The *dermoire* on his arm writhed angrily, and around his neck, a shadow pulsed with the rhythm of his heartbeat just beneath the surface of his skin.

"This is your Change?" she asked, and he nodded. He hadn't said how the actual transition would occur, or how long it would take, and she certainly hadn't expected it to be this intense.

"Hurts." As though his body agreed, it convulsed violently.

"What can I do?"

His lips drew back from his clenched teeth. "I... need... you."

His words washed away the hurtful things he'd said last night. He needed her. "I'm here. Take what you need."

His eyes peeled open. There was no warning. Just his body pinning hers to a tree. She cried out as the bark dug into her spine and his mouth crushed her. "Forgive me," he mumbled against her lips. "Please. Forgive me for what I'm going to do to you."

Shade woke up with a groan. Every muscle ached, his head throbbed, and his skin felt as if it had been bathed in acid. Next to him on the bare floor of the cave, Runa lay curled in a ball on her side. She opened one groggy eye.

"Do you need me again?" she croaked.

He inhaled, took in her scent, the savory aroma of the nonstop sex they'd had. He didn't need her again, but he wanted her. Now more than ever. She was his mate, and he had completed The Change. All his focus, all of his desires, were now concentrated fully on her, and one of his new desires was to fill her with his seed, his young.

And wouldn't that be a disaster. He was possessive enough as it was, could hardly bear the thought of doing what must be done in order to save his life, but if she were carrying his child...

"*No.*" His voice was as hoarse as hers, a result of hours of panting, shouting, and straining during the marathon sex that had taken place in their normal forms all day yesterday, and then all night long in their warg bodies. "Rest. I think it's over."

"Are you sure?"

"Pretty sure." Eidolon's *s'genesis* had been different, had taken place over the course of a few days, with minimal sexual side effects, a result of his months of holding it off with an experimental treatment using his own blood.

Shade's change had been faster and more intense, but thank the gods he'd had a mate to spend himself on.

Shame sat like a weight in the pit of his stomach. All this time he'd been bitching about having a mate, and yet, he'd been happy to use her to make his transition to a fully mature male easier. Hell's bells, he was a bastard.

Images from the last eighteen hours came to him in bits and pieces, erotic images of everything they'd done as he'd felt the *s'genesis* breaking through the surface. Runa had never resisted him, had offered herself as a willing sacrifice to the constant need. Then again, he'd given her little choice.

He touched his throat, winced at the sensitivity. "Do I have a new mark?"

She stroked where his fingers had been. Instead of hurting, her touch soothed. "You have another ring around your neck. Knotted symbols that link to the other ring."

He was fertile now. Closing his eyes, he let her stroke him, felt himself sway toward her. "Are you okay?"

"Fine. What about you?"

He swallowed, opened his eyes, took in the angry bite marks on her shoulder, the welts left by his nails on her back and buttocks. After what he'd done to her, he didn't deserve her concern. He didn't deserve *her*.

With a curse, he shoved to his feet, ignoring her calls as he fled to the waterfall.

"Shade."

"Dammit," he growled, swinging around to her. "What?"

She was nude, gloriously naked, but she hugged herself as if she regretted not getting dressed before she followed him outside. "What would have happened if I hadn't been around for your *s'genesis*?"

"If we hadn't been bonded, you mean?" The cool spray eased his burning skin as he stood there. "I'd have been forced to seek out human and demon females. As many as I needed. I wouldn't have cared about consent or their desires." The idea made him sick, because he doubted he'd cared much about Runa's consent last night, when the worst of it hit him, when he'd felt only the insane, driving urge to spill inside her.

"You didn't rape me, Shade."

His mouth fell open, and he had to snap it shut. He knew she couldn't feel his emotions because she didn't share the link with him, but somehow, she knew what he was thinking. "I didn't give you much choice."

She moved forward, took his hand in one of her delicate ones. "If I'd wanted to defend myself, I could have."

That much was true. During the daylight, she could have shifted into her warg form and kicked his ass. "You should have."

Few Seminus demons survived to their hundred-year mark, but of those that did, fully half died during *s'genesis,* victims of too little sex or killed either by the females they tried to rape or the males trying to defend their females.

"We're in this together now, like it or not," she said, and he almost laughed. They weren't in shit together. She wasn't bonded to him, and he was going to have to kill her to get out of the bond he had with her. This wasn't a pairing made in heaven. It had been thrust upon them in hell.

"So what now?" she asked.

He felt his gaze grow hot no matter how hard he willed it not to. "I can make you pregnant." Her harsh intake of breath was audible even over the roar of the waterfall, and he relieved her worry quickly. "I didn't. You aren't fertile right now."

Her hand was still in his, and he couldn't resist using his Seminus gift to probe her body, to go deep inside her reproductive organs to determine how close to ovulation she was. He could force ovulation if he wanted to, and damn, the temptation made him itch.

She tucked a strand of hair behind her ear and studied him. "Shift into something."

"What?"

"I want to see what happens. Do you have any limitations?"

"We can only shift into similar-sized, live birth species. No egg-layers. We can go up to twice as large as ourselves but not smaller." The females had to be capable of bearing a Seminus's young, and smaller demons wouldn't fare well if forced to give birth to a larger species.

He realized he was stroking her wrist with his thumb, drawing her closer, easing her into relaxation, an incubus trick of seduction. Only this time, it was he who was succumbing. How many human women could have adapted to his world so quickly and with so little fear and reservation? She should be terrified about the changes in him, but she'd rolled with the punches—his raging sexual need last night, the fact that he could impregnate her at will, and now, she wanted him to shapeshift into something potentially horrifying.

She was magnificent. If not for his curse, he'd be thanking his lucky stars that Roag had forced him to mate with her.

"I'm not sure how to shift," he admitted.

"Well, when I shift outside the moon phase, I just picture myself shifting... and it happens."

Eidolon had said something similar, that being in the presence of a demon helped one to turn into that species, but otherwise, the key was concentration. Shade cycled his mind through dozens of different species and in the end decided not to terrorize Runa too much. He settled on a Sora demon. He concentrated... and in moments, he felt the sting of stretching skin, the agony of popping joints, and the next thing he knew, he had bright red skin, long nails, and a whiplike tail.

Cool.

Runa had backed up a step, but she watched him with curiosity, not fear. "You look like a cartoon devil. You just need a pitchfork."

He laughed, because Tayla had said the same thing about Ciska, the Sora nurse at UG. The one who could do amazing things with her tail...

Which gave him a wicked idea.

He whipped his tail up, catching Runa at the waist. She didn't resist as he pulled her toward him, though she swallowed audibly when she noticed his erection. He looked down, and yup, that sucker was worthy of a little trepidation. It pulsed a deep, dark crimson, and the head was broad, the tip glistening with a drop of liquid arousal.

Still, he didn't sense fear from her.

"It's so easy for you, isn't it?" she murmured.

"What's easy?"

"Sex. Seducing women."

Shade drew a finger across the tops of her breasts. "It's what I am." Slowly, he slid his tail down her bare butt. "Spread your legs."

She hesitated for a mere heartbeat before obeying. He slipped his tail between her thighs and feathered the tip over the pad of her sex. She made a sound, the tiny, feminine catch in her breath he loved to hear.

He trailed the fingers of both hands to her nipples, and he used his slightly elongated nails to pluck them gently as he tickled her sex with his tail. What a handy appendage. So maybe this *s'genesis* thing wasn't all bad.

For a mated male, at least.

Dipping his head, he swiped his tongue along the seam of her mouth, demanding that she open for him. When she did, he slid inside her mouth, tasting the faint tang of toothpaste, and he wondered when she'd found the time—and energy—to brush her teeth this morning. Eager to taste more, to take more, he thrust his tongue against hers and started an easy, penetrating rhythm that had her clutching his shoulders and rolling her hips against him with the same carnal timing.

Before Runa, he'd never enjoyed kissing, had detested the intimacy of the act. But he loved how she put her soul into every kiss. She wasn't practiced, but what she lacked in experience she made up for in emotion and effort.

One of her hands dropped between them, and her fingers skimmed over the head of his cock to play in the slick moisture there. Groaning, he threw back his head and let her play, something she hadn't done since this whole nightmare began. Runa had given him so much last night, and it was time to return the favor.

He dropped his mouth to her ear, nipped the lobe lightly. "You smell like me, Runa. Did you know that every time I come inside you, my essence permeates every part of you? Your blood, your hair, your cells." She shuddered, but from his words or the fact that he'd worked his tail between her folds and was stroking slowly, he didn't know. "And your skin, it tastes like me. I want to taste you everywhere."

It was his turn to shudder as he remembered the other night when he'd captured her arousal with his finger and brought it to his mouth. She'd been decadent, smooth and rich with a bite like Irish cream.

His blood pounded through him in an erotic surge that had him dropping to his knees. He worshipped her flat abdomen, skimmed his tongue from her navel to the boundary marked by her soft, caramel curls. At her breathless gasp, he looked up at her. She watched him with wide eyes, and he realized that this was the first time his mouth had been close to this beautiful, feminine place. Even when they'd been dating he hadn't taken the time to love her like this.

*Idiot.* So much time wasted.

"Spread your legs wider," he commanded and, still watching him, she did.

Keeping his gaze on her, he pierced her slit with his tongue. Instantly, her eyes glazed over and her lips parted. The erotic sight would have brought him to his knees if he hadn't already been on them. Desperate for more, he palmed her thighs to hold them apart as he spread her feminine lips with his thumbs.

He captured her hot flesh with his mouth, first licking at her and then sucking in long, gentle pulls. Her hands clutched his hair, holding him, but he wasn't going anywhere. Not when the sweetest nectar on earth and Sheoul was pouring down his throat, lighting him up from the inside out.

"Shade, oh, yes..." She pumped her hips and climaxed hard, her body jerking with such force that he had to hold her in place as he finished her off. When her muscles began to quiver as her orgasm tapered, he pushed to his feet, lightheaded, his body aching for her.

"Do you want me to change back?" he asked as he ran his hands up and down her arms, feeling the strong muscles beneath her silky skin.

"No," she whispered. "This is part of who you are."

Hell's fires. The blast of emotion that came from her rattled his bones and melted his organs. This was dangerous, but he couldn't stop himself. He needed to be inside her.

She wrapped her legs around his waist, and he entered her gently, his size stretching her as he seated himself to the root deep inside. "I'm hurting you," he moaned. "I have to change back."

She grasped his face in both hands and held him with her gaze. "Stay. Please."

He had no choice. Compelled to do her bidding, he began to thrust, slowly. Her tight heat squeezed him with exquisite pressure, and he managed to go slow and easy for a few thrusts before instinct took over. He pumped into her like a demon possessed, which, he supposed, he was. She called out his name, over and over, and each time he heard his name fall from her perfect lips, he had to bite his cheek to keep from coming.

He gave up when she rocked her head forward and bit deeply into his shoulder. His orgasm shot up his spine with such force he felt it blow through his skull. Runa screamed with her own release, her tight clasp milking him through another orgasm, and another, until he lost count.

They collapsed against the wet stone. His legs were so shaky he could barely hold himself up, and he suddenly realized it was Runa's strength that kept him from sliding to the ground into a mindless puddle. At some point he'd taken his true form again. Interesting that he hadn't felt the transformation. Weakly, he checked himself out to make sure all parts were present and accounted for, but as he studied his hands, his heart stopped.

His fingers flickered from solid to transparent and back again. His chest began to cramp as his heart took on a random rhythm dictated by terror.

Damn... *oh, damn.*

Runa arched, bucked with such force his sex slid out of her wet depths. Though he trembled so hard he nearly slipped on the slick stone beneath his feet, he held her through it, and when she eased, he glanced at his hands one more time, and he knew.

The curse had activated.

# Thirteen

"That was amazing," Runa murmured against Shade's shoulder. Drops of water beaded on his skin, and she lapped at them, savoring the cool splash of wetness on her dry tongue. She tasted jungle heat, fresh earth, and powerful male.

He moaned, still leaning on her and pinning her against the wet stone. He held her tight, closer, it seemed, than he ever had. He'd been gentle, caring, his big body shuddering against her. He'd broken her heart a year ago, but she could feel it beginning to heal.

Naturally, Shade couldn't allow the warm fuzzies to last. He pushed away from her, and without looking her in the eyes, he strode into the cave. And was it her imagination, or did he seem to be transparent in places? She'd seen him turn practically invisible in a shadow ... but this seemed different. A side effect of his shift into another species of demon?

She stepped into the waterfall to rinse—how cool was it that he had a natural shower built into his dwelling?—and when she finished, she found him in the kitchen, his hair still wet but dressed in his usual black leather garb.

Including gloves.

His hands shook a little, and tension surrounded him like a blanket. Was he uncomfortable with the closeness they'd shared? Something was up, and he still wouldn't meet her gaze.

"Are we going somewhere?"

Ignoring her question, he tossed her a bath towel and slid a plate across his dining room table. "Eat."

Wrapping the towel tight around her, she stared at the ham and cheese sandwich, and though she was starving, the sudden awkwardness between them unsettled her stomach. "I'm not hungry."

His gaze finally caught hers, and her breath hitched at the sight of the dark shadows in his eyes. "Yes, you are. I can sense it."

Damn him and his senses. He bit into his own sandwich as though ravenous.

"How come I can't sense your hunger?" she asked.

"Dunno. Eat."

Sighing, she sat across from him and watched him chew, watched his throat ripple as he swallowed. That mouth had been on her, and she flushed at the image that was burned into her brain; him, between her legs, his jaw muscles rolling as he'd feasted on her.

"What are you staring at?" he asked. "Do I have something in my teeth, or what?"

She laughed. "No, of course not. I like looking at you. I can't help it. Is that a crime in demonland?"

"I guess not."

A cool draft blew through the cave, sending a chill across her wet scalp. She dragged a hand through her tangled hair. She must look like a drowned rat. "Listen, I know this isn't the ideal situation for either of us, but if you're right, and this bond is permanent—"

"It is."

"Okay, then, it seems to me that we need to work some things out."

He broke a Fresca off the six-pack he'd set on the table and pushed it toward her. "Like what?"

"Like the fact that I don't plan to spend the rest of my life in this cave. The moon cycle is done. Can we go someplace else now?"

"No."

"So you expect me to remain your prisoner for the rest of my life?"

Shade gripped his sandwich so hard mayo dripped from between the slices of bread. "Did you forget about Roag? You killed his female. He'll want revenge."

"How do you know? You said he's insane."

"His insanity only makes him more dangerous. And I know because it's what I would do if someone killed y—" He threw his sandwich down on his plate, knocking the top off kilter. "I don't want to talk about this."

She stared at him. Part of her wanted to kiss him for what he'd said—or almost said—about what he'd do if someone killed her. But the other part wasn't going to get sidetracked by his all too familiar avoidance.

"Well, too bad." She tossed down her own sandwich. "I can't live like this, and I won't. Did it occur to you that I have a life? A job I'm good at? People who will miss me?"

"Actually, no. It didn't occur to me." He laughed bitterly. "Not once in all this time did I think about it. Gods, I'm such an asshole."

"I won't argue that," she muttered.

Angry words fell from Shade's lips, words in a guttural language she didn't know, but she got the gist. He was cursing up a storm. Yet he took a break in the middle of it to fix the top slice of bread on his sandwich, lining it up perfectly with the bottom.

"Who were you talking to on the phone?" he asked abruptly.

Whoa. That made her heart skip a beat. "You remember?"

"I might have been half-crazed with the *s'genesis*, but yeah, it's all coming back."

She swallowed dryly and reached for her drink. "What . . . what did you hear?"

"Enough to know that whoever you were talking to knows about the hospital, and that Kynan is involved."

She broke out in a cold sweat. She'd never been a good liar, and with the bond, Shade would sense her emotions, might know if she was lying about something big. Maybe she could dole out bits and pieces of truth . . .

"I was talking to Arik. I told you that he and Kynan know each other."

"How?"

"What is this? An interrogation?"

"Answer the question." When she said nothing, he leaned across the table. "The longer you stall, the more suspicious I get, and while I can't torture you—unless you want to be tortured—I have no problem with stringing up Ky. Now spit it out."

"Stop bossing me around."

He swore, and this time she understood his raw curse all too well.

"We just did that, buddy. So maybe you could bust yourself out of this grumpy mood and remember that none of this is my fault. And while you're at it, maybe you could wash your mouth out with soap."

Both fists came down on the table with a slam loud enough to startle her, but after a moment, he said quietly, "You're right."

As far as apologies went, it was as much as she'd get, and she knew it. "From the Army."

His dark eyes narrowed. "Is he spying on us?"

"No."

He nodded as if suddenly everything was coming together. "The job you mentioned...you're working for the military, aren't you?"

*Busted.* "No...I..." The lie tangled her tongue, and Shade wasn't buying it anyway, so she looked down and whispered, "Yes."

"What does Kynan have to do with this?" When she said nothing, he sighed. "Help me out here."

Unsure where to start, and afraid to spill more than what might be strictly necessary, she chose her words carefully. "He was a liaison between The Aegis and the Army. He fell off our radar about the time his wife died. We haven't heard from him since. No one in The Aegis has been able to put us in touch with him. So I came to New York to find him."

Obviously, Tayla had known where he was, but she'd kept it from everyone else in The Aegis. Runa had been sent to do more than just locate him. The Army wanted him. Badly. She didn't know why, and it wasn't her place to ask. When orders were issued, orders were followed.

He cut her a sharp look. "There's more. Something you aren't telling me."

"No—"

"When you came to my place, it wasn't because you were pissed at me, was it? You wanted information about Underworld General, didn't you?"

Runa looked away, caught her reflection in the stainless steel refrigerator door. Guilt stared back at her. "Yes."

"You hated me so much that you wanted to bring down me and the hospital." The tone of his voice became gentler. "Not that I blame you."

How could she deny the truth? "It wasn't just that," she muttered, out of some twisted need to make him feel better. "I wasn't lying when I said I wanted to kill the warg who bit me, and that's why I went to your apartment."

"What day was that?"

"Friday. A week before you landed in the dungeon with me."

He ran his gloved hand over his face. "Shit."

"What?"

"I'll bet Roag was trying to nab Wraith. He was supposed to meet me at my apartment that night, but we canceled at the last minute because I needed to come here—"

"With a female," she finished, the bitterness in her voice surprising even her.

He averted his gaze. His shoulders slumped a little, and she actually felt sorry for him. He might be putting up an I-don't-give-a-shit front, but she wasn't believing it anymore.

"Okay," she began, her voice softer than before, "so

how would Roag have known that Wraith would be at your place?"

"Solice knew. She was a nurse at the hospital. She's the one who, ah, tortured me in the dungeon."

"Oh. Well, obviously she didn't know about the change in plans that night, and I got taken instead of you and Wraith."

"Fu—ah, hell's bells." He shook his head. "I'm so sorry, Runa." She didn't have time to be stunned, or to soften up, because he immediately danced away from his apology. "Tell me how involved you are with the military."

As much as she hated talking about this, in a way it felt good to get this huge secret out in the open. Maybe now Shade would understand her need to get back to the real world. "I'm a paid volunteer. They helped me out after the attack."

"Helped you, how?"

"Arik took me to the base, and they tried to cure me of the lycanthropy." She took a deep breath and told him the rest. "The treatments were experimental, and a couple of months after starting them, I gained the ability to shift at will."

"So you think the experiments are responsible for that?" When she nodded, he shook his head. "You should have told me. Eidolon would know better what to look for."

"I didn't know what to expect from you. Or your brothers. I might be a werewolf, but I'm still human, and I can't betray my own people by spilling secrets about the American military. Think about it. If the situation were reversed, what would you do?"

She knew damned good and well he didn't want to admit she was right, and sure enough, he avoided answering by asking another question.

"What did you tell your brother about the hospital when you called him yesterday?"

"Nothing, I swear."

Shade crossed his arms over his broad chest. "Do you know what Kynan told the Army?"

"No."

"What else can you tell me about this military unit that you work for?"

"Shade, please. I can't talk about this."

The look he gave her sent the chill she'd felt earlier straight to her bones. "Then Kynan will."

⁓

Shade stalked away from the table, leaving Runa jaw-dropped and furious at his threat.

Which wasn't really a threat. Dammit, if Ky had any nefarious motives regarding the hospital, if he was secretly working against them...

Fuck.

Well, Runa couldn't yell at him for *thinking* the word.

"Oh, no! You don't get to just walk away from me."

Runa caught up to him in the living room as he headed for the exit. He needed to get out of this place, needed just a few minutes to compose himself before he did something stupid, like wrap her in his arms and promise her he'd make up for everything Roag had done to her. His stomach growled, reminding him of exactly why he couldn't do that; already the curse was affecting him. He'd eaten two sandwiches before she came in from the waterfall, and he felt as though he hadn't taken a bite.

*Relentless hunger.*

One down, three to go.

"Get dressed, Runa," he said, without turning around. "We need to head back to the hospital." The hospital she'd been tasked to spy on. For some reason, the fact that she'd agreed to do it hurt more than it should.

"For more tests, or to torture Kynan?"

"Tests, mostly." Shade could call E to tell him about Kynan, and to give him a heads-up about the Army experimentation on Runa, but he wanted to be there in person. Now, more than ever, UG was a haven. He might be a demon, but he was also a paramedic, and the desire to save lives was almost as strong as his drive to have sex.

With Runa. His mate.

Fuck.

"Shade?"

"What? I didn't cuss." *Way to sound guilty, idiot.*

"I'm afraid."

Did she sense that she was in as much danger from him as from Roag? He swiveled around, a knot of dread twisting his gut. She stood there, chin up and shoulders squared, hair all a mass of wild wetness around her shoulders. "Why?"

"Because I have no control over anything. Your crazy brother wants me dead, I'm bonded to you and can't get out of it, and I couldn't leave you if I wanted to because I don't know how to use the Harrowgates." She swallowed hard enough for him to hear. "You seem to think I should just accept this in stride, and honestly, I've tried...but you're not making it easy. You act like this is all temporary, but at the same time, you say it's permanent. If it was permanent, wouldn't you want to get to know me? At least make an effort to make this work? I don't get it. I really don't."

The tremor in her voice at the very end brought all his

ideas about not hugging her to a grinding halt. He did want to know her. He wanted to know how she grew up. What her favorite movie was, her favorite food, her dream vacation spot. But how could he tell her that as much as he wanted to know these things, he couldn't? Every little bit he learned would draw him closer to her, and closer to his doom.

So instead of explaining any of that to her, he reached for her, knowing he was making a huge mistake. She came to him willingly, folded herself against his chest. She felt good like that, her warmth surrounding him, filling him in places that had been empty and cold for so long.

He nuzzled the top of her head, inhaling the exotic, fresh scent of shampoo and jungle water. "I'm sorry I got you into this."

She tightened her arms around him. "What's done is done. The past doesn't matter."

"Yeah," he said gruffly. "It does. So much of the past affects the future."

Her palm slid up his spine in a comforting stroke. "Tell me about yours. Not about the scars Gem was talking about or anything," she said quickly. "Something nice. Something about your family, maybe?"

He recognized the manipulation for what it was—that need of hers to understand him. But the grief over Skulk's death was fresh, and talking about his family suddenly seemed like the balm he needed.

"I told you my true sire is a Seminus demon. He'd shifted into an Umber and impregnated my mother. Immediately after, she took an Umber as her mate, and when I was born, they were shocked by not only the single birth, but the human-looking infant with tattoos on his arm. Fortunately, Umbers are good parents. They kept me and went on to have more children." Runa's hand kept stroking, coaxing more out of him. "Skulk was the runt of the last litter. Right after that, my Umber father was killed trying to defend our nest from a demon that eats infants."

"That's awful," she said, her hand freezing over his lower back. He wiggled until she got the hint and started rubbing again.

"My mother slaughtered the bastard, but she was devastated over losing her mate. I helped out a lot after that." He felt Runa smile against his chest. "What? What's so amusing?"

"I just can't picture you babysitting a bunch of little girls."

He twirled a lock of her soft hair around his finger. "I love babies. I'd love to have a cave full—" He cut himself off, because he'd never have that. Not with Runa. Not with anyone.

"Kids," she breathed. "That's something I guess we'll have to talk about eventually, huh?"

"Yeah." His voice was hoarse and husky, a powerful combination of Seminus instinct that told him to impregnate her now, and common sense, which screamed at him to run far and run fast.

Common sense won. Barely. "Come on. We need to get to the hospital."

Gem couldn't wait to get off work. After last night's disaster with Kynan, she couldn't bear to see him when he came on shift in an hour.

God, she was so pathetic, lusting after a man who didn't want her except when he was drunk. Worse, even after what had happened last night, she knew that if he walked into the ER right now and crooked his finger at her, she'd fall at his feet like a neglected dog, willing to take whatever scraps its master was willing to give.

*Imbecile.*

The ER Harrowgate flashed, and Wraith strode through. In his arms he carried a bloody, red-skinned demon...

*Ciska. Oh, God.*

Adrenaline kicked her into gear, and she barked out orders to the nearby nurses and techs as she guided Wraith to an empty room. "What happened?"

As Wraith laid Ciska down, she gloved up.

"Dunno," he said, sounding oddly unconcerned. "Found her like this."

"Where?"

"Outside the hospital."

Reaver and nurses joined them, but Gem had a sinking feeling it was too late. The demon had been torn to shreds. Her abdomen lay open, and Gem would be willing to bet that she was missing a few important organs.

*Ghouls. Roag.*

"Someone page Eidolon. And if Shade is around, get him, too." Eidolon could repair damaged tissue, but Shade could affect how the patient's organs functioned, could keep a patient breathing and pumping blood far better than any machine could.

"No breath sounds, left side," one of the male nurses, a vampire, said.

"Tube her," Gem said, and gestured to Reaver. "BP and pulse?"

"One sec," he replied.

Hot breath fanned against the back of Gem's neck, and she jumped, startled.

"So, Gem," Wraith murmured into her ear, "why is it that we've never fucked?"

"Because I don't like you?" And with the way he was behaving while one of their own nurses lay dying, that was true enough at the moment.

His hands came down on her hips, and his teeth scraped her neck. "Leave the nurse. She's as good as dead. Come with me, and I'll make you like me."

"What the hell is wrong with you?" She shoved him away. "Are you high again?"

He laughed, shot her a wink, and strode out of the room. Stunned, she stared after him. Wraith was obnoxious, but as vicious as he could be, she'd never known him to be outright cruel. If anything, she'd have expected outrage and a swift promise of retribution for their mutilated staff member.

"Doctor, look at this."

One of the physician assistants had opened Ciska's mouth. A cloth had been stuffed inside and—oh, Christ—it had been pinned to her tongue. As gently as she could, Gem pulled it free, experiencing a sudden twist in her gut at the writing on the cloth.

*A gift for Wraith. I know what you did.*

Wraith lit up a cigarette right in front of Eidolon in the staff break room. Demons didn't get lung cancer, but E had some leftover human prejudices from his days in human med school, and he hated the smoke. Which was what made lighting up in the hospital so fun.

"Dammit, Wraith," E growled, but he didn't say anything else. Disappointing. Wraith seriously felt the need to work off some tension. Shade had called an hour ago to say he was on his way in and wanted to talk to them, and the wait was killing him, partly because he was worried about Shade, and partly because he had a ton of new information to share with his brothers.

Last night after he left Kynan, he'd gone hunting, but not for blood. He'd tracked down Ramses, a senior member of the Seminus Council, and after that, he sought the advice of an elusive, ancient spellcaster who hated him on sight. He'd had to work off her animosity—in bed—for hours. Lucky for him he didn't wear out easily. And now he was in possession of information that would help both him and Shade.

After that, he'd explored the immediate area around every Harrowgate in Northern Ireland. He'd found nothing, but tonight he was going back to check out the southern part of the island. He *would* find Roag, and when he did, his brother's suffering was going to become legend. Something that centuries later, the most evil demons would tell their spawn at bedtime.

The door swung open, crashed against the wall. Shade strode in, chomping on gum, completely encased in black leather, including his hands. He must have come in on his Harley.

And, Wraith noted with jealousy, he sported a new *dermoire* around his neck. He'd gone through The Change.

"Where's Runa?" E asked.

"MRI." Eidolon's eyebrows shot up, and Shade shook his head. "No, I didn't leave her with any males. Dr. Shakvhan is handling the tests you wanted done."

Wraith blew out a stream of smoke. "Is this a bond thing?"

Eidolon nodded. "For some reason, right after bonding, you get a little overprotective."

Yet another reason Wraith was never, ever going to bond with a female. Nope. He was looking forward to losing himself to the post*s'genesis* world. He wanted to spend his days with no concerns save one. Screwing his brains out. And if he went stark-raving mad, his brothers would kill him.

"So what's up? Is it time to get rid of Runa?"

Shade's gloved hands formed into fists. "Knock it off."

"Shade?" Eidolon asked softly. "You okay?"

His fists unclenched and clenched again, and Wraith got the distinct impression he was hiding something. "I'm good. I just want to be rid of this damned lycanthropy. Now I know what mutts chained in backyards go through. Did you get anything from the tests?"

"Nothing yet. Be patient."

"Patient, my ass. I don't want to go through another full moon." Shade sank down on the couch. "But I might have something that'll help. Runa was experimented on by the military. They were trying to cure her, and whatever they did gave her the ability to shift at will."

Eidolon got that excited look on his face, the way he always did when he was working on a medical mystery. "That explains a lot. Some of her DNA was so abnormal that I was starting to think she had demon somewhere in the family tree. But if experimentation is responsible... you just saved me a lot of time."

Shade leaned forward and braced his forearms on his knees. "We might have another problem. Our favorite Aegi-turned-doctor."

"Kynan? What about him?"

"Apparently, her brother and Kynan were both in the Army. Probably a secret division. Runa is involved as well, and she was sent to find Kynan. They know about the hospital, and I think Kynan told them."

"Fuck." E glanced at his watch. "He's on shift now. Wraith and I will have a little chat with him. Did you hear about Ciska?"

Wraith scowled. "What about Ciska?"

"She died right after you brought her in."

Ciska? *Dead*? Shock and grief collided with confusion. "What? How?" Wraith had been with her just last night. In his office. On his desk. He was supposed to meet her in the on-call room in an hour.

"What do you mean, how can she be dead?" Eidolon asked. "You saw her. She was mutilated."

Wraith flicked his cigarette butt into the sink. "I have no idea what you're talking about."

"You handed her off to Gem. You don't remember?"

"Do you really think I'd forget something like that?"

E stared at him for a moment, his gaze contemplative, as though he was working out how much to believe. Finally, he shoved his hand into his pocket and pulled something out. "There was a message on her. It's addressed to you."

Wraith took the bloody cloth from his brother. *I know what you did.* The writing sent a chill up his spine.

"Hell's rings," Shade growled. "It was Roag who brought her in."

Wraith's stomach bottomed out. "Roag was here? In the hospital?"

"That bastard. That fucking bastard!" Eidolon snarled

and slammed his fist into a cupboard. For a long time, he stood there, hands braced on the counter, head hung low. Wraith recognized that position, the I'm-going-to-compose-myself-before-I-kill-my-brother stance, except for once, he wasn't the brother in question. "What does the message mean?" E finally asked, his voice tight with barely contained rage. "What does he know?"

Wraith's first instinct was to lie, but not to protect himself. The truth would hurt Shade, and he'd already experienced more than enough pain over the last few days. And Eidolon...this might be the last straw for him. Wraith wasn't stupid—he knew E kept him on staff to keep an eye on him, to keep him out of trouble. But after this, E probably wouldn't give a shit anymore.

"Wraith?" Shade's voice was low, soothing. "You need to come clean."

Eidolon swung around, his expression confirming everything Wraith had been thinking. Already disappointment swirled in his dark eyes. Nothing new, there.

Wraith cleared his throat because some big-ass lump seemed to be stuck in it. Both brothers went taut, as though bracing themselves for whatever he'd done this time.

"What happened at Brimstone was my fault. I tipped off The Aegis because I knew Roag would be there." He met Shade's gaze. "I set him up to die."

Closing his eyes, E shook his head, but it was Shade's reaction that concerned Wraith the most. Because of him, Roag wanted revenge, and Skulk was dead.

Shade sat there, his expression shuttered.

"Say something," Wraith said. Begged, really. When Shade remained silent, Wraith took a deep breath, needing to know where his brother's emotions were, but he got nothing. No scent save that of his female. And sex.

"Dammit, Shade! I'm responsible for the situation with you and Runa. I'm responsible for Skulk's death. Don't just sit there!"

But Shade did just that, until Wraith couldn't stand it anymore. He turned away, propped an arm on the wall above his head and closed his eyes to wait. No matter what they did to him, he wouldn't fight back this time. He deserved whatever they dealt.

When Shade finally spoke, his voice was as deadly cold as an arctic wind. "I don't have to ask why. He was out of control. But *goddamn you,* why didn't you tell us a long time ago?"

*Because I didn't want you and E to hate me.* They were all he had in the entire world. They were the only reason he was still alive.

"Shade might not need to ask why you did it, but I do." Eidolon's voice was as hot as Shade's was icy, which meant E wasn't even trying to summon his Justice Dealer calm. "Taking Roag down should have been a group decision, and you fucking know it."

"Right." Wraith wheeled around. "You would never have agreed. Your precious Roag could do no wrong. Me? I can't do anything right. But I've never done to women what he did." Wraith shuddered at the memory of the last human female of Roag's he'd found, the one that put Wraith over the edge, gunning to take down Roag at the next opportunity—which happened to be Brimstone.

"And yet," Eidolon said, "you're looking forward to *s'genesis,* when you could turn into something as evil as Roag. How does that make you better than him?"

The writing on the walls began to pulse as Wraith's temper blasted through him. But after a glance at Shade, who had closed his eyes and sat quietly, probably thinking about Skulk, Wraith backed down. "The difference," he murmured, "is that I don't want the insanity that could come with it." He pegged E with hard eyes. "Roag did. And if it happens, I'll expect you to do what's necessary."

Shade buried his face in his hands. "Dammit, Wraith. Just...fuck."

"I know. I really stepped in it this time. But if you'd seen that woman...if you knew—" He broke off and turned away from his brothers once more. He shouldn't have allowed himself to get pissed. Should have just let them beat the hell out of him. They still could. They still *should*.

After a long moment, footsteps thudded across the black stone tile. He braced himself for a blow, but it never fell. Instead, arms wrapped around him. Eidolon's. A heartbeat later, another, heavier weight settled against him.

Shade.

"Brother," Shade rasped, "it was a stupid thing to do, but you couldn't have known Roag would survive and come back worse than before. So from now on, no more fighting, no more regrets."

Eidolon's voice was as shaky as Shade's. "Roag is trying to drive a wedge between us. To weaken us." He pulled back to turn Wraith around. He cupped Shade's cheek with one hand, and Wraith's with the other. "From here on out, we stand as one."

Shade jerked as if he'd been goosed, and his eyes flared gold. "We test that stand as one thing now," he said, moving swiftly toward the door. "Something's wrong with Runa."

# *Fourteen*

She could feel Him. The One who had turned her into a werewolf, a monster she couldn't escape.

He was here.

The curve between Runa's neck and shoulder where he'd bitten her burned as if his teeth were still buried in her flesh. Her whole body tensed, vibrated with seductively dark power. An oil slick of malevolence floated beneath the surface of her skin, disgusting her even as adrenaline gave her an electric high. She'd read that the relationship between a sire and his *therionidrysi* was powerful and evil.

She felt the truth of that in every cell.

"You can get dressed, now." Dr. Shakvhan helped Runa off the metal table, and while the beautiful succubus fretted over the medical equipment in the room, Runa changed out of her hospital gown and back into her jeans and sweater.

It wasn't easy, not with the way her hands shook with excess energy. Tension coiled in every muscle, all the way to her bones. When Dr. Shakvhan turned her back, Runa darted out the door. She was going to find the werewolf, and she was going to kill him.

Right here in the hospital.

The female came at him. Luc didn't recognize her, but he knew her, and he knew what she wanted.

He caught her by the throat just as the pain struck her. She writhed in his grip, not because he held her a foot off the ground, though that couldn't have been comfortable, but because she'd tried to hurt him, and now she was paying the price. Luc had never tested the Haven spell, had no idea what it felt like to suffer what she was going through, but even if he had, he doubted he'd have much sympathy. Nothing fazed him anymore.

No, that wasn't entirely true. The weird malevolent link he shared with this female fazed him. He felt as if he'd snorted evil-tainted cocaine. The high was incredible, but so was the raw, explosive desire to wreak havoc. He hadn't felt this way since he'd hunted down his own sire and torn him apart with his bare hands.

"Let her go, Luc." Shade's voice was a low, controlled drawl as he and his brothers approached, but his expression was a mask of rage.

"Gladly." Luc opened his palm and let her drop, but Shade caught her before she hit the floor. Too bad.

"Pain," she gasped, holding her skull so tightly her hands were white.

Shade held her against him and shot Luc a look promising murder. "What did you do?"

"*She* attacked *me*."

A faerie nurse nodded from a nearby cubicle where she was draining bloodpans. "He tells it true. Stupid girl."

Shade petted the stupid girl's hair, his glare still black with homicidal intent. "Why would she attack you?"

"Because I sired her."

You could have heard a mouse tiptoeing across the floor with the way the normally noisy ER went dead silent. Frank, one of the lab techs, actually froze midstep as he walked past.

Shadows shifted in Shade's eyes, seething like living things. "*You*?"

"It was the night the slayers tried to take me." The night they'd slaughtered his would-be mate before he had a chance to claim her. "They were on my ass, and she ran into me." He shrugged. "If it's any consolation, I thought I'd killed her." He'd hoped so, anyway. The Warg Council was not forgiving when it came to killing or turning humans, though they definitely preferred the kill over the turn. The Warg Council was made up of born wargs, and if they had their way, they'd eradicate the earth of turned wargs, whom they considered second-class citizens.

Before that night, Luc had been lying low, avoiding catching the Council's attention. He'd retained much of his humanity, had been living among humans, doing the right thing by locking himself up every full moon.

Then the slayers had attacked. They'd broken into his house and into his locked cell where he and Ula had been about to mate. They'd killed her and seriously injured him before he managed to escape. That night screamed through his memories, his nightmares.

*He had no idea how long or how far he ran, keeping to the shadows and ducking behind parked cars, but when the adrenaline ran out and he began to fade again, he was in unfamiliar territory, caught on the edge of the city and well out of his suburban neighborhood.*

*Fire seared his lungs with each breath, and nausea tumbled in his stomach.*

*Ula.*

*A scream ripped from his throat, ringing as a howl through the darkness. Going up on two legs, he opened his mind, sought the nearest Harrowgate. North. Several blocks away. Too far, but his only hope.*

*He loped toward it, no longer bothering with concealment. Operating on instinct alone, he rounded a corner and slammed into a woman. She smelled of rage and hurt that veered instantly to stark, icy terror. The emotions collided with his identical ones, intensifying them in a massive explosion.*

*Out-of-control hunger, the need to take something apart, made him tremble as he towered over her.*

*"Run, Little Red Riding Hood."*

*In beast form, his words came out as a snarl, and she screamed like a fucking B-movie horror actress. The slayers would hear. Panic eroded what little remained of his humanity, and he struck, sinking his teeth into the soft spot between her shoulder and neck. She pounded against his chest, kicked wildly in futile defense as he shook her like a terrier with a rat.*

*"This way!"*

*A slayer's voice broke him out of his murderous rage. The woman moaned, hanging limp from his jaws. In the distance, the sound of pounding footsteps echoed off the surrounding buildings.*

*With a toss of his head, he flung the woman's uncon-*

*scious body behind a Dumpster and sprinted down the sidewalk, bouncing off light posts and street signs in his insane bid to get to the Harrowgate. To the hospital.*

He'd made it to UG, and Eidolon had saved his life. But what remained of his humanity had bled out through the deep wounds the slayers had dealt him.

He'd finally become the monster he'd always feared, but he couldn't dredge up even an ounce of give-a-shit. It was only a matter of time before Wraith made good on the promise he'd made, the one that would ensure that Luc wouldn't prey upon innocent humans.

"Why do you care?" Luc asked Shade. "She's not your mate."

"Yeah, she is."

"She's not marked." Shade's throat bore the mate-mark, but the female's arms were bare.

"I'm aware of that, warg."

Luc shrugged. "Whatever. Just keep her away from me. I'd hate to have to claim First Rights."

Shade's eyes went red, and the female in his arms bared her teeth. "You wouldn't," she snarled.

"Try me."

"You wouldn't live long enough to claim them," Shade spat.

"And you wouldn't live long after you killed me," Luc shot back. "Isn't that right, Doc?"

Eidolon had served as a Justice Dealer for a time, upholding demon law. Warg law stated that any warg may, within the first year of siring another, claim his *therionidrysi* as a mate—willing or not—or kill him or her without consequence. Were Shade to kill Luc in order to prevent him from claiming First Rights, demon law would require Shade's death as punishment.

"No one is killing anyone," Eidolon said. "Shade, take Runa to a patient room. Luc, go home and cool off." He turned to a nearby nurse. "You. Page Kynan. This hospital is falling apart, and it ends now."

Roag followed Shade at a discreet distance as his brother carried his murderous whore of a mate down the hall.

*I'll avenge you, my darling Sheryen.*

He shook with the desire to kill Runa now that she was within reach, but he had to play this smart, and time his revenge with care. If all went well, he could take out his brothers and the whore at the same time. Though maybe he'd let Shade live just so the curse would kick in. Watching Runa die slowly and painfully would definitely bring on the worst effects of the curse, and then he'd spend eternity with those memories running through his head.

The thought made him laugh. Shade didn't break his stride, but he did look over his shoulder, and for a moment, Roag held his breath. He'd taken the form of a male Croucher, an ugly, man-sized demon. He was pretending to be a patient, which allowed him to witness the interesting confrontation between Luc and Runa in the ER, and though Roag knew Shade wouldn't recognize him, the fear still paralyzed him. He was so close to finally getting his revenge, and he couldn't blow it now.

Shade rounded a corner, and Roag breathed again. He needed to get to the lab and the special storeroom where Eidolon kept his rare potions and artifacts. His brother's collection of magical and mythical objects was extensive, and Roag knew exactly what he was after.

But first, in order to gain access to that area, he needed to take the form of a trusted staff member. One whose death would be a major blow to his brothers.

He hurried back to the emergency department, where Luc was heading out the sliding doors to the ambulance bay. Luc walked as if he owned the place, his arrogance topped only by Wraith's. Taking down the grumpy warg would be a pleasure.

Roag slipped into a curtained room and took a form he'd never taken; Shade's. Quickly, he strode out of the ER and found Luc gathering his gear from one of the two ambulances.

"You going home?"

Luc looked up from where he stood on the driver's side of the cab, his gaze wary. "You heard E tell me to take some time off. Why?"

Roag shrugged. "Just wanted to make sure you weren't going anywhere near Runa."

"I was messing with you, Sem. I'm outta here until the First Rights time is up."

"Thrilled to hear it," Roag muttered. "I'm gonna grab something from the rig."

Roag hopped into the box section of the ambulance and snagged the drug box. He had no idea how much of any of the drugs he'd need to kill Luc, but he figured that if he combined them all into the largest of the syringes, he'd at least knock the guy out so he could break his neck. No way was he going up against the warg without insurance.

Just as he slid the box back into place, Luc climbed into the truck. Roag concealed the syringe at his side. He

needed to get Luc out of the rig. The Haven spell safe-
guarded the inside of the ambulances, but the parking lot
was unprotected.

"What are you doing?" Luc's gaze shifted from the
drug box to Roag's face. "I've already done inventory."

Roag rolled his eyes. They inventoried this shit? His
brothers were so fucking uptight.

"This is my hospital. I do what I want, shitshifter," Roag
said in his most taunting, arrogant Shade-voice. Luc was
blocking the back exit, so Roag went through the side door,
hoping Luc would follow. As he stepped down, he feigned
a hard fall. "Ow, fuck. Luc! I think I broke my leg!"

Luc came around the side of the ambulance. "I should
leave you there," he said, but he dropped to his knees at
Roag's side. "Hold still, Sem."

Roag took in the scene. No witnesses. And when
Luc put his hand on Roag's leg, Roag struck. He buried
the syringe deep in Luc's belly and jammed down the
plunger.

Luc roared and slammed Roag into the side of the
ambulance. The impact knocked Roag out of Shade's
form, but by then it didn't matter. Luc was on his knees,
wheezing. Surprise flashed in the warg's eyes, followed,
oddly enough, by a strange calm. If he didn't know any
better, Roag would think Luc wanted to die.

*Happy to help out.*

Slowly, Luc slid to the ground, his chest rattling with
each struggling breath. Death rattles. A beautiful sound,
and one Roag couldn't wait to hear coming out of Runa.

Luc twitched, blew out a breath, and moved no more.
Roag felt for a pulse... it was there, but weak. Luc
wouldn't last another five minutes.

As quickly as he could, Roag dragged Luc's heavy ass into the back of the ambulance. Next, he'd anonymously notify the authorities, tell them Shade had killed Luc to prevent First Rights, and once they nabbed Shade, Runa would be left unprotected.

"Luc?" The female voice floated through the parking lot.

Roag shifted into Luc's form and leaped out of the ambulance. "Yeah?"

Two paramedics, a male and a female, stalked toward him. He closed the rig door, concealing Luc inside.

"The Sup said you're supposed to go home. We're going to be on call today."

Roag eyed the vehicle, cursing his luck. Then again, if he played his cards right, he wouldn't need to keep Luc's form for long. Just long enough to get into the lab and then plant a suggestion in Wraith's head.

Smiling, he strode past the medics. "No problem. I'm outta here."

Shade didn't say a word to Runa as he carried her to a private patient room and placed her gently on the bed. The same eerie red lights that illuminated the rest of the hospital bathed the room in a garnet wash, creating stark shadows against Shade's already sinister, intense features, but his gaze was warm.

"Thank you." She was grateful for his assistance; her head throbbed so badly that she doubted she could have walked to the room on her own two feet. Besides, it had felt good to be cradled in Shade's powerful arms. "But you might have mentioned that the hospital was under a spell that prevents violence."

"I shouldn't have had to," he ground out, but the gentle stroke of his fingers over hers belied his harsh words.

"I'm sorry I humiliated you in your own hospital." She averted her gaze, but looking at the skulls lining the walls didn't exactly comfort her.

"Trust me," he said, using a finger to tip her face back to him. "It would take a hell of a lot more than that to humiliate me in this place."

She sighed, grateful for his understanding. "It's just that I've been searching for the man who attacked me for so long, and I felt him and couldn't stop myself."

Shade's jaw clenched so hard she heard the pop of bone. "Can you still feel him?"

"Yes." The oily taint of evil still shimmered on her skin. She'd give anything to spend an hour under Shade's waterfall right now.

Shade sank down in the chair next to her bed and muttered, "You can feel *him,* but not me."

"I can only feel him when he's very close. Like now." She sat up, wincing at the stab of pain in her head. "He wouldn't really claim—"

"No!" Shade shot to his feet. "I swear to you, he will not claim First Rights."

She'd learned about First Rights when she'd researched werewolves, but hadn't considered the custom to be a true threat since she'd fully intended to kill her sire when she found him. "I'm not sure what would be worse. Having him kill me, or..."

"Don't think about it." Shade crossed to her in two strides and tugged her to her feet and into his arms. "The year will be up soon, and Luc will have no claim on you."

"And who will?" she whispered.

"Oh, Runa…" His heart thundered against her ear, lulling her to relax. She took a deep breath and closed her eyes, reveling in the quiet moment.

They stood like that for a long time, until eventually, the malevolent sludge that had been pumping through her veins melted away. She slumped against Shade in relief. "He's gone. He must have left through one of those gates."

"We should go, too."

"Back to the cave?" When he nodded and backed away, she shook her head. "I told you I don't want to spend the rest of my life as your prisoner."

"What you want is irrelevant."

Damn him. "How can you be so caring and protective one minute, and then a total asshole the next?"

"Roag has been inside the hospital, Runa. He killed one of our nurses just to show us he could. I've got to keep you someplace safe."

The news that Roag had been in this building made her wobble. Shade's arm shot out to steady her. "It's okay. I have you."

His thumb rubbed absently on her arm—the one that should bear his mate-markings. She pulled out of his grip, and he didn't try to catch her again. "This has something to do with the fact that I'm not marked, doesn't it?" The guilt crossing his face confirmed her suspicion. "Oh, my God," she breathed. "The bond isn't working both ways. That's why you're keeping me close. Why you're holding me captive at your cave. You're afraid I'll leave you."

His gloved hands began to shake. He clenched them at his sides. "You have every reason to."

"What would happen if I did?"

"You know I need sex several times a day, and now I can only get it from you. If you left me, I'd be compelled to hunt you down, and if I couldn't get to you for some reason, within days I'd go insane and die."

She sucked in a startled breath. "Oh."

"Yeah. There's a reason so few of my species take mates." He explained in detail, and God, no wonder he was determined to keep her at his side.

This situation must be terrifying for him. If circumstances were reversed, she didn't think she'd handle it half as well as he had. From the moment he'd awakened in Roag's dungeon, he'd put aside his own fears to protect her, and then later, after they became bonded, he continued to protect her, making her feel safer than she'd ever felt before. He'd been hard on her, yes, but he'd also complimented her and encouraged her, giving her the courage to believe in herself and to take risks.

For the first time since becoming a werewolf, she didn't feel like an outsider, a freak. As strange as Shade's world was at times, it was where she belonged.

Reaching up, she palmed his cheek and forced him to look down at her. "I swear to you, I won't leave you. And I won't withhold anything you need." It was a relief to know she wasn't bonded to him and that nothing would happen to her if she left him, but she couldn't let him die.

Why her promise should make him miserable, she didn't know, but clearly, she'd said the wrong thing. His jaw tightened, his throat worked on a hard swallow, and his voice took on the harsh rattle of a steaming espresso machine. "For the love of all that's unholy, *stop it*. Stop being so fucking nice. You should hate me."

"Hate you?" she asked incredulously. "God, Shade.

I love you." Her heart pounded at the admission. Shade went ghost-white, and she only made it worse when she tacked on a weak, "I've loved you since the beginning."

"You said...when we were in Roag's dungeon...that you were over me."

She had, and she'd even believed it at the time. But her mother's mantra, uttered every time she learned of another of her father's affairs, made sense now. *You can't truly hate someone you've loved. You can only hurt.*

"I lied, you big lunk," she said softly. "To myself. To you. But the truth is, I love you." She took a deep, shaky breath. "God help me."

Terror whispered to Shade like a phantom's taunt. He wheeled away, put several feet of space between them, but right now it wasn't enough. Several miles wouldn't be enough. "Don't say that. Don't even think it."

"It's true." Her hand came down on his shoulder, and he hissed, jerked out of her grip.

"Dammit, Runa." He cursed the tremor in his voice, hating himself for it. "Why do you have to make everything so difficult?"

"Me? Difficult? I've done everything you've asked of me. You're the one being difficult. You care about me, and don't you dare deny it."

He wanted to, but she'd know he was lying. His body knew as well. The lightheadedness had come back, and he could feel his muscles turn watery. If he took off his gloves, he'd see his hands shimmering in transparency. He was falling for her so hard his heart hurt. The heart that would soon stop beating because the curse would turn it to shadow. Permanently.

"Well?"

"Well what?"

She threw up her hands. "You're impossible."

He stalked toward her, and he gave her credit for standing her ground. He stopped so close their chests brushed. "Were you telling me the truth earlier? If I wanted to take you, right now, right here, where anyone could walk in, would you refuse me? Because you're pissed?"

She raised her chin. "No."

Gods, her spirit excited him. Challenged him. Made him want to find a way to make sure she was his in every way, curse be damned. He tangled one hand in her hair and held her as he lowered his mouth to hers. The first brush of his lips against hers sent a spark of electricity through his veins. When her tongue slipped out to stroke the seam of his mouth, the spark ignited so fast his body became flame.

Runa worked him into a frenzy without even trying. It was time to take back some control. Roughly, he wrenched her head back so she couldn't move, was at the mercy of his mouth as he teased her. Tiny, soft kisses and nibbles made her whimper.

Finally, when he was good and ready, he whispered, "Open for me. Now."

"No."

He froze. "You said you wouldn't deny me."

"But I didn't say I was going to keep letting you control me." One corner of her kiss-swollen mouth lifted into a mischievous smirk. "And that's what you're doing. You want to prove that you've got me wrapped around your finger. Well, screw you. I won't deny you sex. You want it, you can have it. But your other little controlling games? I'll deny you those and fight you every step of the way."

Amusement made him smile even as irritation stirred his blood. Had she still been the Runa he'd dated a year ago, he could have reined her in with a gentle hand, kept her as little more than an outlet for sex with no worries about the curse. But this little fireball she'd become was too hot to handle with anything less than a firm hand. A firm hand and a new angle of approach.

Because he would not kill her—and when he thought about it, he realized he'd known that from the beginning. She would not die because of him. He'd brought the curse upon himself, and Runa would not be made to pay for his sins.

Shade would pay. Either he'd take himself out, or he'd succumb to a fate worse than death. But either way he was going to take Roag with him.

# Fifteen

Kynan had flashbacks of being called into the principal's office as he approached the administrative wing of the hospital. Eidolon had ordered him to appear before him, and Ky had felt his gut knot.

Eidolon's office door was open, and inside, the doctor sat on his desk, arms folded over his chest, long legs crossed at the ankles. Wraith stood in the corner, his blue eyes iced over.

This couldn't be good.

"Close the door." Eidolon's command was as cold as Wraith's gaze. "And then tell me how you know Arik Wagner."

Kynan had to swallow the lump of oh-shit before he could find his voice. "I knew him from my Army days."

"Give me your hand."

Where was this going? Kynan wondered, but it didn't occur to him to disobey. Eidolon took Ky's wrist and pressed his fingers to his pulse. "I'll tell you the truth. You don't have to play lie detector, if that's what you're doing."

"It is," Eidolon said, and for some reason, that stung. "Now, tell me how he knows about the hospital."

Oh, man. Kynan's heart rate revved like a race car engine. He'd done nothing wrong, but what he'd done during his time in The Aegis now felt like a huge betrayal.

"I told him about UG, last year when Tayla told me all about it. But it was before I started working here."

"Who else knows?" When Kynan didn't answer, Eidolon squeezed his wrist. "*Who else?*"

"I can't answer that."

Eidolon's eyes were flecked with angry gold. "You damned well better answer that. I have to protect the hospital."

"There's nothing to worry about."

"Then why did the Army send Arik's sister to find you?"

Not good. "I didn't know he had a sister."

"He does," Wraith said. "And she just happens to be Shade's new mate."

Small fucking world. Small fucking Army. Dammit, he shouldn't be surprised that they had sent someone after him. Though he was no longer active duty, he'd shared information with them—until he started working at UG. After that, he'd all but severed his ties with The Aegis and the R-XR. He helped out Tayla when she needed him, but he avoided The Aegis when he could. There were too many memories, and he didn't like the reminders that he was playing for the other side now.

If the military knew he'd been working with the enemy,

they'd haul his ass in, and they could keep him imprisoned—or worse—for God knew how long.

"Please, Kynan." Eidolon's tone was as close to pleading as Ky'd ever heard it. "Answer the question."

"I can't."

Wraith lunged, and in the span of a heartbeat, Kynan was dragged back into Wraith's body with an arm around his chest, and paralyzed by a finger pushed painfully hard into the base of his skull.

"I was just starting to like you, human," Wraith murmured into his ear. "So I really hope you haven't done anything to jeopardize this hospital." The demon's voice was low and rough as he continued. "Let's see what you've got in your little human mind, 'kay?"

Guardians wore jewelry imbued with magic to help them resist psychic attacks, but Kynan had tossed his ring months ago. Still, he'd learned basic shielding techniques, and he quickly slammed barriers into place around his thoughts.

Wraith laughed. "You think I can't wear those down?"

Suddenly, Ky was on a beach. Alone except for a female figure in the distance, walking toward him. She wore a knee-length, pink sundress, the kind Lori used to wear. A pang of longing shot through him as the woman drew closer. His heart started beating faster. She looked a lot like his wife. She smiled.

Lori's smile.

This was Wraith at work. He knew it, but he couldn't stop himself from gasping, "Lori?"

She closed the distance at a run, threw herself into his arms. The impact and shock knocked him to the ground, taking her with him.

"You're dead," he said. "This is bullshit. Wraith, knock it off."

"Shh." She touched a finger to his lips, silencing him. "Tell me about Arik."

He shook his head. His mind was getting misty, his memories unclear. His barriers were slipping.

"Kynan? Tell me."

"Arik is part of the Raider-X Regiment. Army paranormal division." Fuck. Did he just say that?

"Yes, you said it." She nuzzled his neck the way she did when she wanted to make love slowly. "Did you tell them about the demon hospital?"

He blew out a long, slow breath, but it did nothing to release the tense feeling of wrongness about this. Wraith was … wait … who was Wraith?

"Tell me, love," she whispered.

"Yes, I told them. But not where it is." By the time he learned the location, he was no longer in contact with the R-XR.

"You should tell them."

"Never."

"I've missed you, Ky. I'm so sorry about everything." Her hand slid down his abs until her fingers breached his waistband. She climbed on top of him, rubbed herself against him as Gem had done.

Gem had been so hot, so …

"Ky, please. Love me."

"I loved you so much, Lori." He gripped her waist, flipped her so she was on her back, and yanked her hands roughly above her head. He wasn't going to fall for her shit again. "Until you betrayed me and threw me away," he growled.

She arched her hips, trying to work him into arousal. It wasn't working. "Tell me about the demon hospital. Tell me about what information you've been giving to R-XR."

He frowned. "I haven't contacted them since the night I caught you with Wraith."

*Wraith! You son of a bitch!*

Suddenly, he was standing in Eidolon's office, heart pounding. "Damn you," he whispered. "*Damn you.*"

He lurched away from the demon, but his legs were too rubbery to support him, and he had to catch himself on Eidolon's desk. Closing his eyes, he stood there, hunched over, trying desperately to bring himself fully back into this world. The images of Lori had been so real, even if they'd been wrong. But one thing hadn't been wrong— even if it had been a surprise.

*I loved you so much, Lori. Until you betrayed me…*

*Until.* Holy shit, he didn't love her anymore, did he?

He grappled with his surprise and his nausea as Wraith filled in Eidolon on everything that had taken place inside Kynan's head.

"I regret that we had to resort to that, Kynan," Eidolon said. "But we had to know what you weren't telling us. The R-XR will be our secret as long as they don't fuck with us. I promise."

Kynan nodded, but didn't open his eyes. He got it, knew why they'd been forced to take the information from him if he wouldn't talk. He'd have done the same thing in a similar situation. Had done worse in the name of protecting The Aegis.

"Ky, if you need some time off, take as much as you need." Eidolon left, leaving him alone with Wraith.

"You okay, dude?"

The room spun a little as Kynan swung around to glare at Wraith. "Go to hell."

"Why are you mad at me but not E?"

"Because he's in charge of this place, this staff. He's protecting his hospital. But you..." *You're my friend.*

God, did he really think that? Just because Wraith had stuck his fangs in him? Okay, it was more than that—they'd been sparring in the gym together for months, kicked each other's butts in video games—but that hardly constituted a friendship. He must really be spiraling downward if he believed any different.

"I what?"

"You got off on it."

"You think I liked using your dead wife against you?" Wraith asked quietly.

"You're the one who said you don't care about anyone or anything."

Wraith went taut, as if he were offended. "That doesn't mean I like to see the people around me suffer."

Kynan snorted. "Yeah, you're a real tender guy."

"I would take your pain away if I could, human." The words were spoken so softly Kynan barely heard them, and then Wraith was stalking away as though his feet were on fire.

Awkwardly, because his knees were still weak and his muscles had gelled, Kynan sank into Eidolon's desk chair. What a mess. So much was bouncing around in his head now—Lori and Gem, his relationships with the hospital, The Aegis, the R-XR. He'd used work and alcohol to avoid confronting any of the issues, but now they were all crashing down on him at once.

One thing was clear; he needed to protect the hospital,

and it wasn't just because he liked Eidolon and his brothers. The things he'd learned here would be invaluable to human medicine—if he could convince Eidolon to share the knowledge. Hell, by Kynan's calculations, nearly 10 percent of human diseases and illnesses had demonic roots. Human-demon matings, especially, accounted for a staggering number of maladies, as Gem had confirmed with her past work in a human hospital.

And what was up with Arik's sister being bonded to Shade? He rubbed the back of his neck, groaning as he worked out the kinks. If she'd told Arik that Kynan was working at the hospital, he was screwed. The R-XR would send an entire team after him.

He needed to call Arik.

Once he did that, he'd have one more pressing issue. An issue that kept showing up in his dreams and his nightmares.

Gem.

Surprisingly, Shade didn't say anything about how Runa had stood up to him. In fact, she got the distinct impression that he'd liked it.

Good. Because he was going to be seeing a lot more of that. She knew she'd always been a bit timid, and hell, she could face it—a doormat. But the whole getting-bitten-by-a-werewolf thing had hardened her a little, and surviving Roag's dungeon hadn't hurt. Then there was the fact that Shade had a way of riling her up, and now that she knew how much he needed her...

Shame put some heat in her face as they walked the hospital's dark halls. That he'd said that females have all the power in a relationship with a Seminus demon didn't mean she should abuse that power.

"Where are we going again?" She studied the weird drains running along the hallway and wondered what they were for.

"My office. I need to post the new paramedic schedule." He gave her a sideways glance. "Don't touch that."

She jerked her hand away from the gargoyle statue she'd paused in front of. "Why?" It was beautiful...smooth white marble shot through with black and gold veins.

"He bites."

Shade continued down the hall as she leaped back. She swore one corner of the gargoyle's mouth tipped up just a bit.

"Your hospital is creepy," she muttered, as she hurried to catch up.

Creepy, but at least it didn't smell like human hospitals, with the overpowering odor of disinfectant layered on top of the more subtle, but much more disturbing, stench of disease and death. Just thinking of the smell made her shudder, brought back gut-wrenching memories of her mother, attached to machines as she lay dying. Of her father in the same hospital, years later.

"So, uh...how long have you been a paramedic?" she asked, partly to get her mind off the reasons she hated hospitals, and partly because she was genuinely curious.

"A little over forty years. I go through human paramedic programs every ten years or so to catch up on the latest technology and techniques."

"That's dedication." She scooted behind him to let a monstrous, two-headed thing pass by. "So why did you become a paramedic?"

He sighed, letting her know he was humoring her. "My breed's gifts are meant to aid in seduction and reproduction, but they can also be used for healing. When my brothers and I started the hospital, I decided I'd rather not spend a ton of time in school to become a doctor." He shrugged. "Besides, paramedicine allows me to pick up patients and drop them off. I don't have to hang around and get involved with them like E does."

"You don't have to get attached."

"That's one way to look at it."

She figured that with Shade, that was the *only* way to look at it.

They turned a corner, and she nearly ran into an iron cage containing some sort of winged demon. Its cruel, sharp beak and wicked black talons told her more than she wanted to know about its diet. It hissed and flapped one of its wings—the other had been immobilized in a cast.

"What the heck is that thing?" she asked as she carefully skirted the cage.

"It's sort of the demon equivalent of a vulture."

"Shouldn't it be at a demon veterinarian's or something?"

She watched in awe as he stopped next to the cage and stuck one hand inside to pet its spiky feathers. The thing made a high-pitched chirping sound.

"Yes, but as you can probably guess, demon vets are rare, and most work topside, in human veterinary clinics. Someone brought this creature in, and E won't turn down anything for care other than a few select species. He even treated a dog Skulk brought in."

A sad smiled tugged at his mouth. She reached for

him, taking his hand in hers. She hoped to comfort him, but he tensed, and with a sigh, she pulled away. "So," she said, mainly to change the subject, "are most paramedics like you?"

He made some clicking noises at the winged thing, and it rubbed its scaly head on his hand. "What? Antisocial?"

"Yeah. I mean, I did notice that Luc is also a paramedic, and he didn't strike me as Mr. Party Animal."

Fury blasted from him, a heat wave that hit her at the same time as his curse. "I want to gut him for hurting you."

"So that's a yes?"

"No." He took off down the hall again, and she had to jog to catch up. "A lot of EMTs and paramedics choose the work because they get off on the adrenaline rush. You never know what you're getting into when you go on a call. Could be walking into a raging battle. Skulk liked—" He broke off, his fists clenched.

"I wish I could have met her," she said softly.

He came to a halt and swung around to her. "Why?" There was no malice in his question. Just curiosity.

"Because you loved her, and from what I can tell, that's not something you do often."

His mouth tightened even as his eyes softened. Slowly, tentatively, he pushed her hair back from her face, his touch gentle, barely a whisper on her skin. Still, his touch made her nerve endings spark.

"Hell's gates," he murmured. "I wish..."

"What, Shade?" She leaned into his hand, nuzzling the warm skin. Playfully, she nipped the heel of his palm and watched as his eyes grew darker, his lids coming down to watch her with sensual intent. "What do you wish?"

Abruptly, he dropped his hand and spun away to continue down the hall, his gait faster and heavier than before. "Nothing."

*Impossible man.* She knew enough about him by now to know to choose her battles, and this was not the time to fire a first shot, so she didn't push it. Instead, she followed him to an area that opened into office spaces.

As they walked past office doors, she realized that the only windows were between the hall and the offices—the offices had no outside views. Come to think of it, neither did the hospital.

"We're underground, aren't we?" she asked, suddenly feeling stupid for not realizing that earlier.

"Technically, we're in New York City, beneath an abandoned parking garage."

She looked around in awe. "Your demon contractors are really something else."

He grunted in agreement, and then grunted again when Kynan exited an office and bumped into Shade.

"Kynan," Shade growled. "We need to talk."

"Your brothers already dressed down my ass, so let's forgo the fun, 'kay?"

"Kynan?" Runa eased around Shade to speak to the man she'd been sent to find, the reason she was in this crazy mess in the first place.

Kynan frowned. "So you're Arik's sister."

She nodded, a bit awestruck at coming face to face with the man who had survived a battle his own team and enemy forces hadn't survived, and had single-handedly brought down a Fangorg demon. But was he also a traitor to the human race?

"Does the Army know where I am and what I've been doing?"

"Yes." *Thanks to me.*

She gave him credit for his poker face. If he was worried, it didn't show. He merely nodded and looked pointedly at Shade. "I hope you know I wouldn't do anything to compromise this hospital." He turned back to Runa. "Good to meet you."

He took off, and she waited until he'd disappeared to ask Shade, "Do you believe him?"

"Yeah," he said. "The guy is like a human version of Eidolon. He's got this pesky, annoying sense of honor."

She gasped in mock horror. "How horrible. You should probably kill him. Immediately."

His eyes locked onto hers, and for a moment she thought she'd irritated him. Again. But slowly, one corner of his mouth came up.

"What?"

"Your inner wolf suits you." Color flooded his face and he stalked away as though just realizing he'd proved her right when she called him a liar for saying he didn't care.

Now she just had to get him to admit it.

# *Sixteen*

Shade had itched to keep Runa at his side while he worked in his office, but she'd been right when she confronted him about his control issues. So although it killed him, he let Runa explore the admin area while he caught up on the paramedic schedule and handled other issues that had come across his desk while he'd been being tortured in Roag's dungeon. And it was a serious pain in the butt to write with gloves on, but he didn't dare take them off, and not just because he didn't want his brothers or Runa to see. He didn't want to see himself fading away, either. Easier to pretend everything was happy, happy, joy, joy.

"Can I get something to drink from the break room?" Runa called out.

"Go for it. Don't leave admin."

"I told you you don't need to worry about me taking off."

"Just be careful. Some of our staff members aren't

angels." That was true enough, but mainly, now that they knew Roag had been ballsy enough to come into the hospital, he didn't want to take any chances.

He heard her wander off, and when he heard footsteps again, he was too engrossed in his work to think they might belong to anyone but her.

Until Wraith filled the doorway, turmoil rolling off his body. "Take off your gloves."

*Shit.* "Screw you."

"Don't make me take them off for you."

Shade's heart went double-time. Wraith knew. At the very least, he suspected. "Why don't you tell me what's gotten up your ass."

Wraith looked up at the ceiling, and Shade knew this wasn't going to be good. Then again, with Wraith, it never was. "I meant to tell you this earlier. I went to the Seminus Council. Know what they said when I asked if they knew of any matings to wargs?"

"No idea, but you're going to tell me, aren't you?"

Wraith nailed Shade with an uncharacteristically serious stare. "One, Shade. One mating that ended in disaster. The bond was one-sided. Sound familiar? Wargs can't bond with our species, so when she went into heat, she took another warg as a lifemate, and together they killed the Seminus."

"I'm not worried about it," Shade said, though he felt like he was going to hyperventilate.

"Does that mean you're ready to put her down?"

"Wraith..." Shade's voice was a low, guttural growl.

"You said you're going to kill her. It's time."

Shade launched out of his chair and took his brother to the ground. Wraith's fist tunneled into Shade's side, sending white-hot bursts of agony through his midsection. Anger gave him the willpower to get through it, and fists flew, the sound of leather on skin as satisfying as anything. One of Wraith's blows caught him in the mouth hard enough to make him see stars and taste blood. Shade slashed downward with his elbow, catching Wraith in the throat, and that fast, Wraith was done playing.

In an instant, Shade was flying backward. The desk broke his launch, and nearly his spine as well. Wraith struck with his foot, connecting with Shade's thigh. Pain and fury shot through him in a haze of red, though somewhere inside he knew Wraith was pulling his punches, because he could have easily broken Shade's leg.

Shade rolled, closed his fist around Wraith's ankle and dragged him toward him. Wraith's knuckles filled Shade's vision, and he turned just in time to avoid a solid blow to the nose. Still, his brother's punch crunched into his cheek, and a whole lot of ache sheared through his face. Roaring with rage, Shade dove on top of Wraith and jammed a knee into his gut. Wraith grunted, a major victory, since his brother usually suffered pain in silence.

Hands gripped his shoulders and wrenched him off his brother. Wraith rolled away, his eyes as gold as Shade's own must be, his fangs extended.

"Knock it off!" Eidolon roared, stepping between them. Shade ignored E and lunged for Wraith, but E caught him around the waist and slammed him back into the wall. "You need to check up, brother." Eidolon snarled, a vicious, nasty sound. "What were you thinking?"

"I was thinking I'd rip Wraith's head off!"

Eidolon shoved him again. "Beating on Wraith isn't

helping anything." Shade wasn't listening. He wanted a piece of Wraith.

Wraith moved in close. "Ask him why he won't take his gloves off, E."

The taste of blood filled Shade's mouth. "Shut the fuck up!" he snapped, still glaring at Wraith, who glared right back.

Eidolon released Shade. "What's this about?"

"I was just heading to Ireland to hunt for Roag when Luc stopped me." Wraith didn't take his eyes off Shade as he spoke to E. "Said he'd seen Shade fading out. That's why I came here. To talk some fucking sense into Shade."

"Yeah, that was working real well." Eidolon stepped back, mouth thinned in irritation.

"Go ahead, Shade. Take off the gloves. Prove you aren't falling for your little wolf." Wraith shook his head. "She helped you through The Change, but you don't need her anymore. You said you'd kill her. Stop stalling."

Eidolon frowned. "Shade? You okay?"

No. No, he wasn't. Splinters of pain ripped through him. But it wasn't his pain. It was Runa's. He craned his head around to the door, where she stood, her face pale, her chin trembling.

She'd heard. Her sorrow slammed into him. Tears. Betrayal. Oh, hell's fucking rings, she knew.

"Runa," he rasped, but she dropped the soda in her hand and bolted down the hall. Cursing, he tore free from E's grip, but before he made it to the door, Wraith tackled him, slamming him back against the wall again.

"We'll get her. You need to let her go. Now. Forever."

"*No!*" Shade didn't possess half of Wraith's fighting skill, but somehow he exploded out of Wraith's grip and

out of the office. He had to get to Runa before his brothers
did. Before E or Wraith killed her out of love for Shade, or
before Roag did the same . . . out of hate.

⌐

Runa careened through the hospital, her eyes stinging.
The burn of betrayal swept through her veins like wildfire,
searing everything in its path. That son of a bitch! She'd
thought he cared, even if he didn't admit it. For the second
time, he'd betrayed her, and she'd let it happen. This time,
though, he would take more than her heart.

He'd take her life.

*Fool me once, shame on you. Fool me twice, shame on
me. Fool me thrice . . . I end up dead.* She had to get out of
this hospital.

Panic made it hard to breathe as she searched for an
exit. They were underground, but she knew ambulances
somehow drove from the hospital through New York City
streets, so there must be a way out. She knew about the
Harrowgate in the ER, since that was what they'd been
using to come and go, but could she use it? She'd watched
Shade operate it . . . surely she could at least get herself to
safety. Somewhere close to the Army base. If Arik could
get to her before Shade did, the Army could protect her.

*You don't need her anymore.*

Wraith's words cut through her like a chilled knife.
She'd stood there, waiting for Shade to tell his brother to
fuck off. He hadn't. Then Wraith's next words had stopped
her heart cold.

*You said you'd kill her.*

Oh, God.

She burst into the ER, and when a blue-skinned nurse

brought her head around a hundred and eighty degrees to stare at her with blinding white eyes, Runa skidded to a halt. Calm down, she told herself. Calm. She couldn't afford to attract attention.

Ahead, the Harrowgate shimmered, a curtain of undulating light. She walked toward it with purpose, as if she owned the hospital and knew exactly where she was going.

As she reached the gate, the lab technician who had taken her blood joined her. "You leaving?" Frank asked. "I'm off shift. I'll share the gate with you."

"Runa!" Shade's voice, faint but strong, echoed from down the hall.

Her heart skipped a beat. She had to hurry, and maybe this guy could help her use the gate. "Yes. That would be nice. Thank you."

They stepped into the arch and were instantly engulfed in eerie darkness. The only light came from the glowing maps on the smooth, black walls. Frank seemed to be waiting for her to make the first move. Her heart pounded as she searched for the crude map of the United States she'd seen Shade manipulate.

"Looking for this?" he asked, tapping an outline she didn't recognize. Instantly, a map of the States popped up, and he tapped New York.

"No...I wanted—" She snapped her mouth shut. She couldn't let a hospital staff member know where she was going, to Washington, D.C., and the secret military installation where she worked. "Yes, yes, that's fine. Thank you."

"New York City...which gate?"

She had no idea. She studied the map, looking for an exit point near her house. There were two. She fingered one, and instantly, the gate opened up into a dark, wooded park. It occurred to her that trotting through a park at night wouldn't be the brightest thing she'd ever done, but it was probably far safer than being at the hospital where demons wanted to kill her. Besides, she could shift into a werewolf if she ran into trouble. She was definitely safer among even the worst humans than...

Humans. Frank was human.

Humans couldn't use the Harrowgate.

Which meant that the person standing next to her was not Frank.

*Oh, my God.* Chills skittered up and down her spine, but she forced herself to remain calm, to take deep, even breaths. She mumbled a polite, "Thank you," and stepped out of the gate and onto the grass, her knees trembling.

She took one step. And another. Another...so far, so good.

And then, a low, ominous growl sneaked up behind her, growing louder. Swallowing the lump of terror in her throat, she turned.

The demon in the archway was charred, twisted. Evil radiated from it like the devil's furnace.

Roag.

The scream built in her throat even as he reached for her with his ruined, clawlike hands. "You little bitch. I'm going to skin you alive for what you did to Sheryen."

She ran. Ran faster than she ever had, stumbling once and nearly going down. A flapping sound reached her ears at the same time as a brush of air, and a winged demon landed with a hard thump in front of her. It grinned, revealing huge, serrated, sharklike teeth. Red eyes drilled hatred directly into her skull.

She didn't stand a chance against Roag in her current form, but she couldn't shift—she'd be vulnerable for the few seconds of her transformation. She needed time.

She plowed her fist into the creature's scaled belly, followed by a brutal kick to its groin. *Thanks for the training, Arik.*

Roag roared, spitting yellow bile that stung her skin as it landed on her arm and neck. She darted to the right, toward an area of the park she knew well. The foliage was dense, difficult for a demon the size of the winged thing to navigate.

Her lungs burned with the need for oxygen, but she kept going, until the stitch in her side became crippling and her legs were ready to give out. At the edge of the park, she dived into the ditch running alongside, and the moment she hit it, she concentrated, bringing out the wolfy side of her.

The snap of bone and tear of skin brought with it the ecstasy of power, and in moments, she was crouched in the grass behind a shrub, her enhanced hearing picking up the crunch of tree leaves and twigs as Roag ran toward her.

He burst out of the trees, only this time, he'd taken the one form that frightened her more than Roag's burned-out shell.

Shade.

"Runa? It's me. You're safe now."

Not only was she not that stupid, but if Roag thought that she'd run to Shade like a well-trained dog, he was not just insane, he was delusional. She remained where she was, waiting for him to come closer.

Roag's gaze swept the area, and then his eyes zeroed in on her hiding place. "I know you're there."

She launched herself. Over the shrub and into his big chest. They went down in a tangle.

"Fuck," he grunted, and wow, Roag definitely had Shade's mannerisms down pat.

He swept his arm in an arc, throwing her against a tree trunk. She slammed into it but came immediately to her feet. In this body, she was bigger than Shade, her strong, furred legs holding her upright as she looked down on him.

"Runa, listen to me. " His voice was soft and comforting, and, she realized, it was his paramedic voice. Roag really knew his stuff, because it damned near worked on her. "I don't want to hurt you. Change back to yourself, and we'll talk about this."

She lunged. This time, her jaws closed around his throat as her claws sank into his shoulders. Warm blood coated her tongue, spurring her on. She clamped down...only to get a mouthful of fur.

Suddenly, the demon beneath her was a warg, the huge black beast Shade had turned into the nights of the full moon. His snarl vibrated both his body and hers. They rolled, a knot of claws and teeth, slashing at each other until fur flew in tufts through the air.

She held her own until Roag hooked a leg around her and flipped her, face-first, into the grass. His low growl hung in the night air as he held her down, his jaws clamped down on the back of her neck, his sharp claws digging into her ribs. He outweighed her by half, his weight keeping her pressed into the ground...and oh, God, his erection pressed into her hip.

Tears of rage and helplessness stung her eyes. Roag was going to kill her. She knew that. But not before he tortured and raped her. In her head, she screamed, hoped Shade could sense her terror. Then again, maybe he'd ignore it, hoping someone else would take care of her for him.

She should have stayed at the hospital. Shade wanted to kill her, but at least he'd have made it quick.

⸺

Runa's body was stiff beneath Shade's, her muscles tensing for another struggle. He wrapped himself tighter around her. They were both bleeding, though he'd definitely borne the worst of the damage. He hadn't wanted to hurt her, and he'd paid the price for holding back.

None of this had gone as planned. Shade had reached the hospital's Harrowgate as it closed, catching a glimpse of Runa inside. When he saw Frank, his blood had congealed. Frank couldn't use the Harrowgate.

Shade had nearly gone insane while he waited for the gate to reopen. Only Eidolon's calming presence had kept him level, and the moment the gate flashed with the ready signal, he and his brothers shot inside. He had no illusions that they'd come along to help him find Runa. They wanted Roag.

Shade's link to Runa had vibrated with her terror, leading him right to her. Eidolon and Wraith had gone after Roag—Shade guessed that the creature he'd seen take flight from the trees had been their brother.

He hoped they caught him, but right now what mattered was the werewolf pinned beneath him.

She was panting from exertion, trembling with rage that veered sharply to fear, effectively shutting down his libido, which had spun up during their battle. Did she think he was Roag?

Then again, she'd have every reason to be more terrified of him.

The thought tore at him. He wasn't a monster. He wasn't.

So why did that feel like such a lie?

"Runa..."

Her name came out as a harsh growl, and he realized he was still in the warg form he'd taken to defend himself against her attack. Slowly, carefully, he disengaged his teeth from the back of her neck but kept his weight on her. Beneath him, she tensed even more.

He concentrated, brought himself back to his Seminus form. God, she was huge, and he realized he was taking a risk.

"Runa. It's me."

Her answer was a nasty snarl. Not encouraging.

"I can prove it. Roag wouldn't know how we met, right?" He rubbed his face in her silky fur as he spoke into her ear, which twitched, tickling his lips. "He wouldn't know I took you outside your coffee shop and that you were so hot, so tight, I nearly came before I was fully inside you."

He let his senses fire up to listen for approaching enemies, and he heard the quickening of her breath as he reminded her of why they were so damned good together.

"He wouldn't know that my favorite part of making love to you is afterward, when you come apart in my arms while I watch."

Her breath caught, just enough to let him know that she didn't doubt his identity, and his words hadn't left her unaffected.

"Yeah, you know it's me. I need you to change back. I

can explain what you heard." Tension radiated from her, as well as confusion, and a spike of hurt at his words. "Please, *lir*—" He cut himself off. *Lirsha*? Was he going to say it? Lover. Beloved.

Hell's rings.

"Talk to me. Please."

Her entire body trembled, but she remained as she was.

In the distance, he heard voices. Human. Too far away to worry about, but they needed to move this elsewhere. Most demons were invisible to humans unless the demon wanted to be seen. But werewolves and humanoid demons like his species were clear as day.

"I'm going to back away. No sudden moves." He eased off her and to the side, where he sat on his heels and planted his hands on his thighs, trying to appear as nonthreatening as possible. Since he was now naked, his clothes shredded and on the ground, he figured he looked about as nonthreatening as he could. He risked a glance at his extremities, and felt lead in his gut even though he knew what to expect. Shimmering transparency that had spread from his hands to his wrists, from his feet to his ankles.

Immediately, Runa shoved to all fours and swung around to him, baring her massive teeth. Damn, she was big. And beautiful. Her toffee fur glinted in the light of the moon, and her eyes glowed like amber coals.

"Come back to me." His voice was pleading and gravelly, because everything was on the line now. She could kill him or leave him, but either way, he'd die.

For a moment, the air went still. Runa made a soft noise, and then the transformation began, sparking hope. Knowing she was self-conscious about it, he looked away until the gruesome sounds of muscle and tendon snapping back into place came to an end. When he looked again, she was standing there in the night air, as naked as he was.

"We have to go someplace safe," he said softly, knowing how lame that sounded.

"Safe?" She laughed bitterly. "With you? That's a joke, isn't it? Why did you bother saving me from Roag when you could have just let him do the job for you?"

"I know what you heard, but I swear to you, I'm not going to kill you."

"You'll leave that to one of your brothers?"

"They won't touch you. I won't let anyone hurt you, Runa."

She wrapped her arms around herself and shivered. "But you were going to."

"Yes," he said bluntly, because there was no way to sugarcoat the truth.

Hurt flashed in her eyes, and right now he'd do anything to make it better, but they were long past that. "You must truly be desperate to get out of the bond. I didn't realize you hated me so much."

Gods, he wished that were true, and it pissed him the hell off that he couldn't rein in enough discipline to make it happen. "That's the problem," he muttered. "I don't hate you enough."

"Are you serious?" She gaped at him, making him feel about two inches tall. "You are, aren't you? You *want* to hate me? What kind of jerk *wants* to hate someone?"

She shook her head as though trying to make his words come together in a way that made sense.

"Look—" He broke off at the sound of approaching

footsteps. Instantly, he leaped to his feet and shielded Runa from the intruders he hoped would be at least one of his brothers. A sane one would be good.

"Who is it?" Runa whispered.

"Just stay behind me."

Two demons emerged from the foliage, and Shade's heart froze. They were different species—one a Night-lash, and the other a pre*s'genesis* Seminus, whose *der-moire* revealed that they shared a great-great-grandsire. Both wore the uniform of the Carceris, demons who captured and held other demons accused of violating demon law.

The Nightlash stepped forward. "Shade, son of Khane, you are accused of slaughtering a warg in order to interfere with First Rights. What say you?"

Runa gasped. "You killed Luc?"

"As much as I'd like to take credit," Shade said, "I didn't do it."

The Seminus inclined his head. "That will be an issue for the Judicia to determine. Your response is noted. You will now submit to our custody."

Like hell he would. The Judicia would get to the bottom of the matter, but he couldn't afford to be locked away until he was found innocent. Not with Roag gunning for Runa. He would not leave his mate unprotected.

He smiled. "Of course. Give me a moment to say good-bye." Before the Carcers could refuse, he turned to Runa, who was looking at him with a mix of confusion and residual anger. Anger he could feel in the taut stiffness of her body. "You're going to run," he whispered against her ear. "Head for the Harrowgate. I'll be right behind you. If

I don't join you within two minutes, either find Eidolon or use the gate to get to the hospital. Understood?"

"No, I don't understand."

"Just do it—" A hand closed on his arm—the Night-lash. Shade struck, a closed fist to its ugly face. "Run, Runa!"

Naturally, Runa did the opposite. She attacked the Seminus, catching him by surprise as he tried to assist the Nightlash. Shade had forgotten how well she fought, but he didn't have time to admire her moves. He'd trained with Wraith for decades, but the Nightlash was bigger and stronger, and it took precious moments to gain the upper hand.

Shade took a quick double-tap to the abdomen, and then he dropped, spun, and with a sweep of his legs, caught the Nightlash in the knees.

The demon hit the ground and rolled into a ditch. Leaping to his feet, Shade jammed the heel of his hand in the Seminus's nose. As the demon wheeled backward, clutching his face, Shade grabbed Runa's hand, and they hauled ass to the Harrowgate. Once there, they dived inside, and he tapped the map to take them to Costa Rica.

They stepped out, and hit the ground running. Once they reached his cave, he shoved Runa inside.

"Shit," he growled, as the stone door slid into place. "I am so fucked." And naked. Which normally went well together, but he figured Runa wouldn't appreciate the association. Besides, he needed to cover up the parts of his body that were fading out. He headed for the bedroom, Runa on his heels.

"What was that all about?" she asked.

He tossed her a robe. "Which part?"

"All of it," she said, shrugging into the garment. "But right now I'm wondering if they can find us."

"They have ways of tracking us through the Harrowgate." He tugged on a pair of jeans. "Once they exit the gate, locating my lair won't be easy. Even if they manage, getting inside will be difficult. But hiding out here is our best option, and Roag doesn't know about this place, so he can't tip them off."

"Who were they? Some sort of demon cops?"

"Something like that." He tore through his closet, searching for a sweatshirt and gloves.

"And the Judicia?"

Dammit. Where the hell were all his riding gloves?

"Shade? The Judicia?"

He swore and stalked to his dresser. No gloves. "They're demons that mete out justice. Eidolon served as a Justice demon for a time, so I know what to expect. They'll get it figured out, but I can't afford to spend time in a cell while I wait."

She frowned. "Without...um...me, wouldn't you suffer in a cell?"

He shook his head. "They're specially designed to negate species needs. While imprisoned, vampires don't need to feed, incubi don't need sex...things like that." Yep, those logical, level-headed Justice demons thought of everything. "Do you think I did it?"

"What? Kill Luc?" She shook her head. "I know you didn't. I was within hearing distance of you pretty much the entire time I was at the hospital."

"It had to have been Roag." He pinched the bridge of his nose, though nothing was going to stave off the headache that was starting to throb at his temples. "He must have killed him, impersonated him, and ratted me out to Wraith. He's getting bolder."

Shade grabbed the satellite phone, stepped outside the cave for decent reception, and rang E's cell. His brother answered on the second ring.

"Shade?"

"Yeah."

"You okay? Safe?"

"For now. The Carceris is after me."

"I know. You didn't do yourself any favors by running."

"I couldn't leave Runa unprotected. Unless you and Wraith happened to nab Roag?"

"The bastard got away. And it looks like he broke into the hospital's storeroom."

Shade swore. Roag could have stolen some potentially dangerous materials. "Bro, we have to step up our search for him. And I think you need to get Tay somewhere safe."

"Already handled. She'll stay at Aegis HQ. When we need to be together, she'll come to the hospital, with Kynan as an escort. What's going on with Runa?"

She'd followed him outside, and though she stood calmly at the cave entrance arms crossed over her chest, there was nothing calm about the flames that burned in her eyes. Still pissed about the whole thing about him killing her, he guessed.

"She's fine for now."

"Yeah?" E's voice lowered to a near-whisper Shade had to strain to hear. "Well, something is going on with you. Wraith's worried, and I'm having a hard time keeping him contained."

"Are you saying he's going to go self-destructive?"

"As improbable as this sounds, I think he's trying to keep his act together. Mainly because he's on the verge of hunting you down. He thinks you need help."

That headache started knocking at his skull. "Shit. I don't want him to know about this place."

"Which means you'd better settle down. Unless..."

"Don't go there."

"The *Maluncoeur*, right? You're falling for Runa."

Shade sucked in a harsh breath. "I can't talk about it." Talking about it, voicing it, would make it real, and if it wasn't bad enough already, the moment he truly made it real was the moment he'd disappear forever.

E's curses blistered the airwaves. "I won't let it claim you."

"There's nothing you can do. This is my mess."

He'd fucked up, over and over, starting with the day he'd been cursed. All these years he'd thought of Wraith as the screw-up in the family, but Shade left his little brother in the dust.

# *Seventeen*

⌒

Runa returned to the bedroom and sank down on Shade's bed while he finished talking with his brother, and wondered what she was going to do now. Shade said he no longer planned to kill her, but she wasn't sure what to believe at this point. In any case, he *had* planned to murder her, and that fact left her cold.

God, she was such a fool for trusting him again.

Shade entered the room and stood there, phone in hand. A hand that seemed to be fading into transparency. His hand went entirely invisible, and he dropped the phone.

"Dammit," he breathed, and stared at the phone, not bothering to pick it up.

"What's going on, Shade?"

"I don't want to talk about it."

She shot to her feet. "You know what? I don't give a crap what you want. You owe me."

Maybe it was her imagination, but he seemed to be ashamed. "I can't."

"Can you tell me why you wanted me dead? Is that on the short list of topics you *can* talk about? Was getting out of the bond the only reason you were going to kill me, or was there something else?" When he didn't answer, her control on her temper snapped. She struck him, a hard slap that left her hand numb and a crimson handprint on his face. "God, how you and your brothers must have laughed at me. You must have thought I was so pathetic, so desperate, to swear to stand by you even though I'm not bonded to you."

The dark shadows were swimming in the black depths of his eyes again. "I never laughed at you," he said fiercely. "I *never* thought you were pathetic."

She laughed, the sound bubbling out of her like an evil sludge. "You should. Even I'm disgusted with myself." Shaking her head, she looked around the room. "And you know what the worst part of it is? Even knowing what you were, I fell for you. Again."

"I didn't want that, Runa. I made it clear from the beginning."

"Oh, you did that, and more." Acid dripped from her voice. "Really, I shouldn't blame you. You *did* try to get me to hate you. I was just too desperate for love to see it. So truly, this is my fault. There. Hope your guilt is eased."

She was seriously messed up. As messed up as her mother had been to keep her abusive, drunken, cheating father around. Clearly, Runa had inherited those vile genes. Granted, her father eventually got sober and stopped cheating, but by then Runa had been too bitter to see it. Or to care.

If only she could channel some of that bitterness and rage to aim at Shade. She looked away from him, afraid her genetic weakness would have her falling into his arms. The tools of pain and pleasure on the walls glinted in the dim light, winking at her. Laughing at her.

How many females had they touched? How many females had Shade brought to tears and orgasms with the tools?

Oh, yes, there was the bitterness, welling up and nearly clogging her throat. She could barely speak, but managed to rasp, "I want it gone, Shade. Everything I feel for you. Everything that's made me so like my mother." She stripped off her robe and stalked to the whipping post, an eight-foot-high plank of wood with soft leather cuffs hanging from the top. "Do it. Do it like you've done to all the other females. And don't chicken out this time."

"I won't do this with you, Runa." His voice cracked, and she almost felt sorry for him. "Not again."

"Why not? Why could you do it to the others but not me?"

"They didn't want it for the same reason."

"They wanted it because they've got some sort of darkness in them. And maybe because they like pain. Because pain turns them on. Well, maybe it turns me on, too," she said quietly. "In fact, I know it does, because loving you hurts. And yet, I still come back for more."

"Stop saying that." He stumbled backward, tripped over the phone. "Stop saying you love me."

"Then make it stop. Hurt me. Make me feel on the outside the way I feel on the inside."

"Runa," he moaned. "Don't do this. Please don't do this."

She braced her forehead against the post and closed her eyes, breathing deeply. "You will do this, Shade. You owe me, and damn you, you *will* do this."

Shade's stomach turned over. Turned inside out and upside down. He did owe Runa, but what she was asking for was beyond his ability to give her. And yet, unlike last time, when she believed he wouldn't hurt her, now she believed he would. And she wanted it.

The last time, she'd been curious, but this time, she needed it on a level he couldn't yet understand, and their bond compelled him to give it to her. It was dark, the compulsion, seductive in the way only sin was, and he gave in to it with a shudder.

"Grab the post with both hands." He hated how his voice shook. "If I have to do this, I will not restrain you with the cuffs."

For a moment he thought she'd argue, because he was rapidly learning that Runa's new backbone wasn't the only uncooperative bone in her body. But eventually, she did as she was told, grasping the post so tightly her knuckles flushed white.

For the first time ever, he wished he had Wraith's gift. How he'd love to get in her head and make her think he'd given her what she wanted.

His gut churned even as his body hardened at the way she had exposed herself to him, her lithe form braced against the wood, her hair tumbling in wild waves to the middle of her back. Gently, he brushed her hair forward over her shoulders. She gasped, a quiet sound of hunger. Gods, she wanted this. He hissed in response, his own hunger rising no matter how hard he tried to tamp it down.

Maybe he could distract her, give her the illusion of pleasure and misery . . . heavy on the pleasure.

He allowed himself to relax, to hope his plan worked. She wasn't stupid, his Runa, and he'd have to be convincing.

"Square your shoulders," he barked, and she jerked in surprise. But she obeyed. Nice. As a reward, he skimmed his fingers over her high, round butt. Slowly, he circled her, letting his hand trail around her waist, his fingertips just brushing her mound. When she sucked in a breath, he smiled. "Humans are the most vulnerable when they are naked."

"What about demons?"

"Some are. But not me." He peeled out of his restrictive clothing. "I'm most powerful when naked." He stopped in front of her on his second pass. "No more talking. You will not speak unless I give you permission." From her enraged expression, he guessed she hadn't expected that. "What's the matter, little wolf? Did you think this would be entirely physical?" He brought his mouth close to her ear. "What I do to females takes place as much in the head as on the body."

He inhaled, took in the heady, mixed scent of irritation and desire.

"That's not what I want," she snapped.

Good. Maybe she'd give up on this insanity. He hoped it would happen before he got sucked in too deeply. Right now he could still think, but the more she wanted something, the more clouded his mind would become, until he would be little more than an animal operating on instinct. Instinct and her wishes.

"What did I say about talking out of turn?" He slapped her bottom hard enough to leave a nice, pink handprint. He rubbed the spot he'd slapped, caressed the hot skin until she began to moan and push back into his palm.

Damn, but he loved to touch her, to stroke her. Loved hearing the little sounds she made when she was aroused. He inched his hand lower, between her legs. Silken honey coated his fingers as he slid them back and forth, finding an easy rhythm that made her breath come faster.

His cock turned to steel, and he had to clench his teeth against the desire to take her like this. "Your safe word is shadow. Say it. Remember it."

"S-shadow," she whispered, arching into his hand.

"Good. That's very good."

This was going to be easier than he'd thought. He smiled as he eyed the toys on his wall and selected the bat, a leather-wrapped stick with a flap of soft leather on the business end. Wielded properly, it left a pleasant, gentle sting. Used in conjunction with reward, it gave great orgasms disguised as punishment.

He slapped the flap against his palm, and she jumped at the crack of leather on skin. "You're going to tell me what drives this desire of yours, aren't you?"

Her eyes flared in surprise. "What?"

"Eyes down," he said sharply, and delivered a whack across the front of her thighs.

She cast her gaze at the floor. "I won't tell you anything. Not like this."

"That's how this works, Runa."

"I'm not stupid," she murmured, still looking at the floor. "I tell you, which releases me from the guilt, right?"

Her gaze snapped upward, slamming into his. "But you have to beat it out of me."

He swallowed. Sweated. Panicked.

"You thought you could trick me? You thought I'd cave in after a little spanking? Like I haven't had the ever-living shit beaten out of me before? Well, fuck you, Shade. Fuck you if you think I'm such a wuss." She struck out, knocking the bat from his hand. "Get something serious. That."

He followed her gaze to the bullwhip. Bile bubbled up in his throat. He picked up the bat. "No."

Runa said nothing. Merely wore him down with the force of her will. Which was far stronger than his. What a fool he'd been to ever think of her as weak. He'd never met anyone stronger.

*Focus. Bluff.*

"First," he said, making damned sure his voice was forceful, "you'll tell me who beat you." He had a feeling he knew, after her brief comment about her father, but he wanted to get as much out of her as he could without hurting her, and the beating thing had been an unexpected revelation.

When she said nothing—*now* she decided to be quiet—he slid the bat up the inside of her leg. He made slow, small circles on her inner thigh until she began to tremble. He could smell her anticipation, but whether it was because she was waiting for pleasure or punishment, he didn't know.

"My father, okay? It was my bastard father."

He slid the flap of leather up to lightly brush her sex. As far as rewards went, it was minor, but her moan of relief made it seem much larger.

"Spread your legs more...oh, yeah, that's it." He kept

stroking her, feathery brushes over her core. "And what did you do to deserve it?"

She squirmed, but her feet remained rooted in place. "Nothing."

"Then why did he do it?"

"He was...an alcoholic."

This was going well. She seemed to have forgotten the bullwhip crap. He increased the pressure, letting the soft leather slide between her folds so each stroke kissed her clit.

"Alcohol rages, then." A sudden, alarming vision of her beneath her father's fists plowed through Shade's brain. During sessions like this, memories often popped into his head, but this was something he felt to the soul. He wanted to kill that man for what he'd done to Runa.

And now it made sense, why she was encouraging him to use violence against her. She truly had hated her father, was probably hoping the same treatment would help her to hate Shade. She had to know it wouldn't work, had to know this was about getting to the root of her pain, but her logical mind hadn't brought her to that place where she could admit it yet.

"Where is he?" he growled, before he could stop himself.

"Dead." The pain in her voice made him fumble the bat, and it clattered to the floor. "He took off when I was a teen. Didn't see him again until he was on his deathbed."

"Why...why does it bother you that he's dead, if you hated him?"

She swiveled her head around so she was glaring at him. "I didn't hate him at the time he died, and if you want more, you know how to get it."

He eyed the bullwhip. "You don't need that," he said, in a final, desperate attempt to change her mind, but she shook her head.

"You know that's not true."

Unfortunately, she was right, and he hated it. Hated himself. With heavy steps, he moved to the wall and removed the whip from its hook. It felt like lead in his hand, which, naturally, chose now to be solid, and he swore upon everything that was holy and unholy that he would destroy the whip after tonight. He would destroy everything in the room.

Breathing deeply, he turned back to her. "Where was your mother when your father was abusing you?"

Her eyes sparked. There was a story there, but it was a story she wasn't ready to share. Not without enticement.

He walked over to her and used the whip, coiled like a rope, against the back of her thighs. Not hard enough to hurt, but hard enough to make her yelp in surprise. "Tell me."

"At work. She never knew."

"Are you sure about that?" he asked softly, because he grew up with a mother who knew every time one of her young sneezed, even if she was a thousand miles away, and he suspected that human mothers were no different.

"She didn't know," Runa said through clenched teeth.

"You're lying." He slapped her with the whip again, a little harder.

"No." Her voice held a tremor, because now they were getting down to it. Her fears were surfacing.

"She knew, but you've never been able to admit it to yourself."

"No!"

A shockwave of need hit him so hard he had to take a step back. She wasn't going to go any deeper into her fears unless he got tougher on her. The whip vibrated in his palm with the force of her need, and his arm raised no matter how urgently he whispered, "No," over and over.

The whip came down on her bare back, lightly, but it left a pink streak that immediately began to swell into a welt. Runa didn't make a sound, but he did. Deep in his throat, he cried out.

"Your mom knew. And she did nothing to protect you. Admit it, Runa. Admit it or we're never getting past this."

A sob escaped her. "She...I can't."

"You can, and you will." His arm raised again. The tip of the whip left another mark on her back and a much, much bigger scar on his soul.

"Yes," she whispered. "She knew. She had to. But she didn't do anything." A tear rolled down her cheek, and he longed to wipe it away. "Why didn't she do anything? He hurt me. He cheated on her. He spent all their money on whiskey, even when it meant we went hungry."

As emotional as her memories were, as good for her as it was to get them out, there was so much more she needed to release. He could feel the darkness in her still, and he couldn't seem to drop the whip. He was no longer in control of his actions, his body reacting only to her wishes. This had gone past the point of no return, and now the only way to stop this session was for her to speak the safe word.

His arm raised. "Runa, say the safe word." Nausea roiled in his belly. *Please, please say it.*

"We're—" She swallowed hard. "—we're not done."

Fuck.

He couldn't stop himself, and this blow struck near her shoulder blade. He tried to say he was sorry, but the words wouldn't come. He'd never been sorry before—this was his nature, the kind of demon he was. He couldn't fight the instinct to cleanse souls any more than he could fight his need to breathe. But this was killing him.

"Where's the guilt coming from, Runa? The darkness?" His voice was strong, even though inside he was quaking. "I sense it in you. I've *always* sensed it in you."

She shook her head.

"Tell me!" he snapped.

"I hated him," she cried. "And I hated her for not leaving him."

He couldn't tear his gaze away from the powerful, lean ropes of muscle in her back as they quivered, not with fear or pain, but with rage. "Everyone hates their parents at some point."

"Not like I did. I wanted her to leave him. I was bad, did things to make him mad so she'd see that he needed to go."

"You were a child—"

"Stop it!" she screamed. "It was more, so much more."

An instant urge to comfort her overwhelmed him. He reached for her, but drew his hand back with a hiss.

His hand was invisible. Fucking gone all the way to his elbow. Terror squeezed the air right out of his lungs. He looked at his other hand. And didn't it just fucking figure that the hand holding the whip was solid as the stone surrounding them.

The muscles in his arm tensed as it began to climb into striking position again. He knew better than to attempt to stop it, but he had to try. He was rewarded with a sensation like scalpels sliding under his skin.

The whip slashed downward, and Runa grunted in both misery and pleasure. Shade's field of vision began to narrow and mist over as his subconscious took over the work he knew he wasn't strong enough to handle.

"How was it more?" He heard his voice, all business, totally foreign.

"Mom finally gave him an ultimatum, and he got sober. Turned into a model husband and dad. But it was too late." She made a strangled sound of anguish.

Shade stepped close, his entire body shaking as he brushed his lips over every pink mark he'd made in her gorgeous skin. "Why was it too late?"

*Please, Runa, talk. I don't want to have to do it again.*

"Because I already hated him," she moaned. "I was sixteen. I caught him with another woman."

Shade's pulse rate shifted into overdrive. They were at the precipice now, and he could feel the guilt and blackness rise up, holding her in its grip but not quite ready to be banished.

"What did you do?"

"Arik begged me to not tell, but I did. I did and I enjoyed the knowledge that I'd be breaking my mother's heart...oh, God, I *enjoyed* it!"

The force of her guilt ripped into him. "Did you succeed in breaking up your parents?"

She nodded. "My mom...she killed herself. But it was for nothing, Shade."

His blood ran cold. "Why?"

Her head dropped forward and her shoulders slumped, and how she remained standing on her feet was beyond his comprehension. "He was dying. And...and he told me that when I saw him with the woman, he was ending things. My mom...*oh, God, Shade.*"

"What is it?"

Runa sobbed. "She didn't need to know about the woman. It was over and had been for a while. If I hadn't told her..."

"Runa, you can't blame yourself." The words were lame, probably the same ones she'd heard from her brother over the years, and they hadn't worked so far.

Only one thing would, and his blood chilled when she asked for it.

"More, Shade. Please, more!"

"I can't." And yet, the whip in his hand whispered dark things. The handle burned in his palm as though it was growing roots that sank into his skin and tapped into the most evil part of what made him a demon.

"Hurt me," she whispered. "Stop holding back. *Make me pay.*"

His fist clenched around the handle. His bond mark around his neck throbbed, reminding him that a female—his mate—was asking for something. Instinct demanded that he respond even as his mind screamed in protest.

His arm raised. No. *No!* Sweat poured down his temples with the effort he spent to drop the whip. It clattered to the ground. Clenching his teeth, he endured the agony that came from resisting his nature.

*Must. Resist.*

But his feet began to move, stiffly, awkwardly, taking him to the wall. He watched in horror as his hand took a flail from its hook, one with braided leather straps that hung like dreadlocks from the handle. At the end of each dread was a tiny, sharp spur made of bone.

"Hurry, Shade." Runa's voice was a magnet, pulling him close to her.

Again, his arm raised. His mind screamed and his organs cramped as he brought the flail down as hard as he could.

On his own chest.

Pain tore through him. Sweet, crippling agony.

Runa gasped. "What are you doing? Stop it!"

"I...can't." Somehow, the pain lightened his own burden, his own guilt over his failures in his past, and at the same time, he rejoiced in being able to spare Runa. "I will bear this pain for you," he swore. "If one of us has to bleed, it will be me. It'll *always* be me." There was nothing he wouldn't do for her, he knew that now.

"No," she cried, reaching for him, but he snapped her wrists into the manacles above her head. "Oh, Shade." Tears rolled down her face. "I love you. I know it's not what you want, and I'm sorry. But I can't help it."

A wave of warmth flowed out of her like a breeze—the hallmark of freedom. The very air around her felt lighter. She screamed in ecstasy, rocked her hips as the mental and physical release took her. This was what the females he brought here were after, the most intense orgasm of their lives, one that would, in a way, last forever. Nothing felt better than a clean soul free of guilt, regret, and hatred.

And yet, he couldn't drop the flail. Her darkness and guilt had been lifted, but his remained, and he had no idea how to get rid of it.

# Eighteen

Wraith burst out of the Harrowgate into a sweltering jungle. Tracking Shade hadn't been easy, not until his brother's agony reached him, savaging Wraith's mind until finding Shade became as critical as breathing. He'd followed Shade's trail mostly by instinct and with a sense of urgency.

He wasn't the only one tracking Shade.

Eidolon had used his Judicia contacts to learn that the Carceris had set their hellhound loose, and no doubt Roag had joined in the hunt as well. Wraith studied the ground, and satisfied that they hadn't been this way yet, he took off down the lightly worn path leading away from the gate.

The jungle heat embraced Wraith as he shot through the vegetation, his senses tuned to Shade. Ahead. His brother was ahead and he was hurting.

Wraith broke out of the trees and into a small clearing where a waterfall gushed from the cliff above. He might have taken a moment to admire the sight, but he felt as if someone was squeezing his lungs and heart into a pulp, and it was growing increasingly hard to breathe.

*Shade.*

Wraith moved carefully around the waterfall, to a section of rocks that seemed to fit together a little too well. He searched the area, looking for openings, because although nothing indicated that this was anything but a tranquil oasis in the middle of a jungle, he could feel Shade, and his brother was close.

This had to be a cave of some sort, but he couldn't find the entrance. There had to be another way.

He looked up at the river of water streaming over shiny, black boulders. Behind the veil of spray, shadowy recesses hinted at some sort of cavern.

He started climbing. The rocks were slick and rough, but he didn't give a shit that he was tearing up his hands, his jeans, his really cool Hard Rock Café Bucharest T-shirt. Well, he mostly didn't give a shit. The T-shirt, given to him by a Romanian half-breed waitress he'd fucked to get it, held some hot memories.

Fifty feet up and soaked to the bone from spray, he nearly lost his grip and plummeted to the ground, but he caught himself on some sort of thorny vine that hurt like hell. Wincing, he peeled his palm off it and moved in behind the waterfall.

*Paydirt, baby.*

About ten feet above him, he saw a flat, broad shelf that seemed to extend deep into the rock. Carefully, he climbed to it, and pulled himself up. The challenge was powering past the incredible force of the water without being slammed into the pool or rocks below, but finally, he made it. For a second he lay on his back on the smooth stone, gathering his breath, but Shade's agony, like ice-picks in his chest, urged him to his feet.

He moved deeper into the arched tunnel, which was smooth and clean, definitely not natural. And there was a towel lying over a chunk of stone, as if someone had used the waterfall as a shower. As his vision sharpened to accommodate the darkness, he heard sobs.

Oh, shit.

Wraith careened off the cave walls in a frantic bid to find a way inside, and when he found the opening, he nearly tripped over his own feet in his rush. When he entered a strangely modern kitchen, the weirdness registered, but only for a heartbeat.

The sounds of suffering hijacked all his senses, and the only thing he could think about was getting to his brother.

He scrambled through the kitchen, knocking a salt shaker off the table as he passed. "Shade!" He took a corner a little too fast and slammed his shoulder into a door opening...

And then he froze. Every muscle vapor-locked. His heart skidded to a smoking stop. His lungs turned to cement.

Shade was standing in some sort of torture chamber, holding a flail as Runa struggled to free herself from the cuffs around her wrists. She was sobbing, begging Shade to drop the weapon.

A biting chill of shock went through Wraith, and he swayed. Then, as quickly as it had come, the shock fled, its void filling with hot, searing rage.

Wraith launched at his brother and took him to the

ground, pummeling him until he realized Shade wasn't fighting back.

"What the fuck were you doing?" he screamed, but Shade just stared, his eyes glazed and unfocused. Nausea swirled in Wraith's stomach. By the looks of the dungeon, Shade had been doing who knew what to who knew how many females. And hurting himself as well? Why?

"Do you kill them?" he whispered. "Shade, do you torture them and kill them?" His breath came in spurts, burning his lungs. The memories of his own torture at the hands of vampires flashed through his brain in sickening, fast-motion frames.

"No," Shade said, eyes wide. "No, never. Gods, Wraith! How could you think that?" He looked over at Runa. "I have to release her—"

"You aren't going near her." Wraith coldcocked Shade hard enough to knock him out.

The sharp tang of blood hung heavy in the air. As a vampire, he found the smell compelling, seductive, even as his nonvamp side was disgusted by how it had been spilled. Trembling in a way he hadn't done since, well, he couldn't remember when he'd ever been this fucked in the head, he went to Runa.

She was still on her feet, her hands clutching the post to hold herself up. How she found the strength to not slide to the ground was a mystery, and he found himself admiring her strength as he undid the manacles and peeled her fingers away from the wood.

"Hey," he said gently. "It's okay. You're okay."

"Sh . . . Shade?"

"He can't hurt you now."

"He d-didn't . . ."

*Maybe not yet.* Wraith didn't have the medical training or expertise his brothers had, but he knew shock when he saw it. Runa collapsed in his arms, and he carried her to the bed set into the wall. How nice that Shade was able to sleep in his chamber of horrors.

Christ, had he not known his brother at all? He shook his head, because he *did* know Shade. Knew how he'd grown up in a loving household with sisters he adored. Knew Shade's favorite food and drink—fish tacos and Fresca, though not, thank gods, the same meal. Knew that Shade loved movies but generally liked to see them alone because he especially liked sappy romantic comedies.

That Shade didn't jibe with the one who kept a torture chamber. And why the hell hadn't Wraith been able to see Shade's sick secret when he tripped through Shade's mind?

Fuck.

Lying on her stomach, Runa moaned into the pillow. With a shaking hand, Wraith covered her with a blanket, careful not to touch her wrists, which had become abraded as she struggled in her bonds. He looked down at Shade, still knocked out on the floor. What now?

Eidolon. He had to call E. He'd know what to do. He always did.

Wraith fumbled around in his jeans' pocket until he found his cell. No signal. Shock, that, here in the middle of BF Central America.

But even in BF Central America Shade would have a way to contact the outside world. Shade didn't like to be isolated for long. As much as he tried to act all I-don't-need-anyone, Shade was, at heart, a social creature. A sadistic social creature.

*Fuck.*

Wraith did a quick sweep of the cave, finally found a satellite phone, and dialed E. The moment his brother answered, Wraith's calm exterior collapsed like an apprentice sorcerer's first spell.

"E, we got trouble. Oh, man, oh, man—"

"Calm down." Eidolon's voice was barely audible over the static. "What's wrong?"

"Shade. It's Shade. I'm at his . . . torture chamber."

Silence filled the airwaves. "Shit."

"You knew?" Wraith realized he was practically screaming, and lowered his voice. "You knew about this?"

"We'll talk about it later. Tell me what's going on. Where is Shade?"

Wraith swallowed dryly. "He's here. He's hurt. And his female . . . just hurry."

"I'll be right there."

Wraith sank onto the bed next to Runa and put his hand on the back of her neck. Closing his eyes, he concentrated on feeding her comforting images. Hopefully, she liked the beach. Piña coladas. Warm sand. Anything that would give her a few minutes of peace to help heal the hell she'd just gone through.

It was only later that he realized that instead of killing her, as he should have done to keep Shade from the *Maluncoeur's* clutches, he'd helped her.

Maybe because deep down, he believed his brother was already too far gone to help.

---

Eidolon left Reaver in charge of the emergency department and went straight to Shade's cave. That Wraith knew about it was not good, but when he saw Runa lying on the bed and Shade unconscious on the floor, he knew it was a whole lot worse than *not good*.

"I got it," he said to Wraith, who stood and let Eidolon take his place.

"Hurry." Wraith's voice was a tangle of worry and pain and fear. Wraith, who generally didn't give a shit about anyone. Eidolon would never figure his brother out.

Eidolon reached for Runa, but hesitated, his palm hovering over her spine. The smart thing to do would be to kill her. Now, while Shade was unaware of what was happening and while she was too out of it to know. He could do it quickly, humanely.

*Humanely.* What a joke. Humans liked to pretend they were superior, above all others, but how superior were people who stoned women to death for cheating on their husbands? Or who made animals fight for amusement? Sure, demons weren't any better, but at least they didn't hide behind religious tenets and cultural tradition to excuse their brutality. Demons pretty much just had the excuse that they were demons.

"E?"

Wraith's voice jerked him out of his thoughts. Eidolon had never been fond of humans and their arrogance, which constantly cracked Tayla up, because she liked to remind him that she'd never met anyone as arrogant as he was.

"I don't think you should do it," Wraith said quietly. "She's been through enough at Shade's hands." He looked down at the floor, but whether he was looking away to hide his embarrassment at being caught showing mercy or he was looking at Shade, Eidolon didn't know.

"We're going to lose him, if I don't."

"We're going to lose him anyway. Look at him. The curse is already active."

An instant, searing pain sliced through him. Wraith was right. It was clear that Shade was in love with Runa. Killing her now might only accelerate the curse. All he had to do was look at Kynan to figure that out. Immediately after Lori's death, his love for her had probably been stronger than ever, tied to his misery over both her murder and her betrayal.

Shifting into doctor mode, he performed a rapid exam, was relieved to see that Runa was suffering more from exhaustion than anything. Shade had held back. He flashed a look at Shade, whose multiple wounds covered his chest, stomach, and shoulders, and then revised his thought. Shade had definitely not held back.

E concentrated until the warm tingle of his healing gift ran down his right arm, and then he put his hand on Runa's shoulder. Instantly, the light pink streaks on her back and the abrasions on her wrists healed. Behind him, he heard Shade struggling to get to Runa, but Wraith sat on their brother, holding him down.

"Let me up," Shade snarled. He grunted in pain, and Eidolon figured Wraith had applied some sort of pressure.

"E, shit," Wraith muttered. "You done with her?"

Eidolon frowned. Shade's lips were drawn back in a pained snarl, and he was reaching for the flail on the floor. Dammit. Eidolon grasped Runa's hand.

"Runa." She rolled onto her side, her glassy eyes blinking as she became aware of her surroundings. "Shade gave you a safe word. You need to say it."

"What?" She tugged the blanket up over her breasts.

"Safe word! What is it? He needs to be released."

She paled. "Shadow," she whispered. "Shadow."

Shade sagged to the floor, stark relief in his expression. "I'm sorry, Runa," he rasped. "So sorry."

"What happened, Shade?" Eidolon asked. "Why are you injured?"

"What the hell is going on?" Wraith demanded.

There was no point in lying or beating around the bush anymore. Eidolon moved off the bed to kneel next to Shade and channel healing waves into him. "It's not as bad as you think, Wraith."

Wraith leaped to his feet and made a sweeping gesture with his hand. "You wanna change your story, bro? Because I'm thinking that these—" he grabbed a pair of handcuffs off the wall "—are exactly what I think. Our brother is one sick puppy." He laughed bitterly. "And I thought Roag was the sick one."

Runa bounded off the bed so fast she nearly knocked Eidolon over. She got right up into Wraith's face. Buck naked. "Don't you dare compare Shade to Roag. You have no idea what you're talking about. Say one more word and I'll drop you."

In all the years Eidolon had known Wraith, he'd never seen his brother speechless.

Runa had just done the impossible.

⌒

Runa spun away from Wraith and knelt on the floor next to Shade, who was ashen and shaky, and much of him was fading in and out. What he'd done for her, how he'd somehow fought her desire for punishment and turned it on himself, well, it was a sacrifice beyond comprehension.

"I'm sorry," he murmured. "So sorry."

She palmed his cheek, feeling the rough scrape of new whisker growth. "No. Don't be. I'm the one who's sorry. What you did for me—"

"I'd do it again."

Her eyes stung. "I know you would." She tugged the comforter off the bed and wrapped them both in it. "Can you feel it? I'm free."

The guilt over her mother's death was gone, as was her anger at Shade. Suddenly, nothing mattered but the bond they shared. She might not be physically marked, but that didn't make the connection any less powerful.

He swallowed. Once, twice. "The darkness in you is gone. But I still can't...Gods, Runa. What I did to you. I've never been able to protect the females in my life. I always hurt them. I hurt *you*."

"Shh."

She pressed her finger against his lips, and he tugged her into his lap and held her so tightly she had to struggle to breathe. The sound of his heartbeat came to her in a rapid-fire punch, nearly drowning out the voices of his brothers as Eidolon tried to explain Shade's gift for releasing females from whatever troubled them. From Wraith's angry words, she guessed it wasn't going well.

Gently, she pushed away, but stayed in Shade's lap. "You need to tell me what's going on with the disappearing act." She glanced meaningfully at his left arm, which flickered in various stages of transparency. She felt him begin to shake beneath her, and her heart nearly broke. Whatever the problem was, it was bad.

"Remember when you asked about the *Maluncoeur*?" When she nodded, he continued. "It's a curse. A curse I brought on myself."

"How?"

He reached up to stroke her hair, but when her hair passed right through his hand, leaving behind only a whisper of air, he dropped his arm. "Do you know how long it took me to stop being angry at the warlock who cursed me? How long I blamed him and not myself?" He shook his head. "I was twenty. My mom went hunting, left me to take care of my sisters. But while she was gone, I entered my first transition."

She nodded, remembering what he'd said and what she'd read about a Seminus demon's maturation process. "You need nonstop sex for days to get through it."

"Yeah. I went out, prowling for females, taking what I needed. And when I say take, I mean it." He blew out a long breath and looked up at the ceiling. "I'd never had sex before the transition hit me, and then when I did, it was insane, fast, violent. I just needed to get off to get through the transition, you know? So when it was over, I wanted it because I *wanted* it. Not because I needed it. Does that make sense?"

Not really, but she nodded, noticed that his brothers had moved to just outside the doorway to give them some privacy, and she wondered how much of this story they'd known and how much was new.

"So instead of going back to the cave to protect my sisters, I pick up this human starlet. We go to her place." His gaze strayed to the tools on the wall. "That's when I discovered that I'd inherited the Umber ability to sense the things females bury deep inside—and that when she needs to be free of it, I can help."

"So you..."

"Yeah. I did. And while I was doing it, her husband came home. It wasn't pretty. We fought. I killed him." Shade shuddered. "But before he died, he cursed me. Cursed me to never know love, because if I did, I'd fade away."

"You'd die?"

"Worse."

She listened in horror as he described what would happen to him. "Oh, my God." She put her hand over her mouth. "That's...that's why you wanted to hate me. You didn't want to—"

"Fall in love with you," he croaked. "But it's too l—"

"Shade!" Eidolon stalked into the room. "Don't say it. Don't say anything else."

She watched in horror as Shade's entire body flickered, and she had a sick feeling that if he actually said he was in love with her, it would all be over. No wonder his brothers had wanted to get rid of her. And though it still hurt that Shade had considered it, she understood.

"It was right afterward that you discovered your sisters, wasn't it?" Wraith asked, and Runa recognized the attempt to get Shade off the subject of his feelings for her.

"Yeah." Shade's voice broke, right along with her heart. "I went back to the cave where I'd left them. They were dead. All but Skulk. If only I hadn't picked up the starlet, maybe they'd still be alive."

Hatred rolled off Shade in waves, along with grief so thick she could practically taste it. "Is that why you think you can't protect females?"

"It wasn't just them. My mother, too. And then there was Skulk—"

"Stop it," she said softly. "I blamed myself for my mother's death for so long, so I know I'm a terrible hypocrite, but none of that was your fault. You did your best. And Shade, you *did* protect me. You got me out of Roag's dungeon. You saved me from him just today. And you lifted me out of that that dark place full of guilt over my past. I've never felt better. We just have to find a way to cure you of this stupid curse."

"There is no cure," Eidolon said. "Not now that he's fallen...ah...yeah, anyway, there's no cure. It can be transferred, but only to a loved one."

Runa felt her hope drain away. Then anger rushed in, and hell no, she wasn't going to lose him now. There had to be a cure.

"Where's the phone?"

Shade frowned. "Why?"

"I'm going to call Arik. Maybe the Army can find something you guys missed."

Wraith snorted. "The United States Army? They couldn't find their dicks with a whore's—"

"Wraith," Eidolon said gently. "We need to take any help we can get."

Wraith said nothing, but he brought her the phone. She thanked him and turned back to Shade. "Just hold on, okay?"

"I will." For Runa's sake he smiled reassuringly, but he had given up hope a long time ago.

God, she wanted to hug him, hold him, make love to him until all of this was forgotten, but she needed to keep her distance. She didn't want to accelerate the curse. And she definitely didn't want him to see that she was on the verge of a breakdown.

She dressed quickly in jeans and a tank top and then left the three guys in the bedroom to call Arik from the TV room. She hoped he'd learned something about the *Maluncoeur*. Pacing the length of the room, she dialed.

Arik answered, but she could barely hear him.

"It's Runa."

He replied, but she couldn't understand him over the static. She moved to the kitchen, where the reception was better, but that made the connection on Arik's end worse. Finally, she stepped out of the hidden cave door. Better. Not great, but she couldn't risk moving too far from the entrance.

"How's this? Can you hear me now?"

"Like a commercial," Arik said, his breathing harsh and rapid.

"Did I interrupt something?"

"Just my workout."

The usual. If he wasn't at the office, he was at the gym. "Look, I have something for you. The *Maluncoeur* I asked you to investigate? It's a curse."

"I know. But that's about all I know."

"Apparently, it can be transferred to a loved one, but there's got to be another way to get rid of it."

"There's not a lot of information for me to go on."

"Do whatever it takes. You've got to find out more, and fast. It's killing Shade. It's some sort of vengeance curse that causes the victim to fade away if he falls in love."

"What are you saying?"

The tears that had threatened earlier fell. "I love him."

"Son of a— He's a demon, Runa!"

"And I'm a werewolf. No one's perfect."

"Not the time for humor, sis." She heard a thump that sounded suspiciously like a fist hitting a wall. "This is unacceptable. I'm sending a team for you."

"You are not," she snapped, and then softened her voice, because getting Arik riled was only going to bring out his hyperprotective, controlling side. "And I don't want the Army messing with the hospital."

"That's not your call. They heal demons there. Our enemies."

Her blood ran cold. "Sounds like maybe that's what I'm becoming."

Arik's curse burned her ear. "We'll discuss this later."

"There's nothing to discuss. I love Shade."

"You can't have it both ways. The military kicks people out for freaking *sleepwalking* if there's a danger that they might spill secrets. You think R-XR is going to let you work for them and then go home to a fucking *demon*?"

"That *fucking demon* saved your life."

No doubt Arik didn't appreciate the reminder. "That doesn't change the fact that this won't go over well with command."

"If they can't deal with it, that's their problem."

"So you're ready to give up your job, your *life*, for Shade?"

The past year came at her in a rush, all the interesting research and exciting missions. All the poking and prodding and experimentation. The loneliness. Shade holding her tight. "I'm not giving anything up."

There was a lot of cursing, followed by a long silence. "Kynan made contact," Arik said finally, but his tone said their conversation about Shade wasn't over. "Said you talked to him."

"Is he going to help you?" *Betray the hospital?*

"He's not playing ball right now, but he'll come around."

She doubted that, not after seeing the expression on Kynan's face. She swatted at some huge insect buzzing around her face. "Look, I need to go, but I'll call later to see if you find out anything."

"I don't like this."

The insect dive-bombed her, and she swatted again, ducked away from it as she spoke. "You've made that clear. Just make the *Maluncoeur* a priority." When he didn't answer, she had a sudden suspicion that he wasn't going to do anything to help. "Remember the bond I mentioned? If Shade dies, I do, too."

"Oh, Jesus."

She didn't even feel guilty for lying. "Yeah. So get the info."

"I will," he breathed. "And Runa?"

"What?"

"I love you."

She smiled weakly, because as crazy as he made her, he'd always had her back. "Love you, too."

She hung up, and the stupid bug, an orange thing with a wingspan of a bat, landed on her neck. She squealed, leaped around a little, and geez, she was a wuss. The creature whizzed away in a flurry of wings, and she sighed in relief. Having grown up in the city, she wasn't big on nature, and this was as natural as it came.

The smells, the sounds...she frowned, becoming aware of the silence in the forest. The last time this happened, Shade had come at her from out of nowhere, his eyes glowing red as the *s'genesis* ravaged him.

"Runa."

She pivoted around as Shade emerged from the brush, dressed as always in black leather. And he was solid. No transparency at all. *It wasn't Shade.*

Her heart threw itself against her ribcage as though leading the charge toward the cave entrance. It was only three yards away, but it might as well have been the distance between goalposts on a football field. She darted toward it. The Not-Shade shot forward, grabbing her around the throat and cutting her off with a strangled cry.

The phone fell from her fingers. She clawed at his hand, kicked at his legs, but he just stood there, his hand squeezing and loathing burning in his eyes.

His features began to swim, half-blotted out by the red spots swimming in her vision. The last thing she saw before darkness swallowed her was Roag's face.

"Take my hand."

Shade stared at Wraith as he sank down next to him. "What?"

Wraith forced Shade's palm into his. "Now say these words: *Solumaya. Orentus. Kraktuse.*"

"Why?"

"Just do it."

Shade jerked his hand away and, still sitting on the floor, tugged on his pants. "Tell me why."

"I didn't have a chance to explain it all in your office, mainly because you were pummeling me—"

"Wraith," E interrupted, "what's going on?"

"I was getting to that." Wraith impatiently shoved his long hair back from his face. "I sought out an old sorceress friend. Enemy, really, but that's all behind us now." Eidolon cleared his throat, and Wraith rolled his eyes. "Yeah, yeah. On with it. Okay, so we know the *Maluncoeur* can be transferred to a loved one, but we didn't know how. She gave me the way."

"The words you just said?" Shade asked.

"Yep. So lay it on me." He held out his hand. "We have to be touching. Glad you put your pants on."

Shade scooted back, wishing he didn't feel so shaky, because he'd be on his feet and out the door if he could. "Are you crazy? I'm not transferring it to you!" He kept backing up, but Wraith stalked him.

"Yeah, bro, you are."

"Fuck. You."

"I'm never going to fall in love, Shade. The curse won't affect me. Ever. So just do it."

Shade shook his head so hard his hair stung his face. "I will *not*."

"Damn you, Shade." Wraith's voice was pure whisper. "You've saved my life so many times. Let me do this for you."

"No. I—"

Shade broke off as a feeling of unease centered in his chest. Evil prickled over his skin and tightened around his neck like a noose.

"Runa," he gasped. "Where is she?" He bounded to his feet, grabbing Eidolon's arm when a wave of dizziness nearly sent him to his knees.

"Probably still talking to her brother," Wraith said.

Shade swore, his head swimming. "Outside. She's outside. Something's wrong."

Eidolon's gaze caught his. "The Carceris."

"Maybe a jaguar got her," Wraith offered, less than helpfully, though at least he was back to his usual self.

E shot Wraith a glare before turning to Shade. "Stay here. Wraith and I will take care of it."

"Like hell," Shade growled. The choking feeling had faded, leaving him unsettled and unable to sense Runa's mood. He could feel her proximity, but even that was fuzzy. He broke away from Eidolon and hauled ass toward the exit.

"Shade, wait! We aren't done!" Wraith followed, and behind him, Shade heard E's curse.

If those Carceris bastards had hurt Runa to get to him, he'd kill someone. Or several someones.

He burst out the side entrance and braced himself for a confrontation with the Nightlash and Seminus he'd seen earlier. No doubt they'd have hellhounds as well, and those beasts loved a good fight. Well-trained Carceris hounds wouldn't kill their target, but they'd fall just short of it. Worse, they were perpetually horny, and what they did to a demon when it was down amounted to a lot more than a little leg-humping.

With Wraith and Eidolon on his heels, he charged down the path to the south side of the cliffs where the waterfall met the pool, not bothering with stealth. Ahead, in the clearing, Runa lay on the ground, her body crumpled next to a tree.

"Son of a—" Something struck him in the head, and pain exploded in his skull. He wheeled toward the source, a slimy Drec demon holding a cudgel.

Wraith struck with the bullwhip. How he'd managed to

grab the thing while on the run was a question for later. His brother wielded it as if it was an extension of his arm, and the Drec's face split open, sending blood and teeth flying.

More creatures burst from the brush, but Shade weaved around them or barreled through them, his entire focus on Runa.

Almost there. Almost...

A massive four-winged creature dropped in front of him. A demon he'd never seen before, a hideous black beast that smelled—and looked—like rotting flesh. Its head was little more than a gaping mouth full of rows upon rows of razor-sharp teeth.

Not good.

Behind him, the sounds of battle raged. He figured his brothers were dealing out the worst of the punishment, but he couldn't look back. The winged thing was between him and Runa, and nothing would get between them ever again.

Shade dropped, swept his leg out to catch the creature in one of its bony ankles. It crashed to the ground but was up in an instant. He struck hard, crunching his fist into its gut. The spongy, wet flesh sucked his hand into the demon's body up to his elbow. Hell's fires, that was nasty.

Shade spun away, bringing his foot up between the thing's legs. It screamed and slammed a heavy wing down on Shade's shoulders. He ducked, taking only a glancing blow, but an explosion of pain and the smell of blood told him the strike had been damaging enough. Another beast landed next to him, its wings stirring up the trees, creating a whirlwind of vines and leaves. Something struck his back, the shock of the impact stunning him.

What the hell was going on? This wasn't a Carceris

operation, not unless they'd changed their methods in recent years.

"*Khroyesh!*"

The word, spoken in Sheoulic, the universal demonic language, meant to stand down, which might have been a relief if it hadn't been uttered in Roag's damaged, deep rasp.

The winged monsters backed away. Roag stepped out from behind one of the things, a barely conscious Runa in his arms. He wore some sort of brace on one hand. Wicked, Freddy Kruger–like extensions gave him sharp fingers where his own should have been.

"Stay where you are," Roag said, bringing the blades to Runa's throat, "or she dies."

"Trust me, brother, you don't want to do that."

Roag raised his eyebrows, dark, sickly things that hadn't completely grown back after the fire. "You aren't in a position to make threats." He nodded at Wraith and E, who were on the verge of being overwhelmed. "Tell them to stop." To emphasize his command, he slashed Runa's cheek with a blade. She whimpered, but through the bond Shade knew she was too out of it to feel much pain.

"Damn you." Shade struggled to keep his voice low and even, when what he wanted to do was scream.

"Do it!" Another flick of a blade opened a gash dangerously close to Runa's jugular.

The scent of Runa's blood filled Shade with a bitter, sharp rage. He wanted to shift form into something horrible and bite Roag's fucking head off. But he couldn't risk Runa, and even if he succeeded in killing Roag, the army of monsters he'd brought with him would probably take them all out.

"Wraith! Eidolon!" He didn't take his eyes off Runa as he shouted to his brothers. "Back off!"

"Not happening, brother." Wraith's words were mushy, gurgled, and Shade suspected his little brother was speaking through split lips and a mouth full of blood. Which meant the taste was on his tongue, and between that and the pain, he'd gone into vampire bloodlust.

Shit.

"Stop him," Roag warned, digging his blades into the delicate skin between Runa's throat and jaw.

Shade's heart hammered hard, and cold sweat broke out on his brow. "E! You've got to stop Wraith. Now!"

Torn between staying as close to Runa as possible and helping E take down Wraith, Shade hesitated, but the sound of Eidolon getting pummeled by Wraith tipped the scales. Shade darted toward them. He caught Wraith from behind, managed to pin his arms to his sides, but only for a moment. Wraith had the advantage on any day, but add to that the bloodlust, and gaining control of him turned into a vicious battle.

They muscled him to the ground, but damn, Wraith was strong and pissed, and with the way his eyes burned red and his fangs had elongated into daggers, Shade doubted Wraith even knew who he was fighting anymore.

Eidolon used his weight to hold Wraith down while Shade channeled power into him, using his gift to slow Wraith's heart and breathing, then reaching deep to cut off the adrenaline flow.

"Ease up, bro. Idle down," Shade murmured, even as he looked over his shoulder to make sure Runa was okay and none of Roag's minions were going to launch a surprise attack.

Bringing Wraith down was agonizingly slow, and most likely futile. As soon as they let him up, Wraith would probably go ballistic on Roag's demons.

"Very, very good," Roag said. "But honestly, I can't believe you two haven't figured out that killing Wraith would make life a whole lot easier."

Eidolon bared his teeth. "You know what would be easier, you fucking—"

"Don't." Shade gripped E's arm and squeezed. "I can't risk Runa."

The wind rustled the leaves in the trees, bringing with it the scent of brimstone. Hellhounds.

"Where'd you get the trackers?" Eidolon eased off Wraith, who leaped nimbly to his feet and stood there, quivering with the amount of restraint it must have taken to not go for Roag's throat.

Roag stroked his blades through Runa's hair, and now it was Shade who had to restrain himself, especially when locks of her gorgeous hair began to flutter to the ground. "What, you think I don't have my own kennel?"

It was on the tip of Shade's tongue to say Roag couldn't control his own female, let alone a hellhound, but with Runa still in danger, Shade kept his mouth shut. Two Carceris officers stepped into the clearing, held prisoner by Roag's minions.

So that was how he'd found Shade. He'd taken the Carceris officers prisoner and forced them to use the hounds to track him. Son of a bitch.

"Shade?" Runa's voice was quiet but steady, and pride swelled in him. He smelled no fear from her, instead her strength permeated the air. "I'm sorry."

"It's okay, *lirsha*."

Roag snorted. "You're fading, you know. I'm thinking it's not *okay*."

A deep, low growl rumbled in Runa's throat. Shade's pulse went tachy with panic. "Runa, no!"

She struck. A double blow, one sharp kick to Roag's shin and a reverse punch to his face. A shockwave of energy hit Shade; she was trying to shift.

"Little bitch," Roag hissed, and buried one of his blades in her shoulder. Her scream rent the air. "This blade is solid silver. You can't shift."

A veil of crimson came down over Shade's vision. He sprang forward, because he was going to tear out Roag's throat. Something pierced his neck. A dart, drugged, no doubt. He fell to the ground hard enough to knock the wind from his lungs. Determined to get to Runa, he yanked the dart from his skin. Eidolon and Wraith's furious shouts told him they'd fallen victim to the same fate.

The last thing he heard before he lost consciousness was Runa's bloodcurdling wail.

# Nineteen

⌒

Kynan stood at the threshold to Gem's apartment, his stomach in knots and his mind fuzzy from the half-dozen shots of liquid courage he'd slammed before coming over. Before Lori died, he hadn't been much of a drinker, but lately he'd been lonely and all too eagerly seeking the kind of embrace only Captain Morgan could give him.

Though he normally didn't fall into the Captain's arms until after noon.

But this morning he'd started early, after calling Arik and confirming that the military knew about his work at UG. Ky had made clear that he wouldn't betray Eidolon or the hospital, and Arik seemed to be cool with that. They'd spent some time catching up, and it had all been cozy—too cozy. His spidey sense was tingling.

The door opened, and Gem stood there, looking surprised and really freaking hot in a black V-neck, cropped sweatshirt that dipped low enough to reveal a hint of crimson bra beneath. Her black miniskirt seemed to be made of the same sweat material and was so short he wondered if she was wearing underwear that matched the bra. Strangely, he got the impression that this was her idea of lounge-around-the-house casual.

"Kynan. Ah, this is a surprise."

"Can I come in?"

She narrowed her gaze at him as though trying to figure out if this was a trick, but she moved aside. Her sweet, citrusy scent came to him as he walked past, and he damned near swayed. *It's the alcohol.*

Maybe, but it wasn't the damned alcohol that was making his dick stand at attention. He entered her small living room and turned to her.

"Were you getting ready to go out?"

"Out?" She looked down at her clothes. "Oh, no. Nowhere special, anyway. I was going to raid the grocery store later. Exciting, huh?"

His dick jerked, because yep, it was excited. Little bastard.

He cleared his throat. Rubbed the back of his neck. Grew some balls to say what he needed to say.

"Yeah, look, Gem. I think we need to talk."

"I think so, too." She propped one hip on the back of her sofa, black leather like all her furniture. Even her lampshade was black. In fact, everything in her living room was either black or stark white. No shades of gray for Gem, but that was no surprise.

"Maybe we could start with why you're still torturing yourself," she said bluntly. "Lori's been dead a year."

He hadn't expected that, and surprise veered quickly

to defensive anger. "There's a time limit on grief?" he snapped. "Is that a demon thing?"

"Why does it always come back to that? I could say I think clouds are pretty, and you'd say they're only pretty to demons."

The fact that she was right only pissed him off more. "What do you expect? I've been fighting them for years. Losing friends to them. Losing my *wife* to them."

"And yet, here you are in a demon's apartment."

"I'm not here to stay."

She crossed her arms over her chest. "Why *are* you here?"

"To apologize. I was an ass the other night. I shouldn't have led you on like that. I used you, and it wasn't fair. I won't do it again."

"You didn't use me. I needed you, you needed me... there's nothing wrong with that."

"We walk in different worlds, Gem."

"Oh, really? Because I see you walking down the same hospital halls I do. I see you wearing the same hospital scrubs bearing the demon caduceus."

Cursing, he jammed his fingers through his hair. "You think I don't know how messed up that is?"

"I think you're immersing yourself in a world you hate so you can hang on to your anger. You don't want to forget your wife's betrayal, do you?"

"You don't know anything," he ground out.

"You think I don't see that it's not demons you hate, but yourself? That you hate the fact that you're starting to like some of us?" She walked up to him, got right up in his face so her breasts brushed his chest. "You hate the fact that you want me. It's driving you nuts, isn't it? Screwing with your head."

"You know what's screwing with my head?" He fisted the hem of her skirt, and his voice plummeted to a low growl. "These skimpy little fuck-me outfits. Do you get off on teasing men? Is it human men you're after? You like to fuck them and then laugh at how you got the unsuspecting, stupid human to screw a demon?"

They were unfair questions born of anger, frustration, and plain old lust. He wasn't sure what he'd hoped to accomplish by asking them, but the pinch to his biceps wasn't it.

"Dumbass."

He blinked. "What?"

"Talking down to someone isn't you, Kynan." Her voice was soft but strong, and surprisingly free of anger. After what he'd said, she should be furious. "I know you're hurting and you're lost, but underneath it all, you're still a decent person."

"Stop saying that! Would a decent person abandon the people he worked with for years? Would he hang out with demons? Would he want to take a demon to b—" He broke off before he could say more, but she knew.

"I would never have taken you for a coward," she said, which got the steam blasting through his veins. "But you are, aren't you? You're so afraid of your own weaknesses that you can't allow yourself to feel anything. To do anything that might go against the mountain of moral superiority you stand on to look down at everyone else."

*Coward?* He was still stuck on that word, one that took him back to his military days, where even the scent of cowardice in someone was a brand he couldn't shake for his entire career. Ky could admit fear—who the hell wouldn't while facing a thirty-foot-tall Gerunti demon with T-Rex jaws and claws as long as a man. But he wasn't a coward.

Except he'd pretty much just proven her point when he'd failed to admit, even to himself, that he wanted her. He wanted to be all over her. Inside her. Making her scream. God help him, he wanted to sink into a demon's body and scour away the rest of his troubles. Just take that last step to cross the line that separated good and bad. Naughty and nice. Pleasure and pain.

The line blurred as he let himself drown in her eyes, but when she licked her lips, the pink tip of her tongue parting them in a slow, sensual sweep, he didn't just step over the line; he sprinted across it.

With no warning, he fisted the hair at the nape of her neck and brought his mouth down to hers. She stiffened. Sealed her lips and denied him entrance. All of his instincts came to bear, the male impulses that demanded he get the female under him, the soldier impulses that demanded victory.

He brought his hard body against her lush one. Heart pounding, he stroked the seam of her lips with his tongue with increasing urgency. He cupped her ass and pressed her against his rapidly growing erection, and with a groan, she went liquid. Her lips parted, and he took immediate advantage.

She tasted good, all sweet fruit and savory spice, and as his tongue tangled with hers, all he could think about was tasting her everywhere. He wanted to take her down to the floor and drive into her so hard she'd scream for more...

And then what? They'd get married and live happily ever after?

Panting, Ky tore away from her. His blood drummed painfully through his veins and his cock. "I can't. This can't happen."

Gem's eyes were glazed, the sheen of lust a beacon to everything that made him male. "Yes, it can. We're adults, Kynan. We don't need permission." Her voice sharpened. "Or is this about your demonphobia?"

He wished it was only the demon thing. "I'm not ready for anything nice, Gem. I'd take you rough and hard, with a big, fat, emotional disconnect." He took her chin in his palm and got in close. "It would be nothing but a fuck, and you'd be nothing but a body to spill into. I can't give anything else right now, and you don't deserve that. I can't give you what you want. I don't know if I ever can. The only thing I know is I've got nothing to offer you but sex." He wheeled away, heard her stepping closer, dammit.

"It's okay," she said. "Ky, I've wanted you for so long. If I'd thought I had a chance with you back when Lori was alive, I'd have tried to get you, and I'd not have cared that you were married."

Her voice, so small, with a touch of a tremor, set him off. "God, Gem, you can do better than me. You *need* to do better than me. You deserve much more than what I can give you."

"Wow, it almost sounds like you respect me. A demon. I mean, really, does a demon deserve to be treated well?" Now her tone was bitter. He ground his teeth because she was right. She was a demon. Why was he worried about her feelings? Her fragility?

He spun around. "So you want it, then? You really want me to fuck you like an animal?"

"Yes," she whispered.

He was on her in an instant. He spun her and bent her over the arm of the chair. With one hand he pushed her skirt up, with the other he released his raging erection. God, the sight of her tight, round ass had him panting even harder, and he took just a moment to stroke the soft skin there. She shuddered and pushed wantonly against him. Unable to wait and not wanting to slow things down, he tore off her underwear—red, as he'd guessed—and sheathed himself in one powerful stroke.

He felt her barrier too late, heard her cry of pain that didn't end even after he'd frozen.

"Fuck." Closing his eyes, he took a deep, shuddering breath. "Why didn't you tell me?"

"Because," she murmured, head bowed so he couldn't see her face, "I was afraid you wouldn't do it if you knew."

Snarling, he pulled out of her. "Damn fucking straight I wouldn't have!" Shit. Shit, shit, shit. He'd already gone soft, so he tucked himself back in his pants and collapsed against the wall before his knees gave out. A virgin. He'd only had one before this.

Lori.

He'd been a virgin himself when they met. He'd just turned eighteen and was shipping out to boot camp. She'd been at the MEPS station, enlisting. It had been love at first sight, and even though he'd never truly hoped to meet her again, they'd ended up stationed at the same base. They'd dated for six months and then got married on a whim. He'd taken her virginity that night, slowly, gently. It had been an amazing experience for both of them.

And now he'd taken Gem's virginity, ruthlessly, and hadn't even given her an orgasm to show for it.

"Dammit, Gem," he said wearily. "Why me? Why did you hold on so long and then give it up for me?"

She turned to him, tugging her skirt down with shaking hands. She didn't look at him as she said, "I've been in love with you for years. Since I first saw you at Mercy General."

Those days seemed so far away. He used to take injured Guardians to a doctor there, one who knew of the battle between The Aegis and demons. Gem had been an intern, and he'd never suspected she was a demon.

"I couldn't bring myself to have sex with anyone else," she continued, "even though I knew I had a snowball's chance in Hades with you." She sniffed and wiped a tear with the back of her hand. "I just...I just wanted to give you something pure. It's all I have. *Had*. Everything else about me is tainted by demon blood. But I had that. And it's always been yours."

Ah, hell. His chest squeezed as if an invisible vise had wrapped around it. Shame made his skin crawl right off him. What was he supposed to say to that?

The ringing of his cell phone startled him, and he hated himself for his shaking hand as he pulled the phone from his pocket. "Go."

"Ky, man, it's Arik. I can't get hold of Runa, and I've got some information that might be important. Do you know how to contact Shade?"

Kynan swore Arik choked on Shade's name, which was no surprise if he knew his sister was mated to him. A demon. "I'll do my best." He hung up. Didn't look at Gem as he said, "I have to go."

He took off without looking back, proving he was the coward she'd said he was.

Awareness swirled around Runa, and with it came blackness so thick she wasn't sure her eyes were open until she blinked several times.

"Runa. *Lirsha*. Wake up."

Shade's worry cut through the darkness. Lifting her head, she winced at the biting pain streaking along the back of her skull. She swallowed, an ineffective attempt to quell the nausea bubbling in her stomach. Where was she?

Orange light flickered at the edges of her vision as she sat up on the cold stone floor, the clank of the chains clamped around her ankles echoing around her. She squinted at the light. Candle flames? No, torches. Familiar. She sniffed the air, taking in the oppressive scents of blood, mold, feces, and terror.

*Oh, God.* She was in Roag's dungeon again. Her stomach lurched, and she leaned over just in time to keep from puking in her lap. Her gut convulsed, emptying its contents in a hot wash. Through her ringing ears, she heard Shade repeating her name, his voice growing more concerned with every passing second.

The memory of her capture slammed into her like a freight train, and she wished she could just pass out again into blissful ignorance. She closed her eyes and considered curling up to do exactly that. She'd done it before, once when her father had gone on a drunken rampage. For three days she'd lain on the floor of her closet, her mind taking her somewhere far more pleasant, somewhere where she wasn't aware of anything going on around her.

Doctors had called it catatonia, and they'd eventually brought her out of it, but she'd never forgotten how easy it had been to go there.

How easy it would be to go there now.

"Runa, baby, stay with me."

Shade knew. Knew what she was thinking, knew her weakness. He'd taken away the guilt that had plagued her for years, but he hadn't taken away the girl she'd been. He kept saying she'd changed in the last year, that she'd grown stronger, but the fact that she wanted to curl up and give up proved how weak she still was.

"Runa." Eidolon's voice, a deep, commanding drawl, brought her up above the fog of self-pity. "Look at me."

Still on her hands and knees, she swung her head around to him. Her vision had cleared, but that wasn't necessarily a good thing. She'd thought she was in a cell similar to the one she and Shade had shared before, but this was worse.

They were in Roag's dungeon, but they'd been imprisoned in the large outer chamber where Roag kept the torture instruments. She'd been chained to the wall, while Shade and his brothers had been stripped of clothing and crammed into individual cages. Shade pressed against the bars of the middle cage as though trying to get as close as possible to her, his body flickering in and out of solidity.

"Oh, Shade," she whispered.

"Listen to me," Eidolon said from his cage on Shade's left. He was sitting against the back bars, arms resting casually on his knees as though he was lounging at home in front of the TV. "The more Shade worries about you, the faster his curse progresses. And if you die, his grief is going to finish him off. You need to hold on. Be strong."

"She is strong," Shade said. His dark gaze bored into her, going obsidian with intensity. "You are. You'll get through this."

Roag stepped out from the shadowed stairwell at the end of the chamber, followed by two burly, ram-headed demons. "And wouldn't that be a good trick? Surviving this, I mean." He swept forward in a fluid, dramatic swirl of black robes.

Wraith, who had been standing in the corner of his cage, head hanging and hair matted to his face with dried blood, hissed. Runa gasped. Wraith looked like, well, a demon. His expression was a mask of rage, his fangs the size of a tiger's, and his eyes glowed like amber tossed in a fire. He was a mass of blood and bruises, far worse off than either Shade or Eidolon, and as Roag approached, Wraith went rabid. He attacked the bars, slamming repeatedly into them as though trying to break every bone in his body so he could squeeze between them. Shade tried to talk him down, but nothing worked.

"He's so excitable," Roag said casually. "Then again, I probably would be, too, if I'd been kept in a cage and tortured for twenty years."

"You've got all of us together now," Eidolon snapped as he shoved to his feet. "What is it you want?"

Behind Roag, the two hulking demons lit a fire in the hearth. "I have a list a mile long, brother. And it begins and ends with pain." Roag smiled. "And that's something you know a lot about, don't you, E?"

Wraith stilled in his cage, head down, shoulders heaving, his gaze drilling into Roag.

"Shut up." Eidolon rattled the bars of his cage. "*Shut the hell up.*"

"What? You don't want poor little Wraith to know how you've suffered for him?"

"E…" Wraith's low growl vibrated through Runa's bones. Something bad, very bad was about to be revealed.

Roag turned to Wraith. "It was probably bad enough to learn that Shade gets off on torturing females. I imagine that knowing what the Vampire Council does to Eidolon once a month won't sit well with you at all. Might even send you completely over the edge. You were never very stable."

"You bastard," Eidolon whispered. "I trusted you. I cared about you!"

Shade shrugged. "I never did. You always were an asshole."

Roag snapped something in another language at his minions, who jammed iron pokers into the fire they'd created, and Runa's blood ran as cold as the Hudson in winter.

"You'll get yours in a moment, Shade." Roag moved closer to Wraith's cage, but not too close, Runa noted. "You know how the Vampire Council leaves you alone? How you can kill and kill and they don't do a damned thing about it? That's because a long time ago, our dear, sweet brother Eidolon volunteered to take the punishment for you."

Wraith went so pale Runa thought he might pass out. "No."

"You piece of shit," Eidolon muttered. "I'm going to take you apart with my bare hands."

"Oh, you'll be taking one of us apart, but that'll come later," Roag promised, not looking away from Wraith. "Now, little brother, do you know what the vamp punishment is for taking more than your quota of humans each month? Do you know that they spend hours brutalizing Eidolon? By the time they're done, there isn't an inch of him that hasn't been bloodied. Here's the fun part. It's been going on for years. I've been making sure of it."

Eidolon's eyes shot wide open. "You. You've been shifting into Wraith's form and doing the killing."

"Wraith flaunts his kills enough to get you tortured without my help, but really, I just like killing humans."

Wraith began to tremble, and his eyes had gone so haunted and so full of pain that Runa could practically feel his misery. "Why, E?" he croaked. "Why didn't you tell me?"

Roag laughed. "Idiot. They didn't tell you because you're a fucking weak little worm. I never did understand why they didn't just let you die in that warehouse."

"Don't listen to him, Wraith," Shade said, his voice a cold, hard command intended to grab Wraith's attention and keep it. "E took the punishment because you'd been through enough already. We didn't tell you for the same reason."

"He hasn't gone through nearly enough," Roag said. "None of you have." He snapped his fingers, and two more demons who must have crept down the stairs while Runa was engrossed in the conversation brought forward a pale female who walked like a zombie.

Which was, Runa realized with horror, because she *was* a zombie. Jesus, it was the female Runa had killed when she and Shade had escaped.

"Oh, you sick fuck," Shade said, as he stared at the female. "You reanimated her."

"Yes, and your mate will be the blood sacrifice I need to bring my love fully back to life."

Shade's lips pulled back in a silent snarl. In a movement so fast Runa didn't see it until it was over, he shifted into some sort of skinny, spindly demon and swiped an extra-long arm through the bars at Roag. Shade's claws caught Roag across the chest, and blood splattered on the wooden rack next to him.

Roag yelped and leaped back. Cold, soulless fury flashed in his eyes. "I'm going to enjoy making you suffer. I'm going to enjoy making *all* of you suffer." He held his hand to his ribs as he turned to Eidolon. "Did I mention the best part of all this? Besides killing Runa in front of Shade and watching him fade away forever? I'm going to remove a few of Wraith's choice parts, skin him, and then make you transplant all of Wraith's good bits onto me."

Runa's jaw about hit the floor. Eidolon's eyes went furious crimson, glowing like Christmas lights. Evil Christmas lights.

"What makes you think I would ever do something like that?" Eidolon's voice sounded like it had been dredged from the deepest pits of hell.

"Because, dear brother, if you don't, I'll torture Tayla in ways you can't begin to imagine."

Eidolon's terror hit her in a blast of cold. "You don't have Tayla."

"Not yet. But I will. She'll be lured to you by your suffering."

Shade shook his head. "Don't listen, E. Remember how Wraith couldn't feel me when I was here?"

"I've removed the dampening spell," Roag said. "She'll

come. And when she does, I'll be ready." He stalked to
the fire, where several irons had been heating. He nodded
to the two burly demons, and they each pulled a glowing iron from the coals. He smiled as he turned back to
Shade.

"Time for some fun, boys."

# Twenty

Kynan had no luck finding Shade or Runa. Hell, he couldn't find Eidolon or Wraith, either. He'd gone back to the hospital and was about to call E again when his cell phone rang—from E's home number. "Yeah?"

"It's Tayla." Her voice vibrated with panic. "Eidolon's hurt. Oh, my God, Kynan, it's bad."

Adrenaline spiked, a freefall dump into the pit of his stomach and a steep mach-climb to the top of his skull all at once, and he struggled to find his calm medic voice. "Slow down and tell me what happened."

A choked sob came over the line. "He called me hours ago from the hospital. Wraith needed him. At Shade's place, I think. Wraith was freaked out about something. I haven't heard from him since. *Oh, God.*"

A cold tremor went up his spine. If the brothers had been together and one was in pain, they were probably all in trouble. "Tayla, listen to me. You can feel Eidolon, right? That's how you know he's in pain."

"Yes. I need to get to him."

"Can you find him? Can you use your bond to locate him?"

"Yes...and he said something about Roag's dungeon being in Ireland. I'm going now."

"You can't go alone. I'll go with you."

"You can't pass through the Harrowgates."

He blew out a breath. He'd forgotten about the restrictions on humans. Only dark-souled or unconscious humans could pass through them, so it looked like he'd need to be knocked out. The very idea gave him the creeps—apparently, humans who woke up inside the gates came out dead.

"We can get around the human restriction," he said. "Meet me here at the hospital."

"I need Gem. Can you find her?"

"I'll call her."

"She's not answering her cell. She was all upset about some asshole dissing her or something...she went to Vamp. Can you get her?"

Shit. Vamp. The Goth club from hell. And he knew damned good and well just who that asshole was.

"Tay, don't do something stupid and go by yourself. Wait until we all get back to the hospital. Got it?"

"Hurry, Kynan."

He hung up and headed straight for Vamp. The Goth club was dark, loud, and weird. Figured it'd be death metal night. Kynan moved through the mass of gyrating bodies, gritting his teeth against the grind of flesh. Half the people wore too much clothing, the other half, not enough. Gem would, no doubt, belong in the latter group, and the thought had him clenching his fists in irritation he had no right to feel.

Ahead, a black and blue head bobbed in the crowd, and he made a beeline for it. He saw Gem before she saw him, and though jealousy burned in his chest at the sight of some tall vampire wannabe dry-humping her as they danced, he couldn't help but stop and admire her.

From her six-inch-heeled black boots to her black micromini skirt, she was all long legs and long-stemmed rose tattoos winding up the inside of her thigh. She wore a red lace-up corset that pushed her magnificent breasts up and out, and the spiked leather dog collar around her graceful neck was connected to the top with a chain. He'd never been attracted to the Goth style or its fashion, but she owned it, and he found himself wanting to be the man rubbing all over her instead of the loser she was with.

That loser was probably going to give her what he hadn't. Would probably take her home and make love to her with care and without anger. Would give her an orgasm while he was moving inside her, kissing her, touching her soft skin.

Except Kynan had a seriously hard time imagining that a guy wearing white makeup, black eyeliner, and black lipstick would be a good lover. Then again, he didn't want to imagine anyone loving Gem.

As though she sensed him, she turned. Her green eyes sparked with surprise and then narrowed with mischief, a definite you're-going-to-get-it light.

She shoved the horny guy off her and shouldered her way through the crowd, never looking away from Kynan. Shit, it was as if he was caught in some sort of spell, and he just stood there like a lump as she walked right up to him so they were touching, her breasts to his chest. She fisted his shirt collar and jerked him as close as possible, straddling one of his legs between hers. No way could she miss the erection burning a hole in her belly any more than he could miss the heat she was rubbing into his thigh.

This was payback, and he knew it. And while he'd love to give her the opportunity to work him up and then walk away, there were lives on the line. Still, he took the time to put his hands on her slim hips and move against her, doing his own version of the dirty dance the vamp poser had been doing with her. And if the way she began to pant was any indication, he was doing it better.

Heat and passion burned in her eyes, and though he knew he shouldn't, he claimed her mouth, fiercely, urgently. Her kiss stole his breath and his thoughts, almost making him forget why he was there. But he did remember, and he forced himself away from her.

"I'm not here for this," he yelled over the scream of the music.

She jammed her fists on her hips. "No shit? I didn't really think you'd come here to fuck me in front of a room full of people when you won't even do it in private."

Yeah, he'd deserved that. "Tayla needs us." He grabbed her hand and dragged her out of the club. She yanked him to a halt outside it.

"What are you talking about?"

He pulled her away from the line of people waiting to get in. "The Sem brothers are missing. Runa, too. Tayla says E is in pain."

"Roag?"

"Probably. We're going to find them."

His cell rang, and he dug it out of his pocket as he and Gem hoofed it toward his Mustang. Arik's name popped up on the caller ID. "Yeah?"

"You find my sister?"

"I have a lead, but I can't get into it right now."

Arik swore. "I'm on my way to New York, but I have something she needs to hear if you get to her first."

Kynan listened, and though he had no idea what the hell Arik was talking about, he promised to relay the message to Runa.

If they survived the night.

Shade waited in his cage. Waited for Roag to come back and continue with his fun.

Fun. Right. Stabbing and beating Eidolon and Shade with red-hot pokers was a shit-ton of fun. At least Roag had taken his minions and girlfriend away so they could suffer in peace for a while.

Eidolon sat in one corner of his cage, concentrating on keeping his pain as buried as possible. He didn't want Tayla to track him, but Shade suspected it was too late. Shade rubbed his thigh where one poker had gone deep, but as with most of his wounds, the heat had cauterized it, so few of his injuries bled.

Though Roag had threatened to let his minions rape Runa, it hadn't happened yet, thank the gods, and neither had they touched Wraith, although he was the one who had been hurt the most.

He'd gone crazy as E and Shade had been burned, stabbed, and beaten. He'd thrown himself against his cage until he was little more than a bloody pulp. Now he stood motionless as a statue, staring at the stairwell Roag had disappeared into. There was murder in Wraith's eyes. Murder and a touch of madness that said he was in a mental place Shade wouldn't want to go.

Wraith hadn't moved or uttered a word in hours, no matter what Shade did or said, and he wondered if his little brother would ever recover from this.

Assuming they survived.

A shudder shook Shade as he thought about the things Roag had planned for them. Death was one thing, but taking Wraith's body parts and skin while he was still alive, and then forcing E to transplant the organs onto Roag... God...*damn*.

Shade rattled his cage, hoping to shake the wildness out of Runa's gaze. "Baby? You okay?"

She hadn't taken her eyes off him, not once since Roag had left. She'd gone as crazy as Wraith when Roag and his minions had been having their fun, and her ankles were bleeding where they'd been rubbed raw by the shackles.

"I'm going to kill him." Her voice was hoarse from screaming, but the power behind her words wasn't diluted. He knew she'd tear Roag's heart out of his chest if she had the chance.

His chest expanded with a great breath, with a rush of blood that filled his heart. Love filled him, so warm, so wonderfully right that his eyes threatened to overflow with wussy-ass tears.

"Shade. Fuck." Eidolon jumped to his feet.

Runa cried out. "Oh, no. Shade, no."

He looked down and felt the ground fall from beneath him. He could barely see his body. He was fading, and at this rate, he had only minutes left to exist.

Kynan, Gem, and Tay stood next to the Harrowgate in UG's ER. Tayla had eaten up valuable hours as she searched the area surrounding the Irish Harrowgates, but once she found the right gate and neutralized the demon guarding it, she'd zapped back to the hospital to grab Ky and Gem.

Gem still hadn't said a word to him since leaving Vamp.

"Did you contact an Irish Aegis chapter for backup?" Gem asked.

"I wish I could," Tay said, "but I can't trust them to kill the bad demons and stop there."

Ky nodded. "Agreed. As helpful as they'd be, we'd have way too much to explain, especially if you two shift form. Besides, we have help."

There was a muffled consensus of agreement from the semicircle of demons surrounding them, hospital staff who insisted on going along. Nearly everyone on duty had volunteered to help rescue E and his brothers, which spoke volumes about their loyalty, when demons were notoriously self-serving.

Tayla smiled as she pulled her red hair into a high ponytail. "Who'd have thought, huh?" She wore her usual red leather fighting clothes—many demons were blind to the color, making it more invisible than black to them.

"Yeah. Demons who aren't all bad. Who knew?" He slid a glance at Gem but looked back at Tay quickly. "Ready to roll?"

"Lock and load." Tay held out her hand, and he pressed one of two syringes he'd prepared into her hand. The contents would knock him out for about five minutes, long

enough to get his human ass through the Harrowgate.
He'd been generous with the dose—he didn't want to be
out longer than necessary, but he definitely didn't want to
wake up midjump. If he was going to die, he'd rather go in
battle than inside a Harrowgate.

"You all know how this works, right?" she began,
addressing everyone. "Once we're out of the gate, I'm
going ahead. I'm sure the bastards will be expecting me,
so I'm going to get captured. You guys follow, and once
I'm inside the castle, you attack while they're busy with
me. Got it?"

Ky didn't like the idea of Tay sacrificing herself, but
they had little choice, and murmurs of assent rose above
the dim hospital noises. Gem hefted a duffel of weapons
onto her shoulder. Tay had various weapons stashed on
her body, as Roag would expect. Ky was weighed down,
as well, the tug of his full weapons harness a familiar
comfort. In addition, he carried a medic kit.

Ky grabbed Tay's wrist before she could dose him. "If
I don't regain consciousness within four minutes after
arriving in Ireland, have Gem stick me with the episol in
my kit."

It was a risk, taking the epinephrine-based stimulant
Eidolon had developed for use in human-demon hybrid
patients, but Kynan needed to be on his feet immediately.

"You got it."

Abasi, a huge male lion shapeshifter, stepped behind
Ky as Tay injected the syringe into Ky's arm. Instantly,
Ky's vision went black, and the last thing he was aware of
was Abasi catching him as he fell.

# Twenty-one

Shade was almost lost to her. Runa couldn't take her eyes off him, couldn't keep the tears from spilling down her cheeks. Eidolon told Shade not to look at her, because doing so seemed to make his transparency worse, but he kept stealing glances anyway. The pain in his eyes sliced at her, and God, she wanted to scream until she lost her voice and her mind.

"It's ti-ime." Roag's singsong sent a shiver down Runa's spine. He led his zombified girlfriend into the dungeon and sat her on one of the autopsy tables he'd set up after he'd tortured Shade and Eidolon. "And I have a present for you."

The sounds of struggle and chains came from within the stairwell, and as Runa watched, three demons dragged a bloody humanoid female into the dungeon. The devastation on Eidolon's face said this was Tayla.

She must have been extremely strong, because the three

demons, though twice her size, were struggling to keep her under control.

"I'm so glad you could join us," Roag said. "Took you long enough. I was beginning to think you didn't care."

"If you touch one hair on her head, you won't get what you want from me," Eidolon swore, and Roag snorted.

"You'll change your mind when my minions are raping her." He pointed to the corner, where a hulking thing with tusks jutting out of its mouth watched, a look of pure evil—and lust—in its eyes. "He goes first." Roag walked over to Runa and released her from her bonds. "Of course, I don't want this one to feel left out."

A burning sensation seared her shoulder, and through the spots in her vision she saw why. Roag had impaled her with something that resembled a silver knitting needle, obviously to keep her from changing form. It also left her too weak to fight, and she hated how limp she was as he dragged her beside his zombie girlfriend.

Clamping Runa's wrist to a massive stone table, Roag wheeled away to grab a wicked, serrated scimitar off the wall. Smiling, he tested the edge.

"This is going to hurt, Runa. It doesn't have to, but where's the fun in that?" He licked the blade, tasted it almost lovingly before speaking again. "See, my darling Sheryen needs your blood, but she also needs your heart. While it's still beating, of course." Roag lovingly stroked Sheryen's cheek.

He returned his gaze to Runa, and in that moment, Roag encompassed everything she'd grown up believing about demons. Evil madness raged in his eyes, a deep hatred for everything good, a love for everything unholy and wrong.

"Master!" A green, antlered thing stumbled out of the stairwell, clutching a bloody stump of an arm. "We're under attack!"

From above, the sound of metal on metal and fists on flesh joined screeches of pain. All hell broke loose as a flash of light nearly blinded Runa, and then, standing where Tayla had been, was some sort of creature. Something that resembled Tayla, but was bigger, with batlike wings and scaly skin.

Not to mention huge teeth and claws. The chains holding the beast disintegrated, and it leaped for Roag.

For a moment, it looked as if the Tayla-thing was going to kick major ass, but as Roag's minions joined in, Tayla began to fall beneath their pounding. Roag, bleeding from a gaping shoulder wound, snarled as he brought his blade down with both hands. Tayla screamed and flashed back to her human form, the blade buried in her abdomen.

Eidolon let loose a keening cry that echoed through the dungeon. A tomblike cold draft accompanied the sound of his anguish, both carrying on long after they should have faded away.

The battle drew closer, but Runa couldn't look away from the sight of Eidolon's mate writhing in pain on the floor.

"See what's going on up there!" Roag barked at one of his demons.

The male who'd been waiting for his turn with Tayla hoofed it—literally—to the stairwell opening as dozens of demons spilled out. Runa watched helplessly as Kynan, Gem, and an assortment of demons, some wearing hospital scrubs, engaged in bloody, violent combat. When Gem took a blow to the head and collapsed to the floor, Kynan whipped a pistol from his leather jacket and blew a fist-sized hole through the chest of the demon that had struck Gem.

Still, even with Kynan's impressive arsenal of weapons, Roag's minions gained the upper hand and were slowly but surely beating down the good guys. Roag stood on the sidelines, hovering protectively over Sheryen.

Time slowed, and Runa felt a punch to the gut each time a friendly demon went down. Her pulse pounded in her ears, muting the screams of pain and the clank of metal on metal. In the cages, Shade and his brothers threw themselves against the bars and kicked at the doors.

"Runa!"

She barely heard the voice, was too engaged in a downward spiral of despair. Roag was winning. She was going to die a horrible death, and Shade was going to suffer for an eternity.

"Runa! The curse…" Kynan swung an odd-looking weapon, a double-ended S-curved blade, at one of the demons he was fighting, cutting a deep gouge in the creature's side. He worked his way toward her, fierce concentration in his expression.

But whatever he intended to tell her would have to wait, because the sharp bite of a blade bit into her breast, and Roag loomed over her, evil intent burning in his gaze.

"No more stalling," he snarled. "It's time to take your heart."

"No!" Shade slammed his entire body against the door of his cage, terror and adrenaline fueling his strength.

The door bowed, but it held. The cages had been made

to hold the strongest of demons, and the spaces between the bars were too narrow to squeeze through no matter what species he shifted into.

Roag looked up from where he loomed over Runa and gave Shade a bone-chilling smile.

Kynan elbowed aside a Darquethoth, getting close enough to Runa to backhand Roag. Roag's head snapped back and blood sprayed from his shriveled nose. The Darquethoth leaped onto Kynan's back, but the human bared his teeth and lunged forward. Shade held his breath, praying to any god who would listen to let Kynan help Runa.

But the Darquethoth seized Kynan by the arm and dragged Kynan away. He shouted at Runa, his words muffled, but whatever he'd said made her eyes go wide. With one last, monumental effort, Kynan leaped, arm outstretched, his blade coming down so close to Runa's wrist that Shade expected to see her hand separate from her arm.

Instead, the chain fell away, and she was free. The silver rod in her shoulder crippled her, but she rolled to the side, catching Roag with her legs. Snarling, she kicked, propelling Roag toward Shade.

The gods had answered, and he wasn't going to disappoint. He caught Roag's arm as his brother hit the cage door. The bars were narrow and his body was fading; he had little chance against Roag, but dammit, he was going to fuck up his big brother as much as he could.

"Family!" Runa's voice cut through sounds of fighting as he yanked Roag against the cage so hard Roag's skull cracked against a bar. "Your curse! Arik!"

Runa was making no sense. "*What?*"

He could hear the harsh rasp of her pained breaths as

she struggled to her feet next to the altar Roag had put her on. "He found another translation for your curse. Loved one... *or family*."

He'd been over this with Wraith. He could be rid of the *Maluncoeur* only if he transferred it to a loved one...

Family. Or... family...

Hell's bones, could it be true? He didn't take the time to think further. He had hold of Roag, and even as his brother started to slip from his grasp, he uttered the words Wraith had wanted him to say.

"*Solumaya. Orentus. Kraktuse!*"

Nothing happened. Fuck.

And then, the air between Shade and Roag began to vibrate. Slowly, Shade's body grew solid, and parts of Roag flashed so milky-transparent that through it, Shade could see Runa's stumbling approach. *Yes!* Excitement renewed his strength, and he held tight to Roag, who didn't seem to notice that he now carried Shade's curse.

Runa snared the key from Roag's belt and leaped back as he swiped at her. One of Roag's minions lunged for Runa, but Gem caught the lizardlike creature around the throat and slammed it to the ground.

"Release Eidolon," Shade shouted to Runa. He was holding Roag too close to the door of his own cage. He couldn't risk her getting hurt.

Once free, Eidolon put Roag on the ground with a fist to the face, and then dashed to Tayla as Runa unlocked Shade's cage. He burst out. Roag's minions advanced, and Roag regained his footing. In a single, smooth motion, Shade braced Runa against the cage and yanked the silver bar out of her shoulder, her strangled cry tearing through him.

"I'm sorry," he breathed. His fingers found the wound,

and he wished he had Eidolon's gift to heal, but all he could do in the split second they had was stimulate the release of endorphins to ease her pain.

"It's okay," she said. "Behind you!"

Spinning, he jammed the heel of his palm into Roag's throat. He'd love to pound the sonofabitch into a pulp, but they needed Wraith's fighting skills. He released his younger brother and stood back. With a snarl, Wraith tore through Roag's team like a knife through tissue paper.

A huge body slammed into Shade from the side. Caught off guard, he lurched into the wall and suddenly was fighting for his life. The demon was strong, far stronger than Shade. It gripped his throat with humanlike hands and used its wings to help steady itself as it tried to squeeze the life out of Shade.

A fallen angel. Gods, what was Roag doing with a fallen fucking angel in his castle?

The angel smiled at Shade's futile struggles. And then, all he saw was fangs and blood. Runa, in her warg form, had ripped one of the angel's wings off its body.

The angel wheeled away, and when Runa made to give chase, Shade grabbed her by the scruff. "Down, girl. They're almost impossible to kill. Let him go."

Roag's agonized scream carried over the sound of battle. He was staring in horror at his hands. Oh, yeah, Roag had discovered the curse. His gaze locked on Eidolon, who was bent over Tayla, his *dermoire* glowing as he healed his mate.

Roag was going to transfer the curse to E.

Shade yanked a battle ax off the wall. In two strides, he was in striking distance.

Of Sheryen.

Roag reached for Eidolon. Shade swung. "This is for Skulk, you sonofabitch."

Sheryen's head separated from her body with a soft whisper. Roag pivoted around, his forward momentum knocking him into Eidolon.

"Sher!" Roag screamed, and for the first time ever, Shade saw genuine pain in his brother's eyes. Roag kept screaming, and gradually, his voice, and his body, faded into nothingness.

"And that," Shade said softly, "was for all of us."

It was over. With Roag gone, his minions no longer held together. Some lost their courage and became easy prey for Gem, Kynan, and the hospital staff, and the rest fled. Wraith, probably more than half insane with blood-lust and the need for revenge, pursued, disappearing up the winding staircase.

Runa shifted, and Shade hauled her nude body against his. "You okay? I'll get E to heal your injuries."

"I can wait. Others need help more than I do."

Shade glanced at E. "How is she?"

Tayla stood, brushing herself off. When many demons shifted, they retained their clothes, and Tayla was one of those fortunate species. "I'm fine. Good as new."

Eidolon seemed as reluctant to leave Tayla's side as Shade was to leave Runa's, but several hospital staff members who'd come to the rescue were in bad shape. Still, Shade took the time to kiss Runa, a lingering, hot meeting of mouths that promised more later. He owed her so much, and he'd spend the rest of his life making up to her what he—and Roag—had done.

Kicking into medic mode, he broke away from her. Some of the injuries were severe enough that Shade had to dip into the medic kit Kynan had brought. Fortunately, since everyone except Runa was a medical professional in some capacity, triage went quickly, though they did lose one physician assistant, a lion shapeshifter who'd been on staff for nearly ten years. Walking woundeds took the more severely injured to the Harrowgate for transfer to the hospital. By the time Shade and Eidolon had done all they could, they were both exhausted.

Someone had raided the rooms in the castle and brought down some of the sacklike tunics Roag's minions wore, so Runa and Shade donned them while Eidolon used the last of his energy to heal Runa, Gem, and Kynan, and when he was done, Shade made him take a seat on a wooden stool before he fell over. Tayla crawled into his lap and wrapped herself around him.

"Got all the bastards." Wraith stumbled out of the stairwell, a mass of blood and gaping wounds. "And Solice." He swayed and hit the stone floor with a crack of kneecaps. "That bitch."

"Shit."

Shade darted to him. He and E reached their brother at the same time, each grasping one shoulder to hold him up, and both sending waves of their power into him. Eidolon's energy began to knit the massive injuries together, but the process was slow . . . E was drained. Cursing softly, Shade probed for internal injuries. Fortunately, Wraith's organs were intact, but he was dangerously low on blood. His head hung so his chin touched his chest and his long hair concealed his face, and Shade wondered if Wraith was too weak to lift it.

"He needs to feed," Shade said, coming to his feet. "Now."

Straw on the floor stirred in the cold drafts and the silence. Gem stepped forward. "I'll do it."

An erotic swirl of lust spun up like a breeze from Wraith, and E raised an eyebrow. "You prepared for that? Because you'll be beneath him with him inside you in about five seconds after he starts feeding."

She swallowed, but nodded. "It's not like I'm a virgin or anything." There seemed to be some subtext there, but fuck if Shade knew what it was.

"No." Kynan moved forward and knelt in front of Wraith. "I'll do it. He's fed from me before."

E stood and shot Shade a look of surprise that had to match Shade's own. When the hell had Wraith taken Kynan's blood? And why? He couldn't imagine Kynan allowing it, but Gem didn't seem surprised. Maybe...nah. Seminus demons didn't do males—they could reach orgasm only with a female. Though he supposed a Sem could screw around with a male as long as a female was present. So had Gem, Ky, and Wraith...

Shade shook his head, needing to clear it. His mind was taking him places he did *not* want to go.

"Will he still need sex?" Runa asked, and Shade nodded.

"Best to have both at the same time, but if he can get blood now, we can find him a female at the hospital."

They backed away as Kynan rolled up his sleeve and offered Wraith his wrist. Wraith's nostrils flared, and before Shade could shout a warning, Wraith sank his fangs into the human's throat. Kynan flailed, convulsed once, and then relaxed.

"I'll bet he doesn't volunteer to do that again," Shade muttered.

After a few minutes, Gem knelt next to Wraith, who

growled at her, his gold eyes viewing her as a threat to his food.

"Easy there," she said softly, as she took Kynan's wrist. "Wraith, you need to stop."

Wraith jerked Kynan closer, taking long, powerful pulls as though trying to ingest as much nourishment as possible before his meal was taken away.

Shade felt for Kynan's pulse on the other side of his neck. It was fast, too fast, and weak. He probed with his power, and yep, the human was too low on blood for comfort.

"Stop, bro. Now."

Wraith sucked harder. Eidolon grasped Wraith's shoulder and tugged him back.

"Dammit, you're killing him." E cuffed the back of Wraith's head. "You're going to kill Kynan. Wraith!"

The gold in Wraith's eyes faded, replaced by electric blue. He disengaged his fangs, blinking as he came out of his bloodlust. Kynan sank to the ground, way pale and way unconscious.

"Hypovolemic shock." Shade caught Kynan's head before it hit the floor. "We need to get him to the hospital." He shoved his arms beneath Ky's limp body, but Wraith locked his hand around Shade's wrist.

"I'll carry him." The determination in Wraith's voice left no room for argument. His brother needed to do this.

"Fine," Shade said, "but step on it."

# Twenty-two

Kynan lay unconscious in the hospital bed, hooked up to an IV delivering B-positive blood. Shade stood quietly at the foot of Ky's bed, Runa at his side. Wraith sat close to the rails, head in hands and looking as if he'd been through the Neethul slave pits a few times.

"He's going to be okay, man." Shade clapped his hand on Wraith's shoulder, now covered, like the rest of them, in scrubs, and his brother looked up, dark circles ringing his bloodshot eyes.

"That's what Gem said."

"She wouldn't lie."

Wraith nodded. "I'm just going to wait until he wakes up."

"And then?"

"There's something I gotta do."

Shade knew better than to lecture Wraith about eating junkies or getting into fights, and after Roag's little revelation about E being tortured when Wraith went over his monthly allotment of kills, Shade had a feeling that Wraith would be careful from now on. At least, he'd be careful not to kill. Careful with his life? That was another question.

Shade squeezed Runa's hand, and they slipped silently out into the hall, where E was waiting. Tay and Gem were talking a few doors down, giving them some privacy.

"How is he?" E asked.

"Ky or Wraith?"

"Both."

"Ky's looking better. Wraith..." Shade shook his head. "I don't know."

"I'm glad Roag's torment is eternal," Eidolon muttered.

"You and me both, bro."

E gazed absently into the room, and then he turned back to Shade. "I have some good news. First, Luc's alive."

"Say again?"

"Luc. You know, Runa's sire?"

A surge of possessiveness had Shade clenching his teeth, but Runa stroked his fingers with her thumb, bringing him down. "Yeah, you could've not mentioned that part." The sire thing stuck like a bone in his craw. "So how's he alive?"

"One of your new EMTs found him. He resuscitated him, got him on life support, and after that it was a waiting game. I just checked on him. He's out of his coma and pissed as hell. Says some burned thing disguised as you tried to kill him. Also says we just put off the inevitable by saving him."

"That boy needs an attitude adjustment." Shade narrowed his eyes at E. "Hold up...when did you learn he survived?"

"After we lost Roag in the park and you went back to your cave with Runa. I meant to tell you, but..."

"Roag grabbed us." Shade took a deep breath and asked Runa the question he really didn't want to know the answer to. "Can you sense Luc?"

She grinned. "I can't feel a thing."

Eidolon cleared his throat, and Shade knew there was some doctorish know-it-all speak coming up. "His death, however brief, must have severed the connection, like what happened to us when Roag died. I have a theory about that—"

"What's the other good news?" Shade cut him off, because really, he didn't give a shit and wasn't going to look a gift hell stallion in the mouth. Not that he'd do that, anyway, because the things breathed fire.

E didn't miss a beat. "Thanks to your information about Runa's Army experimentation, I was able to narrow my focus."

"You saying you have a cure?"

Eidolon nodded. "I'm close. I was able to isolate the proteins that caused your infection. I should have a vaccine ready in a couple of weeks. Month, tops."

*Yes.* Shade wanted to shout to the heavens. Wanted to grab Runa and twirl her around until they were both dizzy. "What about Runa?"

She touched Shade's shoulder, and her hopes and fears transmitted to him in a surge of electricity. Eidolon's expression quickly brought them both back down to earth.

"You can't cure her," Shade muttered. "Why not?"

"A warg's bite alters human DNA," Eidolon explained. "Whatever the military did to her affected the way her genes synthesize proteins. Those proteins allow her to shift at will, and they're also what infected you—without altering your DNA. I can destroy the proteins in both of you, and it'll cure you . . . but all it will do to her is end her ability to shift at will."

Runa blew out a long breath. "And I'd still grow fur during the full moon."

"Yes," Eidolon said. "I'm sorry."

She shook her head. "It's okay. I'm getting used to being a werewolf. It's been handy a couple of times. And hey, the quadrupled lifespan alone is worth it."

Gods, that was something he hadn't considered. If she became human again, he'd lose her way too soon. He couldn't handle that. Breaking the bond wouldn't physically kill him, but a broken heart would.

She squeezed Shade's shoulder. "Get yourself cured. You've had enough to deal with without having the werewolf thing on top of it."

He didn't deserve her, but man, he was so lucky to have her. He hated Roag with every cell in his body, but the bastard had given him Runa. It hadn't seemed like a gift at the time, but now he would never regret the bond he had with her, even if it didn't go both ways.

She knew what he was thinking. "I'm not going anywhere," she said. "Markings or no, you're mine. I love you, Shade."

He drew her hard against him. "But with the bond being one-sided, you still can't feel me. If I need you, if I'm hurt—"

"I'll never be far from you. We'll work it out."

"Damn, I love you."

She sighed, a sweet, soft sound he'd never grow tired of hearing. "Agree to the shot."

"I'm not so sure I want it now."

Eidolon backed away to give them a chance to talk.

"Don't turn this down," she said. "This is your chance to be free."

"Maybe I don't want to be." He drew his finger along her jawline, enjoying the way her champagne eyes darkened to a smooth, swirling caramel. "Maybe I like what we do to each other during the full moon. What we do to each other when we wake up, and the moon is still stirring us."

"We'll still have that. You can shapeshift into a warg any time you want."

"Shade." Eidolon came close again, bringing Tay with him. "There's something else to consider. Your offspring."

"What about them? Runa isn't human anymore, so they'll be born full-blooded Sems."

"Yes, but they'll also be wargs."

"Runa wasn't a born warg, so that shouldn't happen." Humans who were turned into werewolves gave birth to normal human babies—unless conception took place while the mother was in beast form—but those born as werewolves usually gave birth to werewolves no matter how the young were conceived.

"I think the experimentation could have screwed with that. If we cure the lycanthropy in you, I can use your antibodies to create an immunization for your children. Even those conceived in beast form during a breeding heat."

Shade blew out a breath. He didn't want the cure for himself, but he wouldn't wish lycanthropy on his offspring. Without mates, full-moon nights would be dangerous for them and any female who got in their way. "Fine. Do it."

Runa reached for his face with both hands and brought his mouth down hard against hers. "I love you," she said, against his lips. Her voice was a deep, husky rasp that lit him up the way only she could. "And you know how I'm going to show you?"

He pulled back a little. "How?"

"You know that thing you never let me do when we were dating?" Her gaze flickered to the rapidly growing bulge in his pants, and he took in a ragged breath.

The image of her on her knees, taking him into her mouth...*damn*. "I couldn't let you," he croaked. "My semen is an aphrodisiac. I wouldn't have been able to explain why you went mad with lust afterward."

Her wicked grin cut off his words and his breath. Nearly stopped his heart, as well. "Not that I've ever needed an aphrodisiac with you, but it sounds interesting." She licked her lips, the little vixen, and that was it. He was done for, beyond the point of no return.

He grabbed her hand and turned to E. "I'm outta here. Call if you need me, but do *not* call any time soon."

E opened his mouth, but Tayla walked up to them and shot E a shut-up look. *Way to go, slayer.* He started toward the Harrowgate, wondering which of his two places he'd take Runa to, but dammit, both his apartment and his cave were a good walk from the exit point. Again, Runa knew what he was thinking, and she tugged him to her.

"Do you think there's an empty exam room available?"

Amusement—and not a small amount of lust—bubbled
through him. "Could be needing it for hours..."

"Days," she said, with a naughty smile.

His insides liquefied and his outside went harder than
stone. "Oh, yeah. Let's go."

Eidolon watched Shade whisk Runa away, their aroused
state obvious to his incubus senses. His own body stirred
to life, so when Tayla wrapped her arms around him and
whispered, "Do you think there's more than one exam
room open?" he didn't hesitate.

He slid a glance at Wraith on the way past Kynan's
room and prayed that Wraith, too, would find the peace he
so desperately needed.

But Eidolon couldn't shake the feeling that in Wraith's
case, prayers went unheard.

The obnoxious beeping of hospital equipment pierced the
dark depths of Kynan's dreams and yanked him into real
life. Where there was a demon parked next to the bed.

"Wraith?" Kynan blinked, trying to get the grit out of
his eyes. He felt as if he'd been asleep for a week. Maybe
he had. And why the hell was he in the hospital?

As a patient?

Wraith sat forward in his chair, propping his forearms
on his spread knees. "'Sup, buddy."

Buddy? Kynan blinked again. He wasn't at UG. He was
in the Twilight Zone.

"How...what happened?" The moment the words
passed his lips, he remembered the battle in the Irish castle. But he'd only taken minor injuries, and Eidolon had
healed those. "How did I get here?"

Wraith rubbed the back of his neck and looked down at his feet. "Yeah, ah . . . that's sort of my fault."

This was just getting weirder and weirder. Wraith was never uncomfortable, and as far as Kynan knew, the demon had never regretted anything in his life. But he was definitely doing the I-fucked-up shuffle.

"What do you mean, it's your fault? What did you do?"

"Nothing much, really. Just nearly drained you of blood."

Frowning, Kynan searched his memory. After the battle, they'd triaged and treated the injured. Wraith had gone after the escapees. He'd returned, bleeding and battered . . . and in desperate need of blood. Yeah, it was coming back. Including how Gem had volunteered to be Wraith's donor, and Kynan had nixed that right quick. And it wasn't as though he hadn't fed Wraith before.

Only the first time had been about Ky's need to connect with Lori on some level. To understand even a little of what had gone on in her head the night she'd been in Wraith's arms. But the second time Wraith had come to Kynan's vein had been about keeping him off Gem.

It had also been about helping the demon, because as pissed as Ky'd been at Wraith for what he'd done to him in E's office, he was also grateful. Wraith had helped him make peace with his feelings for Lori, and even though the rest of his life was still fucked up, at least that part of it had healed.

"What else?"

Wraith's head snapped up. "What do you mean, what else?"

"I mean, why the long face?"

"I nearly put you in the grave, you stupid human!"

Ah, now there was the Wraith they all knew and loved. "Good to see that guilt hasn't affected your utter lack of tact."

"Good to see nearly dying hasn't affected the fact that you're an asshole," Wraith shot back.

Kynan grinned. "Now that the pleasantries are out of the way, why don't you tell me what I missed while I was out."

That fast, the awkwardness in the room dissipated. The tension in Wraith's shoulders, the embarrassment that he'd been caught giving a shit about someone, disappeared.

"Gem hardly left your side," Wraith said, back to his cocky self.

Kynan blew out a long breath. "She's a doctor."

Wraith snorted. "She wants to *play* doctor."

"Let it go, man."

"Dude." Wraith's eyes bored into him. "You need to tap that."

"It's not that simple."

"Why not?"

"Says the incubus."

Wraith rolled his eyes. "You humans are so damned weighed down by morals. It's sex. Your body is made for pleasure. Why not enjoy it?"

"Morals are not my issue." Kynan didn't know what the hell his issue was anymore.

"Then what? Don't BS me and say you aren't hot for her."

"Well, duh. Look at her."

Wraith waggled his brows. "I do."

"That's not a screaming endorsement. If it breathes, you look at it."

"As E likes to point out, breathing is optional."

Sighing, Kynan threw his head back and stared at the heavy-duty lift chains hanging from the black ceiling. Somewhere in the hospital, something screeched. "I don't know, man. Lori really fucked with my head."

"You've made peace with that now."

The reminder that Wraith had invaded his mind chafed a little, but he was right. "It's not that. I don't know if I can trust anyone like that again."

"So who says you have to get that serious with Gem? See what I mean about you humans? Didn't you ever do the man-whore thing when you were younger?"

"I was pretty young when I met Lori."

"And you didn't fuck around on her?"

Kynan snorted. "Nope. Stupid me, huh?"

"Sounds to me like it's time you get out of the scrubs you've been hiding in and have a little fun."

Wraith was calling him out. Wraith, who Kynan had thought to be so self-absorbed that he didn't notice anything else around him. The guy was far more observant than Ky—and probably his brothers—gave him credit for.

Wraith shoved to his feet. "Look, dude. I know your wife did a number on you. But you're giving her more power than she deserves. Dump your baggage and get on with your life."

"Isn't that a little hypocritical?"

"Damn fucking straight." Wraith clamped a strong hand on Ky's shoulder. "But I'm about to practice what I just preached. See you around, human."

Wraith strode out of the room, his boots striking the stone floor with heavy, ominous thuds. Kynan had a sudden feeling that whatever the demon was up to was going to have consequences that would roll through the hospital like a never-ending seismic wave.

Knowing he couldn't do anything about it, Kynan swung his feet over the edge of the bed and yanked the IV line out of his hand. He couldn't believe he was going to take advice from Wraith, but the guy had a point. Kynan had spent far too much time drowning himself in work and alcohol, and in the process he'd lost himself. It was time to deal with his demons.

Gem was pouring a cup of coffee when someone knocked at the door to her apartment. "Come in!"

Boots thumped on the floor, and she turned. Kynan stood in the doorway to the kitchen, filling it, owning it, making her breath catch. "Here's the deal," he said, without so much as a hello. "I spent my life doing good, knowing good from bad, fighting evil. I wanted to save the freaking world. And then all of a sudden, evil wasn't so evil, and the people I thought were good were bad. I lost myself for a time, Gem, and I need to get myself back. I went from killing demons to saving them...to wanting to have sex with them." His eyes darkened dangerously, and her breath caught. "But I need to regroup. Figure out where I fit in this crazy world."

The cup in her hand shook. She put it down before she spilled. "So what are you saying?"

"I'm going back to The Aegis."

Her heart plummeted. "You're...leaving us?"

He closed the distance between them in half a dozen strides, halting just inches from her. So close his heat engulfed her, and his rugged, male scent washed a tide of sensual hunger through her blood. "Hell, no. Listen to me. It's not safe for me to be working at Underworld General anymore. I'm pretty sure the military is watching me, and I won't put the hospital at risk. I'll be working for The Aegis, but I'm not going anywhere. I have friends here. E, Shade, Wraith. Tayla." His hand came up to cup her cheek. "You."

Her heart pounded painfully against her ribs. "Friends. That's why you're here? To tell me we're friends?"

"I don't want to be friends." He watched her with those patient, navy eyes of his. "I want to be lovers."

*Oh, yes, yes, yes!* Excitement and joy bubbled through her. This had to be a dream.

Kynan traced her lower lip with his thumb. "I figure that if Tayla can serve in The Aegis while being half-demon and being mated to a demon, I can date a demon."

"You're . . . you're serious."

One corner of his mouth tipped up in a smile as he inclined his head in a slow nod. "Yeah."

Kynan's eyes darkened with longing, and she wondered if her own gaze had become as heated. He slid his hands up her arms, leaving a trail of goosebumps on her skin. When he reached her shoulders, he anchored her in place. Slowly, so slowly she wanted to gnash her teeth, he lowered his mouth to hers.

Someone knocked on the door. "Ignore it," he murmured against her lips.

"I plan to."

The door exploded inward. Kynan wheeled around, shoved her behind him. The next thing she heard was the sound of automatic weapons being brought to bear.

Fuck. Kynan had suspected that the R-XR was watching him, but he hadn't expected them to come out into the open. He figured they'd hang back and watch his movements, his contacts. If they knew about Gem's demon side...he reached back, tucked her more fully behind him, and faced off with the ex–Delta Force operative leading the team. His hair, cut in a severe high-and-tight, was as dark as his expression.

"Lower your fucking weapons, Arik."

Arik gave a curt nod, and his men, all dressed in black BDUs, stood down. "We need to talk."

"Then talk."

"Trust me. We want to do this privately." Arik moved into the living room, and Kynan had no choice but to follow.

"Stay here," he told Gem. "I'll take care of this. Don't worry."

"I'm not." She smiled at him, and then scowled at Arik through the opening. "They're going to pay for my door."

"I'll let them know." He squeezed her hand and then moved off to Arik, though he kept Gem in his sights. He faced off with the other man, doing his best to keep his temper in check.

"What the fuck?" So much for the temper.

"I'm sorry we had to do it this way," Arik said. "But you said you wouldn't come in."

"That's because I wasn't in the mood to be tortured for information."

"You wouldn't be tortured, but that's not what this has been about. The fact that you're working in a demon hospital is, ah, disturbing, and we could use the intel, but that's not why Runa was sent to find you."

"I'm starting to lose my patience, so get to the point."

Arik glanced into the kitchen and lowered his voice. "We need you to come into R-XR."

"No means no, buddy."

"*No* is for when you have a choice."

Kynan clenched his fists. "Tell me why I should go without a fight."

Arik didn't tense up, didn't do anything to provoke. "You know that every military member attacked by a demon is tested by the R-XR."

Yeah, he knew. He'd gone through a battery of tests before the military released him to The Aegis. "So?"

"New technology has become available, and we've run old tests again." Arik glanced down before looking back up, directly into Kynan's eyes. "Something came up in yours. A suspicious gene."

Kynan's stomach took a dive to his feet. "Do *not* say it's a demon gene, Arik. Don't. Even. Say. It."

"That's the thing, Ky. We think it's something else."

"What? Shapeshifter?"

Arik shook his head. "It's got divine coding. I don't know the fancy technical term for it. I'm just the muscle."

"Goddammit, spit it out."

"Fallen angel, Kynan. We think that somewhere perched in your family tree, there's a fallen angel."

Kynan's head swam with denial. "Fallen angels are demons."

"Not always. This was probably an angel who hadn't entered Sheoul yet. Fallen, but not quite demon."

Kynan thought about Reaver, UG's resident fallen

angel. He was in that in-between state, though Kynan had no idea why. The guy never talked about it. As far as Ky knew, no one knew Reaver's story...how he fell and why he hadn't entered Sheoul.

This was just too unbelievable, and had to be a mistake. Had to be. But as much as he wanted to rail against the information, he also had to stay level. The tests could be wrong, but if they weren't, he needed to know what the results meant.

"What does R-XR want with me?" he asked, his voice hoarser than he'd have liked. "Straight up."

"We need to run more tests. Do some research."

"Poke and prod, you mean."

Arik didn't deny it. "Nothing like this has ever been seen before."

Yeah, and Kynan hadn't been born yesterday. The R-XR didn't send armed teams to grab someone they wanted to do *tests* on. "What else?"

A vein in Arik's forehead pulsed, and Kynan knew this was Arik's ace, the card he'd been given to play only if he absolutely had to.

"Jesus, it's not some stupid prophecy, is it? Because those never make sense, never turn out like they're supposed to..."

He met Kynan's gaze with solemn eyes. "It's more than a prophecy, Ky. We're talking about a lock of biblical proportions. And you might be the key."

"The key to what?"

"The end of the world," Arik said grimly. "Armageddon."

The concussion from Arik's bomb rocked Kynan to his bones. His head snapped back, and he stood there in silence for a moment, too stunned and terrified to speak, move, or breathe. Finally, when his lungs began to burn, he sucked in some air and pulled it together. "Give me a second." His legs were wobbly as they carried him to the kitchen.

Gem met him, her eyes watery and her chin trembling. She knew. "You're leaving."

"Yes." There was no way to soften the blow. Though he hadn't expected the blow to hurt him as much. Just when he was getting his life together, just as one wound had finally healed, he'd been knocked back to square one, because even though he wasn't prepared to take Arik at his word, this couldn't be ignored. "I'm sorry, Gem."

He kissed her, putting everything he had into it. And then he walked away.

# Twenty-three

It had been nearly a month since the last full moon—which had been Shade's first shift to a werewolf, and Runa's twelfth. Tonight would kick off Shade's last; Eidolon's vaccine was ready to use after the moon phase was done. But it would be her thirteenth shift, and while many people believed thirteen was a bad omen, Runa had always felt the opposite. Thirteen was her lucky number, so she couldn't understand why she felt so unsettled lately.

Even Shade had been behaving strangely over the last couple of days, had been extra-attentive and plastered by her side. If not for the fact that he'd been called into the hospital for some sort of emergency, he'd not have let her out of his sight. He'd wanted her to go with him, but with the full moon only hours away, she'd needed to prepare.

Smiling, she approached her house. *Their* lair. Shade

had sold his city apartment, and now they spent most of their time at her place, though sometimes, when Runa was feeling extra frisky, they spent their days off at his cave.

Shade had wanted to abandon the cave, but she'd convinced him to keep it. With a little redecorating—which meant getting rid of most, but not all, of his toys—the place had become downright homey. She'd even surprised him by researching his Umber background and then filling the cave with Umber art and woven carpets. When he'd seen what she'd done, he'd been too choked up to speak, but he'd drawn her into his arms and held her as if he'd never let her go.

Which would be fine with her.

Her cell rang as she mounted the old wooden steps. The ring tone unique to her brother sang impatiently as she set down the grocery bags on the porch and dug in her windbreaker's pocket.

"Hey, Arik, you home?" He'd come for a visit last week and had left this morning to head back to the base.

"Yup. Got off the plane about fifteen minutes ago." The clank and whirr of a baggage carousel forced him to raise his voice. "Maybe you could bite me or something, so I can use Harrowgates. Much faster than airplanes."

She laughed. She'd learned to use them, though she still preferred the good old-fashioned feel of a steering wheel in her hands. In fact, she almost always drove to work . . . at Underworld General.

A couple of days after the battle in the dungeon, Runa and Arik had talked things out. After meeting Shade, he'd been willing to keep her secret from the R-XR if she wanted to continue working there, but the idea had made her uneasy. She couldn't put Arik's career in jeopardy if the truth ever came out, and besides, she'd found something even better to do with her time.

She'd approached Eidolon with an idea to take over management of the hospital's cafeteria. The challenge of providing for the needs of dozens of species excited her, and where she'd taken a conservative approach with her coffee shop, she now felt free to take risks. Sure, she wasn't trotting all over the globe to sniff out shapeshifters and were-beasts, but Shade could take her anywhere she wanted to go when she felt the urge to travel.

"Arik, it'd kill you to be locked up three nights a month."

"Maybe." She could hear the smile in his voice. "It was good seeing you so happy, sis."

"I'm very happy," she said. "I know you had your doubts about Shade, but you don't need to worry."

"I'm not. He's obviously devoted to you. Doesn't change the fact that he's a demon, but he did save my life."

"And mine," she said softly.

"Which is why I'm giving him the benefit of the doubt."

"What about Kynan? Is the Army giving him the benefit of the doubt?" She still didn't know what was up with that situation. Kynan had been taken to R-XR headquarters, where he'd been subjected to a battery of tests. He wouldn't talk, and neither would her brother, but Ky had given her a message to pass on to Gem.

*"Tell her not to wait."*

"I can't talk about Kynan. You know that." Arik paused. "There's my luggage. Gotta sail. Love you."

"You, too."

She hung up, and for whatever reason, she looked down

the street. A man stood on the corner, his heated gaze focused on her. A tingle skittered over her skin. Why, she had no idea, but when he jerked his gaze away, she followed it to where another man sauntered up the sidewalk toward her. He was as light as the other man was dark, but something united them.

Something familiar.

Her pulse began to race.

The men glared at each other, both measuring the distance between themselves and her. Their eyes glowed with hunger and impending change, and she drew a startled breath. They were wargs.

Her body flooded with heat and liquid arousal. Oh, God. That was why she'd been so unsettled lately. She was entering her first yearly breeding heat.

She needed to call Shade, and now. Before instinct overruled her mind and caused her to do something stupid, like take one of the werewolves into her cage to mate. Female wargs in heat waited for the males to fight it out, and would then mate with the victor. If she became pregnant during the moon cycle, the pairing would become permanent, as wargs formed bonds similar to those of Seminus demons, and mates were for life.

The men came together in a crash of fists. They were as propelled by instinct as she was, and though they'd started the fight in human form, they'd finish it in beast bodies. Which could turn into disaster in the middle of a residential neighborhood.

"Go," she muttered to herself, because the darkest, most primal part of her wanted to watch, to root for a victor, but the still-human side knew she had to get out of there.

*Shade, hurry...* He'd sense her sudden hunger and was, no doubt, on his way now. No matter what kind of emergency had prompted his trip to UG, instinct would bring him home.

She looked up at the sky, at the rapidly growing darkness, though she didn't need to. Her body told her the moon would be up in a matter of minutes.

Quickly, she let herself into the house and darted to the basement. The unfinished room was large, the soundproofed walls allowing for as much noise as two werewolves could make.

She slipped inside the cage in the center of the room, which she and Shade had enlarged and made comfortable for both of them. She slammed the door shut and spun the combination lock.

The crash of glass sent her pulse into overdrive, and then the men were in the basement with her, launching at each other. *Come on, Shade.* She dug her phone out of her pocket and dialed Shade.

"I'm almost there, babe," he said, without a hello and with panic dripping from his voice. He hung up before she could say a word.

Cursing, she called Tayla. She'd gotten to know Eidolon's mate over the past couple of weeks, and right now, she was their best hope to keep the wargs outside the cage from running amok.

"What's up, Runa?"

"I don't have time to explain. I've got a problem. Wargs in my basement. If they get out of the house..."

"Shit. Okay, I'll gather a team and get them contained."

"Don't kill them."

"I know. We'll be careful."

Runa hung up, wondering if, even after a year of being bonded to a demon, it still felt odd for Tayla to ensure the safety of creatures such as werewolves instead of killing them. Granted, Runa had wanted to kill Luc for what he'd done to her, but she was thankful that she hadn't. He wasn't the most friendly guy on the planet, but he had, in his gruff way, apologized for attacking her.

The apology was unnecessary. She was stronger, tougher, and her longer lifespan would give her plenty of time with Shade. If a cure ever became available, she'd turn it down.

She glared at the men who were tearing apart her basement. She'd be happy to inject *them* with the cure, however.

Shade's roar shook the entire house. His scent flooded the basement as he flew down the steps and leaped into the center of the fray. He was still wearing scrubs, but he wore his usual combat boots, and they caused the rivals a world of pain as he landed kicks as high as their heads.

"Stay in the cage!" he yelled at her, when she reached for the lock.

"But you could just slip inside—"

"I need to win this."

Her heart swelled. After a year of being a were, she instinctively understood his determination. The fights struck her human side as barbaric, but the part of her that was female and warg appreciated the raw thrill of being the prize in an age-old battle for possession.

If Shade's enthusiasm was any indication, he felt the same way. He needed to fight for her. *Wanted* to fight for her. He'd bonded with her as a Seminus demon, but he was compelled to do the same as a warg.

A shiver of both feminine excitement and fear prickled her skin. If he lost...

Shade's boot caught the dark-haired man in the chest, sending him crashing into a shelf of canned goods. As the other man crumpled to the floor, unconscious, Runa let out a relieved breath. One down, one to go.

Testosterone and fury turned the air to soup as the blond launched himself at Shade, slamming them both into the stair railing. The blond nailed Shade with an uppercut that snapped his head back with enough force that his eyes glazed.

"Shade!" She rattled the cage, fumbling for the combination lock as the blond took advantage of Shade's stunned state and pulled a Swiss Army knife from his jeans pocket.

In a sweeping arc, the man brought the blade down. Shade twisted away at the last moment. The blade struck a glancing blow at his shoulder, slicing open his scrub top and leaving a thin red line.

"Son of a bitch," Shade snarled. He whirled, crunching a series of blows into the other male's torso and face with his fists and feet. The knife flew out of the blond's hand, but in about ten seconds it would be useless anyway...

The painful tightening of Runa's skin caught her by surprise. The change was upon them all.

"Hurry, Shade!"

Hands trembling and already beginning to elongate, she shed her clothes. Shade caught the blond by one furry arm and slammed him to the ground, then quickly kicked off his boots. The blond snared his ankle, bringing Shade to the floor with him. They were both more beast than man now, and their snapping jaws and flashing claws brought a whole new element of danger—and excitement—to the battle.

Runa's mind began to go fuzzy, her thoughts hijacked by her growing lust, her body taken over by the scent of battle in the air. The door. She needed to open the door before she was nothing but animal.

She fumbled with the lock, and as the door clicked open, pain tore through her. Her bones cracked and her joints stretched, and through the roar of blood rushing in her ears, she heard the males' groans of agony, as well. This was the worst part of being a werewolf, dealing with the painful transformation.

Through the misery, Shade somehow held on to his determination to win the battle. He palmed the other warg's forehead and slammed his skull into the concrete floor. The sharp crack echoed through the basement, and by the time it had faded away, Shade was there, leaping through the cage door. He slammed it shut, and though he didn't lock it, she didn't care. The transformation had taken her completely.

So had the mating heat.

Shade stood before her on two black-furred legs, a massive, beautiful creature that was as fully aroused as she was. He lunged at her, and she dodged to the side. As much as she wanted him, he had one more test to pass.

He had to best her, as well.

His raw, erotic growl swept through her like a muscle-deep caress, warming her, preparing her for him. Right now she was little more than a raging mass of hormones, and deep inside her womb contracted and her sex clenched. Still, when he reached for her, she slashed him with her claws.

In an instant, he was on her. She snarled, snapping at him with her teeth, but he locked his jaws on her scruff and held her in place. With one last burst of power, she threw herself sideways, dislodging him momentarily as they crashed into the side of the cage.

Her victory was short-lived, and in a blur of fur and fangs, he had her where he wanted her once again, and in one smooth, powerful stroke, he filled her.

Ecstasy exploded through her body, far more than a sexual high. Seminus bond or no, this was her true mate.

Shade's howl joined hers, a celebration in the night.

Shade woke, naked, battered, and exhausted, spooning with Runa, who stirred as he stretched. Wincing at the twinge of sore muscles and aching joints, he stroked her arm. His eyes were still closed, mainly because he planned to go back to sleep for a week.

The last three nights and days had been the most exhausting of his life. Not that he was complaining. He and Runa had mated constantly in both their warg forms and true forms, taking breaks during the day only to eat. Someone, probably Tayla or Eidolon, had left them meat the first night—he didn't recall them coming in to take away the males he'd fought and to lock the cage door so he and Runa wouldn't escape, but he was pretty glad he didn't remember. No doubt they'd gotten an eyeful of werewolf mating habits.

E would never let him live this one down.

Beneath his hand, Runa's silky skin heated. Not just

heated, but seared his palm. He struggled to open his eyes. His vision was blurry, and having Runa's mane of hair in his face didn't help. Groaning, he shoved himself up on one elbow.

"Mmm." Runa yawned. "What are you doing?"

"I'm—" He froze. His breath lodged like a plug in his throat. Her left arm... holy hell.

Runa shot him a concerned look over her shoulder. "What's wrong?"

He couldn't tear his gaze away from her arm. "You're marked. You've got my mate-mark."

"Seriously?" As she squirmed into a sit, her grin hit him right in the heart. "Oh, wow. It's real, isn't it?" Her hand came down on his, and she twined their fingers together as she traced the patterns on her skin. "We're bonded."

"Yeah." Intense emotion made him sound as if he'd swallowed a truckload of crushed glass. "You're mine now."

Her hand stilled, and her gaze locked on his. "I always was. You just couldn't see it."

"I'm so sorry—"

She pressed her fingers to his lips. "You couldn't see it because your life was on the line."

He kissed her hand, as lovingly as he could, letting his lips linger. "You deserved so much better than what I gave you."

"Yes," she said smartly, "I did. But, like you, I couldn't see it." She reached up and skimmed the pads of her fingers over his personal mark at the top of his *dermoire*. "An unseeing eye."

"I always wondered why that was my symbol. E has a

set of scales, but he was born to Justice demons, so that made sense. Wraith's got an hourglass ... we always joke that it's because he's impatient and never on time. But mine ... mine never made sense."

"It's open now."

"What do you mean?"

"Your mark. It's an open eye now. No longer unseeing."

Shade's eyes stung. "Eidolon's scales were unbalanced until he bonded with Tayla." He swallowed, trying not to do something wussy like cry. "He didn't discover the change for days."

"So he's balanced now ... and you're no longer blind."

"Never again."

She rolled over, hooked her leg over his, and drew him in. After the last three nights, he hadn't thought he could get turned on again—not for weeks, at least—but having her naked, heated body rubbing against his triggered sensations he couldn't deny.

The ringing of a cell phone interrupted his inappropriate thoughts.

"I'm not answering," he murmured.

"You need to. It's your brother's tone."

Shade tucked Runa beneath him and let voicemail pick it up. Eidolon was going to have to wait.

Eidolon's voicemail message turned out to be urgent, so Shade and Runa showered, scarfed down breakfast—he made her pancakes, because nothing tasted better than carbs after three nights of raw meat—and sped to UG on his Harley. They found Eidolon in his office, scowling at a stack of paperwork on his desk.

"I finally got the inventory report back for the store-room," he said without a hello. "We have a problem."

Shade took a seat and pulled Runa into his lap. "So Roag definitely got away with something?" When E nodded, Shade cursed. Their brother was gone forever and yet he was still causing trouble. They'd known he'd broken into the storeroom somewhere around the time he'd tried to kill Luc, but they hadn't known what, exactly, he'd stolen. "What did he take?"

"Among other things, Eth's Eye and the mordlair necrotoxin."

Eth's Eye was a crystal orb used for divination, but the other...the name rang a bell, but only vaguely. "And that is?"

"A poison for which there is no cure."

Shade cocked an eyebrow. "And you had it...why?"

"Because I've discovered that in microscopic amounts, it can cure Lecepic Pox in Trillahs."

Hell's rings. "I'm going to guess that Roag wasn't after it to go on some demonitarian mission to save Trillahs from a disease that strikes one in a thousand every hundred years."

"You think?"

Runa's warm hand slid up his back to his neck, where she massaged the muscles that were starting to tense up. "Well, the bastard is, for all intents and purposes, dead. He can't hurt anyone with it."

"I hope you're right," E said, and then rolled his eyes at Shade's amused snort. "Yeah, I'm paranoid."

"No shit."

E gave him a blank stare.

"You need to get laid."

Eidolon's eyes lit up, and Shade knew his brother had Tayla on the brain. Shade pressed a kiss into Runa's neck, because he knew exactly what it was like to have a sexy, gorgeous female on the brain. And on his lap. And on his—

"What's E paranoid about now?"

Shade looked up to see Wraith standing in the doorway, one shoulder braced against the doorjamb, arms crossed and...*holy shit.* This was the first they'd seen of Wraith in a month, which wasn't unusual.

But he sported a facial *dermoire.*

He'd gone through *s'genesis.*

A full year early.

Silence stretched, and Runa's hand stilled on Shade's neck.

"Son of a bitch," Shade muttered.

E leaned back in his chair, arms across his chest, a grave expression on his face. "Is there something you want to tell us?"

Wraith shrugged, like all of this was a big joke. "The sorceress who gave me the transfer chant for Shade's curse? She helped the *s'genesis* along. For a price, of course."

From the sly grin on Wraith's face, Shade could guess what the price had been. He wanted to ask why Wraith had done it, but he knew. As an unmated Seminus capable of doing what their species had been born to do, he'd have few cares or concerns save for one—impregnating females. Wraith had lived in hell for the last ninety-nine years, and while The Change wouldn't erase his past, it would make it seem distant. With no time to think on it and his mind completely full of no thoughts other than where to find the next female, Wraith would, in a way, be free.

Hell, Shade was shocked that Wraith had even bothered to stop by the hospital.

"Why is his mark on his face instead of his neck?" Runa's fingers feathered over Shade's throat, and Shade nearly started purring.

"Because he's an unmated male."

"And he's going to stay that way," Wraith said, shifting his gaze to Runa, who had shrugged out of her jacket. "Hey, she's mate-marked!"

E's head swung around. "How?"

"Cool, huh?" Shade brought Runa's marked hand to his lips. "No idea how it happened. Or why. We woke up this morning, and there it was."

"Last night was a full moon," Wraith mused, and then it was his turn to frown as he looked at Runa. "Were you in season?"

Runa turned about eight shades of red. Shade stroked her arm, tracing the new marks, and answered for her. "Yeah. And I have the fucking scars to prove it. Why?"

Wraith shook his head. "Something Luc told me once. He said wargs only become mated during a she-warg's season, and then, only if she gets pregnant."

Shade's breath caught. "That's what it might have taken to complete our bonding."

"You mean..." Runa's voice was a whisper.

"Let's see." Shade's hand shook as he grasped her hand in his. His *dermoire* shimmered, and warmth spread down his arm as his power entered her body. He traveled through her bloodstream until he reached her womb. He held his breath as he probed—and found what he was looking for. A fertilized egg.

"Shade?"

He had to swallow the lump in his throat before he could talk. "Wraith's right. Oh, man, we're going to be parents." He paused, his power flaring to another egg. And another. "Three of them. We're having *three* babies."

By the stunned expression on Runa's face, he couldn't tell if she was happy or not, but he was grinning like an idiot. Sons. He was going to have three of them.

"Congrats, bro," Wraith said, slapping him on the back on his way out the door. "Better you than me."

With that, Wraith was gone. Eidolon started after him, his worry over Wraith's new condition coming off him in waves. Wraith was an unpinned grenade ready to blow.

But at the door, his brother paused. "I'm happy for you, man. Just don't ask me to babysit." Eidolon grinned, and he was out of there.

Shade drew in a shuddering breath and framed Runa's face in his hands. "Are you okay with this? With everything that's happened to you because of me?"

A slow, radiant smile lit her face. "I'm more than okay, Shade. For the first time in my life, I'm alive. And you gave me that." She trailed a finger down her *dermoire*. "Guess you're still cursed. Cursed to be with me."

"I can live with that," he croaked, his eyes stinging again. Runa brought out the best in him when he'd believed there *was* no best in him.

Being cursed to love Runa was the best curse of all.

Larissa Ione's New York Times
bestselling Demonica series is
back and hotter than ever!

Please see the next page
for a preview of

# *Revenant*

Revenant was one fucked-up fallen angel.

No, wait…*angel*. He'd only *believed* he was a fallen angel.

For five thousand fucking years.

But he wasn't an angel, either. Maybe technically, but how could someone born and raised in Sheoul, the demon realm some humans called hell, be considered a holy-rolling, shiny-haloed angel? He may have a halo, but the shine was long gone, tarnished since his first taste of mother's milk, mixed with demon blood, when he was only hours old.

*Five thousand fucking years.*

It had been two weeks since he'd learned the truth and the memories that had been taken away from him were returned. Now he remembered everything that had happened over the centuries.

He'd been a bad, bad angel. Or a very, very good *fallen* angel, depending on how you looked at it.

Toxic anger rushed through his veins as he paced the subterranean parking lot outside Underworld General Hospital. Maybe the doctors inside had some kind of magical drug that could take his memories away again. Life had been far easier when he'd believed he was pure evil, a fallen angel with no redeeming qualities.

Okay, he probably still didn't have any redeeming qualities but now, what he did have, were conflicted feelings. Questions. A twin brother who couldn't be more opposite of him.

With a vicious snarl, he strode toward the entrance to the emergency department, determined to find a certain False Angel doctor he was sure could help him forget the last five thousand years, if only for a couple of hours.

The sliding glass doors swished open, and the very female he'd come for sauntered out, her blue and yellow-duckie-spotted scrubs clinging to a killer body. Instant lust fired in his loins, and fuck yeah, screw the drugs, she was exactly what the doctor ordered.

*Take her twice and call me in the morning.*

Since the moment he bumped into her at the hospital a few weeks ago, he'd been obsessed, and now, as Blaspheme's long legs ate up the asphalt as she walked toward him, he imagined them wrapped around his waist as he pounded into her. The closer she came, the harder his body got, and he cursed with disappointment when she dropped her keys and had to stop to pick them up. Then he decided she could drop her keychain as often as she wanted to, because he got a fucking primo view of her deep cleavage when her top gaped open as she bent over.

She straightened, looped the keychain around her finger, and started toward him again, humming a Duran Duran song.

"Blaspheme." He stepped out from between two black ambulances, blocking her path.

She jumped, a startled gasp escaping full crimson lips made to propel a male to ecstasy. "Revenant." Her gaze darted to the hospital doors, and he got the impression she was plotting her escape route. How cute that she thought she could get away from him. "What are you doing lurking in the parking lot?"

Lurking? Well, some might call it that, he supposed. "I was on my way to see you."

She smiled sweetly. "Well, you've seen me. Buh-bye." Pivoting, her blond ponytail bouncing, she headed in the opposite direction.

Back to the hospital.

With a mental flick of his wrist, he changed into jeans, cowboy boots, and a NASCAR T-shirt, and turned his shoulder-length hair from black to brown before flashing around in front of her, once again blocking her path. "Maybe this is more to your liking?"

She gave him a flat stare. Clearly, rednecks weren't her thing.

Giving it another try, he went ginger and short with the hair, and decked himself out in a business suit. "How about this?"

More staring. He switched back to goth biker chic and stopped fucking around. "Come home with me."

"Wow." She crossed her arms over her chest, which only drew his attention to her rack. *Niiice.* "You get right to the point."

He shrugged. "Saves time."

"Were you planning to wine and dine me at least? You know, before the sex."

"No. Just sex." Lots and lots of sex.

He could already imagine her husky voice deepening in the throes of passion. Could imagine her head between his legs, her mouth on his cock, her hands on his balls. He nearly groaned at the imaginary skin flick playing in his head.

"Oh," she said, her voice dripping with sarcasm. "You're charming, aren't you?"

Not once in his five thousand years had anyone ever called him charming. But even uttered with sarcasm, it was the nicest thing anyone had ever said to him.

"Don't do that," he growled.

"Do what?" She stared at him like he was a loon.

"Never mind." Dying to touch her, he held out his hand. "You'll love my playroom."

She wheeled away like he was offering her the plague instead of his hand. "Go to hell, asshole. I don't date fallen angels."

"Good news, then, because it's not a date." And he wasn't a fallen angel.

"Right. Well, I don't fuck fallen angels, either." She made a shooing motion with her hand. "Go away."

She was rejecting him? No one rejected him. *No one.* Having been raised in a dungeon, with torture specialists and executioners as his playmates, he hadn't exactly learned the art of seduction or even polite conversation. But sex . . . he spoke that language fluently.

She started to take off again, and he blinked, confused. This wasn't right. He had his sights set on her, and she was supposed to surrender. This was something new. Something . . . titillating. The confusion morphed into a sensation he welcomed and knew well; the jacked-up high of the hunt.

Instantly, his senses sharpened and focused. His sense

of smell brought a whiff of her vanilla-honey scent. His sense of hearing homed in on her rapid, pounding heartbeat. And his sense of sight narrowed in on the tick of her pulse at the base of her throat.

The urge to pounce, to take her down and get carnal right here, right now, was nearly overwhelming. Instead, he moved in slowly, matching her step for step as she backed up.

"What are you doing?" She swallowed as she bumped up against a massive support beam.

"I'm going to show you why you need to come home with me." He planted both palms on the beam on either side of her head and leaned in until his lips brushed the tender skin of her ear. "You won't regret it."

"I already told you. I don't fuck fallen angels."

"So you said," he murmured. "Do you kiss them?"

"Ah...no, I—"

He didn't give her the chance to finish her sentence. Pulling back slightly, he closed his mouth over hers.

Strawberry gloss coated his lips as he kissed her, and he swore he'd never liked fruit as much as he did right now.

Her hands came up to grip his biceps, tugging him closer as she deepened the kiss. "You're good," she whispered against his mouth.

"I know," he whispered back.

Suddenly, pain tore into his arms as her nails scored his skin. "But you're not *that* good."

Before he could even blink, she shoved hard and ducked out from under the cage of his arms. With a wink, she strutted away, her fine ass swinging in her form-fitting scrub bottoms. She stopped at the door of a candy apple red Mustang and gave him a sultry look that made his cock throb.

"Give up now, buddy. I can out-stubborn anyone." She hopped into her car and peeled out of her parking stall, leaving him in the dust.

Blaspheme was practically hyperventilating as she drove through New York City's crowded streets, wishing she'd taken the Harrowgate to work today. But no, she'd chosen to drive from her Brooklyn apartment to Underworld General one last time, a sentimental stupidity that had not only taken up precious time, but had also run her straight into a fallen angel who somehow, after a short, unpleasant verbal exchange at the hospital a few weeks ago, thought they needed to date.

No, not date. Just have sex.

Her entire body heated at the thought, something it had no business doing.

But gods, he was incredible. Standing in the UG parking lot, he'd looked like a giant goth biker, wrapped in leather and chains, his massive boots sporting wicked talons at the tips. Even the backs of his fingerless gloves were adorned with metal studs at the knuckles. She'd always hated the tough-guy bullshit, but Revenant had fucking *owned* it. She got the impression that he lived his life that way; if he wanted it, he owned it.

Even when he'd changed his look, he'd still been like something out of a magazine or movie. The cowboy boots had made her want to take up riding—not necessarily horses— and the business suit had given her some racy desk fantasies.

He wasn't going to give up on her, was he? At least, not without a fight, which she was going to give him. She couldn't afford to have a fallen angel sniffing around.

Cursing, she fumbled through her purse for her cell phone and dialed her contact from the moving company. Sally answered on the second ring.

"Hi, Bonnie," Sally said, using the name Blaspheme adopted when dealing with humans. "The movers said they'll be done loading your belongings for the second shipment to London by the end of the day."

"Good," Blas said. It would be nice to go directly to UG's new London clinic directly, rather than having to use the hospital's emergency department Harrowgate to get there. "I should be there in an hour—" The Call Waiting beep interrupted. "Can I get back to you? My mother is ringing in."

Sally's cheerful, "No problem," was followed by a promise to make sure the movers would take wonderful care of Blaspheme's things and not to worry, and a moment later, Blaspheme's mother was on the other line.

"Hi, Mom." Blaspheme slammed on her brakes to avoid rear-ending a piece-of-shit truck that apparently hadn't come equipped with a turn signal *or* brake lights. She shot the driver the finger through her front windshield.

"Blas." Her mother's raspy voice came from right next to Blaspheme.

Screaming, Blas dropped the phone. "Holy shit!"

She opened her mouth again to yell at her mother for popping into the car from out of nowhere, but when she saw the blood, her voice cut out. Deva, short for Devastation, sat in the passenger seat, every inch of her body covered in blood. The broken end of a bone punched through her left biceps, and a deep, to-the-femur burn had wrecked her right leg.

"Oh, gods," Blaspheme gasped. "What happened?"

Her mother lifted her trembling hand from her abdomen, and Blas got an eyeful of bowels poking through the laceration that stretched from just above her navel to her hip bone.

The injury itself was grave enough, but emanating from it was a vibe Blaspheme couldn't place. Whatever it was, it felt...wrong. And very, very fatal.

"I—" Deva sucked in a rattling breath...and slumped, unconscious, against the window.

"Mom!" The POS truck moved, allowing Blaspheme to whip the Mustang around a corner to head back to Underworld General. She automatically reached out with her mind to find a Harrowgate, and although she located one a block away, there was nowhere to park, and no way she could abandon the vehicle in the middle of the street.

Damn, it would be nice to be able to flash like the normal offspring of a fallen angel, but that wasn't an option for Blaspheme. It would never be an option.

On instinct, she gripped her mother's wrist and tried to channel healing energy into her, but that talent had been rendered useless a long time ago.

*Dammit!*

"Just hold on," she told her mom as she wove her car through the streets, narrowly avoiding sideswiping a cab and a messenger on a bike.

She whipped into the underground parking lot owned by the hospital but off-limits to the human public, drove through a false wall, and practically skidded to a halt in a stall in the hospital's hidden parking lot. Then, for a split second, an eternity, really, she hesitated.

Everyone at the hospital believed Blas was a False Angel. She could come up with an explanation as to why her mother wasn't the same species, but doing so could raise questions. Questions from the one person she was pretty sure was already suspicious.

A mere two weeks ago, Eidolon, Underworld General's founder and chief of staff, had been just cryptic enough in his warning to stay away from Revenant that she'd been paranoid ever since.

Her mother groaned, and suddenly, it didn't matter what Eidolon suspected. Her job…hell, her *life*…was at risk, but so was Deva's, and she couldn't let her mother die.

Quickly, she leaped out of the vehicle and ran through the sliding doors to the emergency department.

"I need help!" she barked, and in an instant, Luc, a werewolf paramedic, and Raze, a Seminus demon physician, rushed outside with a stretcher.

Moments later, Blaspheme was in an exam room, gloved up, while Luc checked vitals and Raze channeled his healing power into Deva. His scowl indicated that he was having trouble.

"Her stomach ruptured," he said. "Dammit, there's a tear in her transverse colon. I can heal the tears right now, but she needs surgery to clean out the contaminants." He looked over at Blas. "It's a huge risk, though. I know you're aware that False Angels don't respond well to anesthesia."

Shit. Blaspheme did not want to reveal the truth about her mother—and potentially, herself—but she couldn't compromise Deva's health by sending her into surgery with doctors who thought she was something other than what she was. Maybe she could play fast and loose with the facts and hope no one dug too deep.

Blas glanced up as she prepared an IV site in the back of her mother's hand. "She's not a False Angel."

Raze cocked an eyebrow. "But you said she's your mother."

"She's my *adoptive* mother," she lied. "She's a fallen angel." At least the second part was the truth.

Raze's hand jerked, and he cursed under his breath. She understood his shock; fallen angels were rare, they were mostly evil assholes, and as far as Sheoulic denizens went, they were at the top of the food chain.

Raze's ginger hair, longer in front than in the back, fell over his eyes as he leaned in for a closer look at Deva's abdominal wound. "This is strange."

Those weren't words you wanted a doctor to say. She attempted to summon her most useful FA ability, what was commonly called X-ray vision, used by False Angels to determine the health or virility of their potential victims. As a medical professional, Blas had found a better use for it.

Sadly, it barely flickered before snuffing out. Great. Another False Angel ability was failing. How long before they were all gone and her true identity was revealed?

"What's strange?" she asked.

"I can't heal her. Nothing's happening."

"What?" Blas looked up from inserting an IV catheter into Deva's vein to stare at the incubus. "Are you out of juice?"

He held up his right arm, which was covered in glowing glyphs from his throat to his fingers. "My power is at full charge. I'm telling you, it's not me. It's her."

*The vibe.* What if the weird vibe coming off her mother was somehow interfering with Raze's powers?

Raze glanced over at her. "Can you take a look inside her and tell me what's going on?"

"I just tried," she said. "I think I'm too emotional."

Raze nodded, apparently buying her bullshit story for the X-ray failure.

Her mother groaned, and her eyes flickered open. Her hand fumbled for Blas's. "Alone," she rasped. "I need to talk to you alone."

Blaspheme looked up at Raze. "Arrange for an OR. We'll get her into surgery right away. And page Eidolon. I want him on this." Despite Blas's fears of discovery, she needed him. As the most skilled, most experienced doctor in the entire underworld, Eidolon just might be the only one who could save her mother.

Raze and Luc took off, leaving her alone with Deva.

"Mom," she said quietly. "What's going on? What happened?"

"Angels," she said, and Blaspheme's stomach churned. "I was attacked by angels."

Which explained the vibe and Raze's difficulty healing her. Some angelic weapons caused injury that couldn't be repaired using supernatural means.

"Where were you?" Blaspheme squeezed her mother's hand when Deva's eyes closed. "Hey, stay with me. Where were you when they attacked you?"

"Home," she rasped. "They found me, Blaspheme."

A chill crawled up her spine. "They?" She had a sickening feeling she knew who *they* were, and she prayed she was wrong.

Deva coughed, spraying blood. "I think...I think they were Eradicators. They found me." She sat up, clawing at Blaspheme's hand, desperation and terror punching through the haze of pain in her eyes. "Which means they're also looking for you."